I0593711

Julian Emperor of Rome, John Duncombe,  Libanius, Jean-P.-R. La Bletterie

**Select Works of the Emperor Julian**

and some pieces of the sophist Libanius - Vol. 2

Julian Emperor of Rome, John Duncombe,  Libanius, Jean-P.-R. La Bletterie

**Select Works of the Emperor Julian**
*and some pieces of the sophist Libanius - Vol. 2*

ISBN/EAN: 9783337275853

Printed in Europe, USA, Canada, Australia, Japan

Cover: Foto ©Andreas Hilbeck / pixelio.de

More available books at **www.hansebooks.com**

# SELECT WORKS

OF THE

# EMPEROR JULIAN,

AND

SOME PIECES

OF THE

## SOPHIST LIBANIUS,

TRANSLATED FROM THE GREEK.

WITH

Notes from PETAU, La BLETERIE, GIBBON, &c.

TO WHICH IS ADDED,

The HISTORY OF THE EMPEROR JOVIAN,

From the French of the Abbé De la Bleterie.

By JOHN DUNCOMBE, M.A.

IN TWO VOLUMES.

Him Poefy, Philofophy, deplore.
The fcepter'd Patriot, who diftinctions wav'd,
Lord of himfelf, by Pagan rites enflav'd;
Whom all, but Chriftians, held their common friend,
Whofe very errors had a virtuous end.　　　Irwin.

———

VOLUME THE SECOND.

———

LONDON,
Printed by J. NICHOLS;
For T. CADELL, in the STRAND.
MDCCLXXXIV.

# CONTENTS OF VOL. II.

# THE

# EPISTLES

## OF

# JULIAN.

---

Απασαις μεν απασας νικων, τα δ'αυλα τι των ΕΠΙΣΤΟΛΩΝ.
" Superior, as he was, to all men in all his writings, in
" his EPISTLES he was superior to himself."

LIBANIUS.

---

\*₄\* Of the Epiſtles of Julian, the nine firſt were printed in Greek, with other Epiſtles by various hands, by Aldus, Rom. 1499, 4to. and afterwards in Greek and Latin, at Geneva, 1606, folio. The xth was preſerved by Socrates in his Hiſtory, III. 3. The xıth, and thoſe that follow, as far as the xLyıth, were in like manner publiſhed among the Epiſtles of various writers. The xLıxth was taken from Sozomen, v. 16. The Lth, Lıſt, and Lııd were firſt publiſhed in Greek by Peter Martinius, together with the Miſopogon, and the other Epiſtles, illuſtrated by a Latin tranſlation, Paris, 1567 and 1583, 8vo. Petau therefore firſt tranſlated thoſe three, and alſo the Lıııd, and the following, as far as the Lvııth, which, together with the Epiſtle of Gallus to Julian, Bonaventure Vulcanius publiſhed at Leyden, 1597, 12mo. at the end of the Epiſtles and Problems of Theophylactus Simocatta. The Lvıııth and Lıxth, but doubtfully blended together, were firſt publiſhed by Nicholas Rigalt, who alſo added a tranſlation, at the end of his *Funus Paraſiticum*, Paris, 1601, 4to. But in the edition of Petau, by the advice of Rigalt himſelf, it was divided into two, both mutilated, the former having no concluſion, and the latter no beginning. At length the former was ſupplied from a MS. by the learned and ingenious Lewis Anthony Muratori, in his *Anecdota Græca*, Padua, 1709, 4to. The Lxth and the two following were firſt publiſhed by Petau, from a copy of an old MS. lent him by Patricius Junius. The Lxıııd, which Martinius and Petau have given in Greek only, but very imperfect and incorrect, Ezekiel Spanheim amended and ſupplied from the MS. of Allatius, and firſt added a Latin verſion. Muratori has alſo publiſhed three other Epiſtles of Julian, the Lxıvth, Lxvth, and Lxvıth, from the ſame MS.

FABRICIUS.

For an account of the other Epiſtles, ſee the notes.

## Epiſtle I.  To * * * * †.

I THOUGHT that you had long ago arrived
in Ægypt; and recollecting what I have often
faid, " Happy," cried I, " are the Ægyptians in
" the plenty with which they have long been fup-
" plied by the Nile, but happier are they now
" in the poſſeſſion of your Muſe, a bleſſing, in
" my opinion, fuperior even to the Nile: That
" river, by flooding, enriches their country ; but
" you, by your eloquence, improving the minds
" of their youth, endow them with the treaſures
" of wifdom, like Plato and Pythagoras, their
" former vifitors."

Such were my reflections, little thinking that
you, in the mean time, were not far diftant. At
the receipt, therefore, of your letter I was at firſt
fo much furprifed, that I thought it an impofition,
and could not believe my eyes. But when I pe-
rufed the contents, convinced that fuch elegance
could flow from no other pen, how great was my
delight ! I then entertained hopes of foon feeing
you here, and I rejoiced that your own country
would foon be bleſſed with your prefence, however
fhert might be your ftay. On this fubject you
feem to have brought a ludicrous charge againſt

---

† The name of the fage, to whom this Epiſtle is addreſſed, is not known.        LA BLETERIE.

me. For though I allow that the air is such as
you represent it, that the water is as brackish as
the ocean, and that the bread is made of barley;
all which, out of regard to your country, you
have by no means exaggerated; yet, my good
friend, you are much indebted to her for having
furnished your mind with philosophy. But be-
ware how you despise the luxuries of Ægypt.
Wise Ulysses, though he inhabited a small and
rocky island, could not be tempted either by the
charms of Calypso, or the promise of immortality,
to prefer them to Ithaca. Nor was any Spartan, I
imagine, ever induced by the recollection of his
coarse domestic fare to complain of Sparta. But
I know what has occasioned your bringing this
charge against me. You are fond of money, and
in that pursuit being disappointed, you sigh with
regret, and envy the Nile and the wealth that it
produces. This, you say, makes you desert your
country, and renders your person as inelegant as.
that of Chærephon *. But I rather suspect that
you are detained by some kind nymph, and are
sensible at last of the power of love. Be this as
Venus pleases! Mean time, farewell; and may I
soon hail you the father of a family!

* Chærephon was a writer of tragedies. He celebrated
the actions of the Heraclidæ. But being greatly emaciated
by his nocturnal lucubrations, he became a vulgar joke.
The name of " owl" was also given him. See *Erasm. in
Chil.* p 685.

He was a disciple of Socrates. His nocturnal studies procured him the name of νυκλεξις, " bat;" and his paleness the
epithet of πυξινος, " the man of box."      LA BLETERIE.

Epistle

## Epiſtle II. To Prohæresius *.

WHY ſhould I not ſalute the excellent Pro- A. D.
hæreſius, a man as exuberant in language 361.
as a river in water, when it overflows its banks;
and in eloquence, the rival of Pericles †, except
that he does not embroil Greece? Be not ſurpriſed
at my adopting the Lacedæmonian brevity. Sages,
like you, may make long and verboſe orations;
but from me to you a little is ſufficient.

* One of the Chriſtian profeſſors who ſhut up their
ſchools in conſequence of Julian's edict. [See Epiſtle XLII.]
He taught at Athens, and his reputation extended over
the whole empire. The city of Rome had erected a ſtatue
to him as large as the life, with this inſcription, " The
" queen of cities to the king of orators." He had received from the Emperor Conſtans the honorary title of
" general of the Roman armies." Julian, it is ſaid, exempted him from the general law, and allowed him to retain his ſeat without changing his religion. But Prohæreſius had the delicacy not to avail himſelf of a privilege
which would have rendered his faith ſuſpected. Eunapius,
an admirer and a diſciple of this ſophiſt, but a great enemy
to the Chriſtians, relates this fact differently.
                                              La Bleterie.
On the eloquence of Prohæreſius, Eunapius has fully
enlarged. But Suidas ſays, that Julian, in order to pique
him, preferred Libanius.                      Petau.
Libanius, in one of his Epiſtles, recommends him to
Maximus, " as an ornament to the world by his eloquence,
a good man, and one to whom both Rome and Athens had
erected a ſtatue of braſs." His death was celebrated in a
remarkable epigram by Nazianzen, preſerved by Mutatori
in his *Anecdota Græca,* p. 1.
    † As to the oratory of Pericles, ſee Cicero *de Oratore,*
XXXIV.

B 3                                    Know

Know, then, that my affairs are much embarraffed and diftracted. With all the reafons of my return, if you intend to compile a hiftory, I will moft accurately acquaint you by tranfmitting the original letters and other authentic evidence. But if you determine to profecute your prefent ftudies for the remainder of your life, you fhall have no caufe to complain of my filence.

---

### Epiftle III. To Libanius *.

A. D. 362.

THOUGH this is now the third day, the philofopher Prifcus † is not yet arrived, and a letter from him feems to intimate that he will defer his journey. As you have forgotten your promife, I muft remind you of it by demanding my debt. This debt, you well know, it is no lefs eafy for

---

* For an account of this fophift, and fome of his epiftles, fee Vol. I. p. 303.

† A Platonift, whom, at the folicitation of Maximus, fprung from the fame fchool, the Emperor fent for from Greece. He was fo referved and myfterious in what he knew, as even to tax thofe, who communicated their learning, with prodigality and profanenefs. But when he condefcended to difplay his own talents, he difcovered a profound knowledge of the fyftems of the ancients. The court did not corrupt him, and, inftead of becoming a courtier himfelf, he endeavoured to render the courtiers philofopers.

He was one of the philofophers that attended Julian to the Perfian war, and with whom he harangued in his laft moments on the nature of the foul. He was called in queftion in the reign of the Emperor Valens; but his innocence was immediately acknowledged. La Bleterie.

you

you to difcharge, than it is agreeable to me to receive. Send me therefore your oration, and that
divine difcourfe; but, by Mercury and the Mufes,
fend them foon. For thefe three days, be affured,
you have much wafted me, if what the Sicilian
poet fays be true,

Lovers in one day grow old *.

If this be a fact, as no doubt it is, you, my good
friend, have trebled my age.

I have dictated this letter in the midft of bufinefs. I could not write to you myfelf, as my hand
is more tardy than my tongue. But my tongue
alfo is at prefent tardy and inarticulate through
difufe. Farewell, my deareft and beft loved
brother!

---

Epiftle IV. To ARISTOMENES †.

IS an invitation neceffary from me to you, and
muft friendly offices never be anticipated? Let
us take care not to introduce fuch a troublefome
cuftom

A. D. 362.

* Theocritus, Idyll. XII. by Fawkes.
† This, was, without doubt, a man of learning, and
perhaps a philofopher. From the conclufion of the Epiftle
it may be fuppofed, that he was zealous for the Pagan religion, and perfectly well acquainted with the ceremonies.
This Epiftle feems to have been written by Julian, when
he was in Cappadocia; where he ftaid fome time in his way
from Conftantinople to Antioch. LA BLETERIE.
In the MS. of Voffius it is addreffed " to Ariftoxenus."
PETAU.

cuftom as that of expecting a friend to be as
ceremonious as a common acquaintance. If I am
afked, " How can you and I be ftyled friends, as
" we are not yet acquainted ?" I anfwer, Why do
we profefs ourfelves friends to thofe who were
born a thoufand or even two thoufand years ago ?
Becaufe they were good and virtuous. We wifh
to refemble them. And though as to myfelf I
am confcious of being in fact far otherwife, in
inclination I am certainly not far diftant.

But to ceafe trifling, if you come uninvited, you
will be cordially welcome; but if you expect an
invitation, you here receive it. Therefore, by
Jupiter the Hofpitable, haften hither, I intreat
you, as foon as poffible, and fhew us, among the
Cappadocians, a true Greek *. For as yet fome
                                        facrifice

---

The lxxxixth Latin Epiftle of Libanius, b. iii. feems to
confirm the former reading, being addreffed " to Arifto-
" menes," and much on the fame fubject. Being fhort, I
will add it in Englifh:

" You wifh, I hear, to be known to me. Be affured
" that you have gained your wifh, as I am better acquainted
" with nothing than with you. For who can be ignorant
" of the fplendor of fuch a genius? Befides, my love for
" you is fuch, that I love myfelf fcarce more. Confe-
" quently, command my fervices, if any thing fhould offer
" in which I can be ufeful."

* Ανδρα εν Καππαδοκαις καθαρως Ελληνα. " A pure Greek
" among the Cappadocians." The reftorer of the Greek
religion could not but be difpleafed with Cappadocia.
t. Caefarea, the capital of the province, was almoft entirely Chriftian. The temples of Jupiter and Apollo, the
tutelar deities of the city, had been long deftroyed. Even
in the reign of Julian, the Chriftians had juft pulled down
                                        the

the temple of Fortune, the only one that remained. This prince, not contented with confiscating the effects, moveable and immoveable, of the churches, enrolling the clergy in the moft defpicable militia, and putting to death thofe who had affifted in the deftruction of the temple of Fortune, erafed the town from the number of cities, fubjected it to taxation, and made it refume the name of Mazaca, which it bore before Tiberius gave it the name of Cæfarea. 2. In Cappadocia the Pagans themfelves could not be agreeable to Julian. Befides his complaining of their want of zeal, their Paganifm was apparently blended with the religion of the Magi. Strabo, a native of the province, fays, (*Geogr. l.* xv.) that, in his time, " there was a great " number of Magi, called *Pyræthi*, and feveral temples of " the Gods that were worfhipped in Perfia. Large in- " clofures were feen there, where thofe Magi kept up the " facred fire on an altar," &c. The fame author feems to fay, that thofe inclofures, called *Pyræthean*, were appendages to the temples of Anaïtis and Oman. The ftatue of the latter was carried in proceffion. More than three centuries after Strabo, St. Bafil, a Cappadocian alfo, and contemporary with Julian, being confulted by St. Epiphanius as to the origin of the Magi, and concerning the Magufæi, replied, that " the former were a nation ori- " ginally tranfplanted from Babylonia into Cappadocia, " and diffufed throughout all the country. They wor- " fhipped fire, and condemned the killing of animals, " though they fcrupled not to eat them when they had " been killed by others. They had neither any law in " their marriages, nor books, nor teachers, nor any rules " but their ancient cuftoms. They were alfo unfociable " with all men, and incapable of reafoning." The Magufæi could not be very different from the Hypfiftarii, a fect in which Gregory, the father of St. Gregory Nazianzen, was born. He informs us, that " the Hypfiftarii, " or worfhippers of the Moft High, profeffed to adore one " God only. They defpifed idols, and facrifice," which muft probably be underftood with fome reftriction, as the fame St. Gregory elfewhere fays, that " his father had " been fubjected to the idols of animals. They reverenced " fire and lamps; and though they were not circumcifed, " they obferved the fabbath and the diftinction of meats."

From

3

sacrifice with reluctance, and the few who have zeal, want knowledge *.

---

## Epiftle V. To the moft honoured THEO-DORA †.

ALL the books which you fent me, and alfo your letter, I received with pleafure by the excellent Mygdonius ‡. And though I have little leifure (the Gods know I do not exaggerate) I return you this acknowledgment. Farewell, and favour me with more fuch letters.

From thefe teftimonies it may be inferred, that the tenets and rites of the Perfian religion had made a great progrefs in Cappadocia, but had undergone feveral alterations. They were certainly adopted, in fome degree, even by thofe who embraced the Greek religion ; a mixture highly offenfive to Julian, who thought that the re-eftablifhment of Hellenifm, in its purity, was the chief purpofe of his exiftence.

LA BLETERIE.

* Εθελονίας μεν, ακ' ειδοίας δι θυειν, "Willing, but not know-" ing how, to facrifice." Like thofe Chriftians, who, St. Paul fays, had *a zeal of God, but not according to knowledge.* Rom. x. 2.

† This literary lady I apprehend to be the fame who is addreffed by Libanius in the following fhort Epiftle (the MCCXCIXth). " We, in return, invite you to come hither, " and leave the fea. For it is better that you fhould live " foberly with us than that we fhould feaft with you." By this fhe appears to have been a perfon of fortune as well as learning.

‡ This alfo was a friend of Libanius, as appears from two Epiftles to him, the CCCCLXXIft and the DXVIIIth ; in the firft of which that fophift fays, " he was like a pa-" rent to him at Athens."

Ep:ftle

## Epiſtle VI. To Ecdicius, Præfeſt of Ægypt *,

**T**HOUGH you write to me on no other ſubject †, you ought, however, to have written concerning that enemy of the Gods, Athanaſius,

A. D.
362.

* It appears from Epiſtle L, that Ecdicius was very
remiſs in writing to Julian even on ſubjeſts in which he
was the moſt intereſted. La Bleterie.

Ecdicius ſtudied oratory at Athens with Libanius, as
appears from ſeveral of his Epiſtles.

† After the tumult of Alexandria had ſubſided, by the
maſſacre of George [ſee Epiſtles IX and X], Athanaſius,
amidſt the public acclamations, ſeated himſelf on the
throne from which his unworthy competitor had been pre-
cipitated. Julian, who deſpiſed the Chriſtians, honoured
Athanaſius with his ſincere and peculiar hatred . . . He
again baniſhed the archbiſhop from the city; and he was
pleaſed to ſuppoſe, that this act of juſtice would be highly
agreeable to his pious ſubjeſts. The preſſing ſolicitations
of the people ſoon convinced him, that the majority of the
Alexandrians were Chriſtians; and that the greateſt part
of the Chriſtians were firmly attached to the cauſe of their
oppreſſed primate. But the knowledge of their ſentiments,
inſtead of perſuading him to recall his decree, provoked
him to extend to all Ægypt the term of the exile of Athanaſius. The zeal of the multitude rendered Julian ſtill
more inexorable ; he was alarmed by the danger of leaving
at the head of a tumultuous city a daring and popular
leader ; and the language of his reſentment diſcovers the
opinion which he entertained of the courage and abilities
of Athanaſius. The execution of the ſentence was ſtill
delayed by the caution, or negligence, of Ecdicius, Præfeſt
of Ægypt, who was at length awakened from his lethargy
by this ſevere reprimand. Gibbon.

The death of Athanaſius was not expreſsly commanded ;
but the Præfeſt of Ægypt underſtood that it was ſafer for
him

naſius, eſpecially as you have long been acquainted with our edicts againſt him. I now ſwear, by the great Serapis, that if that enemy of the Gods does not leave Alexandria, or rather Ægypt, before the calends of December, the cohort that you command ſhall be fined a hundred pounds of gold *.

him to exceed, than to neglect, the orders of an irritated maſter. The archbiſhop prudently retired to the monaſteries of the deſert, and lived to triumph over the aſhes of a prince, who in words of formidable import had declared his wiſh, that the whole venom of the Galilean ſchool were contained in the ſingle perſon of Athenaſius.          *Ibid.*

Not contented with baniſhing Athanaſius, the Emperor gave perhaps ſecret orders to put him to death; or at leaſt Ecdicius, to ingratiate himſelf with Julian, who ſeemed diſſatisfied with his negligence, took a reſolution to deliver Paganiſm for ever from ſo formidable an enemy. Be it as it may, Athanaſius went up the Nile in order to retire into the Thebais, when he was informed that he was purſued. " Fear nothing," ſaid he to the companions of his flight. " Let us ſhew, that he who protects us is greater than " he who perſecutes us." Saying this, he made the boat ſteer back towards Alexandria. They ſoon after met the aſſaſſin, who aſked them if they had ſeen Athanaſius, and whether he was far off? He is very near, they replied. ' If you make ever ſo little haſte, you cannot fail to over- ' take him.' The aſſaſſin went on making haſte, in vain. Athanaſius returned to Alexandria, and there remained concealed.          La Bleterie.

The three Epiſtles of Julian, which explain his intentions and conduct with regard to Athanaſius, ſhould be diſpoſed in the following chronological order, xxvi, x, vi.          Gibbon.

M. de la Bleteric has, by miſtake, placed the xth before the xxvith.

* From the excellent diſcourſe of Mr. Greaves on the *denarius*, the Roman pound of gold, the uſual method of reckoning large ſums, may be computed at forty pounds ſterling.          Gibbon.

4000 pounds ſterling therefore would have been the fine.

You

You know, that, flow as I am in condemning, when I have once condemned, I am much flower in pardoning *.

*P. S. In his own hand.*

It grieves me extremely to fee all the Gods defpifed by him. None of your tranfactions, will give me fo much pleafure as to hear that the wicked Athanafius, who has prefumed in my dominions to perfuade fome Greek women of rank to be baptized, is expelled from all parts of Ægypt †.

---

## Epiftle VII.  To Artabius ‡.

BY the Gods, I would neither have the Galileans put to death, nor fcourged, unjuftly, nor be in any other manner ill-treated. I think it, never-

A. D. 361.

---

* Surely this, and the other letters relating to Athanafius, fhew that Julian did not practife that indulgence and moderation towards the Chriftians which he fometimes boafted of. For no fault is alleged againft Athanafius, except that he was " an enemy of the Gods," and made convicts to Chriftianity from among the Gentiles.
                                        Lardner.

† Mr. Gibbon tranflates this paffage thus: " Under " my reign the baptifm of feveral Grecian ladies of the " higheft rank has been the effect of his perfecutions;" and adds, " I have preferved the ambiguous fenfe of the " laft word (δωκισθαι) the ambiguity of a tyrant who wifhed " to find, or to create, guilt."

‡ This Artabius, I imagine, is unknown. What is here given as an Epiftle of Julian is perhaps a fragment of fome edict. There cannot be a doubt that this prince publifhed fuch a one at the beginning of his reign, declaring Paganifm the religion of the empire, and at the fame time forbidding

nevertheless, highly proper that the worshippers of the Gods should be preferred to them. By the madnefs of the Galileans * the empire was almoft ruined ‡, but by the goodnefs of the Gods we are now preferved. We ought therefore to honour the Gods, and alfo religious men and ftates.

## Epiftle VIII. To George ‡.

A. D. 362. " YOU are come, Telemachus §," fays the poet. I have now feen you in your letter. I have there feen your divine mind in miniature, like a large ftatue copied on a fmall feal. For

forbidding the Chriftians to be ill-treated. This therefore muft have been written in 361.    La Bleterie.
    This edict fufficiently indicates what treatment the Chriftians were to expect in his reign.    Lardner.
   * It was his fancy to call the Chriftians Galileans. In this appellation there was no reafon or argument. But it might anfwer Julian's purpofe to make them appear contemptible in the eyes of weak people.    Ibid.
   † It is certain, that the Arian perfecution produced great evils in the ftate. Conftantius, defirous of being a divine, neglected the duties of an emperor. In order to hold councils, he ruined the public carriages, and expended immenfe fums, &c. But it is unjuft to charge the Chriftian religion with faults which it condemns even when committed for its fupport. Of all religions it is beft calculated to render a ftate happy.    La Bleterie.
   ‡ The procurator, or one of the receivers, of the Cæfar. Epiftle LV is alfo addreffed to him, with the addition of Καθολικω, which the MS. of Voffius has annexed to this.
   § Ηλυθες, Τηλιμαχι. In Odyff. XVI. 23. Ηλθις, κ. τ. λ. the beginning of the welcome of Eumæus to that prince on his return from Pylos.

much

much may be expreſſed in little. The wiſe Phidias * was not only celebrated for his Olympic
and Athenian ſtatues, but alſo for compriſing works
of real art in ſmall ſculptures. Such, it is ſaid,
were his graſshopper and bee, and perhaps his
fly †, each of which, though the braſs was formed
by nature, ſeemed animated by art. But in theſe,
it may be ſaid, the appearances of truth might be
owing to the ſmallneſs of the inſects. Obſerve then
his Alexander hunting on horſeback ‡, whoſe
whole dimenſions do not exceed the ſize of a
finger-nail: Each figure, however, is ſo wonder-
fully executed, that Alexander even wounds the
beaſt, and with his looks terrifies the ſpectator.
But the horſe refuſing to rear up, even in this

---

* This excellent Greek ſculptor, in the year of Rome
323, finiſhed the ivory ſtatue of Minerva, ſo much extolled
by the ancients, and conſidered as the maſter-piece of his
art. He placed it in the citadel of Athens. Afterwards,
being baniſhed from that city, he retired into the province
of Elis, where he was killed, after finiſhing the ſtatue of
Jupiter [of ivory alſo, according to Pliny] which he placed
in the temple of Delphi, and which has been reckoned one
of the wonders of the world.      MORERI.

† Theſe do not occur among the works of this artiſt
enumerated by Pliny, in his Natural Hiſtory, xxxiv. 8.
though he ſays, that, " in ſmall works Phidias had equal
magnificence." Julian does not ſpeak of them as then
extant—φασιν is his expreſſion, " it is ſaid." A graſshopper
and locuſt of Myron are mentioned by Pliny, as celebrated
in the poems of Erinna.

‡ Here Julian ſeems to refer to ſome well-known work
then in being, (probably at Rome or Conſtantinople). The
expreſſion is Σκοπει, " Behold." A hunting-match of Alexander by Myron, is mentioned alſo by Erinna, as we learn
from Pliny.

theft

theft of motion, moves by art. The same impreffions, my excellent friend, you have made on
me. For having been often crowned victor in the
lifts of eloquent Mercury, your writings, though
few, are excellent, and remind me of the Ulyffes
of Homer, who, by only faying who he was, terrified the Phæäcians *. Therefore, if my friendship
can be ferviceable to you, you may freely command
it. That even the meaneft can be ufeful, princes
may learn from the moufe, whofe gratitude preferved the lion †.

---

* In Odyff. IX. 19. Ulyffes tells Alcinous and the
Phæäcians who he is, by faying, Εμ' Οδυσευς Λαιρλιαδης,
    Behold Ulyffes, fam'd Laërtes' fon,
but no terror or confufion, on their part, is mentioned,
nor is his narrative difcontinued till b. XI. Perhaps Julian
has fubftituted by miftake (trufting to his memory) " the
" Phæäcians" for " the fuitors," who are indeed faid (XXII.
42 ) to have trembled at hearing " who Ulyffes was."
    ————————— confus'd the fuitors ftood,
  F om their pale cheeks recedes the flying blood.
                         POPE. 53.

† Alluding to the fable of the moufe, who, having been
preferved by a lion, in return extricated her benefactor from
a net, by gnawing the meflies.
    To this fable Libanius alfo alludes, in his XLVIIth
Epiftle: " We mice endeavour more to affift you lions, than
" you lions, us ;" and that proverb, which Synefius ufes,
" he prefers a moufe to a lion," feems not unknown to the
ancients, applied to thofe who promife much, but perform
little.                      WOLFIUS.

Epiftle

Epiſtle IX. To Ecdicius, Præfeɛt of Ægypt.

SOME delight in horſes, ſome in birds, and others in wild beaſts *. I, from my childhood, have always been inflamed with a paſſionate love for books †. I think it abſurd to ſuffer theſe to fall into the hands of wretches whoſe avarice gold alone cannot ſatiate, as they are alſo clandeſtinely endeavouring to pilfer theſe. You will therefore oblige me extremely by collecting all the books of George ‡: He had many, I know, on philoſophical

A. D. 362.

---

* Αλλοι μιν ιππων, αλλοι δι ορνιων, αλλοι θιριων ιρωσιν. M. de la Bleterie has tranſlated this, *Les hommes naiſſent avec des goûts differens*, and ſays, " Some delight in horſes, &c. (as in " the original) would have had no grace in French." The Engliſh language is not ſo faſtidiouſly delicate. Our affected neighbours might with equal reaſon object to that ſimilar paſſage of the Pſalmiſt " *Some truſt in chariots, and ſome in horſes,*" &c.

† Thus was truly Julian, what Cicero terms himſelf, *belluo librorum.*

‡ Surnamed, from his parents, or his education, the Cappadocian. He was born at Epiphania in Cilicia, in a fuller's ſhop. From this obſcure and ſervile origin he raiſed himſelf, by the talents of a paraſite, firſt to a lucrative commiſſion, or contract, to ſupply the army with bacon, and afterwards, by his profeſſion of Arianiſm, to the primacy of Ægypt, vacant by the expulſion of Athanaſius. His entrance was that of a Barbarian conqueror; and he oppreſſed, with an impartial hand, the various inhabitants of his extenſive dioceſe. Under the reign of Conſtantius, he was expelled by the fury, or rather by the juſtice, of the people, and it was not without a violent ſtruggle that the civil and military powers of the

phical and rhetorical fubjects, and many on the
doctrine of the impious Galileans. All thefe I
would have deftroyed *; but left others more
valuable fhould be deftroyed with them, let them
all be carefully examined. The fecretary of
George may affift you in this difquifition, and if
he acts with fidelity, he fhall be rewarded with
freedom; if not, he may be put to the torture †.

I am

ftate could reftore his authority, and gratify his revenge.
The meffenger who proclaimed at Alexandria the acceffion
of Julian, announced the downfall of the archbifhop.
George, with two of his obfequious minifters, were igno-
minioufly dragged in chains to the public prifon (Nov. 30.
A. D. 361.). At the end of twenty-four days, (Dec. 24.)
the prifon was forced open by the rage of a fuperftitious
multitude, impatient of the tedious forms of legal proceedings. The enemies of Gods and men expired under
their cruel infults; the lifelefs bodies of the archbifhop
and his affociates were carried in triumph through the
ftreets on the back of a camel; and the inactivity of the
Athanafian party was efteemed a fhining example of evangelical patience. The remains of thefe guilty wretches
were thrown into the fea.

The meritorious death of the archbifhop obliterated the
memory of his life. The rival of Athanafius was dear and
facred to the Arians; and the feeming converfion of thofe
fectaries introduced his worfhip into the bofom of the Catholic church. The odious ftranger, difguifing every circumftance of time and place, affumed the mafk of a martyr,
a faint, and a Chriftian hero; and the infamous George of
Cappadocia has been transformed into the renowned St.
George of England, the patron of arms, of chivalry, and
of the garter.                                    GIBBON.

* It was mean in Julian to wifh that all Chriftian writings
might be deftroyed. It was beneath a philofopher to entertain fuch a thought.                           LARDNER.

† The deceitful and dangerous experiment of the criminal *queftion* (as it is emphatically ftyled) was admitted,
rather

I am not unacquainted with this library; for when
I was in Cappadocia, George lent me several books
to be transcribed, which I afterwards returned
to him. ...

---

### Epistle X. To the People of ALEXANDRIA *.

IF you do not revere Alexander, your founder †,   A. D.
and more especially that great God, the most   362.
holy Serapis ‡, have you no regard for your
country,

rather than approved, in the jurisprudence of the Romans.
They applied this sanguinary mode of examination only to
servile bodies, whose sufferings were seldom weighed by
those haughty republicans in the scale of justice or humanity; but they would never consent to violate the sacred
person of a citizen, till they possessed the clearest evidence
of his guilt.             GIBBON.

  * This public Epistle [occasioned by the massacre mentioned in a note on the last, p. 17.] affords us a very lively
proof of the partial spirit of Julian's administration. His
reproaches to the citizens of Alexandria are mingled with
expressions of esteem and tenderness. " He suffered his
" friends," (says Ammianus), " to assuage his anger."
                                      *Ibid.*
  Socrates has transcribed this Epistle, and so has M.
Fleury.
  In speaking of George, he did not mention the two
officers who had been massacred with him; because, not
designing to revenge their death, which was most atrocious,
he was ashamed to seem to forgive it. His letter is full of
noble sentiments. I would not affirm, that, after having
written it, he was not in his heart pleased with those who
had furnished him with the subject. The Arians circulated
a report that the partisans of Athanasius were the authors
of the death of George; but the latter need no other
apology than the Epistle of Julian himself, which only accuses the Pagans.            LA BLETERIE.

country, for humanity, for decency? I will add, for me also, whom all the Gods, particularly the great Serapis, have thought proper to appoint ruler of the world *, and who ought to have been informed of the outrage that you have committed? But anger perhaps has misled you, and rage, which, subverting reason, often instigates the most enormous crimes, has, by a sudden impulse, urged you to perpetrate, as a people, such wickedness as in others you have justly abhorred and detested.

† Alexander the Great built this city, as one of the most glorious monuments of his conquests, about 330 years before Christ. Its situation was most advantageous, between the sea and one of the arms of the Nile. Alexandria became not only the first city in Africa, after the destruction of Carthage, but in all the world, next to Rome, as Herodian styles it. It is at present subject to the Turks. Selim subdued it in 1517, with the rest of Ægypt, and the country which composed the empire of the Mammelus. The city is almost entirely ruined, and it has no more than 8000 inhabitants. Its haven, however, is very good and commodious, and it has still some trade.     MORERI.

‡ A false deity which the Ægyptians adored. The Romans had often forbidden the sacrifices of Serapis to be celebrated in their cities. The idol of which the Emperor Hadrian, and afterwards Julian, wished to have a copy, was composed of all kinds of metals, wood, and precious stones. The temple and statue were demolished in the time of Theodosius the Great, A. D. 389, in consequence of a sedition excited at Alexandria by the Pagans.     Ibid.

* It is observable, that Julian was so addicted to the idolatry of the Ægyptians, that, though he worshipped so many Gods of his own country, he professes himself indebted to Serapis alone even for the empire. On this account perhaps he caused himself to be represented on coins, together with Serapis, or alone, with the name of Serapis inscribed, as if he were that deity.     BARONIUS.

But

But tell me, I adjure you, by Serapis, what were the crimes that incenfed you againft George ? You will anfwer, no doubt, " He exafperated " againft us Conftantius of bleffed memory ; he " brought an army into the holy city ; the king " of Ægypt * feized the moft holy temple of " God, defpoiling it of the ftatues, the offerings " and ornaments ; being juftly provoked, on our " endeavouring to fuccour the God, or rather to " prevent his treafures being pillaged, he with " equal injuftice, wickednefs, and impiety, dared " to fend againft us an armed force, fearing " George perhaps more than Conftantius, if he " had treated us with lenity, inftead of conftantly " acting like a tyrant."

For thefe reafons therefore, being enraged at George, the enemy of the Gods, you have again

* Ο Βασιλευς της Αιγυπτυ, rex Ægypti: fo it is expreffed in the edition of F. Petau. He thinks, however, that we fhould read ςρατηγος, (dux) or επαρχος, and M. Spanheim in-ferts that correction in the text. But that is not neceffary. Julian ftyles Artemius " king," or tyrant, of Ægypt, in derifion, on account of the outrages which he was charged with having committed, and for which the Emperor had juft caufed him to be beheaded. LA BLETERIE.

Some months after the tribunal of Chalcedon had been diffolved, the notary Gaudentius and Artemius, duke of Ægypt, were executed at Antioch. Artemius had reigned the cruel and corrupt tyrant of a great province. His merit, who demolifhed temples, and was put to death by an apoftate, has tempted the Greek and Latin churches to honour him as a martyr. But as ecclefiaftical hiftory attefts that he was not only a tyrant but an Arian, it is not al-together eafy to juftify this indifcreet promotion. GIBBON.

C 3                                   polluted

polluted the holy city, inftead of bringing him to a legal trial before the judges. In that cafe, there would have been no murder, no crime; by a juft fentence you would have been entirely acquitted, and by punifhing the impious author of thefe incurable evils you would have reftrained all who defpife the laws, all who dare to infult fuch flourifhing ftates and cities, and think that their own ufurped power is aggrandifed by cruelty. "

Compare with this epiftle that which I fent you not long ago; obferve the difference, and recollect how much I then commended you. But now, though I would gladly praife you, by the Gods I cannot, fo heinous is your guilt. For the people have dared, like dogs, to worry a man, without being abafhed, nor have kept their hands pure to approach the Gods, the purifiers of blood. But " George," you allege, " deferved fuch a " punifhment." Allowed, and one even more fevere. " And for us," you fay. This alfo I will grant, but not by you. For you have laws, which you all ought to obey and revere; and though fome individuals tranfgrefs them, yet ftill the republic fhould be well governed, you fhould obey the laws yourfelves, and not violate thofe which have hitherto been conftantly well adminiftered.

This is nobly done by you, men of Alexandria, in my reign, who, from my reverence towards God, and from a regard to my grandfather *, and

* Conftantius-Chlorus.

my

my uncle and namefake *, who governed Ægypt and your city, efteem you with a brotherly affection. The undefpifed authority of a good and ftrict government will never fuffer the abandoned wickednefs of its fubjects to pafs unpunifhed. A defperate difeafe muft be cured by rough prefcriptions. For the reafons above-mentioned I adminifter to you, however, the mildeft, this epiftle and reprimand, which I hope will have the more effect †, as you are by origin Greeks, and the laudable and illuftrious ftamp of that noble defcent ftill remains in your fentiments and actions.

*Let this be communicated to my citizens of Alexandria.*

* Julian, afterwards Count of the Eaft. See Epiftle XIII. Note *:

† I cannot fuppofe that he flattered himfelf with correcting the Alexandrians, merely by reprimands. Their tumults, which generally arofe in the theatre, were fo frequent, that the government hardly deigned to take notice of them. It found, no doubt, that they did themfelves fufficient juftice, for there was always fome blood fpilt. They were as foolifh as the inhabitants of Antioch, and much more wicked. LA BLETERIE.

Epiftle

---

### Epiftle XI. To the BYZANTINES .

ALL your fenators we have reftored to you, and alfo thofe of fenatorial families, whether they have attached themfelves to the Galilean religion,

* This title feems to me faulty. I do not think that any Emperor, efpecially in a law, has given the name of Byzantium to the city of Conftantinople. But this is not my only reafon for thinking that this law of Julian was not addreffed to the inhabitants of New Rome. Whatever was the city to which Julian wrote, he declares to the citizens that he admits into their fenate thofe who by birth, or any other means, obliged to take their feats there, fhould allege fome exemptions and privileges, by way of excufe. I have often mentioned the zeal of Julian to fill up the council of the cities. But that he had occafion to employ his fovereign authority to retain in the fenate of Conftantinople, or to recall to it, thofe who ought to have been members of it, cannot be conceived. I know, that, at leaft, till the reign of Theodofius the Great, this fenate was not in all refpects equal to that of Rome, without being able to afcertain in what that inequality confifted. But it was, without doubt, a very auguft affembly, efpecially when Conftantius and Julian had augmented its prerogatives. With regard to the Eaft, it was confidered as the public council of the Roman nation. It there held in the political order the fame rank which that of Rome held in the Weft. The fame titles were given to both fenates. The Emperors gloried in being members and chiefs of both, &c. Thus, though the place of fenator, even in the two capitals, was attended with very great expences, it muft have been the object of the ambition of individuals; and we fee that one of the methods which was employed to efcape municipal dignities, obfcure and ruinous honours, was to obtain, when they could, the place or title of fenator either

ligion, or have taken any other method of ab-
fenting themfelves from the fenate, fuch as have
filled any public office in the metropolis * excepted.

either of Rome or Conftantinople. One law of Conftantius
had fuffered ecclefiaftics, in certain cafes and on certain
conditions, to quit the *curiæ*, or municipal fenates ; and it
is probable that Julian, as well from hatred to Chriftianity,
as from zeal for the *curiæ*, was defirous to make the ecclefiaftics fit there again ; as we fee by one of his laws,
XII *cod. Theod. tit.* I. *De decurionibus l.* 51. *Decuriones, qui ut
Chriftiani declinant munia, revocentur.* But who can be perfuaded that he wanted to force them to be fenators of Conftantinople ? That would have been a ftrange kind of perfecution. I could add many other reflections, were I not
apprehenfive that they would make this note degenerate
into a differtation, perhaps curious, but certainly mifplaced.
I think I have faid enough to prove, that the word Βυζαν-
τιοις, which appears in the title of this Epiftle, has been
put by miftake, inftead of fome other fimilar word, which
I will not endeavour to reftore, becaufe I fhould only advance very uncertain conjectures.          La Bleterie.

From this Epiftle it fhould feem that the place of fenator
was confidered as a burthen rather than as an honour ; but
the Abbé de la Bleterie has fhewn that this Epiftle could
not relate to Conftantinople. Might we not read, inftead
of the celebrated name of Βυζαιhοις, the obfcure but more
probable word Βισανθηνοις? Bifanthe, now Rhodofto, was a
fmall maritime city of Thrace.          Gibbon.

* Εν τη μητροπολι. I fuppofe Rome and Conftantinople.
          La Bleterie.

Epiftle

## Epiſtle XII. To Basil *.

A. D. 361, or 362.

" YOU do not declare war †," ſays the proverb. But I add, from the comedy, "O
" meſſenger of golden words !" Come then, ex-
emplify this, and haſten hither. You will come a
friend to a friend. Conſtant attendance on public
buſineſs is fatiguing to thoſe who diſcharge it negli-
gently; but thoſe with whom I act are diligent and
induſtrious, and in every reſpect deſerving. I embrace therefore this opportunity, without neglecting public buſineſs, to take ſome relaxation. For
being ſtrangers to the courtly hypocriſy (which
you perhaps have experienced) of loading with

* There is not a word in this Epiſtle which can autho-
riſe the ſuppoſition of its being addreſſed to Baſil the Great.
The name of Baſil was not uncommon. Who this was is
unknown. As to the Epiſtles of Julian to St. Baſil, and
from St. Baſil to Julian, which are printed with the works
of that father, they are unworthy of either, both as to
their ſtyle and matter. Their ſpuriouſneſs is viſible at the
firſt glance. LA BLETERIE.

† Ου πολεμον αγγελλεις. A common ſaying, when any one
brings good news to a town, as war is the moſt calamitous
of all things: and yet with the rumour of it many people
at preſent are delighted; namely, thoſe who feed on the
miſeries of mankind. Julian has doubled the proverb; as the
following expreſſion, χρυσον αγγειλας επων, taken from the
Plutus of Ariſtophanes, is alſo proverbial. They are the
words of the old men, who ſupply the chorus, to Carion,
who had informed them of the approach of Plutus. They
are alſo adopted by Plato in his Phædrus; and again in his
IIId book De Legibus. ERASMUS.

praiſes

praises those whom it really detests, with mutual freedom we accuse; when neceffary, and blame each other, yet are as cordial as the greatest friends. Hence it happens, envy apart, that I find study a relaxation, and thus ftudious as I am, I feel no anxiety, and fleep ferenely; as when I have watche., I have watched not for myfelf alone, but alfo for others. Thus far perhaps I have been trifling with you through mere idlenefs, and, like Aftydamas *, I have praifed myfelf. But I fend this to inform you, that the company of a fage like you will be highly ferviceable to me. Haften therefore; as I have faid before, making ufe of a public carriage †, and when you have ftayed here as long as you pleafe, you fhall be conveyed wherever you think proper.

---

Epiftle XIII. To his Uncle JULIAN ‡.

A. D. 361.

IT is now the third hour of the night, and having no fecretary, as they are all employed, I with difficulty write you this. I am living, thanks

to

* An actor who, being ordered a ftatue in the theatre, for his excellent performance of Parthenopæus, infcribed his own elogium; whence the proverb, *Aftydamas fe ipfum laudat.* See Erafmus *in Chiliad.* p. 627. It is alfo ufed by Julian, in his LIXth Epiftle, and by Libanius.

† The government furnifhed carriages to thofe who travelled by order of the prince; and thefe were then called public carriages. L.A BLETERIE.

‡ Afterwards Count of the Eaft, the Emperor's maternal uncle. He had alfo been præfect of Ægypt. (See Epiftle X.)

4 At

to the Gods, and have been preferved from doing
or fuffering incurable evils.   The fun, whofe affiftance I particularly requefted, and alfo royal Jupiter, can atteft, that I never wifhed the death of
Conftantius, but that I rather wifhed the contrary.
Why then did I wage war? Becaufe the Gods
exprefsly commanded me, promifing me fafety if
I obeyed, but, if I hefitated, that which all the
Gods avert! By appearing openly in arms I
thought I might intimidate him, and thus accom-
modate matters more eafily; or, if a battle fhould
prove inevitable, I determined to rely on Fortune
and the Gods, and to wait whatever their goodnefs fhould determine.

---

### Epiftle XIV,   To LIBANIUS *.

I READ yefterday moft part of your oration †
before dinner; and after dinner, without in-
termiffion, I finifhed the remainder.   How happy

At his requeft, being alfo an apoftate, and hating the
Chriftians with lefs diftinction than his nephew, Julian
pardoned the Pagan murderers of George at Alexandria.
As foon as Julian had heard in Illyricum of the death of
Conftantius, he wrote this Epiftle to his uncle by the
meffenger whom he difpatched with the news of that interefting event.    LA BLETERIE.

* One MS. adds Σοφιτη και Κοιαιτωρι, " Sophift and
Quæftor." See the firft note on Epiftle xxvii, which is fo
fuperfcribed.

† Perhaps this was the oration in praife of Julian, which
is mentioned by Suidas; or perhaps one of the two that
are publifhed.    BARONIUS.

are

are you to be able thus to fpeak, or rather, thus
to think! What a difcourfe! what judgment!
what an underftanding! what wifdom! what arguments! what an arrangement! what ftrength!
what language! what harmony! what compofition!

---

Epiftle XV. To the Philofopher MAXIMUS *.

ALEXANDER of Macedon is faid to have   A. D.
flept upon the poems of Homer, that, night   361.
and day, he might be converfant with his martial
inftructions.

---

* The boldeft and moft fkilful mafter of the Theurgic
fcience, by whofe hands Julian (after having imbibed the
firft rudiments of the Platonic doctrines from Edefius) was
fecretly initiated at Ephefus, in the twentieth year of his
age.
    As foon as Julian had taken poffeffion of the palace of
Conftantinople, he difpatched an honourable and preffing
invitation to Maximus; who then refided at Sardis, in
Lydia, with Chryfanthius, the affociate of his art and
ftudies. . . . His journey through the cities of Afia difplayed the triumphs of philofophic vanity; and the magiftrates vied with each other in the honourable reception
which they prepared for the friend of their fovereign.
Julian was pronouncing an oration before the fenate, when
he was informed of the arrival of Maximus. The Emperor immediately interrupted his difcourfe, advanced to
meet him, and, after a tender embrace, conducted him by
the hand into the midft of the affembly; where he publickly acknowledged the benefits which he had received
from the inftructions of the philofopher. Maximus, who
foon acquired the confidence, and influenced the councils,
of Julian, was infenfibly corrupted by the temptations of
a court. His drefs became more fplendid, his demeanour
more lofty, and he was expofed, under a fucceeding reign,
to an enquiry into the means, by which the difciple of
                                          Plato

inftructions *. But I fleep with your epiftles as fo
many Pæonian medicines, and am no more weary
of perufing them, than if they were new and juft
received. To give me therefore in your corre-
fpondence a picture of yourfelf, write, I intreat
you, and fail not to write frequently. Or rather
come, with aufpicious omens; and be affured that,
during your abfence, I cannot be faid to enjoy life,
except while I am reading your letters.

Plato had accumulated, in the fhort duration of his favour,
a very fcandalous proportion of wealth. Three other
Epiftles (xvɪ, xxxvɪɪɪ, and xxxɪx.) in the fame ftyle of
frendfhip and confidence, are addreffed to this philofopher.

GIBBON.

Maximus and other philofophers accompanied Julian in
his Perfian expedition; and, when he was mortally wounded,
fome of his laft words were a metaphyfical argument with
Maximus and Prifcus on the nature of the foul, having
Socrates no doubt in view. See Ammianus, xxx. 5. He
was fined and imprifoned in the reign of Valens, and at
laft beheaded for magic by Feftus, pro-conful of Afia, in
374.

Though Maximus was greatly refpected, and much
admired by the Emperor Julian, and many learned Heathens,
as a great philofopher, and was alfo reputed to have commerce with the Gods, I do not think he was a wife man.

LARDNER.

* Of all the remains of antiquity, Alexander had the
greateft efteem for Homer, who, he thought, was the only
writer who had perfectly defcribed that wifdom by which
empires fubfift; and fuch was his paffion for him, that he
was ftyled "Homer's lover." He ufed to carry his works
always with him; and even when he went to bed, he put
them and his fword under his pillow, calling them his
" military viaticum, and the elements of martial virtue."

FREINSHEMIUS.

Epiftle

## Epiſtle XVI. To the ſame.

THE fable ſuppoſes, that the eagle, when he
would try his genuine brood, carries them
unfledged into the air, and expoſes them to the
rays of the ſun, that by the teſtimony of that God
he may diſtinguiſh the true from the ſpurious off-
ſpring. But I offer my writings to you as to
eloquent Mercury: and if they can bear your
penetrating ray *, you will judge whether they
are fit to be publiſhed. If not, throw them away,
as ſtrangers to the Muſes; or plunge them, as
ſpurious, in the river. Thus the Rhine, the decent avenger of adultery, does juſtice to the
Celts †, by overwhelming illegitimate infants with
his

* Την ϲην αϰλινα in one MS. which ſeems preferable to
αϰονν (" hearing") the common hearing, as it continues the
metaphor.

† On examining all the paſſages in which Julian has uſed
the word *Celtes*, I have obſerved that he makes it ſometimes
ſignify the Gauls, ſometimes the Germans, and at other
times both of them. I think that it is employed in this
latter ſenſe here. Claudian (*in Rufin. l.* 11.) reckons
among the Gauls thoſe to whom he aſcribes the cuſtom of
making their infants undergo the trial of water, by plung-
ing them in the Rhine:

Thus the fierce Gauls with yellow locks proceed,
Whom the ſwift Rhone or ſlower Arar breed,
Or whom, new-born, the Rhine's deep current try'd,
Or whom Garumna waſhes with his tide,
When ſwell'd with torrents from the troubled main,
The refluent river floats the cover'd plain.
JABEZ HUGHES;

But

But this poet does not afcribe to them this cuftom exclufively of the Germans. The nations fettled on the two banks of the Rhine muft have had nearly the fame manners and the fame cuftoms, becaufe many of thofe who inhabited the left fide of that river were of German origin. We know alfo that the Germans plunged their children in cold water as foon as they were born, to afcertain whether they were ftrong, and to inure them to the cold, as did many other nations, and as, it is faid, feveral in America do at prefent.

As to the intention of proving the legitimacy of infants, it is probably a fable invented by the Romans. Seeing them plunge in the Rhine thofe children of whom fome perifhed through weaknefs of conftitution, or by the mifmanagement of thofe who bathed them; and judging, by their own corruption, of that of other nations, they imputed to the Germans fome views which they had not, and an anxiety from which the prudence of the women fufficiently preferved their hufbands. Be that as it may, the moft ancient authors who mention this motive are Julian, Gregory Nazianzen, and Libanius; but many have mentioned it fince; among others, Nonnus, Theophylactus, Euftathius, &c. I know not whether Claudian fhould be added, as he does not mention the object of the trial. According to the author of a Greek epigram, quoted by Cluvier (*German. l. 1.*) infants were expofed on the Rhine in a buckler. When a fable is once invented, circumftances never fail to be added. I fhall obferve, however, that Julian, who in two paffages mentions this trial, fpeaks of it as a report in his fecond Panegyric on Conftantius; inftead of which, in this Epiftle to Maximus, fubfequent to that difcourfe, he expreffes himfelf in an affirmative manner: a difference the more remarkable, as in the fame Epiftle he takes care to relate only as a fable what he fays of the eagle and his young ones. Ὁ μὲν μῦθος ποιεῖ τὸν αἰτὸν, κ. τ. λ. *Fabula fingit aquilam*, &c. But, after all, it is probable that Julian was really certain of the fact, that he had feen the nations bordering on the Rhine plunge their children in that river, but that he was miftaken as to the motive. LA BLETERIE.

' The other paffage, to which M. de la Bleterie alludes, is the following, in the iid Oration: " It is faid, that, " among the Germans, there is a river, which is an in- " fallible judge of chaftity, which neither fighing mothers,

" nor

his flood; but such as he acknowledges to be of
a pure origin he supports above the water, and
again delivers into the hands of the trembling
mother, rewarding her with the safety of her child,
as a testimony of her uncorrupt and irreproachable
nuptials.

---

## Epistle XVII.    To Oribasius *.

WE are told by the divine Homer, that there
are two gates of dreams, and that their
credit, as to future events, is different †.  I think
you

A. D.
358.

" nor fathers dreading the event for their wives and chil-
" dren, can perfuade to conceal their fhame, being always
" true and fincere."
     That in thofe days of darknefs and ignorance fuch a fu-
perftition might prevail, may eafily be believed, when we
confider, that in much later times female chaftity was as
abfurdly fubjected to the teft of another element; and that
even in our own country, polifhed as it is, and in our own
memory, the aged of the fame fex have been expofed to
a trial fimilar to that above-mentioned, and drowning has
been deemed the only method of exculpating them from
the charge of witchcraft.
     * Of Pergamus.  He was phyfician to Julian, and one
of the four domeftics whom Conftantius allowed him to
retain when Cæfar. (See the Epiftle to the Athenians,
p. 78.) Oribafius attended him to the Perfian war, and in
his laft moments tried in vain all the refources of medicine.
This letter muft have been written in Gaul.
     The Chriftian Emperors afterwards ftripped him of all
his fortune, and banifhed him among cruel Barbarians, by
whom and their kings he was much efteemed, probably for
his fkill in phyfic or furgery. He was then recalled to his
native country, had his eftate reftored to him, and married

you have had a clear infight into futurity ‡. And

a wife with a large fortune. This we learn from his life, among thofe of the fophifts, by Eunapius, who mentions him as living when he wrote, which was about the year 400, above forty years after his going into Gaul with Julian. Suidas fays, that Oribafius was of Sardis, and both he and Photius mention feveral of his works, particularly thefe four : i. " An abridgment of the works of Galen," in feveral books. ii. " The fentiments of other phyficians, " as well as Galen," in feventy books. Both inferibed to the Emperor Julian. iii. " An abridgment of the other " two," in nine books, to his fon Euftathius. iv. " Another " compendious reprefentation of the principles of medi- " cine," in four books, inferibed to Eunapius (probably his biographer), at whofe defire it was compofed. LARDNER.

The Cæfar had rejected with abhorrence a mandate for the levy of an extraordinary tax; a new fuperdiction, which the præfect [Florentius] had offered for his fignature ; and the faithful picture of the public mifery, by which he had been obliged to juftify his refufal, offended the court of Conftantius. We may enjoy the pleafure of reading the fentiments of Julian, as he expreffes them with warmth and freedom in a letter [the above] to one of his moft intimate friends.                    GIBBON.

† OdyfT. xix. 562.
Immur'd within the filent bower of fleep,
Two portals firm the various phantoms keep;
Of iv'ry one, whence flit, to mock the brain,
Of winged lies a light fantaftic train :
The gate oppos'd pellucid valves adorn,
And columns fair incas'd with polifh'd horn,
Where images of truth for paffage wait,
With vifions manifeft of future fate.        FENTON.
Virgil has imitated this in Æneid VI. 893.

‡ It is obfervable, that Julian ufes this language to an intimate friend. Can his belief then in dreams be doubted ? In what remains of his books againft the Chriftian religion, he affirms that " Æfculapius often cured him by remedies " which he had difclofed to him." The Pagans believed that that God appeared to them in their fleep.
                                   LA BLETERIE.
                                        the

the fame I myfelf alfo have had to-day *. A lofty
tree † grew, I thought, in a fpacious room, with
its branches bending down to the ground, and
from its root fprouted another, fmall and young,
and very flourifhing. For this plant I was very
anxious, fearing left it fhould be rooted up, together with the tree. Approaching nearer, I faw
the large one fallen to the ground, but the fmall
one not only erect, but raifed into the air. Seeing
this, I exclaimed, with much concern, " What a
" downfall is this! The root, I fear, will perifh
" alfo." One, who was a ftranger to me, then
faid, " Obferve with attention, and be not afraid!
" For as the root ftill remains in the ground,
" the plant is unhurt, and will fix more firm-
" ly ‡." Such was my dream; what it portends
God knows.

* Even in his fleep the mind of the Cæfar muft have
been agitated by the hopes and fears of his fortune. Zofimus relates a fubfequent dream.　　　　GIBBON.

† This tree is Conftantius, and the fhoot Julian himfelf.
　　　　　　　　　　　　　　　LA LETERIE.

‡ He here plainly intimates, that he fhould fucceed
Conftantius. To the fame purpofe is the following paffage
of Ammianus, xxi. 2. " As Cæfar Julian was brandifhing
" a buckler, which he was exercifing with various motions
" in the field, the pegs, by which it was faftened to-
" gether, being fhaken out, the handle alone remained,
" which he grafped hard in his hand. And all that
" were prefent, being terrified by the bad omen," ' Let
" ' no one,' he faid, ' be alarmed : I grafp firmly what
" I held !'

D 2　　　　　　　　　　　　　　As

As to that wicked and effeminate wretch *, I am very defirous to learn, when he thus difcourfed concerning me, whether before we met, or fince: inform me as far as you are able. He well knows, that frequently, when he oppreffed the provincials, I was more filent than I ought; not hearing fome things, not admitting others, not crediting a few, and imputing many to his friends and favourites. But when he thought proper to endeavour to brand me with infamy by fending me bafe and fcandalous memorials to fign †, what was the proper ftep for me to take? To be filent, or to revolt? The former was foolifh, mean, and odious; the latter was juft, manly, and liberal, but, on account of fome prefent circumftances, inconvenient. How then did I act? In the prefence of many, who, I knew, would acquaint him with it, I faid, " He will " certainly alter his plan, its injuftice is fo ap- " parent." Hearing this, inftead of acting with difcretion, he did what, by heaven, a common tyrant would have fcrupled, and that almoft before my eyes. In fuch a fituation, what conduct could one, who is a zealous obferver of the precepts of

* Τὰ μιαρὰ ανδρογυνα. He means Florentius, præfect of Gaul. LA BLETERIE.

See the Epiftle to the Athenians, p. 92. Petau and others underftand this of the eunuch Eufebius.

† A fcheme to augment the capitation. *Ibid.*

This, in the reign of Conftantius, was in Gaul twenty-five pieces of gold, annually, for every head. The humane policy of his fucceffor reduced the capitation to feven pieces. GIBBON.

Ariftotle

Ariftotle and Plato *, with propriety adopt? Should I abandon the wretched people to the mercy of thefe extortioners, or fhould I not, to the utmoft of my power, protect them, reduced as they are, by that profligate crew, to the laft gafp †? Shall I punifh a military tribune, when he deferts his poft, with immediate death, and not deem him worthy even of interment; and fhall I abandon my own ftation, when I am called upon to defend the oppreffed; a ftation, in which I was placed by God himfelf? If difgrace muft be my portion, a pure confcience is no fmall confolation. Would to heaven, that I were ftill bleffed with fuch an excellent friend as Salluft ! ‡ If, on this account, I fhould be fuperfeded, I fhall not be concerned; as a fhort time

* It is plain that his illuftrious actions proceeded from pedantry at leaft, as much as from virtue. LA BLETERIE.

† In the original, To κυκνιον εξαδυσι, " they fing the fong " of fwans." Julian here adopts the ancient poetical idea of the dying melody of this bird. And the fame expreffion of the " fwan-fong" is proverbially ufed to this day, in the fame fenfe, in Sweden. Yet even among the ancients it was doubted by Ælian, denied by Pliny, and ridiculed by Lucian, and by modern naturalifts it is generally exploded. Some, however, have fupported it. Mr. Jodrell, in his elaborate illuftrations of Euripides, after employing thirty-four 8vo pages on the fubject, recapitulates the modern evidence on both fides; and a late writer in the Gentleman's Magazine (for 1782, p. 420.) wifhes " Mr. Hunter " would afcertain the capabilities of this common b rd for " fuch enchanting melody," as he has thofe of the Curan-Outang for fpeech; and queries " whether it may not ‹-- " fide, like that of bees and other flying infects, in the " motion of the wings."

‡ An officer of great merit, by nation a Gaul. See the Confolatory Oration on his departure, or recall, in Vol. I.

D 3                              well

well fpent is preferable to a long courfe of evil *.
The Peripatetic philofophy is not, as fome think,
more pufillanimous than that of the Stoics. In
this only, I apprehend, they differ; the former is
more fanguine and lefs fyftematical; the latter
more cool and prudent, urging a tenacious ad-
herence to opinions.

---

### Epiftle XVIII.   To the Philofopher
### Eugenius †.

D ÆDALUS, it is faid, formed waxen wings
for Icarus ‡; and endeavoured by art to fur-
pafs nature. Though I admire his art, I cannot
commend his prudence, in venturing to truft the
fafety of his fon to diffoluble wax. But if I had
the power, according to the wifh of the Teian
lyric, to be changed into a bird §, I would not
fly to Olympus, or on any amorous purfuit, but to

* Such a conduct almoft juftifies the encomium of Mamertinus; *Ita illi anni fpatia divifa funt, ut aut Barbaros do-
mitet, aut civibus jura reftituat; perpetuum profeffus aut contra
hoftem, aut contra vitia, certamen.*   GIBBON.

† There is great reafon to fuppofe that this Eugenius
was the father of Themiftius. For he alfo was a philofopher, and of no fmall reputation, if the teftimony of
his fon may be credited. See the IId oration of Themiftius.                                        PETAV.

‡ See Ovid. Metam. VIII. Fab. 3.

§ No fuch paffage occurs in any of the Odes of Ana-
creon that are known to us, or fo ftyled. See a note on
the Mifopogon, p. 291. The idea is, certainly, Anacreontic.
the

the tops of your mountains, that, as Sappho fays,
Thee, my care, I might embrace *.
·· Nature, however, having confined me in the
prifon of a human body, and not allowing me to
elevate even my words on high, with fuch wings
as I have I purfue you, with my writings, thus
endeavouring to be with you as much as poffible.
Homer ftyles words " winged †," becaufe they can
fly any where, like the fwifteft birds, and make
what excurfions they pleafe. But do you, my
friend, write alfo. For you have an equal, if not
a larger, fhare of the wings of words, to enable
you to reach your friends, and, as if you were
prefent, every where to afford them delight.

## Epiftle XIX. To Ecebolus ‡.

PINDAR thinks that the Mufes are of filver §,
comparing the clearnefs and fplendor of their
art to the moft fplendid of all fubftances. The
wife

---

* Ινα ση, το μιλημα τημον, περιπλυξωμαι.
This alfo muft be in fome Ode of Sappho that has not
been preferved,

† Επια επιροιηλα, Il. I. 201, II, 7. and innumerable other
places. Thus alfo Virgil,
————————————— verbis,
Quæ tuto tibi magna volunt. Æn. XI. 380.
‡ The preceptor of Julian, a fophift, whofe confcience
was fo fupple, that he was conftantly of the religion of the
fovereign, and perhaps, in reality, of none. Under Conftantius he inveighed againft the Gods of the Pagans.
Afterwards he declaimed for them, when his pupil Julian

had

wife Homer ftyles filver " fhining *," and water
" filvery †," as glittering by the bright rays of
the fun, and by its own fplendid form. Fair Sappho
calls the moon " filvery," and fays, " on this ac-
" count all the other ftars are obfcured ‡." Some
therefore may fuppofe that the Gods abound with
filver more than gold. For that filver is more fit for
the ufe of mankind, and better than gold, as being
more eafily attainable, and much more pleafing and
commodious, is not my idea, but that of the ancients.

had opened the temples again. And as foon as he heard of
the death of that prince, he acted the part of a penitent by
proftrating himfelf at the doors of a church, and, in a
lamentable tone, exclaiming to the faithful, " Trample me
" under foot : I am like falt that has loft its favour."
He made Julian promife, with the moft dreadful imprecations, never to be the difciple of Libanius ; precautions
likely to give Julian a greater tafte for that fophift.
                                        LA BLETERIE.

§ Pindar, in his VIIIth Ifthmian, ftyles the Mufe
" golden," (χρυσιαι); but I do not find that the epithet
" filver" is fo applied in any of his works now extant.

* Αιγληεντα.

† Αργυριον. Neither of thefe epithets are to be found fo
applied in the Index of Homer by Seberus. They muft
therefore be in fome work that has not reached us. Water
indeed is often ftyled " fplendid," (αγλαοι) both in the Iliad
and Odyffey.

‡ This alfo muft be taken from fome poem of Sappho
that is loft. The only paffage in which the moon is mentioned in her few remaining works is in a fragment,
and that without the epithet, which the tranflator has
added:

Δεδυκε μεν α σιλαινα,
Και Πλειαδις, κ. τ. λ.
The Pleiads now no more are feen,
Nor fhines the [filver] moon ferene.          FAWKES.

                                        There-

Therefore, if for a piece of gold, prefented by you, I return filver, as of equal value, think not the favour lefs, nor imagine, as in the cafe of Glaucus, that the exchange of armour is difadvantageous to you; and even Diomed perhaps exchanged his filver,* arms for gold, becaufe he thought thofe much more ufeful and more proper, like lead, to blunt the point of fpears.

What you wrote has occafioned this jocularity. But if you would fend me gifts more valuable than gold, write, and fail not to write inceffantly. For a letter from you, however fhort, will be preferred by me to the moft coftly prefents.

---

## Epiftle XX.  To Eustochius.†‡

A. D.
362.

T HE wife Hefiod thinks, that our neighbours ‡ fhould be invited to entertainments, that they may feaft and rejoice together, as well as lament and mourn together, when they meet with any unexpected misfortune. But I think, that our friends, not our neighbours only, fhould be

---

* Ἀργυρα χρυσων. In Homer the arms of Diomed are of brafs: χρυσια χαλκαων. Il. VI. 236.
M. de la Bleterie has not tranflated this Epiftle.

† A native of Paleftine, an eloquent orator, mentioned by Libanius in feveral of his Epiftles. In one of them he fays, " Euftochius, by his manners, conciliates every one; " they render thofe who are fierce gentle," &c.

‡ Works and Days, I. 340.
No friends forget, nor entertain thy foe,
Nor let thy neighbour uninvited go.    COOKE, 457.

invited; becaufe a neighbour may be an enemy,
but a friend cannot, any more than white can be
black, or hot cold. That you are my friend, not
only now, but have long been fo, and that your regard for me has never varied, if there were no other
evidence, my love and efteem for you would fufficiently prove. Come then, and partake the confular feftivity *. The public road will convey
you, and you may command one carriage, and a
fupernumerary horfe †. To complete your wifhes,
I have invited the friendly Enodia and Enodius to
meet you.

* It was a cuftom for the confuls elect to invite their
friends to the confulfhip, which was on the calends of
January; this was called *rogare ad confulatum.* And fometimes the confuls elect not only invited their friends by
their own letters, but alfo by the letters of the prince
himfelf caufed them to be afked to their confulfhip by his
agent; which honour, Libanius, in his oration on his own
life, p. 67, fpeaking of the conful Richomeres, fays, was
firft offered to him. Be that as it may, that the cuftom
was frequent in thofe times we learn from the 5th and 6th
books of the Epiftles of Symmachus. And of the fame
kind is this Epiftle of Julian.     VALOIS.
' Julian invited Euftochius both as prince and conful, which
he was the fucceeding year. Salluft the fecond was his
collegue.
† This παριππος I interpret to be a fingle horfe, a third,
in addition to the two that drew the carriage, which horfe,
for the greater expedition, king Theodoric, in an Epiftle
preferved by Caffiodorus, forbade to carry more than an
hundred pounds weight. The fame indulgence is granted
by Julian to Ætius, in Epiftle xxxi.     PETAV,
This is alfo omitted by M. de la Bleterie.

Epiftle

## Epiſtle XXI. To CALLIXENE *, Prieſteſs of Ceres.

TIME alone evinces men to be juſt. So we were taught of old. Let me add, pious and religious. But you ſay, the love of Penelope for her huſband was alſo thus demonſtrated. To this I anſwer, who can prefer, in a woman, conjugal love to piety, without being thought to have ſwallowed large draughts of mandragora †? And who that

* It is plain, by this Epiſtle, that Callixene had been moleſted, on account of her religion, for twenty years, that is, during almoſt the whole reign of Conſtantius. The date of it may evidently be fixed to the time of the journey which Julian took to Peſſinus. — LA BLETERIE. See note * next page.

The enthuſiaſm of Julian prompted him to embrace the friends of Jupiter as his perſonal friends and brethren; and though he partially overlooked the merit of Chriſtian conſtancy, he admired and rewarded the noble perſeverance of thoſe Gentiles who had preferred the favour of the Gods to that of the Emperor. Thus he praiſes and rewards the fidelity of this prieſteſs, and thus, in Epiſtle xxvii, he applauds the firmneſs of Sopater of Hierapolis. GIBBON.

† Mandragora has ſuch a ſoporific quality, that, if we credit Pliny, (xxv. 11.) large draughts of it are fatal. It is alſo called Circean, becauſe its root is ſuppoſed to be uſeful in love-philtres. Therefore thoſe who neglect their duty, and fall aſleep, are ſaid " to have drunk much man- " dragora." ERASMUS.

Thus Shakſpeare, in Othello:
—— Not poppy, nor mandragora,
Nor all the drowſy ſyrups of the world,
Shall ever medicine thee to that ſweet ſleep
Which thou hadſt yeſterday. Act III.

confiders

confiders the times, and compares Penelope, though
praifed almoft univerfally for her conjugal fidelity,
with the pious matrons who lately hazarded their
lives, and, in addition to thefe evils, twice the
length of time, can juftly put Penelope in competition with you? —

Difregard not thefe praifes. All the Gods will
reward you. We, for our part, will honour you
with a double priefthood, and to that, which you
had before, of the moft holy Goddefs Ceres, we add
the priefthood of the great Mother, the Phrygian
Goddefs at facred Peffinus *.

* The ftatue of Cybele had been removed from this
temple to Rome by Scipio Nafica many centuries before.
See Livy, xxix. 10. and Pliny, v. 32. When Julian arrived
on the confines of Galatia, in his way to Antioch, he quitted his route to vifit Peffinus. And probably he compofed
there, in honour of the Mother of the Gods, that hafty
difcourfe which is ftill extant, as " it coft him," he fays,
" not a whole night," εν βραχει νυκτος μερει, after venting
his anger on two Chriftians, one of whom had pulled down
the altar of the Goddefs.

The Peffinuntians had fuch an indifference for the
Mother of the Gods, their ancient protectrefs, that it is
no wonder that this priefthood was vacant. Julian confers
it as Sovereign Pontiff, the head of the Pagan religion.

LA BLETERIE.

Epiftle

## Epiſtle XXII. To Leontius.

THE Thurian hiſtorian ſays, that " mens ears
" are leſs faithful than their eyes *." But
as to you I diſſent, and my eyes are leſs faithful than my ears. For though I were to ſee you
ten times, I ſhould never truſt my eyes ſo much as
I now truſt my ears; having heard, from one of
unimpeached veracity, that, as you excell others
in every thing elſe, you excell yourſelf in acting,
as Homer expreſſes it, both " with hands and
" feet †." Allowing you, therefore, the uſe of
arms, we have ſent you a complete ſuit of armour
proper for the foot, being lighter than that of the

* Thus Horace, in his Epiſtle to the Piſos,

—————————— What we hear
More ſlowly moves the heart than what we ſee.

Julian ſtyles Herodotus, the author of this ſaying, " the
" Thurian," becauſe he lived and died at Thurium, in
Magna Grecia. It is taken from his Clio, ſpeaking of
the queen of Candaules, whom he wiſhed to ſhew naked
to his friend Gyges.

† When we mean to expreſs our utmoſt endeavours, we
ſay, " with hands and feet." For by the " hands" is declared induſtry in performing, and by the " feet" ſwift-
neſs in forwarding, an undertaking. Thus Hom. Il. XX.
360.  Erasmus.

horſe;

horfe; and have enrolled you among our domeſtic
guards, who confiſt of fuch as have borne arms,
and ſerved in the army *.

----

### Epiſtle XXIII. To Hermogenes, formerly Præfect of Ægypt.

A. D.
361.

ALLOW me to ſay, with the poets,
    How bleſs'd beyond my hopes am I!
How much beyond my hopes have I heard of my
eſcape from that many-headed Hydra †! I do
not mean my brother Conſtantius (whatever he
was), but the wild beaſts who ſurrounded him,
whoſe eyes nothing could elude, and who made
him more ſevere, who in his own diſpoſition was
not the mildeſt, though he ſeemed ſo to many.
But he is no more. On him therefore, as the ſaying is, light lie the earth! As to them, I would not
have them, Jupiter knows, treated with the leaſt
injuſtice; but as many charges are brought againſt
them, I allow them a trial ‡. In order to be
                          preſent,

----

* Symmachus, Epiſt. 67. l.III. "For to ſuch veterans
"a prerogative is due, that they may have the rank of
"guards, as a reward for their long ſervices." Petau.
  This Epiſtle is omitted by M. de la Bleterie.

† Πολυκεφαλον [iu one MS. τρικεφαλον] υδραν. Hermogenes
was, like himſelf, converſant with the Greek poets.
                                     Gibbon.
‡ To conduct this enquiry, Julian named ſix judges of
the higheſt rank in the ſtate and army; and as he wiſhed
to eſcape the reproach of condemning his perſonal enemies,

2                                       he

prefent,. haften hither, my dear friend, even beyond your ftrength ; for, by the Gods, I have long wifhed to fee you : and as I have had the great fatisfaction of hearing that you are well, I now command you to come.

Epiftle XXIV. To the moft excellent SERAPION *.

SOME prefent their friends with panegyrics; but I, as a delicious repaft, have fent you a hundred of our long-ftalked, dried figs †; a gift whofe beauty far exceeds its value. Ariftophanes fays, that " dried figs are the fweeteft of all things, " except honey ;" and he is afterwards of opinion that not even honey is fweeter ‡. The hiftorian Herodotus thought that a true folitude was fufficiently defcribed by faying, " it has neither figs,

he fixed this extraordinary tribunal at Chalcedon, on the Afiatic fide of the Bofphorus, and transferred to the commiffioners an abfolute power to pronounce and execute their final fentence, without delay, and without appeal. They were a fecond Salluft, Præfect of the Eaft, Prefident ; the eloquent Mamertinus, one of the confuls elect, and four generals, Nevitta, Agilo, Jovinus, and Arbetio. *Ibid.*

* A fenator, probably, of Conftantinople.

† Pliny (*l.* xv. *c.* 18.) mentions, among the various kinds of figs [twenty-nine in all], thofe of a purple colour (*porphyritides*) with very long ftalks. PETAU.

‡ The only two paffages in which Ariftophanes mentions figs, are in his Knights, act II. fc. 2. and his Acharnians, act. III. fc. 3. and in neither of thefe are they compared with honey. Julian muft therefore refer to fome play, or work, that is not extant.

" nor

" nor any thing elſe that is good *." As if no fruit
excelled figs, and where there were figs, nothing
good could be, wanting. Homer praiſes other
fruits for their ſize, their colour, or their beauty;
·but to the fig alone he gives the appellation of
" ſweetneſs †." Honey he calls " new ‡," fearing
leſt he ſhould inadvertently ſtyle that ſweet which
often happens to be bitter: on the fig alone he

* Herodotus, in the firſt book of his hiſtories, thus
proves the excellence of figs: " You are preparing to
" make war; Q king, againſt men who wear breeches,
" and other garments, of leather, who feed, not on what
" they like, but on what they have, inhabiting a rugged
" country; they have no wine, by Jove, but are water-
" drinkers; nor have they figs to eat, *nor any thing elſe*
" *that is good*."                          ATHENÆUS.
The above is part of the ſpeech of Sandanis, a Lydian,
who in vain attempted to diſſuade Crœſus from invading
Perſia.

† In the garden of Alcinöus, Odyſſ. VII. 117. Συκαι τι
γλυκεραι. κ. λ. τ.
 The bluſhing fig with luſcious juice o'erflows, POPE, 148.
And again, XI. 589. among the fruits that torment Tan-
talus, where though the line in the original is the ſame,
Broome drops the epithet, and ſubſtitutes two of his own:
——Figs ſky-dy'd a purple hue diſcloſe.
" Homer's epithets," ſays Euſtathius, " are excellent.
" For it is obſervable, that the poet gives every tree an
" epithet ſuited to its peculiar nature. Thus the apple is
" " beautiful," and its fruit, as he expreſſes it, " ſplendid"
" (αγλαος) he therefore ſtyles the apple a " ſplendid-fruited
" tree" (αγλαοκαρπος); among the autumnal fruits, the fig,
" by way of eminence, " ſweet," and the olive " verdant."

‡ Μελι χλωρον, part of the entertainment given by Neſtor,
in Il. XI. 630. and by Circe in Odyſſ. x. 234. Pope renders it in one place by " freſh," and in the other by
" new-preſſed." The Latin tranſlator of Julian has made
it *flavum*.

                                    beſtows

beſtows this peculiar praiſe, as on nectar, becauſe of all things the fig only is ſweet. " Honey," ſays Hippocrates, " is ſweet to the taſte, but quite " bitter when digeſted * :" and I am of his opinion; for that it breeds bile is generally allowed, and gives the humours a different favour ; which ſhews that it is in its nature rather bitter than ſweet. For it would never change to bitter, if it were not ſo originally, and afterwards became the reverſe.

But the fig is not only ſweet to the taſte, but eaſy of digeſtion. It is ſo uſeful to mankind, that Ariſtotle deems it an antidote againſt all poiſons, and ſays, that " for no other reaſon it is introduced at " the beginning and cloſe of meals; as, in pre " ference to every thing elſe, affording a ſacred re " medy againſt the injuries of food." That the fig is conſecrated to the Gods, and in all ſacrifices is placed on the altar, and is better for perfumes than any frankincenſe, is not merely my opinion; but all who are acquainted with its uſe know that ſuch alſo is the opinion of that ſage the Hie-

---

* Hippocrates ſays this, though not in theſe words, in ſubſtance, in his work *de internis affectionibus*, but of honey boiled : " Boiled honey is heating, and adheres to the " belly ; but after it is digeſted, it ferments, and the belly " ſuddenly ſwells, and burns, and ſeems as if it would " burſt." Galen alſo, in his iiid book *de facultate alimentorum*, ſays, that " honey, in its nature, is ſubtle, and by " its acrimony ſwells the belly before it can be digeſted, ſo " as to be voided. Therefore by correcting this we render " it fitter for digeſtion and concoction." And this is done by mixing it with water, and boiling both together. For then, being clarified, it digeſts eaſily.    PETAU.

rophant *. The excellent Theophraſtus †, in his
precepts of husbandry, explaining what kinds of
trees can be grafted on others, and the manner of
engrafting them, commends, I think, above all,
the fig-tree as capable of admitting various ſorts,
and as being ſingular in eaſily bearing at the ſame
time grafts of every kind, if you ſplit any of its
boughs, and engraft upon them the ſhoots of other
trees; ſo that it often reſembles a whole orchard,
diffuſing, like a beautiful garden, the variegated
ſplendor of different kinds of fruit. And while
the fruits of other trees continue but a ſhort time,
and attain no age, the fig alone ſurvives the year,
and accompanies the growth of the ſucceeding
fruit ‡. Homer therefore ſays, that, in the garden
of

---

* Ανδρος σοφυ και ιεροφανlu. I ſuppoſe that Julian here
means the Eleuſinian pontiff, peculiarly ſtyled *Hierophantes*,
or a revealer of ſacred things. He was obliged to devote
himſelf to the divine ſervice, and lead a chaſte and ſingle life.
He was attended by three officers, a torch-bearer, a herald,
and one who aſſiſted at the altar. (See Epictetus, *l.* III.
*c.* 21. and Potter's Greek Antiquities, vol. I. *c.* 20.) This
pontiff was ſuppoſed to be more profound even than Maximus in the ſcience of Theurgy. And Julian muſt have
been well acquainted with his ſentiments, as he initiated
him in the myſteries at Eleuſis, and was afterwards invited
by that prince to the court of Gaul, to perfect his ſancti-
fication. I am not confident, however, that the interpretation which I have given is the true one.

† Theophraſtus has treated on figs, and on the grafting
of them in the 11d book of his *Hiſt. Plant. c.* 1. and 7. and
alſo in his 1ſt book *de Cauſis, c.* VI.　　　　PETAU.

‡ Theophraſtus alſo mentions ſome wild fig-trees which
bore twice, and others thrice, in a year, as in the iſland
of Ceos. The late Mr. Markland, in an ingenious illuſ-
tration

of Alcinöus, fome fruits grew old upon others *;
which, as to other fruits, perhaps may feem a
poetical fiction, but, as to the fig, is confiftent with
truth, becaufe of all fruits it is the moft lafting.

Such, I think, is the nature of the fig in general;
but of all figs ours is far the beft; as that is fuperior to all other fruits, ours is fuperior to all other
figs, and though it excells every other kind of fruit,
it is, in its turn, excelled by ours. And, to continue the comparifon, it not only furpaffes, as is
fit, all others, but even in thofe particulars, where
it feems inferior, it really excells. Nor is this
undefervedly our peculiar lot. For it was juft,
I think, that the true city of Jupiter, and the
eye of the whole Eaft, I mean the holy and moft
fpacious Damafcus, as fhe is pre-eminent in every
thing elfe, in the elegance of her facred rites,
the magnificence of her temples, the happy tem-
perature of her climate, the beauty of her fountains, the number of her rivers, and the fertility

---

tration of Mark xi. 13. adopted from Bifhop Kidder, refers
" thofe who will not be convinced that the tree fhould
" have figs on it at the time of the Paffover," to the above-
paffage of Julian. See Bowyer's Critical Conjectures and
Obfervations on the New Teftament, 4to, p. 65.

* Odyff. vii. 117.
Each dropping pear a following pear fupplies,
On apples apples, figs on figs arife:
The fame mild feafon gives the blooms to blow,
The buds to harden, and the fruits to grow.
POPE, 154.

of her foil *, fhould alfo be unrivalled in this wonderful fruit.

This tree will not bear tranfplanting, nor will it leave its native foil, difdaining, like an indigenous plant, to grow any where but in the colony. Gold and filver are probably produced in various places; but our country is fingular in giving birth to a plant which will not flourifh in any other. As the wares of India, and the filks of Perfia, and all the valuable productions of Æthiopia, by the law of commerce are exported to all other parts of the world, fo this our native fig is tranfmitted by us into all other countries; nor is there a city, or an ifland, to which its admirable flavour is unknown. It graces even royal banquets; of every entertainment it is the boaft and ornament; nor is there any cake, or wafer, or conferve, or any other kind of confectionary, that is comparable to it in fweetnefs, fo much does it excell all other dainties. Other figs are eaten in the autumn, or are dried for that purpofe; ours alone are fit for either purpofe; they are good on the tree, and when they are dried they are ftill better. And were

---

* Damafcus is fituated in a very fertile plain at the foot of Mount Libanus, being furrounded by hills in the manner of a triumphal arch. It is bounded by a river which the ancients named Chryforrhoas, as if it flowed with gold, and it is divided into feveral canals. Damafcus has ftill a great number of fountains, which render it extremely agreeable. Its fertile and delightful meadows, covered with fruits and flowers, contribute alfo to its fame.

MORERI.

S

you to obferve their beauty when growing, how they hang from every bough by long ftalks, like fo many cups, and furround the tree in a circular form, thus exhibiting various charms, you would fay, that what a necklace is to the neck, fuch is this appendage to the tree. In the art of preferving them, there is alfo no lefs ingenuity than there is pleafure in eating them. For they are not, like other figs, thrown together in heaps, and promifcuoufly dried in the fun; but, firft, they are gathered carefully from the trees, and then they are hung againft a wall, by briars or twigs, that they may be bleached by the action of the pure rays of the fun, and may alfo be fecured from the attacks of animals and birds, being protected by the prickles as by fo many guards.

In the praife of their origin, flavour, beauty, confection, and ufe, my epiftle has been fportive. Let me now inform you, that the number a hundred is more honourable than any other, and contains in itfelf the perfection of all numbers. I know indeed that the ancient fages preferred an odd to an even number *. . . . . Homer feems to me

* Thus Virgil, *Ecl.* VIII. 75.—*Numero Deus impare gaudet.* Some paragraphs that follow in the original, being only a trifling play on the number a hundred, I have omitted, " as affording," in the words of M. de la Bleterie, " neither " entertainment nor inftruction." The French tranflator indeed has omitted the whole Epiftle, and reprobates it in his preface, as one of thofe " which turn on mere trifles." " I would fuppofe," he adds, " that this piece is only a

" profti-

me to have given in his poem, not lightly or in-
confiderately, a hundred-folded fhield to Jupiter * ;
as he meant by this obfcurely to intimate either
that he appropriated the moft perfect number, and
that which would moft honour him, to the moft
perfect God, or perhaps becaufe, as no number
but a hundred defcribes the world, which, on account of its rotundity, is difplayed in the circular
form of a fhield, that intelligence which is fo apparent in the world is alfo expreffed by a century
of circles.  For the fame reafon, hundred-handed
Briareus is placed near Jupiter, and contends with
the Father to give an idea of his perfect ftrength
by a perfect number.  Pindar alfo the Theban,

***

" proftitution of wit and learning, and perhaps a criti-
" cifm; for it appears, by the Letter itfelf, that fuch
" elogiums were fafhionable."  Wit and learning, however, are never more difplayed than by giving importance
and charms to trifles.

   * The paffage alluded to is in Iliad II. 447.
     The dreadful Ægis, Jove's immortal fhield,
     Blaz'd on her † arm, and lighten'd all the field :
     Round the vaft orb a hundred ferpents roll'd,
     Form'd the bright fringe, and feem'd to burn in gold.
                    POPE, 526.
This fnaky Ægis, but without the number, is defcribed
alfo in Il. V. 738.
   But to make amends (which I wonder Julian fhould
omit) the helmet of the Goddefs is defcribed as ἑκατον πο-
λιων πευλεεσ' αραρυια, either, as Euftathius fays, " becaufe
" it could cover a hundred warriors, or becaufe it had the
warriors of a hundred cities engraved upon it."  Pope adopts
the latter, but amplifies the idea :
   So vaft, the broad circumference contains
   A hundred armies on a hundred plains.      920.

    † Minerva's.

                             when

when he celebrates the flaughter of Typhœus in a
triumphal fong, and afcribes the ftrength of this
greateft of giants to the greateft king of the Gods *,
beftows fuch extravagant applaufe on him, for no
other reafon than his being able to deftroy this
hundred-headed monfter with one blow; as if no
giant was able to contend with Jupiter but he
alone whom his mother had armed with a hundred
heads, and as if no God but Jupiter was worthy
of the conqueft and deftruction of fuch a giant.
Simonides, the Lyric poet, thinks it a fufficient
commendation of Apollo to ftyle him Εκαιον, and,
in preference to any other title, adorns his name
with this facred diftinction, becaufe he flew the
ferpent Python, it is faid, with a hundred arrows;
and he delights rather to be ftyled Εκαιον than
Pythius, being diftinguifhed by that as by a fur-
name †. The ifland Crete, the nurfe of Jupiter,
as a reward for his birth and education, is now
honoured with a hundred cities ‡. Homer ftyles
Thebes

* This muft probably be in one of the Olympics that
are loft, as no fuch paffage, or "triumphal fong", is
extant.
† This feems a forced conftruction. Apollo's name
Εκαλος is naturally derived from his fhooting at a diftance,
like ικηξολος, fo often applied to him by Homer, and I do
not recollect his being any where ftyled Εκαλος. The above-
mentioned paffage of Simonides is not in his few remaining
fragments collected by Henry Stephens.
‡ Il. II. 649.
Crete's hundred cities pour forth all her fons. POPE, 790.
It is obfervable, that in the Odyffey, XIX. 174, only
— Ninety cities crown the fea-born ifle. FENTON, 197.
E 4

Thebes " hundred-gated *," but gives this praise
to no other, becaufe there is a wonderful beauty
in a hundred gates. I fay nothing of the heca-
tombs † offered to the Gods, of the temples a
hundred feet wide ‡, the altars with a hundred
bafes, the hundred rooms, the hundred-acred fields,
and other things, divine and human, which are included in the appellation of this number. This
number adorns the eftablifhments both of war §
and peace ‖, it exhilarates the military centuries,
and with its addition honours the title of the
judges.

on which Euftathius remarks: " Crete is ' ninety-citied,'
" in the Odyffey, which is ' a hundred-citied' in the
" Iliad, from an accidental circumftance; for it is faid
" that ten cities were deftroyed by Idomeneus, at his re-
" turn from Troy, when Leucus poffeffed it, whom, being
" his fon by adoption, he left guardian of the kingdom,
" " a foftered fnake," as Lycophron ftyles him; but thofe
" ten cities are faid to have been rebuilt after the Trojan
" war. Others underftand ' hundred-citied' here not in
" a determinate fenfe, but merely as ' many-citied.' For
" ' a hundred' was fometimes fo ufed on account of the
" diftinction of that perfect number, like ' a hundred
" fringes,' and the warriors of ' a hundred' cities. Thus
" ' hundred-citied' Crete is ' many-citied." Virgil has
followed the Iliad: *Centum urbes habitant magnas.* Æn.
III. 106.

　　* Εκατομπυλοι. Il. IX. 383.
　　That pours her heroes through a hundred gates,
　　　　　　　　　　　　　　　　　　POPE, 503.
　　† The facrifice of a hundred oxen.
　　‡ Εκατομπεδος. Such, as appears from Plutarch, was the
temple of Minerva, in the citadel of Athens. SPANHEIM.
　　§ Centurions, captains over a hundred foot each.
　　‖ *Centumviri*, judges chofen, three out of every tribe,
to hear and determine certain civil caufes.

　　　　　　　　　　　　　　　　　　　I could

. I could add more, did not the rules of epiſtolary compoſition forbid. Pardon me, if I have ſaid too much. Should it, in your opinion, attain mediocrity, the laudable attempt ſhall be communicated to others, ſuch is my confidence in your judgment. But if another hand ſhould be neceſſary to make it anſwer its intention, who better than you can poliſh this epiſtle ſo as to enable it to delight its readers?

---

## Epiſtle XXV. To the COMMUNITY of the JEWS *.

FORMER times were not ſo grievous to you on account of the yoke of ſlavery, as on that of your being oppreſſed by ſurreptitious decrees, and

A. D. 362.

* We are informed by ſome or all our eccleſiaſtical hiſtorians, who write of Julian, that he ſent for ſome of the chief men of the Jewiſh nation, and enquired of them, why they did not now ſacrifice, as the law of Moſes directed. They told him, that " they were not to ſacrifice " at any place, except Jeruſalem; and the temple being " deſtroyed, they were obliged to forbear that part of " worſhip." He thereupon promiſed to rebuild the temple at Jeruſalem. And we ſtill have a letter of Julian, inſcribed, " To the Community of the Jews," which, however extraordinary, muſt be reckoned genuine. For Sozomen expreſsly ſays, that " Julian wrote to the patriarchs " and rulers of the Jews, and to their whole nation, de- " ſiring them to pray for him, and for the proſperity of " his reign." That is an exact deſcription of the letter which is inſcribed (as above). It was writ in the year 362, as Bleterie ſuppoſeth; in the beginning of that year, ſay Tillemont and the biſhop of Glouceſter. LARDNER.
Aldus

and obliged to pay large fums into the treafury;
of which I faw much with my own eyes, and have
learned more from the edicts which were preferved

Aldus (*Venet.* 1499.) has branded this Epiftle with an
*α γνησιος*; but this ftigma is juftly removed by the fubfequent editors, Petavius and Spanheim. It is mentioned
by Sozomen (v. 22.) and the purport of it is confirmed by
Gregory (*Orat.* IV. *p.* 111.) and by Julian himfelf, Fragment, p. 295.                                              GIBBON.

What Gregory Nazienzen, in his fecond invective, tells
us of the conference that followed this letter, plainly fhews
it to be genuine. " Julian," he fays, " affured the leaders
" of the Jews, that he had difcovered from their facred
" books, that the time of their reftoration was at hand."
It is not a mere curiofity to enquire what prophecy it was
that Julian perverted; becaufe it tends to confirm the truth
of Nazianzen's relation. I have fometimes thought jt
might poffibly be the words of the Septuagint in Dan. IX.
27. *Συνλεια δοθησιται επι την ερημωσιν*, the ambiguity of which
Julian took the advantage of (againft helleniftic Jews, who,
it is probable, knew no more of the original than himfelf),
fignifying *the tribute fhall be given to the defolate*, inftead of
*the confummation fhall be poured upon the defolate*. For the
letter in queftion tells us he had remitted their tribute, and
by fo doing, we fee, was for paffing himfelf upon them
for a fecond Cyrus.                                       WARBURTON.

It feems that the Jews, after the deftruction of Jerufalem,
preferved a fort of monarchy till the beginning of the Vth
century. They had in Paleftine an Ethnarch, or chief of
their nation, who, by the toleration of the Romans, was
invefted with great power. He ftyled himfelf alfo Patriarch.
His place was hereditary, and defcended from father to fon.
All the fynagogues of the Eaft and Weft paid him tribute,
under the pretence of contributing to the fupport of the
Rabbins, who applied themfelves in Judea to the ftudy of
the law. Thofe whom he commiffioned to levy this tax
were ftyled *Apoftles* or *Envoys*. Thefe patriarchs, who had
made themfelves very odious by their extortions and rapines,
did not exift in 429. See M. de Tillemont's *Hiftoire des
Empereurs*, tome I.                                       LA BLETERIE.

                                                    againft

againſt you. The tribute again ready to be levied upon you I have revoked; this infamous impiety * I have reſtrained; and the decrees againſt you remaining in my offices I have deſtroyed, that none may be able to circulate ſuch an impious report. Of theſe great oppreſſions the memorable Conſtantius, my brother, was leſs guilty than ſome men, barbarous in their underſtandings and wicked in their minds, who frequented his table; whom, arreſted by my own hands, and thrown into dungeons, I put to death, that no memorial of their deſtruction might remain among us †.

Deſirous

---

* Ασιϐημα. Julian, deſirous of flattering the Jews, conſiders them as a ſacred nation, who could not be injured without impiety. LA BLETERIE.

† From this part it appears to have been written early in his reign, on his firſt coming to Conſtantinople, when he purged the city and palace of ſpies and informers, and the like peſts of a corrupted court. WARBURTON.

The chamber of juſtice, created by Julian, proceeded againſt the favourites and miniſters of Conſtantius with the utmoſt rigour. But that Julian thruſt any of them into dungeons " with his own hands," no where appears, and is not even probable. It muſt therefore be deemed a moſt extravagant exaggeration; or we muſt ſuppoſe, that the words ιν χιρσιν εμαις λαϐομινος were added by ſome Jew. Though with Meſſrs de Tillemont and Fleury, I have made uſe of this Epiſtle in the Life of Julian, I own nevertheleſs, that this paſſage makes me in ſome meaſure ſuſpect it, and ſtrikes me much more than the ſtyle of the Epiſtle, which ſeems to me written with much leſs purity than the others; for, after all, it is not neceſſary for it to have been dictated by Julian himſelf, or that all his ſecretaries ſhould have been pure writers. It might alſo, as well as ſome others, have been written in Latin. LA BLETERIE.

In

Defirous to fhew you ftill greater favours, I have urged my brother Julus *, your moft venerable patriarch, to forbid the tax which you ftyle apoftlefhip, and no one fhall opprefs you by ex-acting fuch for the future, that you may enjoy eafe and fafety in all my dominions, and may be ftill more fervent in your prayers for my empire to the moft excellent God, the creator of all things †, who

In the ftrange boaft of his perfonal atchievement in thrufting down the delators into dungeons " with his own " hands" the Imperial character is fo little preferved, that the learned M. de la Bleterie is almoft tempted, on this fingle circumftance, to give up the letter as a forgery. But he here forgets what he himfelf had before mentioned of the ftrange efcapes of this fantaftic monarch : " St. " Gregory Nazianzen fays, that Julian drove away with " cuffs and kicks the poor who came to folicit favours from " him." *Life of Julian*, b. IV.     WARBURTON.

* Julian in this refcript forbids the affeffments and tributes which the patriarchs of the Jews ufed to exact by apoftles. Of the Jewifh patriarchs, fee *lib*. xvi. *Cod. Theod. tit*. 8.     PETAU.

† This language of Julian is by no means a proof that the letter is forged. We fhall fee, in the conclufion, that he believed that the God of the Jews was the *Demiurgus*, who had created, or rather arranged, the univerfe. The *Demiurgus*, or Λογος, proceeded eternally, fubftantially, and of himfelf, from the firft God, named The Being, the One and the Good. Whether the Platonifts admitted a diftinction of nature between The Being and the *Demiurgus*, or whether they only acknowledged a diftinction of perfons, or laftly, whether they confidered the *Demiurgus* as an attribute of The Being, it is certain that they gave even the *Theurgus* the name of the firft, the Supreme God. It was the *Theurgus* whom Julian worfhipped under the name of the Sun-King, meaning not the orb which ftrikes our eyes, but an intelligence which pre-

who has condefcended to crown me with his own
pure hand. Thofe who labour under any anxiety
muft neceffarily be timid and difpirited, and cannot elevate their hands with confidence in prayer;
but thofe who are utterly free from care rejoice
with their whole hearts, and more frequently and
more effectually offer their devout fupplications to
God that the ftate may be governed in the beft manner agreeably to my wifhes. In this alfo you are
deeply interefted; that, after having happily terminated the Perfian war, I may dwell in the holy city
Jerufalem *, which you have long defired to fee
inhabited,

prefides over that orb, and holds the fame rank in the intelligent world which the material fun holds in the fenfible,
LA BLETERIE.

* Julian did not wait fo long before he gave the Jews
fome proofs of his affection, or rather of his hatred to the
Chriftians, by the project which he formed of re-building
the temple of Jerufalem; a project, which, as Pagan writers
themfelves atteft, was confounded by one of the moft aftonifh-
ing and beft attefted miracles mentioned in hiftory. *Ibid.*
. On this remarkable event Mr. (afterwards Bifhop) Warburton, publifhed, in 1750, his Difcourfe, entitled, Julian,
&c. (occafioned by Dr. Middleton's Free Enquiry into the
miraculous Powers) written, it is generally thought, with
temper and candour, though Mr. Gibbon brands it " with all
" the peculiarities which are imputed to the Warburtonian
" fchool," and charges the author with " revealing the
" fecret intentions of Julian, and, with the authority of a
" theologian, prefcribing the motives and conduct of the
" Supreme Being."
. Dr. Lardner, however, (Jewifh and Heathen Teftimonies, vol. IV. p. 47—71.) doubts the truth of this
miracle. His reafons are drawn from Julian's own writings
(the

inhabited, and in that, reſtored by my labours, may with you glorify the Moſt High *.

(the above paſſage in particular, which intimates his intention of re-building Jeruſalem after his return ,from the Perſian war, which never happened), the improbability of his allotting money for ſuch an expenſive work when he was juſt ſetting out for Perſia, the credulity, in other inſtances, of Ammianus, the incredible miracles, or pretended miracles, with which the hiſtory of this event is loaded by Chriſtian writers, there being no occaſion, at that time, for ſuch a miraculous interpoſition to hinder that undertaking, and the ſilence of ſeveral Chriſtian contemporary writers, particularly Jerom, Prudentius, and Oroſius. He concludes thus : " Let not any be offended " that I heſitate about this point. I think we ought not " too eaſily to receive accounts of miraculous interpoſitions " which are not becoming the divine Being. There are " many things ſaid of Julian, which all wiſe and good " men do not believe." But let us hear another excellent writer.

The interpoſition certainly was as providential as the attempt was impious. . . There are indeed many witneſſes to the truth of the fact, whom an able critic † hath well drawn together, and ranged in this order: " Ammianus Mar- " cellinus an Heathen, Zemuch David a Jew, who confeſ- " ſes that Julian was *divinitus impeditus*, ' hindered by God, " in this attempt,' Nazianzen and Chryſoſtom among the " Greeks, St. Ambroſe and Ruffinus among the Latins, who " flouriſhed at the very time when this was done ; Theo- " doret and Sozomen, orthodox hiſtorians, Philoſtorgius an " Arian, Socrates a favourer of the Novatians, who wrote " the ſtory within the ſpace of fifty years after the thing " was done, and whilſt the eye-witneſſes of the fact " were yet ſurviving." But the public hath been obliged with the beſt and fulleſt account of this whole tranſaction in Dr. Warburton's Julian, where the evidence for the miracle is ſet in the ſtrongeſt light, and all objections are clearly refuted, to the triumph of faith and the confuſion of infidelity. Biſhop NEWTON.

* The blind ſuperſtition and abject ſlavery of theſe unfortunate exiles muſt excite the contempt of a philoſophic

† Whitby's general Preface, p. xxviii.

Emperor;

To THE PRINCIPAL PHYSICIANS. An Edict *. 12 June, 362.
That the medical art is falutary to mankind, experience clearly demonftrates. The philofophers therefore juftly teach that it came down from heaven; for the weaknefs of our nature, and the frequent diforders to which we ·are liable, are by that corrected. Therefore, as reafon and juftice · require, and according to the example of former. princes +, we, from our benevolence, exempt you, for the future, from the fenatorial functions.

· Dated at Conftantinople, on the 4th of the ides of May, in the confulfhip of Mamertinus and Nevitta.

Epiftle

Emperor; but they deferved the friendfhip of Julian by their implacable hatred of the Chriftian name. GIBBON.

* This law was, without doubt, written originally in Latin. An abridgement of it is found, with the title and date, in the Theodofian Code, XIII. t. 3. de medicis et profefforibus. It is addreffed ad archiatros. The title of archiatri was given to the phyficians of the Emperor, and to thofe who practifed phyfic in the two capitals. It is therefore to the phyficians of the court, and to thofe of Rome and Conftantinople, that this law of Julian is addreffed. LA BLETERIE.

+ The Imperial laws exempted the principal phyficians from every public office. They could not be obliged to be members of the council, nor to exercife the magiftracies in the municipal towns. If they became fenators of Rome or Conftantinople, they enjoyed fome honours and privileges annexed to that office, without being required to difcharge its functions, or to bear its burthens, &c. See the Theodocian Code, at the title juft quoted, and the notes of Godefroi. Thefe privileges were as early as the reign of Auguftus. They had been confirmed by a great number of Emperors, and very recently by Conftantine, whofe laws are ftill in being. But it is well known that Julian was the declared enemy of exemptions, and that he loved to undo what Conftantine had done. The phyficians therefore were uneafy. Julian, however, maintained them

4

in

## Epiſtle XXVI.   To the ALEXANDRIANS.
### An Edict *.

A. D.
362.

ONE who had been baniſhed by ſo many Imperial decrees ſhould have waited at leaſt for
one edict † before he returned home, inſtead of
contumeliouſly inſulting the laws, as if there were
none in being.   For we have not allowed the Galileans, who were baniſhed by Conſtantius, of

in their privileges.   The Latin text ſeems to give them more
than is granted to them in the Greek.   *Securi à moleſtiis mu-*
*nerum omnium publicorum reliquum tempus ætatis jugiter agi-*
*tabitis.*   The Greek only ſays, των βελιυλικων λειτεργηματων.
It is remarkable that the exemptions of the profeſſors,
though they were the ſame as thoſe of the phyſicians, and
though Conſtantine had confirmed them by two laws, were
not attacked.   It was notorious that Julian's love of literature, and of thoſe who taught it, exceeded his hatred of
exemptions, and even of Conſtantine.      LA BLETERIE.

* Athanaſius had been baniſhed once by Conſtantine,
and twice by Conſtantius.   He was in his third exile when
Julian recalled all thoſe whom Conſtantius had baniſhed
on account of religion.   Prudence did not allow Athanaſius
to avail himſelf of this recall while his ſee was occupied
by George of Cappadocia.   But ſoon after the death of the
uſurper (ſee p. 18.) he returned to his church, where the
Pagans did not ſuffer him to remain long in quiet.   They
repreſented to the Emperor that Athanaſius would pervert
the whole city, and that, if he continued there, not a ſingle
Heathen would ſoon be found there.   Their complaints
determined Julian to iſſue this edict.            *Ibid.*

† This was not neceſſary, as Julian had, without diſtinction, recalled all thoſe whom Conſtantius had baniſhed
for the " madneſs" of the Galileans.            *Ibid.*

bleſſed

effed memory, to return to their churches *, but only to their countries. Yet I hear that he moſt audacious Athanaſius, with his uſual inſolence, has again uſurped what they call the epiſcopal throne; and that this has not a little diſpleaſed the people of Alexandria †. We therefore command him to depart from the city on the very day that he ſhall receive the letter of our clemency; and if he remain there, he may expect a much ſeverer puniſhment.

---

## Epiſtle XXVII. To the Sophiſt and Quæſtor LIBANIUS ‡.

ON my arrival at Litarbe §, a town in Chlcis, March, I found a road where were ſome remains of 363. the Antiochian winter camp. One part of it was; moraſſy;

---

* Whether Julian thought of this diſtinction at firſt, or whether it was an after-ſtroke, that this prince employed it only againſt Athanaſius is glorious to that prelate.

LA BLETERIE.

This explication ſeems evaſive, and perhaps was now firſt thought of.

LARDNER.

† This was the " pious" people who tore " men in pieces " as if they had been dogs." [See Epiſtle X.]

LA BLETERIE.

‡ It appears that Julian had given Libanius the honorary title of Quæſtor. But Eunapius reports, that Libanius refuſed the honorary rank of Prætorian Præfect, which one of the ſucceſſors of Julian would have given him; as leſs illuſtrious than the title of Sophiſt (*in vita Sophiſt.* p. 135.) The critics have obſerved a ſimilar ſentiment in one of the Epiſtles (XVIII. *edit. Wolf.*) of Libanius himſelf.

moraffy; the other hilly, and extremely fteep; over
the morafs loofe ftones were placed by chance, and
not artfully cemented, as roads are in a manner built
n other places, where, inftead of fand, the ftones
are laid in mortar, as in a wall. Paffing this with
fome difficulty, I reached my firft ftage *, about
the ninth hour, where I faw in the hall the principal part of your fenate †. Of the fubject of our
converfation, though perhaps you may have heard
it already, if the Gods permit, I will inform you.
From Litarbe I proceeded to Berea ‡, where Ju-

In this Epiftle Julian gives the journal of his march from
Antioch to Hierapolis.      La Bleterie.
 He informed Libanius of his progrefs in an elegant
Epiftle, which difplays the fertility of his genius, and his
tender regard for the fophift of Antioch.    Gibbon.
 § This place Euagrius mentions, *l.* v. *c.* 12, and fays, it
was three hundred ftadia from Antioch.    Petav.
 * It is fingular that the Romans fhould have neglected
the great communication between Antioch and the Euphrates.       Gibbon.
 † The martial impatience of Julian urged him to take
the field in the beginning of the fpring; and he difmiffed,
with contempt and reproach, the fenate of Antioch, who
accompanied him beyond the limits of their own territory,
to which he was refolved never to return.    *Ibid.*
 ‡ Now Aleppo. The inhabitants of this place are recorded with honour in the *Acts of the Apoftles,* ch. xvii. for
the *readinefs of mind* with which *they received the word,*
preached by Paul, *and fearched the fcriptures daily whether
thofe things were fo.* By Julian's account, they ftill adhered
to their Chriftian principles, receiving, as Mr. Gibbon expreffes it, " with cold and formal demonftrations of re-
" fpect, the eloquent fermon of the Apoftle of Paganifm."
 St. Bafil has addreffed two Epiftles to the inhabitants
of Berea, applauding their piety. See his works, vol. III.
p. 1026.

            piter,

piter, by the cleareſt omens, declared all things
auſpicious. Staying there a whole day, I viſited
the caſtle, and royally ſacrificed to Jupiter a wh:t:
bull *. With the ſenate I converſed a little on
matters of religion, but though they all praiſed
my diſcourſe †, a few only were convinced by it;
however, they were ſuch as, before I ſpoke, I
thought ſenſible; the others aſſumed a kind of
licence, and ſeemed totally deſtitute of ſhame.
Men are apt to be extremely abaſhed at qualities
that are laudable, ſuch as fortitude of mind and

---

* He was more a ſuperſtitious than a legal obſerver of
ſacred rites, ſacrificing innumerable cattle without parſi-
mony, ſo that it was thought, if he had returned from
Perſia, oxen would have been wanting; like Marcus Cæſar,
of whom, we are told, it was ſaid, " White bulls to Marcus
" Cæſar:" ' If you conquer, we periſh ' AMMIANUS.
To Capitoline Jupiter white victims only were ſacrificed
in triumph. See *Turneb. l.* 29. 26;

† The ſon of one of the moſt illuſtrious citizens of
Berea, who had embraced, either from intereſt or conſcience, the religion of the Emperor, had been diſinherited
by his angry parent. The father and the ſon were invited
to the Imperial table. Julian, placing himſelf between them,
attempted, without ſucceſs, to inculcate the leſſon and
example of toleration; ſupported, with affected calmneſs,
the indiſcreet zeal of the aged Chriſtian, who ſeemed to
forget the ſentiments of nature, and the duty of a ſubject;
and at length, turning towards the afflicted youth, " ſince
" you have loſt a father," ſaid he, " for my ſake, it is
" incumbent on me to ſupply his place."
Julian alludes to this incident [above]; which is more
diſtinctly related by Theodoret (*l.* III. *c.* 22) The intolerant ſpirit of the father is applauded by Tillemont,
(*Hiſt. des Empereurs, tom.* IV. *p.* 534.) and even by La
Bleterie (*Vie de Julien, p.* 413.) GIBBON.

piety;

piety; but in the bafeſt actions and ſentiments *, in ſacrilege and puſillanimity, they have the confidence to glory.

Batnæ next received me, a place to which I never ſaw any ſimilar but Daphne †. But though Batnæ may now vie with Daphne, not long ago, when the temple and the image were in being, I ſhould, without ſcruple, not only have compared Daphne to Offa, Pelion, Olympus, and Theſſalian Tempe, but even have preferred it to them all. The place above-mentioned is dedicated to Olympic Jupiter and Pythian Apollo. But on the ſubject of Daphne you have compoſed an oration ‡, ſuch as no other mortal,

Of thoſe who live in theſe degenerate days §, with his utmoſt efforts, could have written, and, I think, not many of the ancients. Why therefore ſhould I enlarge upon what has ſo elegantly been deſcribed by you? Far be that idea!

---

* Μαλακια γνωμης και σωμαλος. It is not ſurpriſing, that by the Pagans that abſtraction and contempt of the world, with which the goſpel inſpires every true Chriſtian, ſhould be deemed meanneſs of ſpirit. But why is not Julian aſhamed to blame in the Chriſtians thoſe virtues whoſe very ſhadow he adored in the philoſophers? See his Epiſtle to Themiſtius.                                        LA BLETERIE.

† See an elegant deſcription of Daphne by Mr. Gibbon, in a note on the Miſopogon, Vol. I. p. 280.

‡ This lamentation is ſtill extant in the works of Libanius, and compoſes his IXth Oration. It is entitled, " A " Monody on the Temple of Apollo at Daphne, conſumed " by fire, or, as it is ſaid, by lightning." It is tranſlated in this volume.

§ Hom. Il. V. 304.

I

At

At Batnæ (though the name is barbarous, the town is Greek) we inhaled the fumes of incenfe from all the adjacent country, and faw victims every where prepared. This, though it much pleafed me, feemed rather too fervent and foreign to religion *. For facrifices fliould be offered in private, far from all public roads and paffengers, and all that is required is a fupply of victims and offerings. But this by proper care may be eafily corrected.

Batnæ is fituated on a plain fkirted by a grove of cypreffes, none of which were old or decayed, but all were equally young and flourifhing. My palace was by no means magnificent, being conftructed of clay and boards, and having nothing ornamental. Nor could the garden vie with that of Alcinöus †, but rather refembled that of Laërtes ‡. There was alfo a fmall grove of cypreffes, and a row of thofe trees was planted along the walls : in the middle were pot-herbs and fruit-trees of every kind. I facrificed there in the evening, and again early in the morning, as was my conftant cuftom every day ; and as the rites were aufpicious, we proceeded to Hiera-

---

* He too clearly difcerned that the fmoke which arofe from their altars was the incenfe of flattery, rather than of devotion.　　GIBBON,

† Odyff. VII. 112.

‡ Ibid. XXIV. 204.—Laërtes cultivated land.
　　The ground himfelf had purchas'd with his pain,
　　And labour made the rugged foil a plain.
　　　　　　　　　　　　　　　　POPE, 235.

F 3　　　　　　　　polis,

polis *, where we were met by the citizens, and I
was received as a gueſt by one whom, though I
had ſcarce ever ſeen him before, I had long
eſteemed. Though you are well acquainted with
the reaſon, I cannot deny myſelf the pleaſure of
repeating it; for to hear and ſpeak of theſe perſons
is always nectar to me. Sopater, the father-in-law
of this, was a diſciple of the moſt divine Jambli‑
chus †. Did I not love all that were connected
with him, I ſhould deem myſelf guilty of the

* Hierapolis, ſituate almoſt on the banks of the Eu‑
phrates, had been appointed for the general rendezvous of
the Roman army, who there paſſed the great river on a
bridge of boats, which was previouſly conſtructed.

GIBBON.

The ancient and magnificent temple, which had ſancti‑
fied, for ſo many ages, the city of Hierapolis, no longer
ſubſiſted; and the conſecrated wealth, which afforded a
liberal maintenance to more than three hundred prieſts,
might haſten its downfall.        Ibid.

† Of Chalcis, a Pythagorean philoſopher, the diſciple
of Porphyry, and uncle to the philoſopher of the ſame
name, to whom Julian has addreſſed ſix ſubſequent Epiſtles,
and whom M. de la Bleterie ſuppoſes to have been here
meant; but as I underſtand that the father-in-law of this
Sopater (then dead) had been his diſciple, it ſeems rather
more applicable to the elder Jamblichus. The elder Sopater
was probably that Platonic philoſopher who was put to
death by Conſtantine the Great, being ſtyled by Suidas and
others, " a diſciple of Jamblichus."

The French tranſlator alſo ſtyles this Sopater of Hiera‑
polis the " ſon-in-law" (as well as " pupil") of Jambli‑
chus, for which I can ſee no authority in the original, or
in any other author. Let the reader judge. Ιαμβλιχυ τυ
Σωπατ͵ρος, τηιν κηδιςης ιξ οσυ. In the French,
Sopatre eſt l'eleve et le gendre du divin Jamblique, meaning the
youngeſt of theſe philoſophers, then living.

worſt

worſt of crimes. But there is another reaſon ſtill more cogent. Having often entertained at his houſe my couſin and my brother *, and, as might well be ſuppoſed, being ſtrongly urged by them to apoſtatiſe from the Gods, he had the great merit of never being infected with that contagion.

Theſe particulars, immediately relating to myſelf, I now communicate to you from Hierapolis. As to military and civil tranſactions, you ſhould be preſent to ſee and obſerve them yourſelf. For, be aſſured, if they were diſtinctly related, they could not be compriſed in a letter of twice the length of this. But, as I am writing, I will briefly men-tion them. I have ſent an embaſſy to the Sa-racens †, urging them, if they are ſo inclined, to join us. This is the firſt article. Next, I have diſpatched, as was proper, ſome obſervant ſpies, leſt any deſerter ſhould acquaint the enemy with our motions. Add to theſe, I have decided a mili-tary diſpute ‡. I am perſuaded, with lenity and juſtice.

* Conſtantius and Gallus.

† A wandering people in the deſerts of Arabia [who ſtretched from the confines of Aſſyria to the cataracts of the Nile], warlike and ſelf-intereſted, dangerous enemies and burthenſome friends. *Nec amici nobis unquam nec hoſtes optandi*, are the words of Ammianus. The love of rapine and war allured ſeveral of them to the imperial ſtandard, though Julian ſternly refuſed the payment of the accuſtomed ſubſidies. La BLETERIE.

‡ Στρατιωτικην δικην. M. de Tillemont ſuſpects that this relates to a fact mentioned by St. Chryſoſtom. Being

F 4                                                          ready

juſtice. I have procured excellent horſes and
mules, and my army is aſſembled. The boats are
filled with corn, or rather wi h biſcuit and vinegar.
What a long letter would it require to tell you
how each of theſe points was accompliſhed! What
was ſaid on every ſubject you may eaſily gueſs.
As to the happy omens *, having recorded them
in many letters and books, which I every where
carry with me, why ſhould I trouble you with the
repetition?

ready to paſs the Euphrates, Julian made an attempt to
gain ſuch of his ſoldiers as were ſtill 'Chriſtians. Some
ſuffered themſelves to be ſeduced, but the reſt refuſed, and
the Emperor did not dare to 'caſhier them, for fear of
weakening his army.                                        Ibid.
  * Infatuated with his expedition, he ſaw every thing in
the beſt light, and only kept a regiſter of what he conſidered
as happy preſages. He paſſes over in ſilence the fatal accident which happened when he made his entry into Hierapolis. Fifty ſoldiers were cruſhed to death by the fall of
a portico, and many more wounded. Ammianus xxiii. 2.
                                                           Ibid.
  Another bad omen is mentioned by Ammianus at Batnæ
in Oſdroena (after the date indeed of this letter), fifty men
being alſo killed there by the fall of a ſtack of ſtraw.
  Julian ſtayed three days only at Hierapolis, and then
proceeded to Carrhæ in Meſopotamia, fourſcore miles
diſtant.
  This is the laſt Epiſtle of his writing that is extant.

Epiſtle XXVIII. To Duke GREGORY *.

A SHORT letter from you is ſufficient to give me great pleaſure. Being much delighted therefore with what you have written, I return you many thanks. The love of our friends ſhould be meaſured, not by the length of their epiſtles, but by the extent of their affection.

Epiſtle XXIX. To ALYPIUS †, the Brother, of CÆSARIUS.

SYLOSON ‡, it is ſaid, came to Darius, re- minded him of a cloak which he had for- merly given him, and in return requeſted Samos. Darius

A. D. 361, or 362.

---

* Though the military Counts and Dukes are frequently mentioned both in hiſtory and the codes, we muſt have recourſe to the *Notitia* for the exact knowledge of their number and ſtations. The ſecond of thoſe appellations is only a corruption of the Latin word, which was indiſcriminately applied to any military chief. All theſe provincial generals were therefore dukes. GIBBON.

The Greek word is ηγεμων, which M. de la Bleterie tranſlates *Commandant des troupes.*

† Among the friends of the Emperor (if the names of Emperor and of friend are not incompatible) the firſt place was aſſigned by Julian himſelf to the virtuous and learned Alypius. The humanity of Alypius was tempered, by ſevere juſtice and manly fortitude; and while he exerciſed

his

Darius afterwards was much elated, thinking that he had returned a great prefent for a fmall one.

But his abilities in the civil adminiftration of Britain, he imitated, in his poetical compofitions, the harmony and foftnefs of the odes of Sappho. [See the next Epiftle.]    GIBBON.

‡ This minifter, who is ftyled by Ammianus " a man of an amiable character," and who, like himfelf, was a native of Antioch, afterwards received from his mafter, juft before he fet out for the Perfian war, the extraordinary commiffion to rebuild, in conjunction with the governor of the province, the temple of Jerufalem. But the attempt was defeated, as Ammianus, a Heathen and a contemporary, relates (XXIII. 1.), by a miraculous interpofition, " dread- " full balls of fire (metuendi globi flammarum), breaking out " frequently near the foundations, and rendering the place " inacceffible to the fcorched and blafted workmen." The truth of this miracle, Mr. Gibbon queftions, and even Dr. Lardner has doubted. The reafons adduced by the latter have been briefly mentioned, p. 62. " A philofopher (fays Mr. G.) " may ftill require the original evidence of " impartial and intelligent fpectators.". But Ammianus alfo was " a philofopher," and therefore, no doubt, " required" and had the " original evidence" of his fellow foldiers, of his friend and countryman Alypius, in particular ; and would not rafhly have named him, and related a fact, which, if falfe, muft have been imme- diately contradicted. In the reign of Valens, after having been long in a private ftation, Alypius and his fon Hierocles, a youth of an excellent difpofition, were both apprehended on a charge of poifoning. Alypius was de- prived of his eftate, and banifhed. And the fon, when he was leading to execution, was happily faved. How is not mentioned. Amm. XXIX. 1. Yet Libanius (Ep. XXV. &c.) mentions this Hierocles as perifhing in the earthquake at Nicomedia, in 358.

‡ Sylofon was the brother of Polycrates, tyrant of Samos. See Herodotus, l. III. c. 140. and Ælian. Var. Hift. l. IV. c. 5. He gave his cloak at Memphis to Darius, when that prince was only one of the guards of Cambyfes. Julian relates the fame ftory in his IIId Oration.

" The

But Sylofon found it a woeful gift *. Compare my conduct with that of this prince., In one re-fpect I have the advantage. I did not want to be reminded, but retained the remembrance of you unimpaired, and on the firft opportunity that God gave me I ranked you, not among my fecond but my firft friends. So much for the paft.

As to the future, will you allow me (for I am a prophet) to predict? We fhall be more fuccefsful, I doubt not, if Nemefis be propitious. For you need not a prince to affift you in deftroying a city, but I require the affiftance of many in re-building thofe that have been deftroyed †. Such is the pleafantry of my Gallic and barbarous Mufe ‡. Come with the aufpices of the Gods.

P. S. *In his own hand-writing.*

---

" The cloak of Sylofon," (η Συλοσονῖος χλάμυς) is adduced by Erafmus (*Chil.* p. 352.) as a proverb applied to " thofe " who boaft and pride themfelves on their drefs." And (he adds) " it may be properly faid of thofe to whom a fmall " gift, feafonably beftowed, returns with large intereft;" and then relates, as the origin of it, the above ftory from Herodotus.

* Sylofon was put in poffeffion of Samos, but the city being taken, it was pillaged by the Perfians, fo that he only reigned over a defert.          La Bleterie.

† This perhaps may allude to the forty cities in Gaul, which, Zofimus fays, the Barbarians deftroyed, and Julian rebuilt. See the Epiftle to the Athenians, Vol. I. p 84.

‡ Julian fomewhere fays, [Ep. LIV.] that his refidence in Gaul had made him a Barbarian, fo that he had almoft forgotten Greek. He would have been forry to have been taken at his word.          La Bleterie.

There

There is ready for you plenty of game, goats
and sheep *, which we hunt in our winter-quarters.
Come to a friend who loved you before he knew
your worth.

---

## Epiſtle XXX. To the ſame †.

I WAS juſt recovering from an indiſpoſition,
when I received the geography ‡ that you ſent
me, nor was the book leſs acceptable for coming
from you. For it contains not only better deſcrip-
tions than any book of the kind, but you have

---

† *. Ἄπις εριφων και της ιν τοις χειμαδιοις θηρας των προβατειων.
This paſſage is obſcure and perhaps corrupted. Does
Julian mean to ſay that the winter did not allow hunting;
and that there was nothing at his table but butcher's meat?
But Julian was not fond of dainties, nor, as I recollect, of
hunting. No more might Alypius. The meaning is, that
the troops of Julian made incurſions, during the winter, on
the territories of the enemy, and carried off flocks and herds.
If ſo, this Epiſtle muſt have been written in the Gauls before the abſolute rupture between Julian and Conſtantius.
Alypius might be then in Britain, where, we know, he was
employed before the reign of Julian. *Britannias curaverat
pro praefectis,* ſays Ammianus Marcellinus.    LA BLETERIE.
Vice-praefect therefore, or vicar, was his proper title,
Britain being one of the dioceſes that were governed by a
magiſtrate ſo named, ſubordinate to the Praefect of the
Gauls.
    † La Bleterie has neglected to tranſlate this Epiſtle. It
was probably addreſſed to Alypius, while he was governor
of Britain.                          GIBBON.
    ‡ This geography ſeems to have been the compoſition
of Alypius. Moreri ſays, " another geographical work
" is alſo aſcribed to him, which was a deſcription of the
" old world."

also

alfo embellifhed it with Iämbics, not " finging a
Bupalian * war," as the Cyrenean poet † exprefles
it, but fuch as fair Sappho would have thought
worthy of adapting to her hymns.  Such a work
it may be proper perhaps for you to give, but
certainly it is moft agreeable to me to receive.
With your adminiftration of affairs, as you ftudy
to act, on all occafions, both with diligence and
mildnefs, I am highly fatisfied. For to blend lenity
and moderation with fortitude and refolution, and
to exert thofe in encouraging the good, and thefe
in correcting the wicked, requires, I am confident,
no fmall degree of genius and virtue.

May you have thefe objects always in view, and
make both fubfervient to your own honour ! The
wifeft of the ancients juftly thought that this fhould
be the end propofed by every virtue ‡.  May health,
and happinefs be your portion as long as poffible,
my moft efteemed and beloved brother § !.

Epiftle.

* Bupalus, a ftatuary, made the image of the poet
Hipponax, who was very deformed in perfon, in ridicule ;;
which he refenting, wrote fuch fevere Iämbics against him,
that he hanged himfelf. This was the common report, which
Horace (Epod. v. 14.) feems to confirm.  But Pliny (xxxvi.
5.) fays, that report was falfe.  Hipponax is reprobated,
by Julian in his Duties of a Prieft, Vol. I. p. 132.

† Probably Callimachus, born, as Strabo fays ( l. xvii.)
at Cyrene in Africa, in the reign of Ptolemy Philadelphus.
Thence he is often ftyled " the Libyan bard."  His hymns
were tranflated by Dr. Dodd.

‡ Thus they made the entrance to the temple of Virtue
the paffage to that of Honour.

§ Little did Alypius imagine, while he was exercifing
his poetical and political talents in Britain, among a people

ae

### Epiftle XXXI.   To Bifhop Ætius *.

A. D.
361.
ALL the reft who were banifhed by the late Conftantius, on account of the madnefs of the Galileans, I have recalled. As to you, I not only remit your banifhment, but, mindful of our old acquaintance, I alfo invite you hither. Ufe a public vehicle as far as my camp, and one fuper-numerary horfe †.

as infenfible to the charms of his poetry as their rocks and forefts, that, in a diftant age, when the Britons could have relifhed his verfes, he would not have been known as a poet, and fcarcely as a governor, eminent as he was in both thofe characters, had not this accidental billet been happily refcued from the gulph of time.

* A celebrated Arian prelate, who had been fent by Gallus to his brother Julian, while he was reader in the church of Nicomedia, to ftrengthen him in the Chriftian religion. See the Epiftle from Gallus to Julian, Vol. I. p. 1.

The death of Gallus had been followed by the exile of Ætius, his divine and confident. He was made re-fponfible for fome of the faults of that unfortunate prince, and the demi-Arians accufed him to Conftantius as a very dangerous herefiarch. The rank of bifhop, which is given him in the title of the above Epiftle, muft have been added by the tranfcribers. Ætius was not a bifhop when Julian wrote to him. But he was foon after or-dained by the bifhops of his party, who then came to an open rupture with the demi-Arians. The credit which Ætius had with the Emperor, who prefented him with an eftate in the ifland of Lefbos, no doubt infpired the Ano-means, or pure Arians, with the boldnefs to complete their fchifm. It does not appear that Ætius, though a bifhop, was ever fixed to any fee.                    LA BLETERIE.

† See note † on Epiftle XX. p. 42.

Epiftle

## Epiftle XXXII. To the Sophiſt LUCIAN.

I WRITE, that I may be entitled to an anſwer. If I offend you by the frequency of my letters, give me, I intreat you, the fame offence *.

## Epiftle XXXIII. To DOSITHEUS †.

I COULD fcarce refrain from tears, and with reafon, when I heard your name mentioned, recollecting your ‡ beloved, noble, and in every refpect excellent father; whom if you imitate, you will he happy, and, like him, render your life honourable; but if you are indolent, you will grieve me, and difgrace yourfelf, for being ufelefs to the world.

* The length of this letter could not offend. Many fcraps, equally infignificant, from Pope, were treaſured up by his friend Richardſon. But, *le jeu ne vaut pas la chandelle.*

† Dofitheus is mentioned by Libanius, in his cxxxiſt Epiſtle, and a ſhort Epiſtle to him from that ſophiſt is preſerved (in Latin) by Zambicari.

‡ In the printed editions it is ημων, a miſtake ſurely for υμων. Julian could fcarce remember his own father.

## Epiſtle XXXIV. To the Philoſopher JAMBLICHUS*.

IT was ſufficient for Ulyſſes to ſay to his ſon, in order to check his high opinion of him,
No God am I; for heaven reſerve that name †.
But I cannot think myſelf a man, as the ſaying is, while I am abſent from Jamblichus. I will allow myſelf, however, to be your admirer, like that father of Telemachus, and though ſome perhaps may think it unbecoming, that ſhall not prevent my loving you. For I know that many who have

---

* This Jamblichus muſt not be confounded with another of the ſame name, who was more ancient (ſee p. 70. note †.) This was the diſciple of Edeſius. Julian has addreſſed ſix Epiſtles to him, [XXXIV, XL, XLI, LIII, LX, LXI.] which I have not tranſlated. To theſe Epiſtles in particular may be applied what M. Fleury ſays, in general, of thoſe which are addreſſed to the ſophiſts, *Elles ſont pleines des louanges outrées, et d'un empreſſement qui marque plus de légereté que d'affection.* LA BLETRÉIE.
Mr. Dodwell (*Exerc. de Pythag. ætate*) ſuſpects the authenticity of theſe Epiſtles, " becauſe they treat on very " trifling ſubjects, more worthy of a ſophiſt than a prince, " and ſhew a greater attention to ſtyle than becomes even " a philoſopher." As to his argument drawn from a miſtake in chronology, in regard to Sopater, that may eaſily be obviated by ſuppoſing there were alſo two of that name, as Julian ſeems to intimate See note †. on Ep. xxvii. p. 70. Libanius has addreſſed ſeven Epiſtles to this younger Jamblichus, of which one is preſerved by Fabricius, Bibliotheca Græca, vol. IV. p. 384.
† Odyſſ. xvi. 187. Broome, 222.

admired

admired fine ftatues, far from detracting from the
praife of the artift, have by their paffion for them
added frefh honour to the work. As to your
humorously ranking me among the ancient fages,
that I am far diftant from them is as certain as that
you are one of them. But you unite not only
Pindar, and Democritus, and the moft ancient
Orpheus, but almoft all the Greeks, who are faid
to have gained the fummit of philofophy, as the
various notes of vocal and inftrumental mufic
combine in a perfect concert. And as Argus, who
guarded Io, is defcribed by the poets as furrounded
with eyes, fo you, the genuine guardian of virtue,
are enlightened by eloquence with the pure eyes
of learning. It is faid, that Proteus, the Ægyptian,
affumed various forms, fearing left he fhould inadvertently appear wife to thofe who queftioned
him *. But as Proteus was really wife, and, as
Homer fays, had much knowledge, I praife him
for his knowledge; but I do not admire his
virtue, as he acted not like a benevolent being,
but an impoftor, in concealing himfelf to avoid
being ufeful to mankind. But who, my noble
friend, does not admire you, not only for equalling Proteus in wifdom, but alfo for never in-
vidioufly withholding from any one that virtue
and perfect knowledge, which you poffefs, of all
things excellent ? Thus, like the fplendid fun, the
radiance of your wifdom enlightens all, both by

* See Virg. Georg. IV. and Ovid. Metam. XI.

　　　　　　　G　　　　　　　inftructing

instructing the present, and by your writings, as far as possible, improving the absent. In this you excell even the illustrious Orpheus, since he wasted his music in the solace of brutes, but you, as if born for the good of mankind, imitate the hand of Æsculapius, and every where diffuse your eloquent and salutary precepts. So that Homer, I think, if he were to return to life, might with much more reason apply that line to you,

— One still living traverses the world *.

For to those who are of ancient stamp, to us in particular, a certain 'sacred spark, as it were, of true and fertile learning is by you alone rekindled and revived. And, O Jupiter the Preserver, and eloquent Mercury, grant, in return, that, for the general good of mankind, the life of the excellent Jamblichus may be prolonged to the utmost extent! If, for Homer, Plato †, and all that are worthy of their society, just vows were of old suc-

---

* Homer. Odyss. iv. 198. Proteus speaking of Ulysses to Menelaus,

Εις δ' ετι τα ζωος καλιευκιλαι ευρυ πονλιϊ,

Otherwise, ευριϊ κοσμω.

Not so well. For the word κοσμος does not occur in Homer in that sense.      CLARKE.

This various reading may perhaps rest on no better foundation than the above passage of Julian, in which his insertion of κοσμω may be accidental, by his quoting (as usual) from memory, or intentional, as better suiting his purpose.

† The Latin translator has added " Socrates," but without any authority from the original; and indeed Julian would hardly have mentioned him on this occasion, as his life, though in an advanced age, was shortened by violence, and the prayers of the virtuous were therefore in that respect unsuccessful.

cefsfully

cefsfully offered, and their lives were thus prolonged, why fhould not a contemporary of ours,
their equal both in virtue and eloquence, be tranfmitted by fimilar vows to the extremeft old age,
and endowed with every bleffing?

---

### Epiftle XXXV. For the ARGIVES *.

IN favour of the city of the Argives much may
be faid by any one who would celebrate their
actions ancient and modern. Of the glory acquired at Troy they are juftly entitled to the
greateft fhare †, as are the Lacedæmonians and

Athe-

* The Argives being oppreffed by the Corinthians, and
fubjected to new exactions, contrary to law, Julian recommends them, as I imagine, to the Pro-conful, faying it
was unjuft that a city, fo flourifhing of old, and, on account of the expence of the facred games, exempted from
taxes, fhould pay a tribute to Corinth towards the amphi-
theatral fports. Corinth was made a Roman colony by
Auguftus, who, at the defire of Julius Cæfar, raifed that
city from ruins. Under this title fhe claimed authority
over feveral cities that were not colonies. That this was
not an edict of the Emperor, but a petition of Julian, then
a private man, appears by an obfervation made in a fubfequent note.                                     PETAU.
   This Epiftle, which illuftrates the declining ftate of
Greece, is omitted by the Abbé de la Bleterie.
   The eloquence of Julian was interpofed, moft probably
with fuccefs, in behalf of a city which had been the royal
feat of Agamemnon, and had given to Macedonia a race
of kings and conquerors.                          GIBBON.
   † It feems ftrange that he fhould afcribe the greateft
fhare in the Trojan war to the Argives, in the fame manner
as he does afterwards to the Lacedemonians and Athenians.

Athenians afterwards. For though both thofe, wars were waged by all Greece, of praife, as well as of cares and labours, the generals may claim a large proportion. But thefe are of ancient date. After the return of the Heraclidæ, the birth-right taken from the eldeft *, the colony fent from thence into Macedonia, and the conftant prefervation of the city, free and independent, from the neighbouring Lacedæmonians, were proofs of no moderate or.

For they attempted nothing afterwards againft the Tro-jans; but by the appellation of " Trojan" he means fome other expeditions which were undertaken by the Greeks againft the Perfians, as if Τρωικα were the fame as Βαρβαρικα.

PETAU.

Agamemnon, the " king of men," was king of Argos (in Achaia), as well as of Mycenæ, but is not fo ftyled by Homer in his catalogue of the fhips, the troops of Argos being there fubdivided from thofe of Mycenæ, and led by Diomed, acting as their general under Agamemnon. " Di-" omed" (as Mr. Wodhull obferves, in his notes on the Oreftes of Euripides), " though he derived his title of " king from Ætolia, never poffeffed that throne, but re-" fided chiefly at Argos (about fix miles only from My-" cenæ), till he fettled in Italy. Euripides, it has been " obferved, perpetually confounds thofe two cities."

* Temenus. The origin of the Macedonian kingdom was derived from the Argives by Caranus (their firft king), brother to Phidon, king of the Argives. On which ac-count, he fays, the anceftors of Philip and Alexander fprung from Argos.

PETAU.

This pedigree from Temenus and Hercules may be fuf-picious, yet it was allowed, after a ftrict enquiry, by the judges of the Olympic games (Herod. l. v. c. 22.) at a time when the Macedonian kings were obfcure and un-popular in Greece. When the Achaian league was declared againft Philip, it was thought decent that the deputies of Argos fhould retire.

GIBBON.

common

common fortitude. Actions similar to those of the
Macedonians against the Persians may also be afcribed to this city; as this was the country of the
latter anceſtors of Philip and Alexander. In later
times it obeyed the Romans, not as a vaſſal, but
rather as an ally; and, I think, partook with the
reſt of the freedom and other privileges which the
Emperors have always indulged to the cities of
Greece. But now the Corinthians *, prone to op-
preſſion, compell that city, which is annexed to
theirs (for thus it ſhould properly be expreſſed)
by the reigning city †, to be tributary to them;
and this innovation, it is ſaid, they have now

---

* Argos, he ſays, was made tributary to Corinth by
the authority of the reigning city, becauſe when the
Achaians were ſubdued by Mummius, and Corinth deſtroyed, all Greece, being aſſeſſed under the name of
Achaia, received a magiſtrate from the Romans, who,
under the Emperors, was ſtyled a Pro-conful, and reſided
at Corinth, which was therefore the metropolis of Achaia,
nay of Peloponneſus, and conſequently of all Greece. See
Pauſanias, in Achaicis, p. 222. and Pliny, Ep. ult. l. VIII.
Seven years before Julian wrote this Epiſtle, the Corinthians had begun to exact a tribute from the Argives towards their wild beaſts and hunting-matches.    PETAU.

† Rome. Julian gives her the ſame appellation in his
ıſt Oration, p. 5. Eunapius, who flouriſhed after the death
of Julian, ſtyles her η βασιλευσσα Ρωμη, in his Prohæreſius.
Themiſtius, though he was ambaſſador from Conſtantinople to Conſtantius at Rome, in his IId Oration, p. 41.
ſtyles the one " the queen of cities," and the other " the
" ſecond." For the ſame reaſon, Rome is repreſented on
ancient coins, and thoſe ſtruck even under Conſtantine or
his ſons, as a woman ſitting, and holding a globe in her
right hand.                          SPANHEIM.

G 3                          practiſed

practifed for feven years, not confidering that
Delphi and Elis are by agreement exempted from
tribute on account of their celebrating the facred
games. For fince there are, as is well known, four
great and moft illuftrious games in Greece, the
Eleans furnifh and direct the Olympic, the Del-
phians the Pythian, the Corinthians the Ifthmian,
and the Argives the Nemean. Why then fhould
thofe retain the exemptions formerly granted, and
thefe, who, on account of the like expences, were
formerly exempted, or perhaps not taxed originally,
now be deprived of a privilege with which they
were once honoured? Befides, Elis and Delphi *,
for thofe highly celebrated games every fifth year,
are ufed to contribute only once; but at Argos
there are two Nemean, as there are two Ifthmian at
Corinth. And at this time alfo two other games

* The Olympic and Pythian games were celebrated once
in five years; the Nemean and Ifthmian twice. For the
Nemean were kept at the beginning of the firft, and, in
like manner, at the clofe of the third year; the one being
in winter, and the other in fummer. Befides the two
Nemean, the Herean alfo were defrayed by the Argives.
Four folemnities therefore, in the whole, were exhibited by
them; on which account they ought juftly to have been
exempted from tribute.                          PETAU.

The firft inftitutor of the Olympic games is unknown,
though it is generally fuppofed to have been Pelops. They
were confecrated to Jupiter, and were performed in the
neighbourhood of Olympia, in the diftrict of Pifa. The
Pythian were celebrated at Delphi in honour of Apollo;
the Nemean at Nemea, in Peloponnefus, in honour of
Hercules; and the Ifthmian in the Ifthmus of Corinth, in
honour of Neptune.

are

are added to thofe at Argos, fo that there are four games in four years. Is it proper then that thofe who exhibit them only once fhould be exempted, and that thefe who exhibit them four times at home fhould be obliged to contribute to others, efpecially as they are not ancient nor accuftomed in Greece? For the Corinthians do not require thefe large fums for the fupport of gymnaftic or mufical performances; but for hunting-matches, which they often exhibit in the theatres, purchafing, for that purpofe, bears and panthers; an expence which they eafily defray by means of their wealth and large revenues; and as many others contribute alfo towards it, they reap the advantage of their own inftitution. But do not the Argives, who are extremely indigent, by thus being made to contribute to a foreign entertainment in another country, fuffer unjuftly and illegally, and in a manner unfuitable to the ancient power and glory of their city? And as they are neighbours, they ought on that account to be more efteemed, if that faying be true,

" ———— Bad muft be your neighbours,
" If an ox perifh *."

But

---

* Ουδ' αι βυς απολοι]ο, ω μη δια κακιαν γει]οσων.
Taken from one of the moral maxims of Hefiod,
Ουδ' αι βυς απολοι]', ει μη γει]ων κακος ειη.
Works and Days, ver. 346.
A correfponding Latin proverb occurs in Plautus:
— *Verum illud verbum effe experior vetus,*
*Aliquid mali effe propter vicinum mali m.*
Mercator, Act. IV. Sc. 4. 31.
Juvenal

But the Argives do not bring this charge againſt
the Corinthians through their ſolicitude for one
ox only, but for many and great expences with
which they are unjuſtly burthened.  The Corinthians might alſo be aſked, whether they would
chooſe to adhere to the ancient laws of Greece, or
adopt thoſe which they have ſince received from
the reigning city?  For if they approve the majeſty of the ancient laws, the Argives are no more
bound to pay tribute to the Corinthians, than the
Corinthians are to pay it to the Argives.  But if the
Corinthians adopt the modern laws, and, becauſe
they are made a Roman colony, contend that they

---

Juvenal, in his xvith Satire, ver. 36. expreſſes his apprehenſion of ſimilar dangers from bad neighbours:

——— *Convallem ruris aviti*
*Improbus, aut campum mihi ſi vicinus ademit,*
*Et ſacrum effodit medio de limite ſaxum.*

If any rogue vexatious ſuits advance
Againſt me for my known inheritance,
Enter by violence my fruitful grounds,
Or take my ſacred land-mark from my bounds.
                                    DRYDEN.
Many other parallel paſſages might be adduced both
from the Latin and Greek writers.
    I am indebted for this note to a writer in the Gentleman's
Magazine for 1783, p. 215.
    Similar humanity to animals and good neighbourhood
are inculcated in the Levitical law.  *Thou ſhalt not ſee thy*
*brother's ox or his ſheep go aſtray, and hide thy ſelf from them:*
*thou ſhalt in any caſe bring them again unto thy brother.  Thou*
*ſhalt not ſee thy brother's aſs or his ox fall down by the way,*
*and hide thyſelf from them: thou ſhalt ſurely help him to lift*
*them up again.*  Deut. XXII. 1, 4. &c.

have

have the dominion over Argos, we will humbly intreat them not to be more affuming than their fathers, nor to new model, or fubvert, to the detriment of their neighbours, thofe cuftoms which their anceftors with found judgement obferved, relying on the decree which they lately obtained, and meanly taking advantage of the ignorance of the advocate who pleaded for the Argives *. For if this caufe had been removed out of Greece, the Corinthians would have had much lefs influence, and its merits, difcuffed by many fkilful advocates, would have been more apparent; on which account it is probable, that the judge, abafhed by the eftablifhed dignity of Argos, would have made a juft decree. Concerning the rights of the city, if you will only hear the orators, and they may be allowed to fpeak, you fhall be acquainted with the caufe from the beginning, and, from their arguments may form a judgement of the whole. On what is faid, that we ought not to credit thofe who are fent hither as petitioners †, it may now be proper to add a few words.

---

* In the reign of Conftantius this difpute between the Corinthians and Argives had been litigated, and the latter loft their caufe through the inexperience of their advocate in law-affairs.      PETAU.

† It appears from this paffage that Julian, then a private man, had been requefted by the Argives to ufe his intereft with the pro-conful of Achaia in their behalf: otherwife he would have commanded with authority, inftead of prefenting a petition; as he himfelf would have put an end to the difpute.      Ibid.

If

If there are any philofophers in thefe times, Diogenes and Lamprias are fuch. They decline the legiflative and lucrative offices of the ftate; but if their country wants their affiftance, they ferve her to the utmoft of their abilities; when the city is in any emergency, they plead caufes, affift in the government, engage in embaffies, and liberally expend their money, thus confuting by their conduct the fcandalous afperfions on philofophy, and difproving that vulgar notion, that thofe who ftudy philofophy, are ufelefs to their country. For their country employs them in thofe functions, and they endeavour to defend the caufe of juftice by our affiftance; but we employ yours.

All that remains for the defence and fafety of the oppreffed is the appointment of a judge both willing and able to make a juft decree. If either of thefe be wanting, if he be either miftaken or unfaithful, juftice muft abfolutely perifh. But though we fhould have a judge agreeable to our wifhes, we have not the liberty of fpeaking *, as we have not appealed; this, they requeft, may firft be allowed them, and that the indolence of him who then pleaded for the city, and managed her caufe, may not entail fuch a burthen on pofterity. Nor can there be any impropriety in granting a new trial. It is fometimes expedient to forego

---

* The advocate of the Argives, when he loft the former caufe, neleted to appeal; therefore the city could not bring a new action, nor demand another trial. PETAU.

fome

some present advantages and opportunities, for the sake of future security. And as life is short, they wish to pass that short space with tranquillity. But that the cause should sink before the judgement-seat, and be transmitted to posterity undetermined, is dreadful; so that, the hazard being so great, it seems better to accept half the advantage, than, by contending, to lose the whole. But those immortal cities, unless a just decree be made, and their mutual animosities terminated, must necessarily be at perpetual variance. For enmity gains strength by time.

I have said *, as the orators express themselves. May justice direct your determination!

* Εἴρηται εν' εμος λογος, analogous to *Dixi*, in Latin.

Epistle

## Epiſtle XXXVI. To Porphyry *,

A. D. 362. THE library of George was large and copious †. It was ſtocked with books of philoſophy of all kinds, and with many of hiſtory; on other ſubjects not a few; and with various writings of the Galileans. Examine therefore carefully the whole, and ſend it to Antioch. Be aſſured, that, unleſs you make a diligent ſcrutiny, you ſhall be ſeverely fined; and as to thoſe who are in the leaſt ſuſpected of having ſecreted any of theſe books, if you cannot induce them, by all kinds of arguments, and adjurations, and in particular by putting their ſlaves to the torture, let them be compelled by force to reſtore them all ‡.

---

* Treaſurer-general of Ægypt. Libanius mentions him in one of his Epiſtles as an excellent friend; and ſays, that he was caluminated and oppreſſed by two Ægyptians, a race " more ſavage than all the wild beaſts of Libya."

† See Epiſtles IX. and X.

‡ This is by no means an inſtance of cruelty in Julian. A confiderable robbery had been committed, and of property much more valuable than it is at preſent. The Romans, on the ſlighteſt ſuſpicions, put their ſlaves to the torture, La Bleterie.

## Epiſtle XXXVII. To Amerius.*

YOUR letter, in which you mention the death of your wife, and expreſs your extreme affliction, filled my eyes with tears. Painful would it have been to hear that any wife, young, chaſte, and engaging, and alſo an excellent mother, was prematurely ſnatched away; but that you have ſuſtained ſuch a loſs gives me peculiar concern. For, of all my friends, Amerius leaſt deſerved ſuch a calamity; a man whoſe underſtanding is ſuperior to moſt, a man whom I highly eſteem.

If I were writing on this ſubject to any other perſon, I ſhould be more prolix in telling him that ſuch is the lot of human nature, that ſubmiſſion

* I know not that this man of letters, apparently a ſophiſt and a Pagan, is elſewhere mentioned. One MS. ſtyles him " Himerius." We are acquainted with a celebrated pro-feſſor of that name, the rival and the collegue of Pro-hæreſius, and who, like him, taught eloquence at Athens when Julian was there. Himerius left ſome diſcourſes, of which there are ſome extracts in the Bibliotheca of Photius. It might be ſuppoſed that this Epiſtle was addreſſed to him, if the MS did not ſtyle him " Præfect of Ægypt." In the reign of Julian that province was governed by Ecdicius; and this Epiſtle is certainly written to one who was a teacher: but it might not be impoſſible for the title of Præfect to be here no more than an honorary title. In thoſe times honorary titles of the greateſt employments were ſometimes given to men of letters. I would not ven-ture, however, to aſſert, they had that of governor of any particular province. LA BLETERIE.

is

is neceffary, that the moft poignant grief admits of confolation *, and, in fhort, fhould ufe, as to a novice, all the arguments that are likely to alleviate affliction. But as I am afhamed of employing to one who inftructs others thofe arguments which are ufed to teach and improve the ignorant, waving every thing elfe, I will relate to you a fable; or rather a true ftory, of a certain wife man, not new perhaps to you, but probably unknown to many, whofe only medicine, mirth, you will find as effectual a remedy for forrow as that cup †which the fair Lacedæmonian is fuppofed, on a fimilar occafion, to have given to Telemachus.

It is reported, that Democritus ‡ of Abdera, finding nothing that he faid could confole Darius

for

---

for the lofs of a beautiful wife, promifed to reftore her to life, if the king would fupply him
with all things neceffary for the purpofe. Darius
ordered him to fpare no expence, but to take whatever was requifite to perform his promife. Soon
after, Democritus told him, that " every thing was
" ready for the completion of the work, one only
" excepted, which he knew not how to procure ;
" but that Darius, as he was king of all Afia,
" would perhaps find no difficulty in providing
" it." On his afking what this important matter
was, Democritus is faid to have replied, " If you
" will infcribe on the tomb of your wife the names
" of three who have never known affliction, fhe
" fhall immediately return to life, this ceremony
" being irrefiftible *." Darius hefitating, and not
being able to recollect any one who had not experienced fome forrow, Democritus laughed, as
ufual, and faid to him, " And are not you, the ab-
" furdeft of men, afhamed ftill to lament, as if

23, or even nine. This philofopher was on his return to
Greece, when Darius II. furnamed Nothus, afcended the
throne, in the year before Chrift, 423. LA BLETERIE.
See Vol. I. p. 21. note †.

* It is in the Greek Ευθυς αυτην αναβιωσισθαι τω της τελευτης
νομω δυσωπεμινη, which Martinius has tranflated thus : *Illam
ab inferis effe redituram ; fore enim ut ejus mortis confuetudine
erubefceret.* I think that it may be reftored by leaving out a
fingle letter. Inftead of της τελευτης, we fhould read της
τελπης, and tranflate it, *fore ut ftatim revivifceret, ejus ceremo-
nia ritu exorata.* The word δυσωπεισθαι fignifies, not only
" to blufh, to be afhamed," but alfo, " to fuffer onefelf
" to be perfuaded, to be moved." *Ibid.*

" you

" you alone were involved in fuch diftrefs, when
" you cannot find one that ever lived exempt from
" fome domeftic misfortune?"

That Darius, an illiterate Barbarian, a flave
both to joy and grief, fhould be told this, was
highly proper ; but you, a Greek, who cultivate
true literature, fhould learn from yourfelf to govern
your paffions. For it is fhameful that reafon fhould
not anticipate the certain effects of time *.

---

## Epiftle XXXVIII.  To the Philofopher
### Maximus †.

A. D.
360. MY ideas crowd fo faft upon me, that they
choak my utterance, fome hindering the
paffage of others.  Whether this be frigidity, or
any thing elfe, you will determine.  But let me
now arrange them in order, and firft return my

---

* If Julian had read the Latin authors (and why fhould
he not have read, at leaft, fome of them ?) I fhould fay
that he has copied this paffage of the letter of Servius Sul-
picius to Cicero : *Nullus dolor eft quem non longinquitas temporis minuat atque molliat.  Hoc te expectare tempus turpe eft, ac
non ei rei tuâ fapientiâ te occurrere.*     La Bleterie.
† This Epiftle was written in Illyricum at the time
when Julian was preparing to march againft Conftantius.
                                                    *Ibid.*
Among the philofophers, Maximus obtained an eminent
rank in the friendfhip of his royal difciple, who communicated, with unreferved confidence, his actions, his fentiments, and his religious defigns, during the anxious fuf-
pence of the civil war.                            Gibbon.
See the firft note on Epiftle XV. p. 29.

thanks.

thanks to the Gods; whofe goodnefs hill allows me
to write *, and perhaps will permit us to meet.
When I was firft made Emperor (the Gods know,
and I, as far as poffible, declared to them, with
what reluctance), I was waging war againft the
Barbarians. After paffing three months in that
fervice, as I was returning to Gaul, I looked round,
and enquired of thofe who came from thence
whether any philofopher, any fcholar, or any one
clad in a woollen coat or cloak, had arrived there.
At length I approached Vefontio †. This fmall
town, now rebuilt, was formerly a large city,
adorned with magnificent temples, and fortified
both by ftrong walls and its natural fituation,
being furrounded by the river Dubis ‡, and ele-
vated, as if in the fea, on a high rock, almoft inacceffible even to the birds, except where an ifthmus joins it to the continent. Near this town I
met a Cynic philofopher, with his cloak and ftaff.

* It is probable that Julian, after his taking the title
of Auguftus, wrote feldom to Maximus, for fear of em-
broiling that philofopher, who dwelt in Ionia, or Greece,
and confequently under the dominion of Conftantius.
LA BLETERIE.

† Now Befançon, the capital of Franche-Comté. Julian
paffed through this town, which had fuffered feverely from
the fury of the Barbarians, after his fourth expedition beyond the Rhine, A. D. 360, in his way to Vienne, where
he fixed his head-quarters for the enfuing winter. See Ammianus, xx. 10. Of the citadel of Vefontio, on a high
mountain, fee Cæfar, de bell. Gall. l. 1. F. Martinius
tranflates it " Danubius."

‡ Now the Doux.

At a diſtance I thought it was you *, and on his nearer approach I imagined that he came from you. He proved to be alſo a friend of mine, but not ſuch as I hoped and expected. He was uſeful to me therefore in one inſtance only, that of giving me reaſon to conclude that your anxiety on my account had prevented your leaving Greece. Witneſs Jupiter, witneſs great Sun, witneſs Minerva, and all ye Gods and Goddeſſes, how much, in my return from Illyricum to Gaul, I trembled for you! And I enquired of the Gods, not that I dared myſelf (for I was not able † to ſee or hear any thing of the ſituation in which you then might be), but I entruſted that office to others. The Gods clearly ſhewed, that ſome troubles would befall you, but that nothing terrible ſhould enſue, nor any wicked device prevail.

I omit, you obſerve, many important events. You are chiefly intereſted to know how ſoon we experienced the manifeſt aſſiſtance of the Gods, and

* This clearly ſhews that Maximus was of the ſect of the Cynics. A Cynic was as vain of his ſtaff and cloak as if he had been decked with all the ornaments of dreſs. But this Maximus muſt be diſtinguiſhed from another Cynic of the ſame name, under the Emperor Theodoſius, who was of Alexandria. BARONIUS.

† He means the danger to which Maximus was expoſed under Conſtantius, and affirms, that he did not venture himſelf to conſult the Gods concerning him, left he ſhould be compelled to hear ſome inauſpicious tidings, as was highly probable. PETAU.

After this, can there be a doubt of Julian's belief in theurgy? LA BLETERIE.

escaped

efcaped fuch a multitude of traitors, killing none
and fpoiling none, but only imprifoning thofe who
were apprehended in the very fact *.

Thefe things perhaps, it might have been better
to fpeak than to write. I am certain, however,
that they will give you pleafure. We worfhip the
Gods publickly, and all the troops that are returning with me profefs the true religion. We
openly facrifice oxen. We have made our grateful acknowledgments to the Gods in feveral heca-
tombs †. They command me to reftore their
worfhip with the utmoft purity ‡. Moft willingly
I obey them. They promife me great rewards, if
I am not remifs. Euägrius § is arrived.

* Soon after Julian was proclaimed Auguftus, an eunuch,
fuborned by the partifans of Conftantius, attempted to
affaffinate him. Julian pardoned him. We learn from hence,
that this was not the only confpiracy which threatened his
life.                                        *Ibid.*

† The legions of Gaul devoted themfelves to the faith,
as well as to the fortunes, of their victorious leader; and,
even before the death of Conftantius, he had the fatif-
faction of announcing to his friends; that they affifted, with
fervent devotion, and voracious appetite, at the facrifices,
which were repeatedly offered in his camp, of whole he-
catombs of fat oxen. " So that the foldiers," fays Ammianus (xxii. 12.) " living grofsly on fat meat, and
" greedy of drink, were carried through the ftreets on the
" fhoulders of paffers-by, from the public-houfes . . . .
" to their quarters." The devout prince and the in-
dignant hiftorian defcribe the fame fcene; and in Illyricum,
or Antioch, fimilar caufes muft have produced fimilar
effects.                                    GIBBON.

‡ He had no doubt of his being raifed up by the Gods
to be the reftorer of Paganifm.        LA BLETERIE.

§ See the firft note on Epiftle XLVI.

Epiftle

---

### Epiſtle XXXIX. To the ſame.

A. D. 362.

**W**ELCOME the coming, ſpeed the parting gueſt *.
Such is the law of the wiſe Homer. But our
friendſhip is ſuperior to that of hoſpitality, being
founded on learning and religion. So that no one
could juſtly charge me with tranſgreſſing this law
of Homer, if I ſhould think proper to detain you
longer with me. But as, I ſee, your diminutive
frame † requires more attention, I allow you to
go into your own country ‡, and have provided
for the convenience of your journey, by giving
you the uſe of a public carriage. May Æſculapius, and all the Gods, conduct you, and bring
you ſafely back to us again!

* This is ſaid by Menelaus (Odyſſ. xv. 74.) when Telemachus, after viſiting him at Lacedæmon, was going to
take his leave.                           LA BLETERIE.
Pope, 84. He has adopted this line in his imitation of
the 2d ſatire of the 1ſt book of Horace. Thus alſo Theocritus, Idyll. xvi. 27. as tranſlated by Fawkes.
With prudent hoſpitality they ſpend,
And kindly greeting ſpeed the parting friend.
† Σωμάτιον, corpuſculum. As from ανθρωπισκος, homuncio,
applied to Athanaſius in Epiſtle LI. it has been inferred,
that the primate of Ægypt was a little man, the ſame concluſion perhaps may be drawn from the above expreſſion
in regard to Maximus; though, in this inſtance, the diminutive is a term of affection, and, in the other, of contempt.
‡ Epheſus. Maximus probably took this journey while
the Emperor was at Conſtantinople.        LA BLETERIE.

Epiſtle

## Epiftle XL. To JAMBLICHUS *.

I AM fo fenfible of the good-nature with which
you blame me, that I think myfelf equally honoured by your letters, and inftructed by your re-
proofs. But were I confcious of the leaft failure of
attention to you, I would certainly endeavour, if poffible, to palliate the fault, or I would not fcruple to
afk your pardon, efpecially as I know that, whenever
your friends indifcreetly violate the laws of friendfhip, you are not implacable. Now then (fince
negligence, or indolence, generally prevents my
accomplifhing what I ardently defire), afcend, as
it were, a tribunal, while I plead my caufe before
you, and fhew that I did not treat you with impropriety, or act with tardinefs or negl.ct.

Three years ago I left Pannonia +, with difficulty efcaping thofe fnares and dangers, of which
you are well apprifed. But when I had croffed the
Chalcedonian ftrait ‡, and approached the city of
Nicomedia §, to you firft, as to the God of my
country, I paid due offerings for my fafety, by
fending you a meffage as a token of my approach,

A. D.
363.

---

* See the firft note on Epiftle XXXIV.
+ Now Hungary.
‡ Now the Bofphorus.
§ This city was then in ruins by an earthquake, which
happened in 358. See a note on an epiftle of Libanius,
vol. I. p. 304. and his Monody on that event, in this vol.

or

or a kind of facred prefent. The letter was configned to the care of one of the Imperial guards,
by name Julian, the fon of Bacchylus, a native of
Apamea *, to whom I the more readily entrufted
it, as he was going thither, and declared that he
knew you perfectly well. After this, I received,
as from Apollo, a facred epiftle from you, ex-
preffing that you had heard with pleafure of my
arrival. Wife Jamblichus, and a letter from Jamblichus, were to me a happy omen, and the dawn-
ing of good hopes. Need I fay how much I rejoiced, and how greatly I was affected by your
letter? For if you have received what I wrote on
that fubject (which was fent to you by one of the
letter-carriers that came from thence), you certainly know the great fatisfaction that it gave me.
And again, when the man who nurfed my children † returned home, I fent you another letter,

in

---

* The metropolis of Phrygia.

† Τω τροφιως των εμαιλυ παιδων. M. de Tillemont, who
takes in its moft rigorous fenfe that fufpicious paffage in the
Mifopogon (p. 244.) in which Julian ironically urges the
reproach of the people of Antioch, that " he *almoft always*
(ως ωιπται) lay alone," and confiders it as a confeffion that
Julian himfelf makes of his incontinence, obferves, in order
to ftrengthen this pretehded confeffion, that Julian, in
this Epiftle (which is one of thofe that I have not tranflated), fpeaks of " the man who had nurfed his children."
" Now," fays M. de Tillemont, " he never had any le-
" gitimate, except a fon who perifhed by the wickednefs
" of the midwife, whom the Emprefs Eufebia, the wife of
" Conftantius, had fuborned. The fact is certain: there-
" fore he had fome illegitimate."

But

in which I expreſſed my acknowledgments for your
former, and alſo requeſted a repetition of the
favour. Afterwards the diſtinguiſhed Sopater *
came to us on an embaſſy, and, as I knew him, I
inſtantly ſprung forward to embrace him, and ſhed

But we muſt not conclude from this paſſage, as M. de
Tillemont does, that there was actually a man who was
charged with the care of the children of Julian. Helena
had a ſon. After her firſt lying-in, ſhe never went her
full time. But at every pregnancy a nurſe was provided.
The ſame perhaps was frequently choſen. It was probably
the huſband of that nurſe whom Julian ſtyles " the nurſe
" of his children." I ſay probably, becauſe a number of
other plauſible reaſons may be ſuppoſed for Julian's having
given ſome one that name. Who knows, for inſtance,
but that it was a man whom he had deſtined for the care
of the children that he hoped to have ? Whether he did
not cauſe ſome children that did not belong to him to be
educated with the tenderneſs of a father ? Or whether it
was not a joke which Jamblichus perfectly underſtood ?
LA BLETERIE.
When Julian ſpeaks of " the tutor of his children,"
who is not named, the expreſſion muſt be underſtood figu-
ratively. For Julian had no children, legitimate or illegitimate. Hiſtorians are quite ſilent about them, excepting that one which he had by his wife Helena, who was not
ſuffered to live. If Julian had any children out of lawful
marriage, and therefore illegitimate, can it be ſuppoſed
that Chriſtian writers would have been ſilent about it ? By
no means. Eumenius, in his Panegyric, recommends to
Conſtantine not only his five children of whom he was the
parent, but his other children likewiſe, as he calls them,
whom he had educated for the bar or the court. In ſome
ſuch figurative ſenſe Julian muſt be underſtood. He intends
ſome young perſons under his ſpecial care. LARDNER.

* See Epiſtle XXVII. p. 70. note †. That this was the
ſame Sopater who entertained Julian afterwards at Hierapolis, though probable, I cannot affirm.

H 4                    tears

tears of joy, dreaming of nothing but you and a
letter from you. As soon as I received it, I kissed
it, held it to my eyes, and strained it close, as if
I had feared, that, while I was reading it, the
features of your face should secretly escape me.
I immediately wrote an answer, not only to you,
but to the excellent Sopater, his son, telling him,
in joke, that I had accepted a common friend from
Apamea as an hostage for your absence.

From that time to the date of my present writing,
I have received no letter from you but that in
which you seem to chide me. If by this appearance of a charge you mean only to urge me to
write, I accept the whole charge with the utmost
joy, and the very letter which I have now received
I deem the highest favour. But if you really
accuse me of having given you the least offence,
who can be more miserable than I in having been
prevented by the negligence of letter-carriers from
giving you the satisfaction that I wish? However,
though I were not to write very frequently, I might
justly claim your indulgence, not on account of
the business in which I am engaged (for I am not
such a wretch as not to prefer you, as Pindar says,
to all my affairs *); but, because there is more

---

* Ασχολιας απασης το καλα σι χεντιον ηγεισθαι. The sense, but
not the Words, of Pindar.

———— τοι τoον, χρυσασπι Θηβα,
Πραγμα κ π αχολιας υπερτερον
Θασαμαι ————                              Isthm. I. I.
Your business, golden-shielded Thebes,
To all my own I willingly prefer.

wisdom

wifdom in being loth to write to fuch a man as you,
who cannot be recollected without veneration, than
in being too prefumptuous. For as thofe who venture to gaze ftedfaftly on the light of the fun,
unlefs they are in a manner divine, and can behold
his rays like the genuine off-fpring of eagles *,
cannot fee what is unlawful to be feen †, and the
more they endeavour it, the weaker are their
efforts; fo he, who prefumes to write to you,
clearly fhews that the bolder he is, the more he
ought to fear. But you, diftinguifhed fage, who,
I may fay, were created for the total prefervation
of Gentilifm, judged right in fending me frequent
letters, and thus, as far as poffible, checking my
indolence. For as the fun (again to compare you
with that deity), when he fhines perfectly bright
with full radiance, is regardlefs whether all the
objects that he illuminates perform their refpective functions with propriety ‡; you, in like
manner, fhould liberally diffufe the light of your
knowledge among all the Gentiles, and not fecrete it becaufe fear or modefty prevents your
hearers from making a reply. Æfculapius does
not heal difeafes from interefted motives, but
every where difplays his humanity, like a kind of
doctrine. You, being the phyfician of noble fouls,

---

* See Epiftle XVI. p. 31.

† Οἷς α μη θεμις οφθηναι. Not unlike St. Paul, α ουκ εξον
ανθρωπω λαλησαι, *not lawful for a man to utter.* 2 Cor. xii. 4.

‡ This paffage in the original being corrupted and mutilated, I can only guefs at the meaning.

I                            fhould

should do the fame, and in every thing obferve the precepts of virtue; like a good archer, who, though he has no adverfary, always exercifes his art againft a proper opportunity. Our views are not the fame, as we wifh to enjoy your aufpicious letters, and you to receive ours. But we, though we fhould write a thoufand times, refemble the play-ful children in Homer, who erect clay-buildings on the fhore, and then foon overwhelm them with fand*: While your letter, however fhort, is pre-ferable to the moft copious ftream. And in truth, I had rather poffefs one epiftle of Jamblichus than all the gold of Lydia.

If you have any regard for your friends (and fome regard you have, or I am much miftaken), do not neglect us, who, like poultry, are always in want of your fuftenance; but write frequently, and forbear not to nourifh us with your good cheer. And if we have been deficient, difcharge at once two friendly offices, that of writing to us, and alfo of writing for us. For fuch a pupil of eloquent Mercury as you are, fhould employ his rod, not in exciting, but in banifhing and dif-pelling fleep, and in this particular, above all, let him be your model.

* Il. XV. 362, where the poet defcribes the Grecian turrets nodding, and the bulwarks falling, when fhaken by Apollo;

  Eafy, as when afhore, the infant † ftands,
  And draws imagin'd houfes in the fands,
  The fportive wanton, pleas'd with fome new play,
  Sweeps the flight works and fafhion'd domes away.

POPE.

† Julian, quoting by memory, fubftitutes παιδι; for ψαμ.

Epiftle

## Epiſtle XLI. To the ſame.

IN obedience to the Delphic oracle, we ſhould have known ourſelves, and not preſumed to ſtun the ears of a ſage like you, whoſe very looks it is difficult to encounter, much more to contend with him in genius, as he combines all the powers of philoſophic harmony. Every muſician, Ariſtæus * not excepted, muſt yield to Pan, when he breathes ſweet melody; and when Apollo warbles to his lyre, all, though they had the muſical powers of Orpheus, would be ſilent. Conſcious, as we are, of our own inferiority, it is juſt that the leſs ſhould ſubmit to the greater. But he who would put human in competition with divine harmony muſt be unacquainted with the cataſtrophe of Marſyas † the Phrygian, and with the river named from him, which flows as a puniſhment to the mad muſician.

* The ſon of Apollo by Cyrene, the daughter of Pe-neus, king of Arcadia. He is ſaid to have diſcovered the uſe of honey, milk, rennet, and other uſeful things. Juſt. Hiſt. XIII. 7. This the poets have turned into a fable. See Virg. Georg. IV. 317, &c. One MS. inſtead of Αριϛαιος, has αριϛος, (" the beſt" muſician.) The fable of Ariſtæus is alſo in the IVth book of the Odyſſey.

† A ſatyr, who challenged Apollo, and, being overcome by him, was flead alive, and changed into a river. See Ovid. Metam. VI. and Liv. XXVIII. 13.

Nor

Nor can he have heard of the fate of Thamyris *,
who unsuccessfully contended in singing with the
Muses. Not to mention the Sirens †, of whom
such of the Muses as conquered them still bear a
wing in their foreheads. All these now suffer, and
will long suffer, for their presumption; we therefore, as I said before, ought to have remained
within our own bounds, and to have been quietly
satisfied with your strains; like those who silently
receive the oracle of Apollo issuing from the sacred

---

* Il. IJ. 595.

 Superior once of all the tuneful race,
 Till, vain of mortals empty praise, he strove
 To match the seed of cloud-compelling Jove!
 Too daring bard! whose unsuccessful pride
 Th' immortal Muses in their art defy'd.
 Th' avenging Muses of the light of day
 Depriv'd his eyes, and snatch'd his voice away.
        Pope, 732.

† As to the wings of the Sirens, see Ælian de natura
anim. l. xvii. c. 23. This contest of the Sirens with the Muses is thus mentioned by Spenser:

 They were fair ladies, till they fondly striv'd
 With th' Heliconian maids for maisterye,
 Of whom they overcomen were, depriv'd
 Of their proud beauty, and th' one moiety
 Transform'd to fish, for their bold surquedry ‡.
     Fairy Queen, b. xi. c. 12. st. 31.

which Mr. Spence justly quotes as one instance (among
many) of this great poet's " misrepresenting the stories and
" allegorical personages of the ancients, the Sirens being
" never represented in antiques with a fish-tail, but with
" the upper part human, and the lower like birds." See
Polymetis, p. 302.

 Ovid, in his Metamorphoses, v. 553. ascribes their trans-
formation to another cause.

‡ Presumption.

shrines.

shrines. But since you lead our song, and by your eloquence, as with the rod of Mercury, rouse us from sleep; we, in the manner of those enthusiasts, who with dances meet Bacchus, when he celebrates his orgies, will join in unison with your Harp, as they in tune and measure accompany the leader of the dance. Accept therefore the orations *, which, by the command of the Emperor †, I lately composed on the celebrated junction of the straits ‡: a small work, if compared with yours, and brass for your gold §; but such presents as we have ‖, we offer to our Mercury. Theseus by no means despised the coarse fare of Hecale **; but, urged by necessity, was satisfied with little. And the shepherd Pan disdained not to apply to his lips the pipe of a young herdsman. Such as it is, then, receive it, and scorn not to bestow great attention on a small poem ††. If it have any merit, both the work and its author will be fortunate in receiving such a token of esteem from Minerva.

* These orations are not extant.
† Constantius.
‡ Does he mean the Hellespont joined by Xerxes?
                                        PETAV.
§ II. VL 236. Julian seems particularly fond of this passage, this being the third time of his quoting or alluding to it in these Select Works.
‖ Οις δε εχομεν ξενιοις—ιςιωνιες. Not unlike that expression of St. Peter, Acts III. 6. Ο δι εχω, τελο σοι διδωνι. Such as I have, I give thee.
** A poor old woman mentioned by Callimachus, as having entertained Theseus with wild lettuce. See Plin. Hist. Nat. xxii. 22, and xxvi. 8.
†† Ολιγω μελει. Could this be one of those which before were styled λογω (" orations?")

And

And fhould a finifhing hand be neceffary to com‑
plete it, difdain not, I intreat you, to fupply its
defects. Thus of old the God appeared to the
archer * who invoked him, and directed his fhaft,
and thus the harper who was playing the Orthian †
tune was anfwered by Apollo in the form of a
grafs-hopper ‡.

_____

### An Edict relating to Profeffors §.

17 June,
362.

PROFESSORS and mafters fhould be diftinguifhed firft by their manners, and in the
next place by their talents. We therefore forbid
any,

_____

\* Paris probably, when Apollo guided his arrow againft
Achilles. See Ovid. Metam. XII.

† A kind of loud mufic ufed by Arion, according to
Ilerodotus. It is introduced by Homer, Il. xi. 11. where

Difcord

—— ——Through the Grecian throng,
With horror founds the loud Orthian fong.

POPE, 13.

‡ I am aware that the Greek word τιτιξ, and the Latin
cicada, mean a different infect from our grafs-hopper; for
it has a rounder and fhorter body, is of a dark green colour, fits upon trees, and makes a noife five times louder
than our grafs-hopper. It begins its fong as foon as the
fun grows hot, and continues finging till it fets. Its wings
are beautiful, being ftreaked with filver, and marked with
brown fpots; the outer wings are twice as long as the
inner, and more variegated; yet, after the example of Mr.
Pope (fee Il. iii. 300,), I retain the ufual term.

FAWKES on Theocritus.

§ I have taken this Epiftle from the Theodofian Code,
xiii. t. 3. De medicis et profefforibus. It is not known from
what

any, whoever they be, to intrude haftily or rafhly
into this important office.   He who would keep
a fchool muft be approved by the council of the
town, and alfo have the fanction of the principal
inhabitants; and, as I * cannot be every where
perfonally prefent, let the decree be fent to me for
examination, that the candidate may have the additional honour of feeing the fuffrages of his fellow-citizens † confirmed by our opinion.

Given at * * * * on the fifteenth of the calends
of July.  Received at Spoleto on the fourth of the
calends of Auguft, in the confulfhip of Mamertinus
and Nevitta.

what place it was dated, nor to whom Julian addreffed it.
It only appears that he wrote it on the road from Conftantinople to Antioch, as he left Conftantinople in the month
of May, and was at Antioch towards the end of July.  It
was made, without doubt, on account of fome profeffor of
Spoleto, a city of Picenum, and confequently was addreffed
either to the Prsefect of the Prsetorium of Italy, or to the
Prsefect of Rome, or perhaps to the Confular of Picenum
(now the march of Ancona), or, laftly, to the inhabitants of Spoleto.  The intention of Julian is plain.  He
referves to himfelf the right of confirming or annulling
the election of profeffors, in order to exclude the Chriftians
from all literary offices:  This law might perhaps be part
of the following edict.  I have therefore placed it here.
                                                LA BLETERIE.
* The Emperors generally fpeak in the plural in their
laws; Julian, however, here ufes the fingular.  *Sed quia
fingulis civitatibus adeffe ipfe non poffum, jubeo,* &c.     *Ibid.*
† The original is, *Hoc enim decretum ad me tractandum
deferetur ‡, ut altiore quodam honore noftro judicio* (M. de la
Bleterie thinks we fhould read *noftrum judicium*) *ftudiis civi-
tatum accedat.*

        ‡ In Gothofred's edition, *referatur.*

Epiftle

## Epiſtle XLII. An Edict, forbidding the Chriſtians to teach polite Literature *.

A. D. 362.

TRUE learning, in my opinion, conſiſts not in words, in elegant and magnificent lan-guage, but in the ſound diſpoſitions of a well-formed

* Two motives induced Julian to reſtrain the Chriſtian profeſſors from teaching: 1. He flattered himſelf, that, in order to keep their chairs, they would change their re-ligion. In this, he did not ſucceed, if, as Oroſius ſays, almoſt all rather choſe to quit them. This, in particular, is affirmed of Prohæreſius, the ſophiſt, of Athens, and of Marius Victorinus, who profeſſed eloquence at Rome. 2. Julian knew, by his own experience, that maſters, when they ſhewed their ſcholars the ancient authors, never failed to inſiſt on the weakneſs and folly of Paganiſm. He was ſenſible how much a Chriſtian maſter can contribute to the progreſs of religion, when he explains profane authors chriſtianly, and equally avails himſelf of the truth and the falſhood which he finds there in order to conduct his pupils to God and Jeſus Chriſt. This is what he wiſhed to pre-vent. But, inſtead of diſcovering his true motives, he em-ploys the moſt lamentable pretext that can be ; ſo that this piece of eloquence is a maſter-piece of ſophiſtry. M. Fleury has inſerted moſt of it in his Eccleſiaſtical Hiſtory.

LA BLETERIE.

His moſt illiberal treatment of the Chriſtians was, his forbidding the profeſſors, who were of that religion, to teach humanity and the ſciences in the public ſchools. His more immediate deſign in this was to hinder the youth from taking impreſſions to the diſadvantage of Paganiſm ; his remoter view, to deprive Chriſtianity of the ſupport of human literature. His own hiſtorian, Ammianus Mar-cellinus, paſſes a ſevere ſentence on this edict, xxi. 10.

WARBURTON.

His

formed mind, and in juſt notions of good and evil, of virtue and vice. Whoever therefore thinks or teaches otherwiſe ſeems no leſs deſtitute of learning than he is of virtue. Even in trifles, if the mind and tongue be at variance, it is always eſteemed a kind of diſhoneſty. But if in matters of the greateſt conſequence a man thinks one thing

His driving from their ſchools ſuch teachers of rhetoric and grammar as profeſſed the Chriſtian religion, was ſevere *(inclemens)*, and ſhould be buried in eternal oblivion.

AMMIANUS.

He enacted no oppreſſive laws . . . . a few excepted ; among which was that ſevere one, which forbade Chriſtian maſters to teach rhetoric and grammar, unleſs they conformed to the worſhip of the Gods.            *Ibid.*

Ammianus has twice mentioned this Edict, and always with diſlike, as a great hardſhip. Oroſius ſays, that " when Julian publiſhed his edict forbidding the Chriſ- " tian profeſſors of rhetoric to teach the liberal arts, they " all in general choſe rather to reſign their chairs than " deny the faith." And Jerom, in his Chronicle, aſſures us, that " Prohæreſius, the Athenian ſophiſt, in particular, [ſee Epiſtle II.] " ſhut up his ſchool, though the Em- " peror had granted him a ſpecial licence to teach." Auguſtine records the like ſteadineſs of Victorinus, who had long taught rhetoric with great applauſe at Rome. But Ecebolus, a Chriſtian ſophiſt at Conſtantinople [ſee Epiſtle XIX.], who had been Julian's maſter in rhetoric, was overcome by the temptations of the times, and with great humiliations intreated to be reconciled to the church.

LARDNER.

This Edict may be compared with the groſs invectives of Gregory (*Orat.* III. *p.* 96.). Tillemont (*Mem. Eccl. tom.* VII. *p.* 1201—1204.) has collected the ſeeming differences of ancients and moderns. They may be eaſily reconciled. The Chriſtians were *directly* forbid to teach ; they were *indirectly* forbid to learn, ſince they would not frequent the ſchools of the Pagans.            GIBBON.

and

and teaches another *, does he not resemble those
mean-spirited, dishonest, and abandoned traders,
who generally affirm what they know to be false,
in order to deceive and inveigle customers?

All therefore who profess to teach ought to be
strict in their morals, and should never entertain
opinions opposite to those of the public; such,
especially, ought to be those who instruct youth,
and explain to them the works of the ancients,
whether they are orators, or grammarians; but
particularly sophists, as they affect to be the teachers, not only of words, but of manners, and insist
that civil philosophy is their peculiar province.
Whether this be true or not I shall not at present consider. I commend those who make such
specious promises, and should commend them much
more, if they did not falsify and contradict them-

---

* If the Christian professors, when they explained in
their schools Homer, Hesiod, &c. had canonised the
doctrine of those writers, the reproaches of Julian would
have been just; yet perhaps he would not have made them.
A book may be esteemed in some respects, and condemned
in others. No one is deceived by this. To explain the
classic authors, to commend them as models of language,
of eloquence and taste, to unveil their beauties, &c. this
is not proposing them as oracles of religion and morality.
Julian is pleased to confound two things so different, and
to erect, under favour of this confusion, the puerile so-
phistry which prevails through his whole edict.

LA BLETERIE.

Thus Homer's Achilles, Il. ix. 312.
Who dares think one thing, and another tell,
My soul detests him like the gates of hell.     POPE.

selves

felves by thinking one thing, and teaching their
fcholars another. What then? Were not Homer,
Hefiod, Demoftpenes, Herodotus, Thucydides, Ifo-
crates, Lyfias, guided in their ftudies by the Gods,
and efteemed themfelves confecrated, fome to Mercury, and others to the Mufes? It is abfurd therefore for thofe who explain their works to defpife
the Gods whom they honoured.

I do not mean (I am not fo abfurd *) that
they fhould change their fentiments for the fake
of inftructing youth; I give them their option,
either not to teach what they do not approve, or,
if they choofe to teach, firft to perfuade their
fcholars, that neither Homer, nor Hefiod, nor
any of thofe whom they expound, and charge with
impiety, madnefs, and error, concerning the Gods,
are really fuch as they reprefent them. For as
they receive a ftipend, and are maintained by their
works, if they can act with fuch duplicity for a few
drachms, they confefs themfelves guilty of the moft
fordid avarice.

Hitherto, I allow, many caufes have prevented
their reforting to the temples; and the dangers
that every where impended were a plea for their
difguifing their real fentiments of the Gods. But
now, when the Gods have granted us liberty, it
feems to me abfurd for any to teach what they
do not approve. And if they think that thofe

* Petau thinks that fomething is wanting here to perfect the fentence.

writers whom they expound, and of whom they
fit as interpreters, are truly wife, let them firſt
zealouſly imitate their piety towards the Gods. But
if they think their ideas of the moſt holy Gods
erroneous, let them go into the churches of the
Galileans, and there expound Matthew and Luke *.
In obedience to your rulers, you forbid ſacrifices.
I wiſh that your ears and your tongues were (as
you expreſs it) regenerated † in thoſe things of
which I wiſh that myſelf, and all who in thought
and deed are my friends, may always be par-
takers.

* Let all the moral truths which are found, or are ſuppoſed to be found, diſperſed here and there in the Pagan
writers, be collected; let all profane antiquity, if I may ſo
expreſs myſelf, be laid under contribution; the ſyſtem
which can be drawn from it will be far leſs valuable
than what we are taught in a few words by the authors of
whom Julian affects to ſpeak with contempt, and will ſo
far only be rational, as it reſembles their doctrine.
                                        LA BLETERIE.
A juſt and ſevere cenſure has been inflicted on the law
which prohibited the Chriſtians from teaching the arts of
grammar and rhetoric. The motives alleged by the
Emperor to juſtify this partial and oppreſſive meaſure might
command, during his life-time, the ſilence of ſlaves, and
the applauſe of flatterers.                GIBBON.

† He ridicules the Chriſtians by the trite application of an
expreſſion uſed by them. Αναγινωσις is commonly underſtood
of baptiſm, the reformation of the new man, and the
change of ſtudies and manners. Therefore forbidding the
Chriſtians to read the books of the Heathens, he ſays, he
would have their ears and tongues cleanſed from all acquaintance with their writings, that what is depoſited
in them may in a manner be born again.        PETAU.

To

To mafters and teachers let this be a general law. But let no youths be prevented from reforting to whatever fchools they pleafe *. It would be as unreafonable to exclude children, who know not yet what road to take, from the right path, as it would be to lead them by fear, and with reluctance, to the religious rites of their country. And though it might be proper to cure fuch reluctance, like madnefs, even by force †, yet let all be indulged with that difeafe. For the ignorant fhould, in my opinion, be inftructed, not punifhed.

* This was fair, but would by no means be accepted. Here the bait was half off the hook, and difcovered, that to draw them to the fchools of the Pagan profeffors was one end of the edict, which he imagined would neceffarily reduce things to this ftate, either to difpofe the Galileans, during their youth, in favour of Paganifm, or to difable them, in their adult age, to defend Chriftianity. So that it appears from hence, his forbidding Chriftian profeffors to *explain* Pagan writers to any audience whatfoever, amounted to a prohibition of *learning* them.　　WARBURTON.

Mr. Gibbon has adopted the fame idea in a former note, p. 113.

† He derides the μυρια Γαλιλαιων (Epift. VII.) and fo far lofes fight of the principles of toleration as to wifh (Epift. XLII.) ακπλας ιασθαι.　　GIBBON.

Epiſtle XLIII.  To ECEBOLUS *.

A. D.
362.

SO mild and humane have been my decrees
concerning the Galileans, that none of them
can ſuffer any violence, or be dragged to the
temples, or be expoſed to any other injury. But
they who are of the Arian church, being pampered with riches †, have attacked the Valentinians, and have dared to perpetrate ſuch outrages at Edeſſa as can never be tolerated in a well-
governed city. Therefore, as they are taught, in
their wonderful law, the moſt eaſy method of entering into the kingdom of heaven, for this pur-

* This is not the ſophiſt under whom Julian had ſtudied,
and to whom he addreſſed Epiſtle XIX. This, no doubt,
was the chief magiſtrate of Edeſſa, the capital of Oſrhoëna,
a province beyond the Euphrates and the Tigris.
                                              LA BLETERIE.
    About the ſame time that Julian was informed of the
tumult of Alexandria, he received intelligence from Edeſſa
of the diſorders which occaſioned this mandate.  GIBBON

  † The Arians were put in poſſeſſion of the church of
Edeſſa, under Conſtantius. They muſt neceſſarily therefore be great perſecutors to retain it under Julian. The
Valentinians derived their name from the hereſiarch Valentinian, who lived in the ſecond century after Jeſus Chriſt,
and who, by a mixture of the goſpel, of Platoniſm, and
the theogony of Heſiod, formed a ſyſtem ſo compounded,
ſo extravagant, that we do not underſtand it, perhaps he
did not underſtand it himſelf.  Some remains of the
Valentinians ſtill exiſted in the Vth century.
                                              LA BLETERIE.

                                                  poſe

pose co-operating with them *, we have ordered all the wealth of the church of the Edessenes † to be confiscated and given to our soldiers, and the lands to be annexed to our demesnes. Thus being poor they may become wise, and not fail of that heavenly kingdom to which they aspire ‡.

We also command the inhabitants of Edessa to refrain from all tumults and seditions §, left, if they provoke my humanity, you yourself should be punished for the public disorders by exile, fire, and the sword.

Epiftle

* Julian might boaft as much as he pleafed of not being a perfecutor. Thofe profane and cruel railleries, which fell from the pen of the fovereign, were in themfelves a cruel perfecution, and muft expofe the Chriftians to the fury of the idolaters, wherever they found themfelves the ftrongeft. In order to ill-treat thofe who are not of their religion, the populace only wait for the leaft fignal from the prince, and frequently not even for that.

LA BLETERIE.

† The effects of the church of Edessa were probably returned to it by the fuccessors of Julian. At leaft, it was very rich in the vth century.          Ibid.

‡ Doubtlefs Julian refers to divers texts of the gofpels ; perhaps to Matth. v. 3. Luke vi. 20. Matth. xix. 21. or fome other parallel places. But few will allow him to be a good interpreter of fcripture, or that he deduces right conclufions from it.          LARDNER.

§ Thefe divifions might perhaps be occafioned by the Arians having feized the church and its revenues, though the greater part of the inhabitants was inviolably attached to the Catholic faith. It is notorious, that, nine years after the death of Julian, in the reign of Valens, the bifhop, the clergy, and the laity, ftriftly deferved the glorious title of confeffors. The women, and even the children, fhared the glory of this confeffion. The Edessenes pretended

that

## Epiftle XLIV. To Libanius *.

RECOVERING lately from a fevere and
dangerous illnefs, by the providence of the
Supervifor of all things, your letter was delivered
to me on the day that I firft bathed. Reading it
in the afternoon, I can fcarce exprefs how much
it confirmed me in my opinion of your pure and
difinterefted benevolence, of which I wifh I were
worthy, that I may not difgrace your friendfhip.
I immediately began your Epiftles †, but could
not finifh them: thofe from Antony to Alexander
I poftponed to the next day. A week after, my
health, by the providence of God, improving to
my wifh, I wrote you this. May you be preferved, my moft efteemed and beloved brother,
{by God, who regards all things! may I fee you,
my beft friend! With my own hand, by your
fafety and my own, by God the fuperintendant

that their city had the honour of being the firft that dedicated itfelf to Jefus Chrift, and fhewed in their archives a
letter which they believed to have been written to one of
their kings by Jefus Chrift himfelf in the courfe of his
mortal life. We may judge to what degree Julian hated
them, and we muft no longer be furprifed at his writing
to Ecebolus, or rather to the whole fenate of Edeffa, fo
bitter and fo threatening a letter. LA BLETERIE.

* This, in one MS. is addreffed " to Prifcus."

† What thefe " Epiftles" were we know not. Poffibly
fome in affumed characters (now loft), fuch exercifes being
common with this fophift.

of

of all things, I have written what I think. ; Excellent man, when shall I see and embrace you? For now, like a difappointed lover, I am enamoured even of your name *;]

Epiftle XLV. To Zeno †.

BESIDES many other proofs of your having attained the fummit of the medical art, to which you have added propriety of behaviour, good-nature, and regularity of life, this teftimony now crowns all, your having turned the whole city of Alexandria towards you in your abfence; fuch a fling, like a bee, you have left behind you. And with reafon; for Homer well obferves,

A wife phyfician, fkill'd our wounds to heal,
Is more than armies to the public weal ‡.

And you are not merely a phyfician, but alfo a mafter to all who practife phyfic, fo that you are to phyficians what phyficians are to others. For this reafon you are re-called from exile, and with great fplendor. If you were obliged to quit Alex-

A. D. 362.

---

* The words between [ ] are added in one MS.

† Some MSS. give Zeno the title of " Chief Phyfician," (αρχιατρω). He was, it appears, a celebrated profeffor of phyfic, a Pagan without doubt, as Julian expreffes to him fo much efteem and affection.

LA BLETERIE.

‡ Il. xi. 514. Pope, 636. The words of Idomeneus on Machaon. It is needlefs to obferve that the ancient phyficians were furgeons,

andria

andria by the Georgian * faction, as the procefs
was unjuft, you may moft juftly return. Return
therefore to your former honour, and let acknow-
ledgements be paid to us by both ; by the Alexandrians for reftoring Zeno to them, and by Zeno
for reftoring to him the Alexandrians.

---

## Epiftle XLVI. To EUAGRIUS †.

INHERITED from my grandmother ‡ a fmall
eftate in Bithynia, confifting of four farms, and
with it I reward your affection to me. It is too inconfiderable to elate a man with wealth, or to confer

* George had equally perfecuted the Catholics and the
Pagans. He muft have procured by furprife fome order of
Conftantius to banifh Zeno ; for if George had only driven
him out by force, this phyfician, fo dear to the city of
Alexandria, would not have waited for an order from the
fucceffor of Conftantius to return thither. LA BLETERIE.

† It is not known to whom this Epiftle is addreffed. It
is very well written ; neverthelefs, it is tinctured with pedantry. *Ibid.*
The name of " Euagrius" occurs in the index to Petau's
edition. I have therefore added it. He is probably the
fame who is mentioned in the conclufion of the xxxviiith
Epiftle.
Libanius has two Epiftles to one of this name, and mentions him in feveral others. He held, it appears, fome
office under the government, and being accufed of fome
mifmanagement in it, was brought to trial, but was acquitted by the intereft of Salluft, whom Libanius thanks
for his good offices.
‡ In the Duties of a Prieft, p. 122, Julian mentions his
inheriting the whole eftate of his grand-mother, which had
been forcibly with-held from him.

felicity,

felicity, but its endowments are by no means un-
pleasing, as you may judge from the particulars.
And there is no reason why I should not be jocular
to you who abound with elegance and wit.   one

It is twenty ftadia * diftant from the fea; and is
therefore undifturbed by trafficking merchants and
clamorous or quarrelfome failors. Yet it is not
entirely deftitute of the graces of Nereus; for it
can always fupply a gafping fifh frefh-caught, and
an eminence near the houfe commands a view of
the Propontic fea, the iflands, and the city which
bears the name of a great prince †; and inftead
of being difgufted by fea-weed, and various other
kinds of filth that fhall be namelefs, which are often
thrown on the beach and the fands, ground-ivy,
thyme, and other aromatic herbs, will afford you
a conftant regale. When with tranquil attention
you have purfued your ftudies, and wifh to relax
your eyes, the profpect of the fhips and the ocean
is delightful. In this retirement I found many
charms when I was a boy, for it has fountains alfo
far from defpicable, a beautiful bath, a garden,
and an orchard; and when I grew up, I was ftill
fo fond of it, that I frequently reforted to it, and
therefore my obtaining it feemed a fortunate circumftance. It affords too a fmall memorial of my
agriculture, a fweet and fragrant wine, which is

* About two miles and a half.
† Conftantinople.

good

good, even when it is new *. In short, you will there see Bacchus and the Graces. The grapes, both when they hang on the vines, and are pressed into the vat, are as odoriferous as roses. But as soon as the wine is in the casks, to speak in the language of Homer, it is

A rill of nectar, streaming from the Gods †.

Why then, you will say, did I not plant many more acres with such vines? Because I was not a very keen husbandman ; and besides, as mine is a temperate cup, and the neighbourhood abounds with nymphs, I provided enough for myself and my few male friends. Such as it is, my dear friend, you will now accept it : however trifling the

---

* In the original, Ουκ' αναμειναντα τι παρα τε χρονε προσλαβειν, literally, " not waiting to receive any thing from time." But the Latin translator has affixed a meaning no less opposite to the intention of Julian, than to fact and observation : *neque temporis diuturnitate vitii quicquam assumit.* Though our Imperial author was no votary of Bacchus, his " cup" (as he says) being " temperate" (νηφαλιο;), he must have known, and meant to intimate, that, in general, old wine is proverbially good, and *vice versâ. A new friend,* says the wise son of Sirach, *is like new wine ; when it is old, thou shalt drink it with pleasure.* Eccl. ix. 10.

† Τε νικταρος εςιν αποῤῥωξ. *Odyss.* ix. 359. POPE, 426. The elogium of Polyphemus on the rich Maronean wine given him by Ulysses. This wine also, like that of Julian,
Breath'd aromatic fragrances around, ver. (210.) 245.
Julian, it appears, had several female friends whom he occasionally mentions, viz. Areta, Theodora, Euodia, &c. but here, to avoid any misconstruction, he takes particular care to specify, that though " there were many nymphs " there" (πολυ των νυμφων δι εςιν), those whom he entertained were " a few of the other sex" (ολιγοι δι ιςι το χρημα των ανδρων.)

I present,

prefent, it is pleafing to a friend both to give and receive, " from houfe to houfe," according to the wife Pindar *.

This is a hafty epiftle, written by lamp-light. Whatever therefore may be its faults, do not criticife them with the feverity of one orator towards another †.

---

## Epiftle XLVII. To the Inhabitants of Thrace ‡.

TO a prince who was avaricious your requeft would feem unreafonable, nor fhould the public revenue ever be injured through any favour to individuals. But as it is our view not to collect from our fubjects as much as poffible, but rather to do them the utmoft poffible good, we remit you what is due. Not indeed the whole, but it fhall be divided; one moiety you fhall retain, and the other fhall be given to the foldiers. Of

* Οικοθεν οικαδι. I have not found thefe words in Pindar. If I have fearched well, it muft be fuppofed that Julian took them from one of the works of that poet which has not been tranfmitted to us.    LA BLÉTERIE.

M. de la Bleterie has not " fearched well." They are both in the vith and viith Olympics.

† This conclufion favours more of the author than the prince.    Ibid.

‡ He remits them the arrears of taxes till a certain time, namely, till the third indiction, or levy, which began in the year of Chrift, 359. This ufed to be ftyled " an indulgence." See Cod. Theod. l. xi. tit. 28. De indulgentiis debitorum.    PETAU.

this

this no inconfiderable part will alfo be yours, as they preferve you in peace and fafety. We remit you therefore, till the third indiction *, all that is in arrear; after that, you muft pay it as ufual. For what we have remitted to you is fully fuffi-cient; and the public revenue we muft not im-pair. I have written on this fubject to the præ-fects, that the favour intended you may have its full effect.

I pray the Gods always to preferve you †.

---

* The name and ufe of the indictions, which ferve to afcertain the chronology of the middle ages, were derived from the regular practice of the Roman tributes. The Emperor fubfcribed with his own hand, and in purple ink, the folemn edict, or indiction, which was fixed up in the principal city of each diocefe, during two months previous to the firft day of September. And, by a very eafy con-nection of ideas, the word " indiction" was transferred to the meafure of tribute which it prefcribed, and to the annual term which it allowed for the payment.

The proportion, which every citizen fhould be obliged to contribute for the public fervice, was afcertained by an accurate *cenfus*, or furvey, and from the well-known period of the indictions there is reafon to believe that this dif-ficult and expenfive operation was repeated at the regular diftance of fifteen years. The cycle of indictions, which may be traced as high as the reign of Conftantius, or perhaps of his father Conftantine, is ftill employed by the papal court; but the commencement of their year has been very wifely altered to the firft of January.    GIBBON.

† This fentence is added in one MS.

## Epiſtle XLVIII. To * * * *.

MY body is on many accounts in an indifferent ſtate of health *; my mind, however, is pretty well. An epiſtle from one friend to another cannot, I think, have a better preface. Of what then does this preface conſiſt? Of a petition, I ſuppoſe. For what? An epiſtolary correſpondence; which, I hope, will confirm my wiſhes, and bring me intelligence of your health and happineſs.

## Epiſtle XLIX. To ARSACIUS, High-prieſt of Galatia †.

THAT Helleniſm ‡ does not yet ſucceed as we wiſh is owing to its profeſſors. The gifts of the Gods are indeed great and ſplendid, and far ſuperior

A. D. 362. or 363.

---

* From this and ſeveral other paſſages, which the reader muſt have obſerved, it appears, that Julian had frequent returns of illneſs, owing probably to his great and conſtant fatigue of mind and body, and to his rigid manner of life.

† This pontiff is not known. I imagine this Epiſtle was written, at the ſooneſt, towards the end of the year 362, as it ſuppoſes that ſome time had been employed in endeavouring to re-eſtabliſh Helleniſm. Sozomen and M. Fleury have thought the whole worth being inſerted in their Eccleſiaſtical Hiſtory. Indeed it would be impoſſible to produce a more honourable and leſs ſuſpicious teſtimony in favour of our religion. But I will not deprive the reader of the pleaſure of

fuperior to all our hopes, to all our wifhes. For (be Nemefis propitious to my words!) not long ago no one dared to hope for fuch and fo great a change in fo fhort a time. But why fhould we be fatisfied with this, and not rather attend to the means by which this impiety § has increafed, namely, humanity to ftrangers, care in burying the dead, and pretended fanctity of life? All thefe, I think, fhould be really practifed by us.

It is not fufficient for you only to be blamelefs. Intreat or compell all the priefts that are in Galatia to be alfo virtuous. If they do not, with their wives, children, and fervants, attend the worfhip of the Gods, expell them from the prieftly function; and alfo forbear to converfe with the fervants,

of making himfelf all the ufeful reflections which the perufal of this piece fupplies.          LA PLETERIE.

The paftoral letters of Julian, if we may ufe that name, ftill reprefent a very curious fketch of his wifhes and intentions.          GIBBON.

‡ This was the ftyle at that time. *Hellenifm* is Heathenifm, or Gentilifm. And Heathens are called *Hellenes*, and Hellenifts, by our Ecclefiaftical hiftorians, Socrates, Sozomen, and Theodoret, efpecially in their hiftory of Julian's reign.          LARDNER.

§ A fingular kind of impiety, which renders man the friend of man, and makes him practife all virtues! To charge good men with hypocrify is the ufual refource of extravagant prejudice and wickednefs. Julian, with all his genius, did not and would not fee that a fociety, fo numerous as the Chriftians then were, does not carry on and cannot even conceive fuch a defign. Hypocrify will never be a popular vice. The multitude, be it what it may, is always honeft.          LA BLETERIE.

children

children, and wives, of the Galileans *, who are impious towards the Gods, and prefer impiety to religion. Admonish also every priest not to frequent the theatre, nor to drink in taverns, nor to exercise any trade or employment that is mean and disgraceful. Those who obey you, honour; and those who disobey you, expell. Erect also hospitals in every city, that strangers may partake our benevolence; and not only those of our own religion, but, if they are indigent, others also.

How these expences are to be defrayed must now be considered. I have ordered Galatia to supply you with thirty-thousand bushels of wheat † every year; of which the fifth part is to be given

---

* Ἀλλα ανιχοιϊλο τ .ν οικιϊων, η υιιιϛ, η τον Γαλιλαιον γαμιϊων, x. τ. λ. I have attempted a new translation of th's passage, not being satisfied with any other which I have met with. In Spanheim's edition the Latin version is, *ne patiantur servos, aut filios, aut conjuges Galilæorum impiè in Deos se gerere, et impietatem pietati præponere.* And much to the same purpose is the Latin translation of this Epistle in Sozomen, made by Valesius, which would be commanding every Heathen priest and his family to become persecutors; which cannot be supposed to be probable. Cave, in the introduction to his History of the Fathers of the ivth century, p. 34. " not suffering their servants, children, or " wives, to be Galileans, who are despisers of the Gods, " and prefer impiety before religion," which cannot be right. For it is a tautology, saying over again the same thing which had been said just before. And yet Bleterie's translation is much to the same purpose: *s'ils souffrent dans leur famille de ces impies de Galiléens.* LARDNER. I have adopted this construction.

† The Latin and French translations add here " and " sixty-thousand *sextarii* (or *septiers*) of wine," words, for which there is no authority in Petau's or Spanheim's edition.

to the poor who attend on the priefts, and the
remainder to be diftributed among ftrangers and
our own beggars. For when none of the Jews beg,
and the impious Galileans relieve both their own
poor and ours, it is fhameful, that ours fhould be
deftitute of our affiftance *.

Teach therefore the Gentiles to contribute to
fuch minifterial functions, and the Gentile villages
to offer to the Gods their firft-fruits. Accuftom
them to fuch acts of benevolence, and inform them
that this was of old the regal office. For Homer
puts thefe words into the mouth of Eumæus :

——— It never was our guife
To flight the poor, or aught humane defpife ;
For Jove unfolds our hofpitable door,
'Tis Jove that fends the ftranger and the poor †.
Let us not fuffer others to emulate our good
actions, while we ourfelves are difgraced by floth ‡,

left

---

* Julian beheld with envy the wife and humane regu-
gulations of the church, and he very frankly confeffes his
intention to deprive the Chriftians of the applaufe, as well
as advantage, which they had acquired by the exclufive
practice of charity and benevolence.        GIBBON.
    Se: the conclufion of the Duties of a Prieft, Vol. I.
p. 142, &c.

† Odyff. XIV. 56. Pope, 65. This paffage is quoted
by Mr. Harris, on the fubject of the Arabian hofpitality.
See his *Philological Enquiries*, part III. ch. 7.

‡ Who doubts but that, before Chriftianity appeared in
the world, the Pagans performed fome humane actions,
and that fome among them practifed fome moral virtues ?
But it was not as Pagans, it was as men that they practifed them : In that they only followed the impreffions of
the law and religion of nature. It was becaufe the corruption

ruption of the heart, the strange idea which the idolaters, at least the people, formed of the divinity, and that monstrous collection of senseless opinions, of scandalous traditions, and of ridiculous superstitions, in which Paganism consisted, had not absolutely extinguished the *light which shineth in darkness.*

The Pagans had a morality, but Paganism had none. It is no less absurd to appropriate virtues to it, as Julian does, than it would be to ascribe to infidelity some virtuous actions, of, no consequence, which escape from infidels. Supposing that they have some probity, it is from temper, from interest, from caprice, because they are men, and often because they have preserved some remains of a Christian education. This epistle of Julian shews, how many virtues, even those which by the pleasure that attends their practice carry with them their reward, were rare among the Pagans. Could the finger of God be mistaken in a religion which renders all virtues common ; which, founded also on all the proofs of which a fact is susceptible, brings into the world a system of morality the most perfect that can possibly be imagined, supports it by the most powerful motives and examples, regulates even the most secret motions of our souls ; in a word, which re-establishes, unfolds, and perfects the principles of the law of nature, almost effaced in the minds of men, and still more in their hearts ?

Let us judge of the necessity of Christianity by the horrid crimes which were committed, and are still committed, in the best-governed Pagan nations. To the disgrace of Philosophy, it will, for instance, be always true to say, that mankind are indebted to the gospel of Jesus Christ for the abolition of the barbarous custom of exposing infants. In this respect the most savage animals rise up in judgement, even at the tribunal of reason, against the Greek, the Roman, and the Chinese.

To deprive our religion of a glory which is peculiar to it it would be useless to say, that Mahometanism has been equally serviceable to humanity. Who knows not, that this false religion supposes and acknowledges the mission of Jesus Christ, and is only a corruption of Christianity and Judaism ? No one can deny, that the Christian religion has at least sweetened the manners, civilised the barbarous people who have embraced it, enlightened, as to his duties, left by negligence we lose our reverence for the Gods. If I hear that you practise this, I shall overflow with joy.

Visit the dukes * seldom at their houses, but write to them often. Whenever they enter a city, let none of the priests go to meet them; but when they resort to the temples, let them be received within the vestibule. When they enter, let none of

.the rudest Pagan, diffused every where some delicacy, of conscience, and, even among those whom it does not alter, a tincture of probity. A Christian, moderately instructed, and of common virtue, knows more in point of morality, and is more philosophical than a philosopher. Those who, like Julian, but with less splendor than he, have abandoned the Christian religion, are more indebted to that religion than they imagine. They, as well as Julian, are indebted to it for the exactest and purest notions of certain moral virtues. It is from that that some have retained those maxims of rigid probity of which they would not have made parade, if Christianity had not given them reputation. It has already been said, that if, which is impossible, the gospel were false, it would be for the interest of mankind to believe it true. LA BLETERIE.

* Or commanders of the troops. See note on Epistle XXVIII, p. 73. Julian, in what follows, seems very attentive to the dignity of the priesthood, by endeavouring to prevent those who were ordained to any holy office from degenerating into mere secular politicians, party zealots, and danglers at the levees (as we now call them) of the great. What so proper to impress them with a just opinion of their own rank and importance as to forbid their mixing in popular assemblies and tumultuous processions, even when intended to give honour where honour was due, and paying idle or even ceremonious visits, and rather to confine them within the precincts of their own temples, where, without offence, they had an undoubted precedence? In the Duties of a Priest, in like manner, the priests are allowed to " visit the dukes and præfects." See Vol. I. p. 138.

their

their guards precede them; but let who will follow them. For as foon as they enter the door of
the temple, they become private perfons. You
yourfelf, you well know, have a right to precede
all who are within it, that being agreeable, to the
divine law. Thofe who are truly pious will obey
you, and none will oppofe you but the proud,
oftentatious, and vain-glorious.

I am ready to affift the people of Peffinus *, if
they can render the Mother of the Gods propitious to them. But if they neglect her, they
will not only be culpable, but, which is more harfh
to fay, will incur my difpleafure †.

No law requires that they my care fhould prove,
Or pity, hated by the powers above ‡.

There-

---

* See Epiftle XXI. p. 43.
† An ungenerous diftinction was admitted into the mind
of Julian, that, according to the difference of their religious fentiments, one part of his fubjects deferved his
favour and friendfhip, while the other was entitled only to
the common benefits that his juftice could not refufe to an
obedient people. GIBBON.

‡ See Odyff. X. 73. What Julian fays here does not
feem to agree with the order which he has juft given to
eftablifh fome hofpitals, where all might be received, Chriftians as well as Pagans. This contradiction, if fuch it
were, would not have been the only one of which he had
been guilty. But it is only apparent. The duties of humanity are ftrictly juft. They are obligatory with regard
to all men. But favours are due to none; and it was fome
favour that the inhabitants of Peffinus had afked of the
Emperor. LA BLETERIE.

Thefe two lines, which Julian has changed and perverted,
in the true fpirit of a bigot, are taken from the fpeech of
Æolus, when he refufes to grant Ulyffes a frefh fupply of

K 3 / winds.

· Therefore affure them, that, if they wifh for my protection, all the people muft fupplicate the Mother of the Gods.

---

## Epiftle L. To Ecdicius, Præfect of Ægypt *.

A. D. 362. " YOU tell me my dream †," fays the proverb. But I am going to tell you what you have feen waking. The Nile, I am informed, has

---

winds. Libanius (*Orat. Parent. c.* 59. *p.* 286.) attempts to juftify this partial behaviour by an apology, in which perfecution peeps through the mafk of candour.    GIBBON,

The lines in Homer are,

Ου γαρ μοι θεμις εςι κομιζεμεν, ꙏδ' αποπεμπειν
Ανδρα, τ' ος κε θεοισιν απεχθηλαι μακαρεσσιν.

His baneful fuit pollutes thefe blefs'd abodes,
Whofe faith proclaims him hateful to the Gods.

POPE, 85.

Julian has altered them thus, at the expence of a falfe quantity, and a jingle :

Ου γαρ μοι θεμις εςι κομιζεμεν, η' ελειαιρειν
· Ανδρας, οι και θεοισιν απεχθωντ' αθαναλοισιν.

· In the laft word, probably, his memory might deceive him, as απεχθωνλαι μακαρεσσιν would have fuited his purpofe and metre as well. The other alterations (και perhaps excepted) muft have been intentional.

* This Epiftle is a good piece of pleafantry on the negligence of Ecdicius. That governor, I fancy, would rather have received a ferious reprimand. Nothing was more interefting to the Emperor and the empire than an account of how many cubits the Nile had rifen in the autumnal folftice, as on that depended the fertility of Ægypt, and the fubfiftence of Conftantinople. Where the waters rofe too much, or too little, the lands could not be fown. "' If the increafe," fays Pliny, '(*l.* v. *c.* 9,) " be only " twelve

has rifen feveral cubits, and overflowed all Ægypt. If you wifh to know the number, it was fifteen on the twentieth of September. This intelligence I received from Theophilus, præfect of the camps. If you had not heard it before, rejoice at hearing it now from me.

"" twelve cubits, the province is afflicted with famine ; if "" it be only thirteen, it ftill fuffers.    Fourteen give joy : "" fifteen fafety; fixteen abfolute plenty."    The Nile fwells from the middle of July to the folftice.    When it is at its greateft height, the canals are opened, to let it in upon the lands.    It returns to its bed in the month of No-vember.    The feeds are then. fown,    The corn is reaped in May.    .                                    LA BLETERIE.

The cubit, by which the rifing of the Nile in Ægypt was meafured, had been ufually lodged in the temple of Serapis [at Alexandria].    Conftantine removed it into a Chriftian church.    But Julian ordered it to be replaced in the temple of Serapis.    His ftatue and temple having been demolifhed, by order of Theodofius I. in the year 391, it was given out by the Gentiles that the Nile would no longer overflow.    Neverthelefs it rofe the following year to an uncommon height.    The cubit was then again re-ftored to the Chriftians.                        LARDNER.

Thales, the Milefian, accounted for the inundation of this river by the Etefian winds blowing againft the mouth of it at that feafon.    But the fame would probably then happen to other rivers where the like winds are known to blow.    The true caufe is probably the melting of the fnows on the mountains of Ethiopia, when the fun comes over them.    Yet thefe winds may contribute to make the over-flow more regular and lafting, as they are an equal balance to the waters, and prevent their running into the fea after thefe have fufficiently fertilifed the land.

† Τε σον οναρ σοι διηγαμαι, "" I tell you your dream." That is, "" I tell you what you yourfelf know better than I." In Suidas this proverb is quoted from fome unknown au-thor, and alfo in Plato De Republ. l. vIII.    It feems derived from thofe who confult interpreters of dreams ; whom fome alfo require to guefs what they have dreamed.   ERASMUS.

K 4                    Epiftle

## Epiſtle LI. To the ALEXANDRIANS *.

A. D. 362.

IF your city had had any other founder, any one of thoſe who, tranſgreſſing their own laws †, had juſtly ſuffered puniſhment for leading a wicked life, and introducing a new doctrine, a new religion, even then it would have been unreaſonable for you to wiſh for Athanaſius. But now, as the founder of your city is Alexander ‡, and your ruler and tutelar deity king Serapis, with the virgin his aſſociate, and the queen of all Ægypt, Iſis, * * * *, you do not act like a healthy city, but the diſtempered part dares to arrogate the

---

* The Catholics, who were, without doubt, the moſt numerous, preſented, in the name of the city, a petition to the Emperor, requeſting the repeal of the order which he had iſſued againſt Athanaſius. The Emperor anſwers their petition by this new Edict. M. Fleury quotes the whole of it. LA BLETERIE.

† Thoſe whom Julian here treats as apoſtates (a reproach ſtrange enough in his mouth), had not abandoned the God of their fathers, to run after ſtrange gods. They believed in the ſecond revelation, which was only the object, the ſequel, and the accompliſhment of the firſt. By dying for the doctrine of their maſter, they have proved that they were not deceivers. The proofs of the fact which determined them to embrace it are of ſuch a nature, that it is impoſſible for them to have been deceived. Could Julian allege any thing ſimilar in juſtification of his change? He has here given us a very remarkable ſketch of his reaſons in the pathetic diſcourſe which he addreſſes to the inhabitants of Alexandria. Ibid.

‡ See Epiſtle X. note †, p. 20.

name

name of the whole. By the Gods, men of Alexandria, I am afhamed, that any of you fhould
avow himfelf a Galilean.

The anceftors of the Hebrews were formerly
flaves to the Ægyptians. But now, men of Alexandria, you, the conquerors of Ægypt (for Ægypt
was conquered by your founder), fuftain a voluntary fervitude to the defpifers of your national
rites, in oppofition to your ancient laws * ; not recollecting your former happinefs, when all Ægypt
had communion with the Gods †, and enjoyed
many bleffings. But tell me, what advantage ‡
has accrued to your city from thofe who now introduce among you a new religion? Your founder
was that pious man § Alexander of Macedon, who
did

* The Hebrews were fubjected to the ancient kings of
Ægypt; the Alexandrians therefore ought to prefer the
Greek religion to the doctrine of the Apoftles : What a
fingular complication of bad arguments ! LA BLETERIE.

† If they recollected it, they recollected but little of it.
Ibid.

Julian makes intercommunity the diftinguifhing character of the Pagan religion. For the Imperial fophift,
writing to the people of Alexandria, and upbraiding them
with having forfaken the religion of their country, in order
to aggravate the charge, infinuates them to be guilty of in-
gratitude, as having forgotten " thofe happy times when
" all Ægypt worfhipped the Gods in common" (ηνικα ην
κοινωνια). WARBURTON.

‡ The Chriftian religion does not promife temporal
bleffings; but, if men practife it, they will be as happy as
they can be on earth. LA BLETERIE.

§ In matters of religion, what authority was that of
Alexander? What conquefts were his, compared to thofe
of

did not, by Jove, refemble any one of thefe, or any of the Hebrews, who far excelled them. Even Ptolemy, the fon of Lagus *, was alfo fuperior to them. As to Alexander, if he had encountered, he would have endangered, even the Romans. What then did the Ptolemies, who fucceeded your founder? Educating your city, like their own daughter, from her infancy, they did not bring her to maturity by the difcourfes of Jefus, nor did they conftruct the form of government with which fhe is now bleffed by the doctrine of the odious Galileans.

Thirdly, after the Romans became its mafters, taking it from the bad government of the Ptolemies †, Auguftus vifited your city, and thus addreffed the citizens: " Men of Alexandria, I ac-
" quit your city of all blame, out of regard to
" the great God Serapis, and alfo for the fake of
" the people and the grandeur of the city. A
" third caufe of my kindnefs to you is my friend

of the Apoftles? I beg the reader to recollect that paffage in the epiftle to Themiftius (p. 24;), where Julian raifes Socrates above Alexander; and to determine whether the juft reafons which he has given for preferring the former are not infinitely more ftriking and decifive in favour of the difciples of Jefus Chrift. Here Julian fpeaks like a true fophift. He was well acquainted with Alexander, and would not have wifhed to refemble him in every thing.
　　　　　　　　　　　　　... La Blererie.
· · * Ptolemy, the fon of Lagus, was one of the generals of Alexander, who fhared his empire. He founded the kingdom of Ægypt.　　　　　　　　　 , ·　　　　Ibid.
· † The family of the Lagides terminated in the perfon of Cleopatra, after having reigned 300 years.　　　Ibid.

　　　　　　　　　　　" Areus."

"Areus *." This Areus, the companion of Augustus Cæfar, and a philofopher, was your fellow-citizen.

The particular favours conferred upon your city by the Olympic Gods were, in fhort, fuch as thefe. Many more, not to be prolix, I omit. Thofe bleffings which the illuftrious Gods beftow in common every day, not on one family, nor on a fingle city, but on the whole world, why do you not acknowledge? Are you alone infenfible of the fplendor that flows from the fun †? Are you alone ignorant that fummer and winter are produced by him, and that to him all things owe their life and origin? Do you not alfo perceive the great advantages that accrue to your city from the moon, from him and by him the difpofer of all things? Yet you dare not worfhip either of thefe deities; and this Jefus, whom neither you, nor your fathers have feen, you think muft neceffarily be God the Word ‡, while him, whom, from eternity, every

---

* The fame who is mentioned in the Cæfars, (Vol. I. p. 193.) and in the Epiftle to Themiftius, (p. 25.)
LA BLETERIE.

† All nature, and the heavenly bodies, in particular, prove the exiftence of a Supreme Being, and declare his power, his wifdom, and his goodnefs. But their fplendor, the regularity of their motions, and the ufes which they render to mankind do not prove that they are governed by fome particular intelligences, and much lefs that they deferve to be worfhipped. *Ibid.*

‡ I have already faid that Julian placed the *Logos*, or Demiurgus, in the Sun. *Ibid.*

Θεον λογον. Taken from St. John, i. 1. Θεος ην ὁ λογος, *The Word was God.*

generation

generation of mankind has feen, and fees, and
worfhips, and by worfhipping lives happily, the
great fun, I mean, a living, animated, rational,
and beneficent image of the intelligible Father *,
you defpife. If you liften to my admonitions †,
* * * *, you will by degrees return to truth. You
will not wander from the right path, if you will
be guided by him, who, to the twentieth year of
his age, purfued that road, but has now worfhipped the Gods for near twelve years.

If you will follow my advice, my joy will be
exuberant. But if you will ftill perfevere in that
fuperftitious inftitution of defigning men, agree,
however, among yourfelves, and do not defire
Athanafius. There are many of his difciples who
are abundantly able to pleafe your itching ears ‡,
defirous as they are of fuch impious difcourfes.
I wifh that this wickednefs were confined to Athanafius and his irreligious fchool. But you have

---

* In another place (*apud Cyril. l.* 11. *p.* 69.) he calls the
fun " God, and the throne of God." Julian believed the
Platonician Trinity, and only blames the Chriftians for
preferring a mortal to an immortal Logos. GIBBON.

Though the Alexandrians faw the fun, they by no means
faw that he was a divinity ; but without having feen the
MAN GOD, they had certain proofs of his miffion ; proofs
which, all united, form, in fact, a complete demonftra-
tion. It is worth obferving, that Julian, in one and the
fame phrafe, fpeaks the language of Pyrrhonifm and that
of credulity. LA BLETERIE.

† Something here is wanting.

‡ Τας ακοας υμων κνησωσας. Similar to that expreffion of
St. Paul, 2 Tim. iv. 3. κνηθομενοι την ακοην.

among

among you many, not ignoble, of the fame fect, and the bufinefs is eafily done. For any one whom you may felect from the people, in what relates to expounding the fcriptures will be by no means in-ferior to him whom you folicit. But if you are pleafed with the fhrewdnefs of Athanafius (for, I hear, the man is crafty), and therefore have peti-tioned, know, that for this very reafon he was banifhed. That fuch an intriguer fhould prefide over the people is highly dangerous; one, who is not a man, but a puny contemptible mortal, one who prides himfelf on hazarding his life *, cannot but create difturbances. That nothing of that kind might happen, I ordered him formerly to leave the city, but I now banifh him from all Ægypt.

*Let this be communicated to our Alexandrians.*

* I cannot convey all the energy of the Greek : Μικρὸ αντρ, αλλ' ανθρωπισκος ευτελης, καθαπερ αλλος, ο μεγας (it fhould be το μιγα) οιομενος πιρι της κιφαλης κινδυνευειν. *Ne vir quidem, fed homuncio nullius pretii, qualis ifte eft, qui de capite periclitari magnum aliquid exiftimat.* LA BLETERIE.
The prefent tranflator may fay the fame.
M. de Tillemont concludes from this text, that Atha-nafius was a little man, and that his perfon had nothing that announced the grandeur and elevation of his mind. The moft, I think that we can conclude from this expreffion of Julian is, that, Athanafius was not of a proper h ig t. I fay, the moft; for it muft be obferved, that it is an Emperor who fpeaks of one of his fubjects, and who affects to fpeak of him in a tone of contempt. Gregory Nazianzen (*Orat.* xxi.) fays, that Athanafius " had the form of an angel," αγγελικος το ειδος. It even appears, that, when he went to meet the Emperor Conftantine the younger, in Gaul, that prince was ftruck with his advantageous appearance. *Ibid.*

Epiftle

## Epiſtle LII. To the Bostrenians *.

Aug.
362.

I THOUGHT that the prelates of the Galll-
leans had been under greater obligations to me
than to my predeceſſor. For in his reign many
of them were baniſhed, perſecuted, and impriſoned;
and numbers of thoſe, who are ſtyled heretics, were
put to death, particularly at Samoſata and Cyzicus;
and in Paphlagonia, Bithynia, Galatia, and many
other provinces, whole villages were laid waſte
and entirely depopulated †. In my reign the re-

* Boſtra, or Boſra, as it is ſtyled in ſcripture, was a
Roman colony, and the capital of Arabia. It had then
for its biſhop a man equally well verſed in polite literature,
and the doctrine of the church, named Titus.
                                              LA BLETERIE.
In this very remakable Epiſtle to the people of Boſtra,
Julian profeſſes his moderation, and betrays his zeal; which
is acknowledged by Ammianus, and expoſed by Gregory,
(Orat. III. p. 73.)                              GIBBON.

† The ſucceſſor of Conſtantius has expreſſed, in a conciſe, but lively, manner, ſome of the theological calamities which afflicted the empire, and more eſpecially the
Eaſt, in the reign of a prince, who was the ſlave of his
own paſſions, and of thoſe of his eunuchs.        Ibid.

Under Conſtantius the Arians, who pretended to be the
Catholic church, had perſecuted not only the orthodox, but
alſo the ſectaries, eſpecially the Novatians, who, without
receiving the council of Nice ſubſequent to their ſchiſm,
were no leſs zealous than the orthodox for conſubſtantiality.
They were the ſubſiſting and unſuſpected proof of the
novelty of Arianiſm; which made them much regarded
by the Catholics, and more odious to the Arians than the
Catholics themſelves.                          LA BLETERIE.

verſe

verfe has happened. For they who had been banifhed are allowed to return, and to thofe whofe
goods had been confifcated, all have been reftored. Such, neverthelefs, are their madnefs
and folly, that, becaufe they can no more tyrannife, or perpetrate what they had projected,
firft againft their brethren, and then againft us,
the worfhippers of the Gods, enraged and exafperated, they move every ftone, and dare to alarm
and inflame the people *; impious towards the
Gods, and difobedient to our edicts, humane as
they are. For we fuffer none of them to be dragged
to the altars againft their will. We alfo publickly
declare, that, if any are defirous to partake of our
luftrations and libations, they muft firft offer facrifices of expiation, and fupplicate the Gods, the
averters of evil. So far are we from wifhing to
admit any of the irreligious to our facred rites
before they have purified their fouls by prayers to
the Gods, and their bodies by legal ablutions +.

The populace therefore, deluded by thofe who
are called the clergy, as the feverity above-mentioned is abolifhed, grow tumultuous. For they
who have been ufed to tyrannife, not fatisfied
with impunity for their paft crimes, but ambitious of their former power, becaufe they are no

* The Arian clergy, who were in poffeffion of a great
number of churches, gave occafion to the invectives of
Julian.　　　　　　　　　　　　La Bleterie.
+ One who fpeaks in this manner was very capable of
having endeavoured to efface his baptifm.　　　Ibid.
7　　　　　　　　　　　　　longer

longer permitted to act as judges *, or make
wills †, or embezzle the estates of others, and appropriate every thing to themselves, all, if I may
so say, pull the ropes of sedition, and, as the proverb expresses it, heap fuel on the fire, and scruple
not to add greater evils to the former by urging
the multitude to commotions.

It is my pleasure therefore to declare and pub-
lish to all the people, by this edict, that they must
not abet the seditions of the clergy, nor suffer
themselves to be induced by them to throw stones,
and disobey the magistrates. They may assemble
together, if they please, and offer up such prayers
as they have established for themselves. But if
the clergy endeavour to persuade them to foment
disturbances on their account, let them by no means
concur, on pain of punishment.

* Julian had revoked all the privileges granted to the
church, and, among them, the law by which Constantine
allowed those who had law-suits to decline the ordinary
jurisdiction, and to apply to the bishops, whose sentences
were to be executed like those of the Emperor himself.

                                        LA BLETERIE.

† Γραφειν διαθηκας, *scribere testamenta*, may here have three
meanings ; 1. to make wills; 2. to receive wills in a public
capacity ; 3. to dictate or suggest wills. Julian had not
deprived the clergy of the right of making wills. This is
proved by the silence of Christian writers. Among the Romans, to the making of the most solemn will no public person was requisite : there only wanted a certain number of
witnesses. The third sense therefore remains. A law of
Constantine, which is still in being, allowed wills to be made
in favour of the church. Julian having abrogated that law,
the ecclesiastics could no longer engage any one to give his
estate to the church by will, and consequently to their advantage, as Julian pretends they had.                    *Ibid.*

I thought

I thought proper to make this declaration to the city of Boſtra in particular, becauſe the biſhop, Titus *, and the clergy †, in a memorial which they have preſented to me, have accuſed the people of being inclined to raiſe diſturbances, if they had not been reſtrained by their admonitions. I will tranſcribe the words which the biſhop has dared to inſert in that memorial: " Though the Chriſtians " are as numerous as the Gentiles, they are re- " ſtrained by our exhortations from being tumul- " tuous." Theſe are the words of the biſhop concerning you. Obſerve, he does not aſcribe your regularity to your own inclination ; unwillingly, he ſays, you refrain, " by his exhortations." As your accuſer, therefore, expell him from the city ‡. And, for

* This Titus, biſhop of Boſtra, taught that we do not die in conſequence of the ſin of Adam, but by the neceſſity of nature ; and that Adam himſelf would have died, if he had not ſinned. In this he was followed by Pelagius.
PRIESTLEY.

† It ſeems as if there was an apprehenſion of ſome commotion in the city of Boſtra. Julian had threatened to make the biſhop, Titus, and his clergy, reſponſible for the whole. The biſhop had preſented, or cauſed a memorial to be preſented, to the Emperor, accounting for his conduct.
LA BLETERIE.

‡ If we did not know how much the mind is narrowed by the ſpirit of party, it would be inconceivable that an Emperor, a man who piqued himſelf on reaſoning, and who publiſhed this himſelf, ſhould be capable of ſuch a trick [tracaſſerie.] I uſe this word, becauſe it is a low one, and I know none more proper to characteriſe the artfulneſs of Julian, who was determined, at any rate, to prejudice in the minds of the people an irreconcilable

for the future, let the people agree among themfelves; let no one be at variance, or do an injury
to another; neither you who are in error, to thofe
who worfhip the Gods, rightly and juftly, in the
mode tranfmitted to us from the moft ancient
times; nor let the worfhippers of the Gods deftroy or plunder the houfes of thofe who rather
by ignorance than choice are led aftray. Men
fhould be taught and perfuaded by reafon, not by
blows, invectives, and corporal punifhments. I
therefore again and again admonifh thofe who embrace the true religion in no refpect to injure or infult the Galileans *, neither by attacks nor reproaches.

proachable prelate, who employed his authority to main-
tain the public tranquillity. This philofophical Emperor,
in an edict which breathes the principles of mutual fupport, foments the flame, which he pretends it is his wifh
to ftifle. If he had banifhed the bifhop, his orders would
have been peaceably obeyed. But does not his advifing
the people to drive him out indicate a defign to excite a
tumult? Some might confider the advice of the Emperor
as an order, and others only as an advice. Hiftory does
not inform us what was the confequence of this affair.
LA BLETERIE.
After this, no inftance of balenefs, or injuftice, will be
thought ftrange. It is remarkable that the author of the
Characteriftics has given us a tranflation of this letter, for
" a pattern," as he tells us, " of the humour and genius,
" of the principles and fentiments, of this virtuous, gallant,
" generous, and mild Emperor." p. 87, &c. 4th edition.
It is true, his tranflation drops the affair of Titus, their
bifhop. So that nothing hinders his reader from concluding
but that the Emperor might be as " gallant and generous"
as he is pleafed to reprefent him. WARBURTON.
* How irreconcileable is this with the above Edict,
{Epiftle XLII.} for which he deferved no fmall reproof from
(is

proaches. We fhould rather pity than hate thofe who in the moft important concerns act ill. For as piety is the greateft of bleffings, impiety, cerr tainly, is the greateft of evils. Such is their fate, who turn from the immortal Gods to dead men *, and their relicks. With thofe who are thus un-happy we condole, but them who are freed and delivered by the Gods we congratulate †.

*Given at Antioch on the calends of Auguft.*

Epiftle

(in other refpects) his chief panegyrift! " It was very un-
" merciful in him (as that excellent writer expreffes it) to,
" forbid the mafters of grammar and rhetoric to teach
" the Chriftians, unlefs they embraced the worfhip of the
" Gods." Amm. Marc. xxv. 4.          SPANHEIM.

* Αποθιων επι τας νεκρας μιλαλεραμμινας. An expreffion fimilar to that of St. Paul, Επιςρεψαι προς τον Θιον απο των ειδωλων :
*Ye turned to God from idols, to ferve the living God.* 1 Thef.
i. 9.

† From this Edict, as well as from other things, it appears that Julian was very fond of Hellenifm, or Heathenifm.
And Sozomen's obfervations appear to be very pertinent.
Julian was very ready to lay hold of every pretence, and to
improve every occafion, to rid himfelf of the Prefidents of
Chriftian churches; efpecially fuch as had an influence with
the people. We fee three inftances of this, in Athanafius of
Alexandria, Eleufius of Cyzicum, and Titus of Boftra, all
of them men of great diftinction.

Julian here makes repeated profeffions of moderation and
equity toward the Chriftians. But the letter bears witnefs
againft him. Titus was one of the moft learned men of
the age. His people were peaceable, and he had exhorted
them to be fo. And yet Julian commands his people to
expell him out of their city; under a pretence, that his
exhortations to a peaceable behaviour implied an accufation
of an unpeaceable temper.

Julian was a man of great ingenuity, fobriety of manners, and good-natured in himfelf. But his zeal for the
religion which he had embraced was exceffive, and de-
                    L 2                    generated

Epiſtle LIII.   To the Philoſopher JAM-
BLICHUS *.

O JUPITER! can it be true that we reſide in
the middle of Thrace, and winter in its ca-
verns, while from the excellent Jamblichus, as
from ſome eaſtern ſpring, letters greet us, inſtead
of ſwallows, though we are not yet allowed to go
to him, nor he to come to us? Who but a Thracian,
or one like Tereus †, can with equanimity ſupport
this?

O royal Jove! from Thrace the Grecians free ‡,
Diſpell theſe fogs, and give us but to ſee

generated into bigotry and ſuperſtition; inſomuch that
with all his pretentions to right reaſon, and all his pro-
feſſions of humanity, moderation, tenderneſs, and equity,
he has not eſcaped the juſt imputation of being a perſecutor.                                                            LARDNER.
    This learned writer has given an Engliſh tranſlation of
the above Epiſtle in his Jewiſh and Heathen Teſtimonies,
Vol. IV. p. 108.

    * See Ep. XXXIV. note *, p. 80.
    † Tereus was a king of Thrace, but ſeems here intro-
duced for his cruelty and brutality. See Ovid. Metam. VI.

    ‡ Ζιυ ανα' αλλα ου ρυσαι απο Θρηκηθιι Αχαιως, altered from Il.
XVII. 645.   Ζιυ πατιρ, αλλα ου ρυσαι υπ' ηερος υιας Αχαιων, the
beginning of the celebrated prayer of Ajax, applauded by
Longinus and others.   The other line is the ſame as in Homer.   Pope has thus tranſlated them:
    ——————— Lord of earth and air!
    O King! O Father! hear my humble prayer!
    Diſpell this cloud, the light of heaven reſtore,
    Give me to ſee, and Ajax aſks no more.                   727.

            3                                    ſome-

fometimes our Mercury, and to falute his fhrine,
and embrace his Images, as Ulyffes is faid to have
done, when, after his wanderings, he at laft faw
Ithaca * ; though the Phæacians departed, after
laying him out of the fhip, like a bale of goods,
in his fleep +. But fleep does not feize us till we
are allowed to fee the great bleffing of the world.
You too are jocofe in faying that I and my companion Sopater ‡ have tranfported Iall the Eaft
into Thrace. For if the truth muft be fpoken,
while Jamblichus is abfent, I feem involved in Cimmerian § darknefs. Befides, you defire one of thefe
alternatives,

* Ulyffes, at his return to Ithaca, Odyff. XIII.
————————With joy confefs'd his place of birth,
And on his knees falutes his mother earth. POPE, 403.
but where Julian found the two other circumftances mentioned above, I cannot fay.

+ Odyff. XIII. 116.
Ulyffes fleeping on his couch they bore,
And gently plac'd him on the rocky fhore, &c.
POPE, 138.

‡ Could this be the Sopater, who afterwards entertained
him at Hierapolis, (fee p. 70.) whom he " had (then)
" fcarce ever feen before ?"

§ The Cimmerians were a people of Italy who dwelt in
a valley, between Baiæ and Cumæ, fo furrounded with hills,
that it is faid they never faw the fun. There was the
Sibyl's grot, and there was fuppofed to be the defcent to
hell.

Great obfcurity, or darknefs, of the mind, is called
" Cimmerian darknefs." This adage arofe from the prodigious darknefs of the Cimmerian region, which Strabo
defcribes in his firft book of his Geography, and quotes
the following paffage from the Odyffey of Homer, XI.
14.

There,

alternatives, either that I would go to you, or that you may come to me; one of which, namely, that I would return to you, and enjoy your advantages, is very defirable to me. The other exceeds all my wifhes. But, as this is not only inconvenient to you, but alfo impracticable, remain at home, fare you well, and continue to enjoy your prefent tranquillity. As to me, whatever the Gods fhall allot, I will bear with fortitude: for it is the character of the virtuous to cherifh good hopes, and to perform their duty; but always to fubmit to fatal necefity.

> There, in a lonely land, and gloomy cells,
> The dufky nation of Cimmeria dwells;
> The fun ne'er views th' uncomfortable feats,
> When radiant he advances, or retreats;
> Unhappy race, whom endlefs night invades,
> Clouds the dull air, and wraps them round in fhades.
>
> BROOME, 15.

Tully alfo mentions the Cimmerians in the 1vth book of his Academic Queftions. And in this country Ovid, in the x1th book of his Metamorphofes, has built a temple to the God of Sleep.                    ERASMUS.

Epiftle

Epiſtle LIV. To GEORGE, the Catholic *.

LET Echo be, as you ſay, a Goddeſs, and talkative, and alſo, if you pleaſe, the wife of Pan †. I ſay nothing to the contrary. Though Nature would teach me, that Echo is the ſound of the voice reverberated by the percuſſion of the air, and reflected back to the ear, yet, by the opinion both of ancients and moderns, as well as by yours, I am induced to think that Echo is a Goddeſs. But what is this to me, who in love to you far exceed Echo? For ſhe does not reply to every thing ſhe hears, but only to the laſt words of the voice, like a coy miſtreſs, who receives the ſalute of her lover on the extremity of her lips. In this as I gladly lead the way, ſo again challenged by you, like a tennis-player, I return the ſtroke. You ſhall not eſcape, but ſhall be convicted by your own letter; and in that image you may diſcover a reſemblance of yourſelf, as you re-

* Epiſtle VIII. is addreſſed to the ſame.
† The Mythologiſts fable, that Echo was deſperately beloved by Pan. See, among others, Hephæſtion in the Writers of poetic hiſtory, publiſhed by Thomas Gale, p. 333.
WOLFIUS.
And thus Libanius ſays to his friend Demetrius, " You " have tranſmitted me ſo ſweet a voice by your epiſtle, " that I was quite captivated by it, and enamoured of its " charms, admiring the beauty of the words no leſs than " Pan admired the Goddeſs !" Ep. ccccxlii.

L 4 ceive

ceive much and return little, not of me, who endeavour to excell in both. But whether you return with the same measure that you receive, or
not, whatever I receive from you is agreeable to
me, and shall be deemed a full and satisfactory
answer.

---

### Epistle LV. To Eumenius and Pha- rianus*

A. D.
359.

WHOEVER has persuaded you that any
thing is more pleasing and beneficial to
mankind than philosophising in ease and security,
is deceived himself, and deceives you. If you
retain your former spirit, and, like a sparkling
flame, it be not suddenly extinguished, I deem you
happy. Four years have now elapsed, and almost
three months more, since we parted; I would
gladly therefore learn what progress you have made
in that time. As to me, it is a wonder that I can
even speak Greek; such barbarism I have contracted in this country†. Despise not oratory,

---

\* These were probably two of Julian's fellow-students,
whom he left with regret at Athens, in 355, when he was
summoned to court by Constantius, and created Cæsar. I
have therefore dated this Epistle as above. I know not that
their names occur any where else.

Among the Epistles of Libanius, preserved (in Latin) by
Zambicari, are two to Eumedius, (III. 237, 8.) which
probably means this Eumenius, especially as in one of them
Andromachus, an Athenian, is recommended to him.

† This expression shews, that Julian was then in Gaul.
It is similar to one in Epistle XXIX. p. 75.

nor neglect rhetoric, nor be inattentive to poetry.
But let your principal study be philosophy; and
on this bestow all your labour, on the maxims of
Aristotle and Plato. Be this your chief work, be
this the base, the foundation, the walls, the roof.
Let the rest be no more than office; which, however, you may finish with more skill than some can
build a mansion. As to what ——— ——— ———
—— This advice is given you by one, who by divine Nemesis loves you both with a brotherly
affection, as having been his school-fellows and
intimate friends. If you retain a regard for me,
my affection will increase. If not, I shall grieve.
And what at length may be the consequence of
continual grief, for the sake of a better omen, I
suppress.

## Epistle LVI. To Ecdicius, Præfect of Ægypt.

IF any thing particularly deserves our serious
attention, it is sacred music. Selecting therefore from among the Alexandrians some youths of
good families, order two *artabæ* * to be distri-
buted every month to each; and some oil, wheat,
and wine. The præfects of the treasury shall supply them with cloaths. They shall be chosen by

* Among the Egyptians, that an *artaba* made twenty
*modii* we are told by Jerom on Isaiah ch. ——— †
Among the Persians it was different, as we learn from
Herodotus, *l.* 1. ROBERTSON.

their

their voices. Mean time, let those who are proficients in that art be informed, that we have allotted rewards for their labours. And, besides these encouragements from us, they may also be assured by those who have a right judgement in these things, that they will profit their souls by purifying them with divine music. So much for these youths. As to what relates to the scholars of the musician Dioscorus; let them cultivate that art with more attention, and they shall receive from us all possible assistance *......................
................................ regard for me,
................................ I ... all grieve.

## Epistle LVII. To the Philosopher ELPIDIUS †.

THE pleasure even of a short letter is great, when the friendship of the writer is measured, not by the conciseness of his epistle, but by the greatness of his mind. Therefore if my present mental salutation be rather short, do not from thence form a judgement of my regard. But as you well know the extent of my love for you, excuse the brevity of this address, and answer it with-

* This Epistle is a proof of the Emperor's great esteem for himself. And indeed it is impossible to read his works without being convinced, that he was ignorant of nothing which was then necessary to be known to render a man an universal scholar. LA BLETERIE.

It is omitted, however, by this translator.

† This philosopher, and the Emperor's kindness to him, are mentioned by Libanius in one of his Epistles to Julian. See Vol. I. p. 305.

out delay. For whatever you send me, though
it be small, I esteem as a specimen of every thing
that is good.

Epiſtle LVIII.    To the ALEXANDRIANS,

Y OU have a ſtone obeliſk *, I am informed, A. D. 362.
of a proper height, but that, as if it were
worthleſs, it lies on the ſhore.    Conſtantius, of
bleſſed memory, had conſtrupted a veſſel on purpoſe to convey it to my country, Conſtantinople †.
But as he, by the will of the Gods, has taken a
fatal departure from hence, that city now requeſts
this preſent from me, being my country, and conſequently more nearly connected to me than to him.
His was a brotherly, but mine is a filial, love ‡;
for

---

* In a remote but poliſhed age, which ſeems to have preceded the invention of alphabetical writing, a great number of theſe obeliſks had been erected in the cities of
Thebes and Heliopolis, by the ancient ſovereigns of Ægypt,
in a juſt confidence that the ſimplicity of their form and
the hardneſs of their ſubſtance would reſiſt the injuries of
time and violence.                                    GIBBON.

† Conſtantius cauſed one of the obeliſks that are ſtill
ſeen at Rome to be tranſported thither from Ægypt.  It is
that which was erected by Sixtus V.  Conſtantius was deſirous of procuring a like decoration for New Rome.
                                             LA BLETERIE.
A veſſel of uncommon ſtrength and capaciouſneſs was
provided to convey this uncommon weight of granite from
the banks of the Nile to thoſe of the Tyber.    GIBBON.
‡ Julian, I think, might have ſaid that Conſtantine loved
the city as his " daughter;" and then he would have had
                                                      no

I was born there, I was educated there, and therefore I cannot be ungrateful to her.*

As your city is no less dear to me than my own country, instead of a triangular stone engraved with Ægyptian characters, I allow you to erect the colossal statue †, which has lately been made, of a man whose resemblance you desire. And as it is generally reported that some persons repose on the top of that obelisk, and pay it adoration ‡,

A. I.
362.

. . . . . . . . . . . . . . . .

no occasion to magnify his affection for that place above *Constantine's.* However, the more to satisfy the Alexandrians, he promises them a column of brass, of a large size, in the room of the Ægyptian obelisk of stone. And thus Julian does what had been blamed in *Constantine.* He robs and strips Alexandria to enrich and adorn Constantinople.

                                                    LARDNER.

† This learned writer, it is observable, has here mistaken " Constantine" for " Constantius." Yet he refers to Span-heim's edition, where we read ‹ μακαρίης Κωνσαντίος.

* In the editions of Julian the Epistle ends here. M. Muratori found the conclusion in a MS. of the Ambrosian library, and has published it in his *Anecdota Graeca*; from whence M. Fabricius has inserted it in his *Bibliotheca Graeca*.
                                        LA BLETERIE.
but I imagine this was a statue of Julian himself.    *Ibid.*

‡ . . . . . θεραπευτὰς καὶ προσκαθεύδοντας αὐτῇ τῇ κορυφῇ.
M. Muratori translates it, *quosdam esse therapeutas qui obelisci hujus vertici indormiunt.* He thinks that these *therapeutae* were some monks, who, no doubt in the spirit of mortification, slept on that obelisk. M. Fabricius adds, that these were certainly some Stylites. But, 1. in order to find therapeutae here, a force must be put upon the text, and no regard paid to the conjunction copulative which connects the two verbs, *cultum adhibitis et indormientes ejus vertici* 2. The Stylites were entirely unknown before the illustrious St. Simeon, who did not ascend his pillar till about the year 423; and it is remarkable that the an-

chorets

it fhould, I am convinced, on account of that fuperftition, be removed. For thofe who fee them
fleeping there, amidft the filth which muft fur-

chorets of Ægypt fent and declared to him, that they
feparated themfelves from his communion, becaufe they
could not approve fo new a kind of life. Nor did they
again unite with this faint till they had had proofs of his
obedience and humility. It is better therefore to tranflate
it as I have done, and to fay that fome Heathens paid adq-
ration to this obelifk. It is well known, that all the obelifks
were dedicated to the fun, a reafon fufficient to miflead
fome Chriftian anchorets ; and the hieroglyphics which were
feen on this might render it ftill more refpectable to idolaters. Some, hoping no doubt to have divine dreams,
went to fleep on the point, or rather near the point, of
this obelifk, which lay on the fea-fhore. The heat of the
climate will not admit a doubt that this was in the night ;
and this nocturnal fuperftition ferved as an occafion and a
pretext for fome diforders which completed the difcredit
of Paganifm. Julian, if I may be allowed the expreffion,
was defirous of removing that *ftone of offence*, and of preferving from this ridicule his unhappy religion, which had
already too much of it. *Ibid.*

This obelifk might be that which Spon faw at Conftantinople in the fquare of the Armeydan, where was formerly the Hippodrome. It is of Ægyptian granite, fifty
feet high, and covered with hieroglyphics. The infcription
on the bafe relates that " Theodofius undertook to erect
" this monument, which lay on the ground, and that Pro-
" clus accomplifhed the work in thirty-two days." Julian, no
doubt, was dead before his obelifk was erected, and Valens
had neglected it. In the reign of Theodofius they were
far from giving the honour of it to Julian, or from faying
that it had been tranfported from Ægypt by the orders of
that apoftate. It may be objected that the obelifk of Spon is
fquare, but that this which Julian mentions was triangular,
τρίγωνος. But this word is a correction of M. Muratori, as
the MS. gives τρίγωνος, which has no meaning. Probably we
fhould read τετράγωνος, efpecially as, according to M. Muratori himfelf, all the other obelifks are fquare. *Ibid.*

round

round the place, and the shameful actions there
committed, can by no means regard this stone as
sacred, and the superstition of those who dwell on
it confirms unbelievers in their infidelity. You
should therefore second me in my undertaking, by
sending this obelisk to my country, which, when
you navigate our seas, receives you with such hos-
pitality, and thus contributing your assistance to
the outward embellishment of that city. Nor can
it be disagreeable to yourselves to have something
of your own extant among us, which, as you
sail towards the city, you may hereafter view with
pleasure.

---

### Epistle LIX *. To Dionysius †.

[MORE prudent was your former silence than
your present defence;] for then, though
perhaps you devised scandal, you did not utter it.
[But now, teeming, as it were, with slander against
us, you pour it forth most abundantly; unless I
ought not to deem slander] and abuse your thinking

* For an account of this Epistle and the former, see
p. 2. In the editions of Rigalt, Petau, and Spanheim, it
is imperfect. The above is translated from a copy in the
*Lux Evangelii* of Fabricius, p. 326. collected by Roſtgaard.
The additions are inferted within [].

† The Medicean MS. has this inscription: Ιελιανος καια
Νααλʋ. The beginning of the Epistle is wanting in the editions.                                          FABRICIUS.

me

# EPISTLES OF JULIAN.

me like your friends; to each of whom you offered
your services unaſked *, but particularly unaſked by
the firſt, and the ſecond only hinting that he ſhould
be glad of your aſſiſtance, you immediately, com-
plied. Whether I reſemble Conaſtus and Magnentius †, faĉts, as the ſaying is, will ſhew. But
you, like Aſtydamas in the comedy, are your own
panegyriſt ‡; and this is evident from what you
have written. For thoſe expreſſions, " intrepidity,"
and " great boldneſs," and, " I wiſh you knew who
" and what I am," and the like; for ſhame! what
boaſting and oſtentation do they exhibit! But, by
Venus and the Graces, if you are ſo bold and noble-
minded, [ why were you ſo fearful of being under the
neceſſity of offending a third time? For thoſe who
have incurred the diſpleaſure of princes, if they
are wiſe, find an eaſe, and perhaps a pleaſure, in

* Suidas: ακλητος, ακυντμος, δεδωκας σιαυλον ακλητον τω δειλιερω.
He alludes to the words of Julian. By προτερον (" the
" former,") underſtand Conſtans (" the ſecond,") ο δευτερος,
is Magnentius. PADRICIUS.

† Conſtans, the youngeſt ſon of the great Conſtantine,
was engaged in a civil war with his eldeſt brother Conſtantine, who was killed in the courſe of it. Magnentius revolted againſt Conſtantius, and uſurped the Weſt.
By comparing Julian to them, Dionyſius perhaps meant
to ſtigmatiſe him with the murder of Conſtantius and uſur-
pation of the empire.

‡ In the MS. σιαυλον επαινης, not φαυλην επαινης, γυναι, as
even Rigalt to Onoſander, in his edition, p. 90. It refers
to Philemon, the comic poet, as appears from the Proverbs
of Apoſtolius, Centur. XVII. 30. and Suidas on φαυλη επαινης.
See alſo Zenobius, v. 100. Julian quotes the ſame proverb
in his XIIth Epiſtle. FABRICIUS.

being

being discharged from business; or if they must be
fined, they suffer in their fortunes; or, the utmost
effect of resentment is that incurable evil, as it has
been called, the loss of life. All these things are
scorned and despised by you, who have renounced
your friend, a man, from common and general report,
well known to us, dull as we are. Instead
of this, you say, you invoke the Gods that you
may not offend a third time. My anger therefore
will not from being good make you wicked. He
that could do this would be a prodigy indeed. According
to Plato, it might indeed have the contrary
effect*. But virtue being perfectly free, you ought
to have no such ideas. You, however, think it a
great matter to slander all men, to utter the bitterest
sarcasms, and to convert the temple of peace
into a brothel.]

Do you think that your past faults are in general
excused, and that your late courage has atoned for
your former cowardice? You know the fable of
Chabrias †. A cat was once in love with a handsome
youth ‡. Learn the rest from the book. What-

---

* De Legibus, vi.

† The words τον Χαβρω are in the Medicean and Barro.
MSS. and this is in the xvith fable of Chabrias, or Babrias,
a Greek poet, who has put the fables of Æsop into
Iambic verse.

‡ Rather, according to our fables, a young man was
in love with a cat. Dionysius could no more divest himself
of his natural pusillanimity, &c. than the cat (transformed
to a woman) could forego her pursuit of mice.
The Latin translator renders it mustela (" a weasel"); but
γαλη signifies also " a cat."

ever you may fay, you will perfuade no one that you were not what you were, and what many have long known you to be. But your unfkilfulnefs and temerity are owing, not to philofophy, the Gods forbid! but rather to what Plato calls " a double ignorance *." For though experience might have taught you, as it has me, that you know nothing, yet you think yourfelf the wifeft of all men, paft, prefent, or to come ; fo great is your ignorance, fo abundant your felf-conceit.

But enough concerning you. Some apology perhaps is neceffary to others for fo readily giving you a fhare in the conduct of my affairs. I am not the firft, nor the only one, Dionyfius, who has been miftaken. Your name-fake alfo deceived Plato †. [And fo did Callippus the Athenian ‡, whom, he faid, he knew to be wicked, but that he was profligate to fuch a degree he never could have fufpected.] And need I add, that the greateft of phyficians, Hippocrates, faid, " in my opinion of " the futures of the head I was miftaken § ? Thus they were deceived in what they ought to have known,

---

* The one is when men ackhowledge their ignorance, the other when they think they know that of which they are ignorant. *In Alcib.* I.

† Dionyfius the younger fent for Plato into Sicily, to inftruct him in philofophy. See the Life of Dion in Plutarch.

‡ A hearer of Plato, who murdered Dion.

§ The following is doubtlefs the paffage to which Julian alludes : " Autonomus of Omilus died of a wound on his " head, on the fixteenth day, having received a hurt by a

known, and even a phyfician was ignorant of a
theorem of his own art. Is it ftrange then that
Julian, hearing that Nilöus *, or Dionyfius, had on
a fudden behaved bravely, fhould be miftaken ?

You have heard of Phædon † of Elis, and you
know his hiftory. If not, read it with attention.
He thought that no one is fo depraved that philofophy cannot cure him, and that it purifies human life from the paffions, defires, and all fuch diforders. For that it fhould be ferviceable to thofe
who are well born, and well educated, is not at all
extraordinary. But if it brings back into the light
thofe whofe minds are ever fo much darkened by
depravity, this feems to me truly admirable. And on
that account, as all the Gods know, I began by degrees to form a more advantageous opinion of you.

" ftone on the futures. I did not think it neceffary to
" open it ; for that the futures themfelves were injured by
" the blow efcaped me." (εκλειψαν δε μη την γνωμης αι εαφαι,
κ. τ. λ.) *Hipp. de morb.* V. 7. 27. The words above quoted,
as from Hippocrates, are, ισφηλαν δε μη την γνωμης αι πεις την
κιφαλην εαφαι. But though in a particular cafe (as above)
this great phyfician had the candour to own himfelf miftaken, it does not follow, nor does it appear, that he was
ignorant of the nature of the futures in general. Julian
trufted to his memory, which, though good, was not infallible.

This candid confeffion of Hippocrates is mentioned alfo
with applaufe by Celfus, VIII. 4. and Plutarch *de profectu
in virtutem*, p. 82.

* Τον Νηλωις. MS. Τον Νηλον.          FABRICIUS.

† A fcholar of Socrates, fo much beloved by Plato, that
he infcribed his divine book, on the immortality of the foul,
*Phædon.*

5                                          Not

Not that I placed you in the firſt, or even in the ſecond, rank of worthies, as you yourſelf perhaps
may know. If not, aſk the excellent Symmachus *,]
for he, I am perſuaded, being naturally diſpoſed
to ſpeak truth, will never utter a wilful falſhood.

[But if you reſent my not raiſing you to the
higheſt, I reproach myſelf for not degrading you
to the loweſt, rank. And I thank all the Gods
and Goddeſſes for preventing me from forming an
intimacy with you, and making you privy to my
counſels, as a boſom friend. Though the poets
have ſaid many things of Fame, as a Goddeſs;
ſhe is rather, if you pleaſe, a Dæmon. For
Fame is not always to be credited; and therefore her nature is dæmoniaçal, being not abſolutely
pure or perfectly good, like that of the Gods, but
allayed with ſome degree of evil †. And though it
may not be proper to ſay this of the other Dæmons,
I know I may ſafely affirm of Fame, that ſhe utters
many falſhoods, as well as many truths ‡. For I

* A Roman orator and præfect, well known by his
epiſtles ſtill extant, and by his writings againſt Chriſtianity,
refuted by Prudentius and St. Ambroſe. Three epiſtles to
him are extant from Libanius, to whom, it appears, he
wrote in Latin, as his letters required an interpreter. He
was conſul in 391.

† And had not the Gods, as well as Fame and the
Dæmons, of Julian and the Heathens, much evil in their
nature? Not to mention the notorious vices of Mars,
Bacchus, Apollo, and the reſt of them; in what was their
Jupiter, their Supreme, ſo pre-eminent as in his debau-
cheries?

‡ *Tam falſi pravique tenax quam conſcia et i.* Virg.

M 2                                    wo. l₰

would by no means be accufed of bearing falfe
witnefs.]

You value your freedom of fpeech at four
*oboli* \*, as the faying is. [But know you not, that
Therfites, among the Greeks, was alfo a free-fpeaker,
and in return was chaftifed by the wife Ulyffes with
his fceptre † ? and that the drunkennefs of Therfites was lefs regarded by Agamemnon than the flies
in the proverb were by the tortoife ‡ ?]

What avails our reproaching others? We fhould
rather be irreproachable ourfelves. If you are fo,
convince me of it. [When you were young, you
told fine ftories of yourfelf to your elders. Thefe
adventures, with the Electra of Euripides §, I pafs

---

\* That is, at ever fo high a rate. Suidas on Τεῖλαρων
οβολων, quoting this paffage of Julian.    FABRICIUS.
He quotes it, as ufual, without naming his author. An
*obolus* was a fmall Athenian coin of filver, weighing about
twelve grains; in our money five farthings.

† Il. II. 199.
———— Cowering as the daftard bends,
The weighty fceptre on his back defcends.  POPE, 336.

‡ Suidas quotes thefe words from an author to me unknown, τω δι Αγαμεμνον. κ. τ. λ. Flies cannot hurt a tortoife,
on account of the fhell with which it is furnifhed. Similar
to this is, " an elephant does not regard a fly." It would
be more pleafant if applied to the mind. A mind fortified
by virtue and philofophy no more fears the attacks of fortune than "a tortoife flies."    ERASMUS.
The paffage above quoted by Suidas is this of Julian,
which has been brought to light long fince the time of
Erafmus. It is alfo quoted anonymoufly by Apoftolius, in
his Centur. XX. proverb. 66.

§ Eurip. Electr. ver. 946. 1122.
I never with the opening morn forbore
To breathe my filent plaints, &c.    POTTER.

6                                          in

in filence. But when you became a man, and
joined the army, you did, by Jove, juft what you
fay of truth; it gave you offence, and you deferted it. By how many witneffes can I prove this,
and thofe not of the vulgar and abandoned, but
fome by whom you yourfelf were repulfed, who
came to us from that neighbourhood?] To depart
from princes in enmity, moft fagacious Dionyfius,
is no proof either of courage or wifdom. Much
more would it become you to conciliate, by your
intercourfe with mankind, their affections to us.
But fuch, by the Gods, will never be your conduct, nor that of thoufands more who are like-
minded.

If rocks dafh againft rocks, and ftones againft
ftones, inftead of being ferviceable to each other,
the ftrongeft eafily breaks the weakeft. I fay not
this with Laconic brevity; for I think on your fubject I feem more loquacious than the Attic grafshoppers *. For your drunken abufe † of me,
with the leave of the Gods, and powerful Nemefis,
I will inflict upon you a deferved punifhment.
" To what purpofe?" you fay. [To reftrain as
much as poffible your mind and tongue, and] to

---

* This is faid of a man immoderately talkative, or
very mufical; becaufe this infect, living only on dew, chiefly
delights in finging. And Socrates, in the Phædron of
Plato, relates that fome who were fo abforbed by mufic
that, neglecting their food, they were famifhed, were
changed by the Gods into grafshoppers.     ERASMUS.

† See the Fragment (from Suidas) on Mufonius.

prevent

prevent your offending [in the leaft] either by
words or deeds; in fhort, to diveft your fcurrilous
tongue of fo much flander, I well know that
the fandal even of Venus is faid to have been ridiculed by Momus *. But you fee that Momus, though
envious of all her beauties, could find nothing but
her fandal to depreciate. May you grow old,
fretted, in like manner, with envy, more decrepid
than Tithonus, more wealthy than Cinyras, and
more effeminate than Sardanapalus, fo as to verify
the proverb, " Old men are twice children! †"

[But why does the divine Alexander feem to you
fo renowned? Why do you profefs yourfelf his
imitator and rival? Is it for that with which the
youth Hermolaus ‡ reproached him? Of that no
one is fo filly as to fufpect you; but of the contrary, for which Hermolaus, grievoufly complaining, fuffered ftripes, and, it is faid, would have
killed Alexander, there is no one who is not per-

---

* Viz. The creaking of it. See Philoftrati Epift. XXI.

† On the word Καλαγηρασκι, Suidas has the above paragraph (not mentioned as a quotation from Julian) with
this addition, " which is faid of thofe who live long. For
" Tithonus, being fuperannuated, was, at his own defire,
" changed into a grafshopper. Cinyras, a defcendant of
" Pharnaces, king of Cyprus, was famous for his riches.
" And Sardanapalus, the laft king of Affyria, fell a victim
" to intemperance and luxurious delights."

‡ " We confpired to kill you," faid Hermolaus, " be-
" caufe you have begun not to govern us as free-men, but
" to tyrannife over us as flaves."        Q. Curtius.

fuaded that you are guilty *. From many, by the Gods, who faid they had a great regard for you, I have heard feveral things advanced by way of extenuating this offence; and one there was who difbelieved it. But he was a fingle fwallow, who does not make a fpring †. Perhaps Alexander appears great to you, becaufe he cruelly flew Callifthenes ‡; or becaufe Clitus ‡ fell a facrifice to his intemperance; and alfo Philotas ‡, and Parmenio ‡; whofe fon Hector was afterwards fmothered in the whirlpools of the Ægyptian Nile, or of the Euphrates, for both have been mentioned §. I omit his other follies, that I may not feem to revile a man, who, though by no means diftinguifhed for virtue, was a moft valiant and excellent commander. Of both which, virtue and

* Hermolaus, a noble youth, of the royal guards, for killing a boar, which the king had deftined for his own fpear, was by his command fcourged; a difgrace which he fo bitterly refented that he wept, and formed the abovementioned confpiracy.    Q. Curtius.

† See Lrafmi Chiliad. xciv.

‡ The cruel deaths of this philofopher and thefe generals are well known, and are related at large by Quintus Curtius. " One," faid Hermolaus, [Clitus] " fprinkled " your table with his blood; another [Philotas] fuffered " more than one kind of death. Parmenio was maffacred " unheard, &c."

§ According to Curtius, as this youth, one of the few dear to Alexander, was attempting to follow him down the Nile, the fmall veffel in which he had embarked, being overloaded, funk. Hector, after long ftruggling with the ftream, at length reached the bank, but there, for want of affiftance, perifhed. Of this, however, Alexander feems to have been innocent. Philotas was alfo a fon of Parmenio.

valour,

valour, you have a lefs portion than fifh have of
hair. Now hear with calmnefs what I advife :
  Not thefe, O daughter, are thy proper cares !
  Thee milder arts befit, and fofter wars *.

What follows, by the Gods, I am afhamed to
tranfcribe. I would have you, however, attend to
it, fince it is highly reafonable that deeds fhould
follow words, and that one who has been remifs
in his deeds fhould never ftart at words. But you,
who revere the fhades of Magnentius and Conftans,
wage war with the living, and, in fome way or
other, afperfe the beft characters. Are the living
lefs able to revenge affronts? This you will by no
means think proper to affirm, be the confidence
which you mention, whatever it may. Rejecting
that plea, will you admit this, that you deride
them becaufe they are infenfible ? Nor is this, I
prefume, the true reafon. For who among the
living is fo ftupid, or pufillanimous, as to think
your good opinion of the leaft importance, and
would not prefer being totally unknown to you, or,
if that were impoffible, would not rather choofe to
be reviled by you, as I am now, than honoured ?
I would by no means err fo egregioufly in my
judgement as not to think your praifes better than
your reproaches. But even this, perhaps, that I
am now writing to you, proves that I am hurt.
By no means, I call the preferving Gods to witnefs; I only wifh to check the intolerable arrogance

* Il. V. 428. Pope, 519.

of

of this reviler, the petulance and prurience of his tongue, the frenzy of his mind, and his fury on all occasions. If I were injured by you, I might by deeds, not words, have a legal remedy, as you, being a citizen, and of the senatorial rank, have disobeyed the command of the Emperor. But for this there was no occasion, nothing but the last extremity requiring it. I did not think proper therefore to subject you to any punishment, but rather chose first at least to write to you, hoping that a short epistle might effect your cure. But as you persevere in these crimes, or rather exhibit to the public the frenzy which was before concealed, let no one, for the future, think you a man, who are not a man, or mistake the fury, which transports you, for courage, or suppose you to be learned who are an utter stranger to literature, as may easily be proved from your epistles.]

None of the ancients, for instance, ever used το φρεδον, to signify " manifest,". * as you have, besides many other blunders, in your letter. No one, in the longest discourse, could express your loose and indecent behaviour, your self-prostitution. For

you

---

* Φρεδον is rather αφανις, ικπεδων, αφανλον. (" Far distant, obscure.)" See Hefychius and Harpocratio. FABRICIUS.

† Among the flagrant crimes of which he accuses Dionyfius, Julian here condescends to arraign his phrafeology, and, like a former Dionyfius, exchanges his sceptre for a rod. Thus a mistake in the meaning of a word, or in the graces of style, is put on a level with treachery and treason, and seems as unpardonable to this Imperial critic, as an offence against the graces of behaviour was to a late British peer.

you feduce, not only fuch as are willing and for, ward, * * * * nor thofe who hunt after public employments, but thofe who, in confequence of a found judgement, act right, [and therefore have been felected by us for their prompt obedience.

You make fair promifes, though not by way of intreaty, or fubmiffion, if we will again employ you in fome place of truft. But fo far is that from my intention, that when others have been admitted, I never fent for you, as I have for many, known and unknown to me, of the inhabitants of that heaven-beloved city, Rome. Such value I fet on your friendfhip; of fuch attention I thought you worthy! I fhall therefore act in the fame manner probably for the future. And this epiftle, which I am now writing, I intend, not only for your perufal, but think it neceffary to be communicated to many more. I will give it indeed to all, for all, I am perfuaded, will readily receive it; fuch a general indignation your infolence and arrogance have excited.

You have here a complete reply, fo that you can defire from us nothing farther. Nor do we wifh any return from you. Make what ufe you pleafe of our letters; for you have fold our friendfhip. Farewell; amidft your banquets abufing me!]

peer. The above criticifm is perfectly in the fpirit of Bentley *verfus* Barnes. But Julian fhould have recollected that this Roman wrote Greek in compliment to him.

Epiftle

## Epiftle LX. To Jamblichus.

YOU came, and acted. For you came, though abfent, by your letter. But, by the ardour of the friendfhip which I feel for you, I do not decline your love †, * * * nor in any refpect defert you, but, as if you were prefent, I view you with my mind, and am with you, though abfent, nor can any thing elfe give me complete fatisfaction. You are never weary of obliging the prefent, and not only delighting, but preferving the abfent by your writings. For being told that a friend was arrived with a letter from you, though I had been three days ill of a pain in my ftomach, and was much indifpofed with a fever, yet hearing, as I faid, that a letter from you was at the gate, like one not mafter of himfelf and divinely infpired, I fprung up and rufhed out to him before he could enter. But as foon as I had taken the letter into my hands, I fwear by the Gods themfelves and that regard for you which inflames me, my pain at once abated, and the fever inftantly fled, abafhed, as it were, at the evident prefence of fome tutelar deity. And when I had opened and read it, what, think you, were my fenfations, or how great was my fatisfaction, praifing immoderately, and loving

† Imperfect.

the

the moſt friendly, as you ſtyle him, * * * * †, who
is really deferving of love, and the miniſter of
good, for being inſtrumental in forwarding to me
your letter, and conſigning it to me, like a bird,
by a favourable and proſperous gale, which not
only gave me the delight of hearing that your
affairs were in a proper ſtate, but alſo recovered
me from illneſs! As to other things, how ſhall I
expreſs what I felt when I firſt read that epiſtle,
or how can I ſufficiently demonſtrate my affection?
How often did I turn back from the middle to the
beginning! How much did I fear, left, when I
had finiſhed it, I ſhould forget it! How often, as
in the circuit and compaſs of a ſtanza, did I carry
back the concluſion to the beginning, repeating at
the cloſe, as in a muſical compoſition, that meaſure
with which the ſong began! And what followed?
How often did I apply the letter to my lips, as
mothers kiſs their infants! How cloſely did I preſs
it to my mouth, as if I had been embracing my
deareſt miſtreſs! How frequently did I accoſt and
kiſs even the ſuperſcription, which, as a well-
known ſignature, you had written with your
own hand; and then fixed my eyes upon it, rivetted,
as it were, by the fingers of that ſacred hand on
the traces of the letters?

† Imperfect. The name of the friend who forwarded
the letter ſeems all that is wanting.

" Much

" Much falutation from us attend you!" as fays the fair Sappho * ; and, not only during our feparation, but fare you well always, not failing to write, and, as is fitting, to remember us! As to ourfelves, there will never be a time, there can never be an occafion, there will never be a difcourfe, in which we fhall not remember you * * * *. And if Jupiter fhall ever allow me to revifit my native country, and again to enter your facred manfion, fpare not the fugitive; but, as a deferter from the Mufes, brought back from flight, bind him, if you pleafe, to your delightful benches, and, when properly chaftifed, reprimand him. I will by no means decline the punifhment, but will fubmit to it voluntarily and chearfully; as to the provident and falutary correction of an indulgent father. But if you will permit me to pronounce my own fentence, I will with pleafure fubmit to this; the being faftened, my noble friend, to your veft, fo as never to be feparated from you, but clofely to adhere to you, and every where to be carried about with you, as fables feign of double men; unlefs they ludicroufly mean it as an allufion to the excellence of friendfhip, exprefling the congenial agreement of each foul in the bond of communion.

* Χαιρε δε και αυτος ημιν πολλα. This muft be in fome poem that is loft.

Epiftle

## Epiftle LXI. To the fame.

I HAVE fuffered, I confefs, fufficient punifhment for my abfence from you, partly in the
fatigues which I endured in my journey, but
chiefly on account of my long feparation from you.
Though I have every where met, with a variety of
accidents, fo as to have left none unexperienced;
though I have fuftained the tumults of battles, the
diftrefs of fieges, the wanderings of flight, with ter-
rors of every kind, and alfo the feverities of winter,
the dangers of difeafes, and many and various other
calamities from Upper Pannonia to the paffage of
the Chalcedonian ftrait, I can truly fay, that nothing has happened to me fo grievous and perplex-
ing, fince my leaving the Eaft, as my not having
feen, for fuch a length of time, you, the general
blefling of the Greeks. Wonder not therefore, if
I fay, a kind of darknefs and thick clouds hang
over my eyes. For, in truth, the fky will be
ferene, the light of the fun more fplendid, and a
moft beautiful fpring of life will, as it were, be
renewed to me, when I can embrace you, the great
ornament of the world. Then, like a darling fon,
efcaped from war, or returned from a long voyage,
and reftored unexpectedly to an excellent father,
relating to you all my fufferings, and the dangers
that I have furmounted, and refting, as on a facred
anchor,

anchor, I ſhall find a ſufficient ſolace for my ſor-
rows. For calamities are conſoled, and ſufferings
alleviated, by communication, and by the knowledge of our friends participated. Mean while I
tender you my beſt ſervices, nor will I ever fail to
write to you, and during the whole time of my
abſence to ſend you ſuch epiſtolary tokens. If
I can obtain the ſame from you, the peruſal of
your letters, like an auſpicious omen, will abate
my grief. Receive mine with complacence, and
be more favourably diſpoſed to make a return.
For whatever good you ſhall expreſs or communicate, I ſhall prefer to the eloquent voice of
Mercury, and the ſkilful hand of Æſculapius.

Epiſtle LXII. †. To **** (Imperfect.)

\* \* \* \* \* \* \* \*
SHOULD not the ſame indulgence, which is
given to wooden blocks, be allowed to men ‡ ? For
ſuppoſe that one inveſted with the prieſthood be
unworthy, ſhould he not be ſpared, till, having
aſcer-

† The Gentiles, who peaceably followed the cuſtoms of
their anceſtors, were rather ſurpriſed than pleaſed with the
introduction of foreign manners; and in the ſhort period
of his reign, Julian had frequent occaſions to complain of
the want of fervour of his own party. See Epiſtles LXII.
and LXIII.                                    GIBBON.
Many of the Epiſtles of Julian are the effuſions of private friendſhip; ſome are public Edicts; while others are
juſtly

afcertained the enormity of his offence, he can be
removed from the minifterial function, and deprived
of the name of prieft, injudiciously perhaps conferred upon him, and may be fubjected alfo to cen-
fure, fine, and other punifhments? If you underftand
not this, you cannot have even a fuperficial knowledge of any thing; for how ignorant muft you
be of what is juft and right, not to know the difference between a prieft and a private man!
And what muft have been your temper, if you have
beaten one to whom you ought to have rifen from
your feat! Nothing can be more fhameful, in you
it is particularly unbecoming, in the fight both of
Gods and men. The bifhops and prefbyters of the
Galileans perhaps affociate with you; and if not
publickly, through fear of me, yet by ftealth and

juftly ftyled by Mr. Gibbon " paftoral letters," and are
dictated by the Emperor as Sovereign Pontiff. In this
pontifical character he addreffes the Epiftle, of which this
fragment only is preferved, to a Gentile prieft, who, for-
getting the nature of his fpiritual warfare, had violently
affaulted and beaten one of his brethren. As a Chriftian
Pontiff would have quoted St. Paul to Titus, *A bifhop
muft be no ftriker*, this Gentile apoftle appeals to the
Didymæan oracle, and then pronounces a fentence of
fufpenfion.

‡ This paragraph is unintelligible, for want of that
which precedes it. Julian perhaps had been fpeaking of
fuch images of the Gods as were worn out and decayed,
which he has mentioned alfo in his long Fragment. " If
" any one," fays he, " thinks, that, becaufe they have
" been once called the images of the Gods, they can
" never decay, he feems to me to have loft his fenfes.
" For then they could not have been the workmanfhip of
" men," &c.

at

at home with your concurrence. But the prieſt
has been beaten. Otherwiſe your pontiff would
not have preferred ſuch a complaint againſt you.
Paſſages from Homer you think fabulous; hear
therefore the oracle of the Didymæan lord, and
conſider whether he rightly admoniſhed the Greeks
of old, and afterwards, in his diſcqurſes, taught
men to be wiſe and virtuous:

They, whom depravity and folly lead
To ſcorn the prieſts of heaven's immortal powers,
And to the wiſe intentions of the Gods
Their own vain thoughts contemptuouſly oppoſe,
In ſafety live not half their days, condemn'd
To periſh by th' eternal Gods, who deem
Their ſervants honour ſacred as their own *.

Not only thoſe, you ſee, who beat or inſult prieſts,
but ſuch as deny them honour are [declared †] to
be enemies to the Gods; ſo that he who beats them
is guilty of ſacrilege. I therefore, as the Sove‑
reign Pontiff of the religion of my country, having
now obtained the præfecture of the Didymæan
oracle, forbid you to interfere in any thing that
relates to the prieſthood for three whole months.
If, within that time, you ſhould appear deſerving,
on my hearing from the chief-prieſt of your city,
I will conſult the Gods whether you ſhall be re‑
inſtated. To this puniſhment, which I inflict upon

---

* This paſſage has been quoted before, in the Duties of
a Prieſt, p. 127.

† Some ſuch word is wanting in the original.

you for your rafhnefs, the ancients ufed formerly
to add, by words and in writing, the curfes of the
Gods. But of this I do not approve, as it never
feems practifed by the Gods. And in other refpects, knowing that the priefts are the minifters
of our prayers, I join my hopes and prayers to
yours, that by many and earneft intreaties you may
obtain the pardon of the Gods.

---

Epiftle LXIII.   To the High-Prieft THEO-
DORE *.

A. D.   THE Epiftle that I have addreffed to you differs
361.        from that which I have tranfmitted to others †,
as I think your friendfhip for me fuperior to theirs.
It is no inconfiderable circumftance, that we have

---

* This High-Prieft Theodore was, as may be inferred
from this Epiftle, a zealous Pagan, the difciple of Maximus, who, like Julian, had been initiated by Maximus,
and inftructed, like that prince, in the principles of theurgy.
This letter is inferted in the edition of F. Petau, but only
in Greek. It had been copied from a MS. fo defective,
that it was not poffible to tranflate it. M. Spanheim, from
a MS. lefs imperfect, has given it, with a Latin verfion,
which is not anfwerable to the reputation of that learned
writer.                    LA BLETERIE.

† Julian had fent, without doubt, a circular letter to
the Pagan pontiffs as foon as he was in peaceable poffeffion
of the empire. As this feems to have been written at the
fame time, I affign it to the year 361.            Ibid.
Julian muft then have been at Conftantinople.

one

one common mafter, and you well remember *. ⚓ .
In a converfation that paffed between us, a few
evenings ago, it gave me great pleafure to hear
him exprefs the higheft regard for you. In my
friendfhips I am ufually very cautious. As for you,
I had never feen you. Before we can love, we muft
know; and before we can know, we fhould try.
But a certain reafon determined me †. I have therefore thought proper to rank you among my friends.
And now I entruft to you an affair very interefting
to me, and highly advantageous to all men. You
will tranfaft it, I doubt not, with propriety, which
will afford me much joy here, and better hopes
hereafter ‡. For I differ in opinion from thofe
who

* He intimates by half a word, and a myfterious air, what
they faw, or thought they faw, when they were initiated
by Maximus.                              LA BLETERIE.

† It is impoffible to guefs this reafon ; but we may partly
difcover, that, in the initiation of Theodore, fomething
happened which induced Julian to conclude that a man
fo agreeable to the Gods deferved to be the minifter and
the affiftant of the apoftle of Paganifm.          Ibid.

‡ As this Epiftle was not written to be fhewn, it proves
to what a degree Julian was fanatical and convinced of
his falfe religion. It fhews, at the fame time, that he
believed a providence, another life, and the immortality
of the foul. He detefted the materialifts. In one of his
works he fpeaks with horror of Pyrrhonifm, and of the
doctrine of Epicurus. He thanks the Gods for having
extinguifhed thofe fects, and caufed moft of the books
which contained their pernicious tenets to be deftroyed,
[See the Duties of a Prieft, p. 134.] Probably the free-
thinkers would not have triumphed in his reign. Why
then

N 2

who think that the foul perifhes before or with the
body *. We rely, however, on no man, but only on
the Gods, as they only can be well acquainted
with thefe things, or rather they alone neceffarily
know them. Men may form conjectures, but
knowledge belongs to the Gods. The commiffion
that I now give you is the fuperintendence of all
the priefts in Afia, both in the cities and in the
country, with full powers to treat every one according to his deferts.

In a high-prieft the principal requifite is moderation, together with kindnefs and benevolence to
the deferving. As to thofe who are unjuft or in-
folent to men, and irreligious to the Gods, let
them be rebuked with boldnefs, or punifhed with
feverity. Whatever is neceffary to be regulated
in common, in order to render divine worfhip as
perfect as poffible, I will foon direct, with many
other particulars. Some of them, in the mean time,
I will here mention, in which it is right for you to

then fhould they defend him? But fome common interefts
often ferve to unite in appearance irreconcileable enemies. *And the fame day they were made friends together;
for before they were at enmity between themfelves.* Of this the
affection which Julian teftified for the Jews is a remarkable
inftance. *Ibid.*

* Thofe who believed the foul to be immortal, and even
the materialifts, diftinguifhed in the foul the intellectual
part, *νϭ,* and the fenfitive part, *ψυχη.* There were fome who
imagined, no doubt, that the intellectual part was withdrawn, and others that it was deftroyed, when they faw the
body reduced to a mere animal life. *Ibid.*

te

be advised by me. For on many of thefe fubjects I fpeak, as all the Gods know, with much
premedi-attoh. In circumfpection no one exceeds
me, and I am an enemy, and have been fo ftyled,
to all innovation, efpecially in matters of religion,
thinking it highly proper to adhere to our ancient
paternal laws *, which were certainly given us by
the Gods. They could not be fo excellent, if they
proceeded from men. But by the prevalence of
riches and pleafures they have been fo neglected
and corrupted, that they require, I think, a new
foundation. Seeing therefore fo great an indifference among us towards the Gods, and all fenfe
of religion banifhed by debauched and luxurious
manners, I have continually lamented in private,

---

* Paganifm, in general, had no religious code, unlefs it
were fome pretended oracles, apparently very modern, as
to the ceremonies which ought to be obferved in facrifices, and the victims which were fuitable to every kind
of Gods. Eufebius quotes fome paffages of thefe oracles
in the fourth book of his Evangelical Preparation. I imagine that the laws which Julian here mentions are principally the ancient rites of every nation, city, and temple.
Thefe rites had in time fuffered various alterations, and in
the decline of Paganifm fome were abolifhed.

Julian, deeply verfed in antiquity, was defirous of reftoring things to their former ftate. As to the wifdom quite
divine which he admires in thefe rites, that is the work of
his imagination. He confiders them as fymbolical. Being
an ingenious and fruitful allegorift, by the force of arbitrary
explanations he difcovered fome wonderful things in the worfhip, as well as in the hiftory, of his Gods. To be convinced
that he every where found all that he chofe, we need only
read his difcourfe " on the Mother of the Gods."

LA BLETERIE.

For those who are diftinguifhed in the fchool of impiety * are fo zealous as to fuffer want and famine rather than tafte fwine's flefh †, or that of any thing ftrangled, or even killed by accident; while we are fo regardlefs of the Gods as to forget the laws of our anceftors, and not even to know whether any fuch exift. But thefe men are in part only religious, as the God whom they worfhip is really moft powerful, and moft benevolent, and governs the vifible world ‡.

They therefore who do not tranfgrefs the laws feem to me to act right. I blame them only for

---

* Δυσσιβιιας σχολη προσχονlας, "Thofe who are attached " to the fchool of impiety." I think that we fhould read προιχοιlας, " the chiefs, the principal teachers." The fequel fhews that this refers to the Jews.    LA BLETERIE.

† This would only prove that Julian fpeaks of the Jews. Indeed the Chriftians, through refpect for the Council of Jerufalem, abftained from blood and things ftrangled longer than the reafons fubfifted on which the prohibition was founded; and the Oriental Chriftians continue to abftain from them ftill. But after God had revealed to St. Peter (Acts xv.) that the diftinction of meats was abrogated, no Chriftian fcrupled eating fwine's flefh, except the Judaifing Chriftians, who were not tolerated till the fecond deftruction of the Jews, which happened under the Emperor Hadrian.    Ibid.

‡ In the books of Julian againft the Chriftian religion, of which St. Cyril, in refuting them, has preferved a confiderable part, this prince fays, in direct terms, that " he " worfhips the God of Abraham, of Ifaac, and of Jacob :" Αν προσκυνων τον Θιον Αβρααμ, και Ισαακ, και Ιακωβ. But it appears, in the fame books, that he means, by this God, the Demiurgus; in which he is miftaken if he makes the Demiurgus, or Logos, of a different nature from the BEING, το ον, τ'αγαθον.    Ibid.

worfhip-

worſhipping God alone, and deſpiſing the worſhip
of other Gods. Hurried into this frenzy by the
pride of Barbarians *, they think that he is hidden
from us Gentiles only. But from the Galilean impiety, like a peſtilential diſtemper † * * * *.
[*The remainder is wanting in the original.*]

. * Whatever incenſe Julian gave the Jews in the Epiſtle
which he wrote to them, this text, and many others, ſhew
that he deſpiſed them. In general, what moſt prejudiced
the Pagans againſt both the Chriſtian and Jewiſh religions,
was their being excluſive and admitting no community with
any other. But they endured the Jews with leſs impatience, and contented themſelves with deſpiſing them, becauſe the latter gained few proſelytes. The barrenneſs, with
which the ſynagogue was ſtruck, made it find grace in the
ſight of our common enemies; but the fertility of the
church alarmed and enraged them. They foreſaw that
ſhe would at length deſtroy their altars. Julian, in particular, kept good terms with the Jews, becauſe they entered into his plan, 1. By their implacable hatred to the
Chriſtians; 2. from the deſign which he had formed to reſtore the nation and the temple, in order to falſify the
ſcriptures. Beſides, the religion of the Jews ordained ſacrifices, and in this point of view was agreeable to Julian,
who, as may be ſeen in his life and his works, had a taſte
for bloody ſacrifices more worthy of a butcher than a philoſopher. LA BLETERIE.

† It is evident that Julian here launched forth againſt
Chriſtianity and the Chriſtians; perhaps in a manner ſo
atrocious as to ſhock the tranſcribers. *Ibid.*

Epiſtle

## Epiſtle LXIV. *. To the People †, cla-
## moroufly applauding in the Tychæum, or
## Temple of Fortune.

A. D.
361.
WHEN I enter the theatre, even privately, you may applaud ; but in the temples be filent, and transfer your applaufes to the Gods. Praifes are much more properly due to them.

* This Epiſtle was firſt publiſhed by Muratori, in his *Anecdota Græca*, from a MS. 700 years old, in the Am-brofian library, and is copied by Fabricius, in his *Biblio-theca Græca*.

In the edition of Wolfius, it is the мccxxth Epiſtle of Libanius. And the editor fubjoins in a note, " I neither " underſtand what Libanius here means, nor the occaſion " on which he wrote this Epiſtle." Yet as Muratori and Fabricius had previoufly given it to Julian, I cannot account for its being there afcribed to Libanius. Surely it feems much more characteriſtic of a prince than of a fophift ; and is befides a fubject, which Julian has difcuffed in the Mifopogon, Vol. I. p. 241, &c.

† Probably ".of Conſtantinople." Fabricius infcribes it *Byzantinis*, like Epiſtle XI. But fee a note on that Epiſtle, p. 24.

## Epiftle LXV. To a Painter *.

* Not being able to fatisfy myfelf as to the meaning of
the firft part of this fhort Epiftle, I will add the original,
with the Latin tranflation of Muratori, by whom this alfo
is preferved:

| Πρὸς ζωγραφον. | Ad Pictorem. |

Εἰ μὲν μὴ εἰχον, καὶ ἐχαρισω *Siquidem non haberem, et mihi*
μοι, γιγγνωμης νοθα αξιος. Ει δι *fuiffes gratificatus, venia dig-*
ειχον μαι, κι' εχρησαμην τι, της *nus effes. Sin autem habe-*
 *rem, neque uterer, Deos ferrem;*
Θεὺς εφερον, μαλλον δι υπο Θεῶν *imo potius, Dii me ferrent. Tu*
εφερομην. Συ μοι αλλωτριον σχημα *vero quare alienum mihi habi-*
πως εδιδως, εταιρε; Οιον μι ειδεις, *tum dedifti, O amice? Qualem*
τοιωτον και γραψον. *me vidifti, talem etiam pingito.*

The meaning of the two laft paragraphs is fufficiently
clear. "But why, my friend, have you given me a foreign
"drefs? Paint me as you fee me." The painter perhaps
had drawn him, like a Roman Emperor, with a fmall beard,
and not like a Grecian Philofopher, with a large one.

## Epiftle LXVI.  To Arsaces, Satrap of Armenia *.

A. D.
363.
ARM, arm, Arfaces, againft the furious Perfians, and haften to join my forces, fwift as
thought.   My martial preparations and determined refolution have one of thefe ends in view;
either

* The feeble Arfaces Tiranus, king of Armenia, had
degenerated, ftill more fhamefully than his father Chofroes,
from the many virtues of the great Tiridates; and as the
pufillanimous monarch was averfe to any enterprife of
danger and glory, he could difguife his timid indolence by
the more decent excufes of religion and gratitude.   He
expreffed a pious attachment to the memory of Conftantius, from whofe hands he had received in marriage Olympias, the daughter of the præfect Ablavius; and the alliance of a female, who had been educated as the deftined
wife of the emperor Conftans, exalted the dignity of a
Barbarian king.   Tiranus profeffed the Chriftian religion;
he reigned over a nation of Chriftians; and he was reftrained by every principle of confcience and intereft from
contributing to the victory which would confummate the
ruin of the church.   The alienated mind of Tiranus was
exafperated by the indifcretion of Julian, who treated the
king of Armenia as his flave, and as the enemy of the
Gods.   The haughty and threatening ftyle of the Imperial
mandates awakened the fecret indignation of a prince,
who, in the humiliating ftate of dependence, was ftill confcious of his royal defcent from the Arfacides, the lords
of the Eaft, and the rivals of the Roman power.  GIBBON.
    This Epiftle, printed, for the firft time, in the *Anecdota
Græca* of M. Muratori, is inferted in the *Bibliotheca Græca*,
[tom. VII. p. 86.] of Fabricius.   It is in very bad Greek,
vulgar, brutal, meanly vain-glorious, without genius, contrary

either to pay the debt of nature, bravely fighting, and exerting my utmoſt efforts, if ſuccefs ſhould attend the Parthians; or, if the Gods ſhould affiſt me, to return triumphant, and to erect trophies

trary to policy; and, what is ſtill more remarkable, it contains expreſſions that could not proceed from the pen of a ſuperſtitious Pagan, at the eve of a great enterpriſe, and in circumſtances where the leaſt word of bad omen was ſcrupulouſly avoided, as capable of being fatal. Can it be ſuppoſed that Julian would have ventured to ſay, even by way of circumlocution, that " he was reſolved to periſh ?" Would he have communicated the prediction that we find at the end of the Epiſtle? Whatever the illuſtrious M. Muratori may ſay of it, I can ſcarce believe that it is the ſame which Sozomen has mentioned; eſpecially as this does not contain all that the Eccleſiaſtical hiſtorian relates. I do not inſiſt on this laſt reaſon, becauſe it may be anſwered, that we have not the whole Epiſtle. But, after all, it is ſo ſtrange a piece, that, inſtead of aſcribing it to Julian, I would rather ſay, which is not neceſſary, that Sozomen was deceived by a ſpurious piece.

LA BLETERIE.

Muratori has publiſhed an Epiſtle from Julian to the Satrap Arſaces, fierce, vulgar, and (though it might deceive Sozomen) moſt probably ſpurious. La Bleterie tranſlates and rejects it.     GIBBON.

And ſo does the preſent tranſlator.

The paſſage of Sozomen, to which M. de la Bleterie refers, is as follows : " He wrote alſo to Arſaces, king of " the Armenians, an ally of the Romans, to join him in " the field. In this Epiſtle, after boaſting immoderately, " and extolling himſelf as fit to reign, and dear to the Gods " whom he worſhipped, and ſtigmatiſing Conſtantius as " puſillanimous and impious, he threatened Arſaces moſt " contumeliouſly. And as he had heard that he was a " Chriſtian, in order to aggravate his reproaches, he ut " tered ſome wicked blaſphemies againſt Chriſt, with great " pride and oſtentation, ſignifying, that the God whom " he worſhipped would by no means defend him, if he " neglected his commands." *Hiſt. Eccl. l.* VI. c. 1.

taken

taken from the enemy. Shake off therefore your inactivity, forego all evasions, and thinking no longer of that Constantine of happy memory *, or of the wealth of the nobles, which was lavished on you and other Barbarians, by the effeminate and too aged † Constantius, now cultivate the friend-ship of Julian, Sovereign Pontiff, Cæsar, Augustus, the servant of Mars and the Gods, the destroyer of the Franks and Barbarians, but the deliverer of the Gauls and Italians. If you have any other design, for I hear that you are very crafty, a bad soldier, a boaster, I shall not be surprised, as you now secrete a public enemy, trusting to the chance of war. To destroy the enemy, we need only the assistance of the Gods; but if Fate, whose decree is their will, should determine otherwise, I shall submit with fortitude and complacence. Know, however, that you, in consequence, will be subjected to the Persian power, your house and your whole family will be destroyed by fire, and the kingdom of

---

* Μακαριτην εκεινον Κωνςαντινον, "That blessed Constantine." Julian would hardly have spoken so favourably of his uncle, the constant object of his hatred and ridicule. It appears by the conclusion of the Cæsars, p. 220, that he rather thought him cursed than "blessed."

† Πολυετης Κωνςαντιε, annosi Constantii. Constantius lived only 44 or 45 years. LA BLETERIE.

In like manner, Julian, in his 1st oration, styles Licinius "an old man," (γεροντος), at the battle of Cibalis in 314, though he was then not so. M. de la Bleterie translates πολυετης "qui n'a vecu que trop long tems ("who had lived too "long.")

Armenia

Armenia fubvertcd. The city of * Nifibis will
alfo fhare your misfortunes. This the Gods revealed to us long ago.

---

### Epiftle LXVII. To the People [of An-
### tioch †.]

SOME are fo audacious as to prophane the fe-  12 Feb.
pulchres and confecrated graves of the dead,  363.
though to remove from them even a ftone, or to
dig the earth, and pull the turf, was always deemed
by

---

* The bulwark of the Eaft, given up to the Perfians by
Jovian, now reduced to 150 houfes. See *Voyages de Niebuhr*,
tome ii. *p.* 300—309.

Be this letter genuine, or not, " Arfaces," as M. de la
Bleterie expreffes it, " attentive only to his own intereft,
" and diffatisfied with Julian, would not leave his own
" frontiers." This prince, in the reign of Valens, was trea-
cheroufly feized, imprifoned, and put to death, by Sapor,
king of Perfia, as Ammianus relates, xxvii. 12.

† I take this law from the Theodofian Code, ix. xvii.
3. *tit.* De fepulchris violatis. It is the only piece of any
length that is left of the Latinity of Julian. It is forcible
and elaborate, but much lefs pure than his Greek. The
reader perhaps will not diflike being enabled to judge for
himfelf. The following is the whole Epiftle.

IMP. JULIANUS A. AD POPULUM.

*Pergit audacia ad bufta diem functorum et aggeres confecratos;*
*cùm et lapidem hinc movere, terram folicitare, et tefpitem vellere,*
*proximum facrilegio majores femper habuerint. Sed ornamenta qui-*
*dam tricliniis, aut porticibus, auferunt de fepulchris. Quibus*
*primis confulentes, ne in piaculum incidant contaminatâ religione*
*buftorum, hoc fieri prohibemus pænâ Manium vindice cohibentes.*

Secundum

by our anceftors next to facrilege. Some take
away the ornaments of tombs to adorn their porticoes or parlours; To prevent, in the firft place, the
criminal impiety of polluting fepulchres, we pro-
hibit it under pain of the punifhment that is due to
thofe who offend the Manes *.

*Secundum illud eft, quod efferri regnovimus cadavera mor-
tuorum per confertam populi frequentiam et per maximam infif-
tentium denfitatem, quod quidem oculos hominum infauftis inceftat
afpectibus. Qui enim dies eft bene aufpicatus à funere? Aut
quomodo ad Deos et templa venietur? Ideoque, quoniam et dolor
in exequiis fecretum amat, et diem functis nihil intereft, utrùm per
noctes, an per dies, efferantur, liberari convenit populi totius af-
pectus; ut dolor effe in funeribus, non pompa exequiarum, nec
oftentatio, videatur.*

*Datum prid. id. Feb. Antiochiæ, Juliano Aug. IV. et
Salluftio, Coff.* LA BLETERIE.

\* The profanation of fepulchres was confidered in all
times among the Romans as a kind of facrilege. Thofe
who dug up the body, or the bones, of a dead perfon were
punifhed with death, if they were of mean condition.
They were confined in an ifland, if they were of genteel
rank. Thofe who deftroyed a fepulchre, or took any thing
away from it, were condemned to the mines, or banifhed.
Conftantine, in a law, whofe object was to render divorces
lefs frequent, and to make the Roman jurifprudence as to
marriage again fomewhat like the gofpel, by reftraining
divorce to certain cafes, fpecifies, among the crimes which
gave a woman a right to repudiate her hufband, murder,
poifoning, and the violation of tombs. *Si homicidam, vel
medicamentarium · vel fepulchrorum diffolutorem maritum fuum
effe probaverit.* III *Cod. Theod. tit.* XVI. *De repudiis.* But
the refpect for the dead, and their tombs, which nature
herfelf feems to infpire, was carried to an excefs among
the Pagans. They honoured the fouls of the dead as divinities, and fepulchres as temples.

The Chriftian religion, which enlightened the world as
to the fate of thofe wretched divinities, and the impiety
of the worfhip that was paid them, no fooner became the

religion-

religion of the empire, than many individuals fell into an
excefs oppofite to that of Paganifm.   A zeal ill underftood,
and, under the mafk of zeal, avarice, always ready to draw
from  the trueft principles falfe conclufions which favour
it, deftroyed tombs, applied the ftones and ornaments to
other ufes, and difperfed the afhes of the dead, in order
to find fome valuable ftuffs, or trinkets, which fuperftition
might have interred with them.

M. Muratori, in his *Anecdota Græca*, has inferted near
eighty fhort copies of verfes compofed by St. Gregory
Nazianzen, againft the violators of fepulchres. As feveral of
them feem made in order to be engraved on the tombs of
his friends, of whom the majority at leaft profeffed Chriftianity, we may infer that the tombs of the Chriftians were
not fpared, were it only by the Pagans, who, without
doubt, ufed reprifals.   The law, above quoted, fhews what
the Emperor Conftantine, long after his converfion,
thought of thefe diforders, which not only outraged
nature, but alfo might render Chriftianity odious, on whofe
account they had become more common, though it had
always condemned them.   However, in the reign of
Conftantine, the laws were not executed with rigour.   It
appears by a law of Conftans, that fome individuals, and
even fome of the magiftrates, had violated them with impunity.   He caufed a fearch to be made for the guilty :
but he moderated the feverity of the ancient laws, and reduced it to pecuniary penalties.   Conftantius renewed and
even augmented it, as he fuffered the pecuniary penalties
to remain, when he re-eftablifhed the punifhment of death.
Other chriftian princes, particularly Valentinian III. ex-
erted themfelves, in like manner, againft this crime.

Julian, who confidered the worfhip of the Manes as an
effential part of Hellenifm, here condemns from fuperftition what thofe princes condemned from a principle of
humanity and Chriftianity, though fome Pagan expreffions
have crept into their ordinances, which, without doubt,
muft be afcribed to their fecretaries.   The firft part of the
law of Julian is in the Code of Juftinian, with fome alteration.   That which favoured too much of Paganifm has
been reformed.                              LA BLETERIE.

If an ancient were to revifit the world, with what af-
tonifhment would he be ftruck in the amphitheatre of the
Academy Royal, which no law authorifes to have dead
bodies

Secondly, we have heard that dead corpfes are carried to interment through large crowds of people and numerous fpectators, a fight, that defiles the eyes of men by its inaufpicious appearance. For what day is well-omened by a funeral? And how can we afterwards approach the Gods and the temples?

For thefe reafons, and becaufe funereal grief loves privacy, and as it is of no confequence to the de ceafed, whether they are interred by day or by night, it is proper that funerals fhould be fecreted from the public view, fo as to be expreffive of forrow, rather than of pomp and oftentation *.

---

bodies! A corpfe was efteemed by the ancients a facred object, which was refpectfully placed under a funeral pile; and he who dared to lay hands on it was declared impure. What would he fay on feeing that corpfe horribly cut and mangled; and all the young furgeons, with their arms ftripped and bloody, joking and laughing amidft thofe dreadful operations!      *Tableau de Paris.*

* Whatever refpect the Pagans had for the dead, by a contradiction, of which I will not here trace the origin, they confidered a human corpfe as the impureft thing in the world. They thought they ought not to enter into a temple on a day when they had attended a funeral. But, delivered from a vain fuperftition, the Chriftians, and perhaps fome Pagans, after their example, paid the laft duties to the dead in open day. Julian was defirous of reviving the ancient practice, and even endeavoured to fupport, by philofophical ideas, the Pagan notions on which that practice was founded. This fecond part of his law is in the Theodofian Code, though it does not appear to have been observed after his death.      La Bleterie.

Of the laws which Julian enacted in a fhort reign of fixteen months [Dec. 361—June 363.] fifty-four have been admitted into the Codes of Theodofius and Juftinian. (*Gothofred. Chron. Legum. pp.* 64—67.)      Gibbon.

*Given at Antioch, on the day preceding the ides of February, Julian Aug. (for the IVth time), and Salluft being Confuls.*

Epiftle LXVIII.   To LIBANIUS *.

YOU have made a proper return to Arifto-    A. D.
phanes † for his piety to the Gods, and his    362.
affection for you; by making what was formerly
a difgrace to him redound to his glory, not only

---

* This Epiftle was copied by the illuftrious Roftgaard
from the Modenefe MS. D. collated with the two Medicean
E. and F. and is not to be found among thofe which have
been publifhed, except, with many more, in the *Salutaris Lux
Evangelii* of our Fabricius, p. 323. But it is here more enlarged. It is thus infcribed: Ιουλιανος Αυτοκρατωρ Λιβανιω τω Σο-
φιϛη χαιρειν.                                   WOLFIUS.
   Libanius anfwers this Epiftle (occafioned by his oration
in defence of Ariftophanes) in his DCLxxth, which fee
Vol I. p. 317. The original of it is inferted by Wolfius, in
his notes on that Epiftle.
   Muratori obferves that in one of the Ambrofian MSS. [at
Milan] there was a fhort Epiftle of Julian, not yet publifhed;
" but," he adds, " the evanefcent letters made me totally de-
" fpair of reading it. I hope, however, that it will fome time
" or other be publifhed, together with fome other remains
" of the Apoftate, by Frederick Roftgaard, a noble Dane.
" For when he was travelling through Italy, and collecting
" the Epiftles of Libanius from various MSS. in order to
" give them to the public, he thought he had fagacity
" enough to decypher alfo this Ambrofian MS."
See the firft note on the next Epiftle.

   † Meaning Ariftophanes, a Corinthian, the fon of Me-
nander, for whom there is an oration of Libanius, in Vol.
II. of Morell's edition, p. 210.          FABRICIUS.

at present, but in future times; as the calumny of Paul *, and the sentence of that judge †, can by no means be compared with your orations. For such fiery proceedings were instantly detested, and, together with t̶h̶e̶i̶r̶ ̶a̶u̶t̶h̶o̶r̶s̶,̶ are now extinct; while your orations delight the true Greeks of the present age, and, unless I am much mistaken, will also delight their posterity.

Be assured, in short, that you have convinced me, [or rather that you have induced me to retract my opinion of Aristophanes, and that I think him superior to all the allurements both of profit and pleasure. Can I refuse to concur with the most philosophical of orators, the greatest partisan of truth? After this, perhaps you may ask, why we have not placed his affairs in a more prosperous

---

* This Paul, who pleaded for the informers against Aristophanes, before the Emperor Constantius, is mentioned in the same oration of Libanius, p. 222.     FABRICIUS.

Julian has stigmatised Paul as a "notorious slanderer," in his Epistle to the Athenians, Vol. I. p. 92. See also Ammianus, XIX. and XXII. He was burnt alive, by the order of that prince, soon after his accession to the empire; a fate to which he seems to allude above by αιθυλα, ("fiery") and συναπισθη, ("extinguished together.") In Fabricius it is αιθυλα, ("at their first appearance.")

Libanius, in the oration above mentioned, says, in one place, "Aristophanes received many severe stripes from "balls of lead" [tied, probably, to strings], "which "Paul thought fit instruments of death;" and in another, that "he had irritated Paul by some expressions suitable "indeed to him, but which it would have been better to "have suppressed."

† The Emperor Constantius.     FABRICIUS.

3     state,

ſtate, and removed every inconvenience attending his diſgrace.

When two their efforts join, &c. *.

You and I will confer together. For you are worthy to be confulted, not only as to the propriety of affiſting a man who devoutly honours the Gods, but alſo in what manner, of which indeed you have given ſome hints. But of theſe matters it will be better perhaps to difcourſe than to write. Farewell, my moſt dear and beloved brother †.]

* Συν τι δυ' ερχομενω, κ. τ. λ. Iliad X. 224.
An expreſſion of Diomed, enforcing the propriety of an affiſtant in his nightly expedition. The ſame meaning is conveyed by our Engliſh proverb, " Two heads are better " than one."

† This was immediately followed by Αντγιων δι χθις τον λογον, κ. τ. λ. (" Reading yeſterday your oration, &c.") which is the XIVth Epiſtle of Julian [ſee p. 28.] publiſhed by Ezech. Spanheim, among his works, as a ſingle Epiſtle, and (as is very probable) totally unconnected with the former.              WOLFIUS.
The concluding farewell is exactly the ſame with that of Epiſtle III. to Libanius alſo.
All that is between [ ] is only in the copy publiſhed by Wolfius.

## Epiſtle LXIX *.    To Soſipater †.

WHEN an opportunity offers of writing to
our friends by a domeſtic, the pleaſure it
affords is much augmented. For thus your letters
convey to them ſomething more than a mere image
of your mind. So fortunate am I at preſent. And
therefore, as I was ſending to you Antiochus, the
tutor of my ſons ‡, I could not omit this opportunity of informing you, that if you wiſh to have
any intelligence concerning us, you may learn it
particularly from him. And if you have a regard
for your friends, and that you have ſome I am
certain, when you have a ſimilar opportunity of
writing, you will by no means neglect it.

* This, and the ſeven following Epiſtles (and alſo great
part of the LIXth and LXVIIIth, as has been obſerved in the
notes on each) were firſt publiſhed by Fabricius, in his *Lux
Evangelii*, 1731, with a Latin tranſlation. He was indebted
for them, he ſays, to Count Chriſtian Danneſhiold de Samſoa
(then lately deceaſed), who purchaſed them in 1726, together with many hundreds of unpubliſhed epiſtles of Libanius, at the public auction of the library of the " moſt
" noble and learned Frederick Roſtgaard," having been tran-
ſcribed by him in Italy, from the Vatican, Medicean, and
Ambroſian libraries. See p. 193, note *.

† Or was it " to Sopater," the ſon-in-law of Jamblichus,
who is frequently mentioned in the XXVIIth, XLth, and
LIIId Epiſtles of Julian ?                     FABRICIUS.
    See p. 70, note †.

‡ This probably muſt be the perſon mentioned by the
ſame appellation (Τροφιας των εαυτυ παιδιων) in Epiſtle XL.
See p. 102, note †.

7                                    Epiſtle

Epiftle LXX. To PHILIP *.

WHILE I was Cæfar, the Gods can witnefs, A. Γ.
I wrote to you, and, I think, more than ³⁶²·
once. Great certainly was the impulfe I felt, but
many and various were my avocations ; and, befides,
as the friendfhip between me and the bleffed † Conftantius, in confequence of my advancement, *as
that of wolves, I was extremely cautious of writing to any one beyond the Alps, left I fhould in-
volve him in the greateft difficulties. Confider
my writing to you now as a proof of my friendfhip, for frequently the tongue refufes to corre-
fpond with the heart. And fubjects perhaps have
reafon to exult and glory in being able to fhew the
letters of princes, difplaying them to the unexperienced, like rings to perfons unacquainted with

* This feems to be the fame to whom there are feveral
Epiftles of Libanius, in [one of] which he fays, that the
letters which he received from Philip were written " not
" with ink, but with a Pegafean liquor." FABRICIUS.
Libanius had two correfpondents of this name, one a
præfect, whom he mentions in his Life, p. 25, and the
other a poet.
It muft have been written in the fpring of 362, probably
at Conftantinople, when Julian was preparing to remove to
Antioch.
† So Julian ufed to ftyle Conftantius, now dead, as he
calls him μακαρίης in his XXXIft and LVIIIth Epiftles, and
in his XXIIId, ικιιιω μιι υ?, ιπαδη μακαρίης ιγιιίω, κυφ* γη.
*Ibid.*

O 3                                              fuch

such trinkets. True friendship is generally found between equals; but there is a second kind, when one has a real, not a pretended, esteem for the other, and though superior in rank and genius, is loved for his good-nature, affability, and discretion. But such epistles are apt to be filled with vanity and trifles. And I often reproach myself for making them too prolix, and being too loquacious, when I should teach my tongue a Pythagorean silence.

I have received your presents, a silver cup, a pound in weight, and a piece of gold coin. I am indeed desirous, as you say in your letter, of having your company here. But now the spring approaches, the trees begin to blossom, and the swallows, though not yet expected, when they arrive, will expell us, engaged on a like expedition, from our houses, and bid us remove to a distant country. Therefore, as we shall pass near you, it will be better for you, if the Gods permit, to meet us in your own neighbourhood. This, I hope, will soon happen, unless something providential prevents: which may the Gods avert!

Epistle

## Epiftle LXXI. To Eutherius *.

W E live, preferved by the Gods †. Offer fa- A. D. crifices therefore to them in acknowledge- 361. ment of my fafety; but not for the fafety of one individual only, but of all the Greeks ‡ in general. If you have leifure to pafs over § to Conftantinople, I fhall think myfelf not a little honoured by your company.

* To this Eutherius I have three Epiftles of Libanius in MS.          Fabricius.
    There are fix in the edition of Wolfius. Julian muft have written this foon after his arrival at Conftantinople in the winter of 361.

† Ζωμεν υπο των Θεων σωθειλες. On the fame occafion Julian ufes an expreffion very fimilar to this in his XIIIth Epiftle, to his uncle: Ζωμεν δια τες Θεες. In the Latin of Fabricius it is mifprinted *Vicimus*.

‡ Meaning the Gentile worfhippers of idols.
                                                        Fabricius.

§ This expreffion (λαζυται) fhews, that Eutherius was then on the oppofite fide of the Bofphorus.

## Epiſtle LXXII.　To the Patriarch *.

THIS is the ſecond letter that I have ſent in
favour of Amogila †, my former having
been rendered ineffectual by the powerful influence
of her oppreſſors. Lamenting therefore the fate
of my former Epiſtle, pay due regard to this, and
make it not neceſſary for us to write a third.

* Mention is made of Julus, the Patriarch of the Jews,
whom he calls " moſt venerable," in the XXVth Epiſtle of
Julian.　　　　　　　　　　　　　　　FABRICIUS.
See p. 50.
This, as has been obſerved of the LXIVth Epiſtle, p.
184. has alſo, by miſtake, been aſcribed to Libanius, being
printed in the edition of Wolfius, as the DCCCXXXVth of
his Epiſtles. There are ſix more ſo inſcribed. But a MS. of one
of them in the Vatican library has the addition of Αιλιοχιωτ.
This therefore, and all of them, were probably addreſſed,
not to the Jewiſh Patriarch, as Fabricius ſuppoſes, but to
the Chriſtian Patriarch of Antioch, who in the year 361 was
Meletius.
† Αμωγιλης. In the copy (above mentioned) aſcribed to
Libanius, the name is Αμμωνιλλης, (" Ammonilla.")
This is followed in Fabricius, by
　　　　　" To ÆTIUS.　(See p. 78.)
" Κοινως μιν απασι, &c. This, in the editions of Petau and
" Ez. Spanheim, is the XXXIſt Epiſtle, p. 405, but inſtead
" of Κοινως, (" in general,") we there read Λοιποις, (" the
" reſt,") and then inſtead of the words μιχρι τυ ςρατοπιδυ
" τυ εμυ, (" as far as [my] camp,") there is only in the
" Medicean MS. μιχρι τυ ςρατοπιδυ. This Epiſtle, by which
" we find the biſhops, whom Conſtantius had baniſhed,
" recalled by Julian, is mentioned by Sozomen, l. v. c. 5."

## Epiſtle LXXIII. To Diogenes *.

AFTER your departure, Diogenes, your ſon
came to me, and ſaid, you were angry with
him, and as much enraged as a father could be
with a ſon : he begged me therefore to intercede
for him, and to reconcile you to him. If his offence be ſlight, and ſuch as may eaſily be forgiven,
yield to nature, and, recollecting that you are a
parent, reſtore your ſon to favour. But if it be
ſuch as cannot be pardoned, you yourſelf are the
beſt judge which is moſt expedient, to act gene-
rouſly on this occaſion, and to conquer the diſpoſition of your ſon by the beſt advice, or to truſt
his amendment, and the reparation of his fault, to
length of time.

* An Athenian philoſopher, to whom there are ſome
Epiſtles of Libanius.                    FABRICIUS.
    In one of them he acquaints Diogenes with the death
. and burial of his wife. He is alſo mentioned by Julian
in his XXXVth Epiſtle. See p. 90. He was the uncle of
Ariſtophanes, the Corinthian, mentioned p. 193.

## Epiſtle LXXIV. To Priscus *.

A. D.
362.

ON receiving your letter, I immediately diſpatched Archelaus †, and gave him ſome
epiſtles for you, with a paſſport, as you defired,
for a longer time. If you are inclined to ſpeculate
the ocean, every thing, under God, will proſper
to your wiſh, unleſs you dread the inelegance of
the Galatians, or a ſtorm. But this will be as God
ſhall think fit. I ſwear to you by him, who is to
me the giver and preſerver of all good, that I wiſh
to live only for the ſake of being uſeful to you.
By you, I mean the true philoſophers; of whom
convinced that you are one, you well know how
much I have loved, and love you, and wiſh to ſee
you. May divine Providence preſerve you in
health many years, my moſt eſteemed and friendly
brother! The excellent Hippia, and your children,
I ſalute.

---

\* The father of the præfect Anatolius. FABRICIUS.
Anatolius was maſter of the offices, and was killed in
the ſame ſkirmiſh in which Julian himſelf was mortally
wounded. He would otherwiſe perhaps have ſucceeded
that prince, as he himſelf is ſaid to have wiſhed. For an
account of Priſcus, ſee p. 6, note †.

† To this Archelaus, as I ſuppoſe, Libanius has four
Epiſtles, in one of which he expoſtulates with him for
env> enviouſly burning ſome of his declamations.

Epiſtle

Epiftle LXXV.  To LIBANIUS, Sophift and
Quæſtor *.

HOW fortunate was our difappointment of a
public carriage ! For inftead of the terror and
apprehenfion attendant on fuch a vehicle, where we
meet with drunken muleteers, and mules, like thofe
in Homer, " pampered with barley †," fuch are
their idlenefs and repletion, and are annoyed with
clouds of duft and the intolerable diffonance of
clamorous drivers and fmacking whips ‡, I now
travel at my leifure on a pleafant fhady road,
abounding with fountains, and having many commodious inns, and when the hour of refrefhment
arrives, I reft wherever I pleafe, beneath the fpacious, fragrant boughs of the plane or cyprefs,
with the Myrrhinufian § Phædrus ||, or fome other
work of Plato, in my hands. As I thus enjoy an
unembarraffed journey, did I not communicate this
pleafure to you, my deareft friend, I fhould think
myfelf inexcufable.

* So ftyled alfo in Epiftle XXVIIth. But here, for a
reafon given below, I fufpect it to be an anachronifm.
† Ακεσησασι. Iliad. VI. 506. xv. 263.
‡ The inconveniences of the public vehicles in thofe
days feem by this account very fimilar to thofe experienced
in our times. Had Julian then been Emperor, or even
Cæfar, all the public carriages, with their motions, would
have been at his command.
§ Of Myrrhinus in Attica.          FABRICIUS.
|| The book of Plato fo infcribed, from his fcholar of that
name.

Epiftle

---

### Epiſtle LXXVI. To the Philoſopher Euclid*.

WHEN did you leave us, that we muſt write
to you? or when do we not view you, as if
you were ſtill preſent, with the eyes of our mind,
ſeeming not only to be conſtantly enjoying your
company and converſation, but alſo taking the ſame
care of your affairs as when you were here? If,
however, you would have me write to you as to
one who is abſent, conſider whether this requeſt
does not prove that you are really abſent. Be that
as it may, if it gratifies you, even in this we readily
obey you. Indeed, according to the proverb, you
will ſpur to the field a free horſe. See then that
you make a ſimilar return, and fail not to be punc-
tual in your replies. Though I am unwilling to
interrupt your labours for the pnblic good, yet,
as I obſerve that you purſue what is excellent, far
from offending I ſhall ſeem to render an eſſential
ſervice to all Greece by diſmiſſing you unmoleſted,
like a generous hound, to track learning through
all her paths, through every footſtep †. If you
have ſuch alacrity as neither to neglect your friends,
nor to diſcontinue theſe purſuits, haſte, and exert
yourſelf in both thoſe courſes.

---

* I do not recollect that this philoſopher is elſewhere
mentioned, either by Julian or Libanius. An Eucladius
occurs in the DCLXXIIId Epiſtle of the latter.
† Βημαζι, otherwiſe Αημμαζι, (" argument.") FABRICIUS.

Epiſtola

Epiſtola LXXVII *. Ad PHOTINUM †.

TU quidem, O Photine, veriſimilis videris et
proximus ſalvare, benefaciens nequaquam in
utero inducere quem credidiſti Deum. Diodorus ‡
autem Nazaræi magus ejus pigmentalibus man-
goneis acuens irrationabilitatem acutus apparuit
ſophiſta religionis agreſtis. * * * * Quod ſi nobis
opitulati fuerint dii, et deæ, et muſæ omnes, et
fortuna, oſtendemus infirmum et corruptorem le-

* This Epiſtle, mentioned by Fabricius, in his *Lux Evan-
gelii*, p. 310. is preſerved by Facundus, biſhop of Her-
mania in Africa, in his book dedicated to the Emperor
Juſtinian, in defence of the " three chapters," as they were
called, which were the writings of Theodore of Mopſueſtia,
Theodoret of Cyprus, and Ibas of Edeſſa, againſt all which
Juſtinian had publiſhed an edict, A. D. 544. See Moſheim,
I. 299. It was printed by Sirmond, at Paris, 1629, 8vo ;
and from that edition, p. 163, this letter is extracted.
This letter of Julian, if not written originally in Latin,
ſeems to have been tranſlated in a very bombaſt ſtyle. He
here threatens his work againſt the Chriſtians. I will not
give it in Engliſh.
† Photinus, biſhop of Sirmium, publiſhed, in the year
343, his opinions concerning the deity, which were equally
repugnant to the orthodox and Arian ſyſtems. His temerity was chaſtiſed, not only by the orthodox in the
councils of Antioch and Milan, held in the years 345 and
347, and in that of Sirmium, whoſe date is uncertain, but
alſo by the Arians, in one of their aſſemblies held at Sirmium, in the year 351. In conſequence of all this, Photinus was degraded from the epiſcopal dignity, and died
in exile in the year 372. MOSHEIM.
For his extravagant notions ſee vol. I. of this hiſtorian,
223.
‡ Of Antioch, biſhop of Tarſus, an orthodox prelate.
See Moſheim, I. 188, and Moreii, article *Diodors d' Antioche.*

gm,

gum, et rationum, et myſteriorum paganorum, et
deorum infernorum, et illum novum ejus deum
Galilæum quem æternum fabuloſè prædicat indignâ
morte et ſepulturâ denudatum confiſtæ a Diodoro
deitatis ! Iſte enim malo communis utilitatis Athenas
navigans, et philoſophans, imprudenter muſicorum
participatus eſt rationem, et rhetoricis confeſti-
onibus odibilem adarmavit linguam adverſus cæ-
leſtes deos uſque adeo ignorans paganorum myſ-
teria omnemque miſerabiliter imbibens, ut aiunt,
degenerum et imperitorum ejus theologorum piſca-
torum errorem. Propter quod jam diu eſt quod ab
ipſis punitur diis. Jam enim per multos annos in
periculum converſus, et in corruptionem thoracis
incidens, ad ſummum pervenit ſupplicium. Omne
ejus corpus conſumptum eſt : nam malæ ejus conci-
derunt, rugæ vero in altitudinem corporis deſcen-
derunt, quod non eſt philoſophicæ converſationis
indicio, ſicut videri vult a ſe deceptis, ſed juſtitiæ
pro certo deorumque pœnæ quâ percutitur com-
petenti ratione uſque ad noviſſimum vitæ ſuæ finem
aſperam et amaram vitam vivens et faciem pallore
confeſtum.

FRAG-

# FRAGMENTS

## OF

## EPISTLES OF JULIAN,

Tranſlated from S U I D A S.

*Article* A M P H I O N.

FOR you have leiſure, you have excellent natural endowments, and, if any
one ever had, a love for philoſophy. Theſe three
uñited were ſufficient to render Amphion the inventor of ancient muſic * ; namely, time, divine
inſpiration, and the love of harmony. The want
of inſtruments cannot be any impediment to theſe ;
and he who is poſſeſſed of theſe three will eaſily
find thoſe. Have we not heard that Amphion not
only invented muſic, but alſo the harp, either by
the wonderful powers of his genius, or ſome divine
aſſiſtance, or ſome unuſual co-operation ? And moſt
of the ancients, by principally attending to theſe
three, ſeem to have philoſophiſed without diſguiſe,
and to have required nothing elſe.

* The lute, on which Amphion played ſo harmoniouſly as
to bring together the ſtones with which the tower of Thebes
was built, is ſaid by others to have been preſented to him
by Mercury. Some ſuppoſe that there were two Amphions,
and that the younger, called the Dircæan, from the river
Dirce, in Bœotia, was the muſician and the inventor of
muſic.

*Article*

*Article* HERODOTUS.

WHO is ignorant of what the Æthiopians said of the moſt nouriſhing food we have? On taſting ſome of our bread, " they wondered", they ſaid, " how we could live upon dung," if we may credit the Thurian hiſtorian *. Thoſe who have treated on the various climates of the earth alſo relate that there are nations of men who feed on fiſh and fleſh, and never, even in a dream, ſaw ſuch diet as ours. If any one of them ſhould attempt to adopt our mode of living, he would fare no better than thoſe who ſwallow hellebore or hemlock.

* Herodotus, ſo called from Thurium in Magna Græcia, where he lived and died. Julian gives him the ſame appellation in Epiſtle XXII. The paſſage to which he here alludes is in the IIId book of that hiſtorian, and is part of the enquiry which the Æthiopians made of the *Ichthyophagi*, or " fiſh-eaters," whom Cambyſes ſent to explore that country. Their king, they ſaid, lived upon bread, explaining the nature of wheat, and that eighty years was the longeſt period propoſed by a Perſian. The Æthiopian anſwered, " I do not wonder, as you live upon dung, that " you are ſo ſhort-lived; and, were it not for this " beverage (wine), you would not live ſo long."

This extraordinary perſon was born at Halicarnaſſus, a Grecian colony in the leſſer Aſia, not long before the invaſion of Greece by the armies of Xerxes. In his youth he retired from his native city to Samos, in order to avoid the arbitrary proceedings of Lygdamis, the grandſon of the famous Artemiſia, who acquitted herſelf with much honour in the naval engagement of Salamis. There he formed himſelf upon the dialect of Ionia, and compiled his
hiſtory

hiſtory, which begins with Candaules and Cyrus, and comes down to the battle of Mycale, towards the latter end of the reign of Xerxes, a period of 120 years. In the mean time he ſpared no pains to inform himſelf of all that was neceſſary, in the beſt manner which he could. To this end he travelled into Ægypt, ſurveyed its chief towns, conferſed with the prieſts of Thebes and Memphis, and penetrated into the principles of their religion and learning; as far as his own ſagacity could carry him, and their recluſeneſs would permit him. He travelled through the ſeveral diſtricts and republics of Greece, ſaw the principal cities of Aſia, and viſited the borders of Thrace, Scythia, and Arabia. Returning, however, after a long voluntary exile, into his own country, he bore a conſiderable ſhare in the expulſion of the tyrant ; but meeting with envy from his fellow-citizens, inſtead of that gratitude which he expected as the juſt reward of his ſervices, he went to Athens, and after about a twelvemonth's ſtay there, departed into Italy with a colony of Athenians, to build a city called Thurium (hence the above appellation) near the ruins of the ancient Sybaris. As ſoon as he had drawn up his hiſtory from the materials he had collected with ſuch infinite diligence and induſtry, he determined to expoſe it to the judgement of all Greece. It happened, that during his reſidence at Athens, beſides the feaſt of Panathenæa where he read his work aloud, the Olympian exerciſes were performed, to which the Grecians reſorted in general from each ſtate, and thus he had a very favourable opportunity of putting his deſign into execution. Many of his auditors had, no doubt, been perſonally engaged in ſome of the battles againſt Xerxes and Mardonius, and not one of them could be unacquainted with the principal facts of a war, ſo honourable to Greece, and ſo inglorious to Perſia. In the midſt of this aſſembly he declared, that " he appeared be- " fore them not ſo much a ſpectator of their games, as a " competitor for the prize of reputation ;" and recited his work publickly a ſecond time with univerſal applauſe. Of this nothing can be a greater teſtimony than that the names of the nine Muſes have been given to the nine books of his hiſtory, as if the compoſition were above the ſtandard of humanity, and the joint labour of thoſe celebrated divinities.

*Article* MUSONIUS *.

⁞ ⁞ . THE drunken abuſe, with which the commander in Greece † has loaded me, you have borne with ſerenity, thinking that it did not in the leaſt concern you. As to your earneſt deſire to be ſerviceable to the city in which you reſide, that is a certain proof of a philoſophical mind. The firſt ſeems to me ſuitable to Socrates, the ſecond to Muſonius. He ſaid that it was wrong for a good man to ſuffer himſelf to be injured by the wicked ‡. For he had the ſuperintendence of the towers when he was baniſhed by Nero.

* For an account of Muſonius, ſee the Epiſtle to Themiſtius, Vol. I. p. 25. note ‖.

† This poſſibly might be Dionyſius, whoſe " drunken " abuſe" Julian mentions in Epiſtle LIX. p. 165. The words in the original are ſimilar, παροινιαν and πιπαρωνηκας.

‡ Though I have literally tranſlated this paſſage, I do not clearly apprehend its meaning, or its connection with what follows.

## *Article* X P H M A.

O UR journey lay through the Hercynian A. D. foreſt *. There I ſaw a moſt wonder- 357. ful ſight (χρημα, εξαισιον). I can confidently aſſure you, that you have never ſeen the like, though I know that there are many of the kind in the Ro- man dominions. But let any one think of the in- acceſſible Theſſalian Tempe, or of Thermopylæ †, or of ſteep and extenſive Taurus ‡ ; and all theſe will ſeem inſignificant when compared in rugged- neſs with the Hercynian foreſt.

* This ſeems alſo to be ſtyled the Hercynian foreſt by Zoſimus, *l.* III. It is at preſent called *der Speſſard*, for- merly a part of the Hercynian foreſt, and is on the left bank of the Mayne, not far from the confluence of the Rhine and Moſelle, as Cluverius ſays, *l.* III. *c.* 7.

VALOIS.

In Cæſar's time this foreſt extended from the country of the Rauraci (Baſil) into the boundleſs regions of the North. Julian mentions his being " ſent into the Her- " cynian foreſt when he had ſcarce arrived at manhood," in the Miſopogon, p. 275 ; and Ammianus, XVII. I. where it is ſtyled *ſylvam ſqualore tenebrarum horrendam.*

† Straits between the mountains of Theſſaly and Phocis, which divide Greece, famous for the defence of Leonidas againſt the Perſians.

‡ The higheſt and moſt extenſive mountains in Aſia.

# INDEX TO THE EPISTLES.

P 3 XLI.

N. B. Thofe tranflated by M. de la Bleterie are
marked with Arabic figures, which fhew the chronological order in which he has endeavoured (as far
as he could) to arrange them. Gallus to Julian,
and Julian to Themiftius, are his two firft. And
thofe to the Athenians and Conftantius he has
omitted.

P 4                         THE

# THE

# L I F E

O F

# L I B A N I U S, the Sophist.

From the Latin

Of John Albert Fabricius, D. D. *

L IBANIUS was born of an ancient and noble family at Antioch, on the Orontes, in the year of our Lord 314. Suidas calls his father " Phafganius ;" but this was the name of one of his uncles †; the other, who was the elder, was named Panolbius. His great grandfather, who excelled in the art of divination, had publifhed fome pieces in Latin, which occafioned his being fup＊pofed by fome, but falfly, to be an Italian. His maternal and paternal grandfathers were eminent in rank and in eloquence; the latter, with his brother Brafidas, was put to death, by the order of

---

* In his Bibliotheca Græca, vol. VII. p. 378.

† Libanius, in his Life (which he fays, p. 19, he wrote when he was fixty), vol. II. p. 6. and 40, and *Orat.* XXIV. p. 534. He mentions, p. 46. that he attained his fiftieth year under Jovian; and, p. 48, his fifty-feventh under Valens.        FABRICIUS.

Diocletian,

Diocletian, in the year 303, after the tumult of the tyrant Eugenius. Libanius, of his father's three sons the second, in the fifteenth year of his age, wishing to devote himself entirely to literature, complains that he met with some " shadows " of sophists." Then, assisted by a proper master *, he began to read the ancient writers at Antioch, and from thence, with Jasion, a Cappadocian, went to Athens, and residing there for more than four years became intimately acquainted with Crispinus of Heraclea, who, he says, enriched him afterwards with books at Nicomedia, and went, but seldom, to the schools of Diophantus. At Constantinople he ingratiated himself with Nicocles of Lacedæmon (a grammarian, who was master to the Emperor Julian), and the sophist Bemarchius. Returning to Athens, and soliciting the office of a professor, which the proconsul had before intended for him when he was twenty-five years of age, a certain Cappadocian happened to be preferred to him. But being encouraged by Dionysius, a Sicilian, who had been præfect of Syria, some specimens of his eloquence, that were published at Constantinople, made him so generally known and applauded, that he collected more than eighty disciples, the two sophists, who then filled the chair there, raging in vain, and Bemarchius ineffectually opposing him in rival orations, and when he could not excell him, having recourse to

---

* This was probably the same whom Libanius freed from the resentment of the Emperor Constantius, as he relates, p. 34.                                    FABRICIUS.

5                                                               the

the frigid calumny of magic. At length, about
the year 346, being expelled the city by his com-
petitors *, the præfect Limenius concurring, he
repaired to Nice, and soon after to Nicomedia, the
Athens of Bithynia, where his excellence in speaking began to be more and more approved by all, and
Julian, if not a hearer, was a reader and admirer
of his orations. In the same city, he says, he
was particularly delighted with the friendship of
Aristænetus †, and the five years, which he passed
there, he styles " the spring, or any thing else that
" can be conceived pleasanter than spring, of his
" whole life." Being invited again to Constantinople, and afterwards returning to Nicomedia, being
also tired of Constantinople, where he found Phœnix
and Zenobius, rival sophists, though he was pa-
tronised by Strategius, who succeeded Domitian as
præfect of the East, not daring, on account of his
rivals, to occupy the Athenian chair, he obtained
permission from Gallus Cæsar to visit, for four
months, his native city Antioch, where, after
Gallus was killed in 354, he fixed his residence
for the remainder of his life, and initiated many

---

* The jealousy of his rivals, who persecuted him from
one city to another, confirmed the favourable opinion which
Libanius ostentatiously displayed of his superior merit.
                                                    GIBBON.

† The death of this Aristænetus, præfect of Bithynia,
who was overwhelmed at Nicomedia by an earthquake in
358, he laments, p. 40, and in his XXIXth and XXXIst
Epistles. See also the following Monody.

in the facred rites of eloquence. He was alfo much beloved by the Emperor Julian, who heard his dif-courfes with pleafure *, received him with kindnefs, and imitated him in his writings. Honoured by that prince with the rank of quæftor †, and with feveral Epiftles [of which fix only are extant ‡], the laft § written by the Emperor during his fatal expedition againft the Perfians, he the more la-mented his death in the flower of his age, as from him he had promifed himfelf a certain and lafting fupport both in the worfhip of idols and in his own ftudies. There was afterwards a report that Libanius, with the younger Jamblichus, the mafter of Proclus, enquired by divination who would be the fucceffor of Valens ‖, and in confequence with difficulty

* Fabricius corrects this miftake in his *Lux Evangelii*.
† See p. 65.
‡ Viz. the iiid, xivth, xxviith, xlivth, lxviiith, and lxxvth.
§ The xxviith.
‖ In the year 373, or 374, whilft Valens was at Antioch, a difcovery was made of a confultation which fome Gentiles had together for finding out the name of the perfon who fhould fucceed the Emperor. There are accounts of it in feveral of our Ecclefiaftical hiftorians, and in divers Heathen authors, particularly Ammianus Marcellinus, who is the fulleft of all, and was then in the Eaft, and poffibly at Antioch. The confeffions made by Patritius and Hilary, both fkilful diviners, he thus particularly relates:

" A tripod made of laurel was artificially prepared, and
" confecrated with certain prefcribed fecret charms and
" invocations. It was then placed in the middle of a
" room, perfumed with Arabian fpices. The charger, on
" which it was fet, had on its utmoft brim the four and
" twenty letters of the alphabet, nearly engraved, and fet
" at due diftances from each other. Then a perfon, clad
                                                      " in

" in linen veſtments, with linen ſocks upon his feet, and
" a ſuitable covering upon his head, came in with laurel
" branches in his hands, and, after ſome myſtic charms
" performed, ſhook a ring, hanging at a curtain, about
" the edge of the charger; which jumping up and down,
" fell upon ſome letters of the alphabet, where it ſeemed
" to ſtay; the prieſt alſo then compoſing certain heroic
" verſes in anſwer to the queſtions that had been propoſed.
" The letters, which the ring pointed out in this caſe, were
" four, Θ, E, O, Δ, which being put together, one that
" was preſent immediately exclaimed, that the oracle
" plainly intended Theodorus" [then ſecond in the ſecretaries office], " nor did we make any farther enquiries,
" being all well ſatisfied that he was the perſon intended,
" though himſelf was totally ignorant of this proceeding."
                            *Cave's Tranſlation.*

Zonaras gives a different account of the method of divination then made uſe of. He ſays, " that the four and
" twenty letters of the alphabet were written upon the
" ground, and at each one was placed a grain of wheat or
" barley. Then, after ſome myſtic forms, a cock * was let
" out, which picked up ſuch grains as lay at thoſe four
" letters." But it is much more reaſonable to rely upon
Ammianus, who was contemporary, and likely to be well
informed. His account alſo is agreeable to that in Sozomen and Zoſimus, who have both mentioned the tripod.

When Libanius ſays, that " Valens hoped to have had
" him alſo accuſed as one of the conſpirators," I take it to
be a mere flouriſh. He was willing to make a merit of
ſome danger with the reſt of his friends, though really he
was ſafe enough.                       LARDNER.

For this conſultation and divination many were put to
death, viz. Simonides and Maximus, philoſophers, the
latter the friend and perverter of Julian, Diogenes, who
had been præfect of Bithynia, and Theodorus, the perſon
named, perhaps with many more who owned the fatal
ſyllables. Theodoſius ſucceeded. Alypius too (ſee p. 73.)
who had been vice-prefect of Britain, was condemned, but
only baniſhed; and his ſon Hierocles, when he was leading
to execution, was happily ſaved, it is ſuppoſed, by a tumult
of the people.

* To this method Fabricius plainly alludes by the word *alectryomantia.*

                                                    The

difficulty efcaped his cruelty *, Irenæus attefting the innocence of Libanius. In like manner he happily efcaped another calumny, by the favour of Duke Lupicinus, when he was accufed by his enemy Fidelis, or Fiduftius, of having written an elogium on the tyrant Procopius †. He was not, however, totally neglected by Valens, whom he not only celebrated in an oration, but ob-

The inquifition into the crime of magic, which, under the reign of the two brothers, was fo rigoroufly profecuted both at Rome and Antioch, was interpreted as the fatal fymptom, either of the difpleafure of heaven, or of the depravity of mankind. Lardner has copioufly and fairly examined this dark tranfaction. GIBBON.

* That future events may be conjectured by the motions of the ftars Libanius does not deny, in an Epiftle [the xivth of Zambicari, l. I.] to Euftolius. That he alfo ftudied the interpretation of dreams may be deduced from Vol. II. of his works, p. 74. FABRICIUS.

† Procopius, a relation of the Emperor Julian, who had haftily promoted him, from the obfcure ftation of a tribune and a notary, to the joint command of the army of Mefopotamia, retired, after the death of that prince, to his ample patrimony in Cappadocia. But being fufpected and ordered to be apprehended by the new fovereigns Valentinian and Valens, A. D. 365, he efcaped from his guards, paffed over to the country of Bofphorus, and, after remaining many months in that fequeftered region, embarked for Conftantinople, and affumed the fovereignty. Being joined by fome Gallic foldiers, whofe numbers rapidly increafed, he fubdued the unarmed provinces of Bithynia and Afia, the city and ifland of Cyzicus, &c. but being at laft deferted by his troops, in two engagements, after wandering fome time among the woods and mountains of Phrygia, he was betrayed by his defponding followers, conducted to the imperial camp, and immediately beheaded.
*Abridged from* GIBBON.

tained

tained from him a confirmation of the law againſt
entirely excluding illegimitate children from the
inheritance of their paternal eſtates, which he ſo-
licited from the Emperor, no doubt, for a private
reaſon, ſince, as Eunapius informs us, he kept a
miſtreſs *, and was never married. The remainder
of his life he paſſed, as before-mentioned, at Antioch, to an advanced age, amidſt various wrongs
and oppreſſions from his rivals and the times, which
he copiouſly relates in his Life, though, tired of
the manners of that city, he had thoughts, in his
old age, of changing his abode, as he tells Euſebius
in his DLIVth Epiſtle [edit. Wolf.] He continued
there, however, and on various occaſions was very
ſerviceable to the city, either by appeaſing ſe-
ditions, and calming the diſturbed minds of the
citizens, or by reconciling to them the Emperors
Julian and Theodoſius. That Libanius lived even
to the reign of Arcadius, that is, beyond the
ſeventieth year of his age, the learned collect from
his oration on Lucian and the teſtimony of Cedrenus;
and of the ſame opinion is Godfrey Olearius, a
man not more reſpectable for his exquiſite knowledge of ſacred and polite literature, than for his
judgement and probity, in his MS. prælections, in

---

* He laments her death, and mentions a ſon, whom he
had by her, in his Life, p. 82. and in ſeveral of his Epiſtles.
In others it appears that his name was Cimon ; that his
father ſent him to ſtudy at Athens, and that he died before
him.

which;

which, when he was profeſſor of both languages
in the univerſity of his own country, he has given
an account of the life of this ſophiſt.

The writings of Libanius * are numerous, and
he compoſed and delivered various orations, as well
demonſtrative as deliberative, and alſo many fic-
titious declamations and diſputations. Of theſe
Frederick Morell † publiſhed as many as he could
collect in two volumes, folio, in Greek and Latin. In
the 1ſt vol. Paris, 1606, are XIII. Exerciſes (*Pro-*

* The voluminous writings of Libanius ſtill exiſt; for
the moſt part they are the vain and idle compoſitions of
an orator, who cultivated the ſcience of words; the productions of a recluſe ſtudent, whoſe mind, regardleſs of his
contemporaries, was inceſſantly fixed on the Trojan war,
and the Athenian commonwealth.          GIBBON.

† The Latin tranſlation of Morell has been obſerved by
many of the learned to be often obſcure, and in numberleſs
places to have miſtaken the ſenſe of Libanius. Whoever
therefore ſhall undertake another edition of this author,
muſt new tranſlate many paſſages, eſpecially in the 11d
volume. It is ſaid, nevertheleſs, that Morell applied to
his verſion with ſuch intenſe application, as not to ſuffe.
himſelf to be interrupted by an account that his wife was
at the point of death, if we credit Iſaac Voſſius, in Colo-
meſius, p. 99. of his works: " I have heard from M.
" Voſſius, that while Frederick Morell was employed on
" Libanius, ſome one came to inform him that his wife
" was very ill:" to which he replied, " I have only three
" or four ſentences more to tranſlate, and then I will go
" and ſee her." Another coming to tell him that ſhe was
dying; " I have only two words," ſaid he, " I will be
" there as ſoon as you." At laſt, being informed that his
wife was dead, " I was very happy," he anſwered coldly,
" ſhe was an excellent woman."          FABRICIUS.

*gymnaſmata)*

*gymnasmata*) XLIV Declamations *, and 111 moral
differtations, and in the 11d vol. Paris, 1627, are
the Life † of Libanius, and xxxvi other orations,
moſt of them long and on ſerious ſubjeᶜts.

Beſides what are contained in thoſe volumes,
and his Epiſtles, ten other works of this ſophiſt
have been ſeparately publiſhed, moſt of them orations ‡, and in the *Excerpta Rhetorum* of Leo
Allatius,

---

* That his Declamations were " poſſeſſed, read, and
" thought worthy of being imitated by many," appears
from an Epiſtle of Libanius to Archelaus [xlivth of Zambicari, *l.* 1.], who, from envy, had committed ſome of them
to the flames. Eraſmus (I. 559.) has tranſlated the 1ſt of
them, the " oration of Menelaus," which Morell has
adopted *verbatim*, without acknowledgment, (I. 189.) his
name being prefixed as the tranſlator of them all.

† Libanius has compoſed the vain, prolix, but curious
narrative of his own life, of which Eunapius (p. 130—135.)
has left a conciſe and unfavourable account. Among the
moderns, Tillemont, Fabricius, and Lardner have illuſtrated the character and writings of this famous ſophiſt.
GIBBON.

‡ Of theſe, as of all the others, Fabricius has given
the titles and ſubjeᶜts. The Vth of them, " an oration
" for the Temples," that they may not be deſtroyed, to
Theodoſius the Great, 390, firſt publiſhed by Godefroi,
Geneva, 1634, 4to. is tranſlated into Engliſh by Dr. Lardner, in his Jewiſh and Heathen Teſtimonies, Vol. IV. p.
137—158, with Obſervations. The VIth, " On reveng-
" ing the death of the Emperor Julian," addreſſed to the
ſame Theodoſius, 379, was firſt publiſhed, from the Bod-
leian MS. by Olearius above-mentioned, Leipſic, 1701,
8vo. to which he afterwards added a Latin tranſlation, and
learned notes, at the deſire of Fabricius, which he publiſhed, in Bibliotheca Græca, Vol. VII. p. 145—179, with
the original, and alſo with the VIIth, " To thoſe who
" called him troubleſome," 373 ; and the VIIIth, " To
" the Antiochians, on appeaſing the reſentment of the
" Emperor"

Allatiùs, Greek and Latin, Rom. 1641, 8vo. are
xxxix Narrations, vii Defcriptions, and vii more
Exercifes of Libanius, with tranflations by Allatius. His unpublifhed works are,

1. Many hundred Epiftles * yet concealed in various libraries, a mode of writing in which it appears he excelled by the teftimony even of the
ancients, particularly Eunapius and Photius; and
of that the perufal of them will eafily convince
the intelligent reader; for they abound with Attic
wit and humour, and every where recommend
themfelves by their pointed concifenefs no lefs than
by their elegance and learning †.

2. Several

"Emperor" [Julian], 363, both for the firft time, and a
correct copy of the " funeral oration on Julian," with
tranflations of them all by the fame Olearius.

* Eleven years after Fabricius printed the above, John
Chriftopher Wolfius, his pupil, friend, and collegue, affifted
by the collections of Frederick Roftgaard, a noble Dane,
(fee p. 196.) publifhed at Hamburgh, in one volume, folio,
1738, with learned notes, MDCV Epiftles of Libanius, in
Greek and Latin, two-thirds of them collected from various
MSS. to which he added DXXII Epiftles of the fame author,
in Latin only (xc of them duplicates, being alfo in tha
Greek), tranflated from the originals, collected in Greece,
and publifhed at Cracow, about the middle of the XVth
century, by Francis Zambicari of Bologna, and republ fhed
there by John Sommerfeld, M. A. 1504. See Vol. I. p.
330, note *.

† The critics may praife their fub:le and elegant brevity;
yet Dr. Bentley (Differtation upon Phalaris, p. 487.)
might juftly, though quaintly, obferve, that " you feel by
" the emptinefs and deadnefs of them, that you convirfe
" with fome dreaming pedant, with his elbow upon his
" defk."                                    GIBBON.

2. Several Orations, as in a MS. of the Barberini library, of excellent character, moſt correctly written on vellum, from which Allatius aſſerts *, that all the publiſhed works of Libanius might alſo be given much more correct and perfect.

3. Various Declamations, in the above MS. and one in the Vatican library.

And that there are many MS Epiſtles, Orations, and Declamations of Libanius in the Imperial library [at Vienna], Neſſelius has obſerved, affirming alſo that ſeveral Greek ſcholia are frequently inſerted in the margin.

Though ſo many of the writings of this ſophiſt are preſerved, there is no doubt that many both of his Epiſtles and Orations have been loſt †.

The MDLXXIVth Epiſtle of Libanius occurs among thoſe of Phalaris, and is inſcribed to Antimathius, n. XXVII.

It is thought at preſent by almoſt all the learned, Bentlev, the prince of critics (*viro* κριτικωτατω) at their head, that theſe Epiſtles of Phalaris may juſtly be aſcribed to ſome ſophiſt. It may be worth while to conſider whether all of them perhaps were not fabricated by Libanius. I recollect, at leaſt, that in my notes I have frequently compared the phraſes and expreſſions of Phalaris with thoſe of Libanius. See, for inſtance, the notes on Ep. MCXLI.    WOLFIUS.

* *Præf. ad Excerpta Rhetorum Græcorum.*

† Of XI of theſe, mentioned by Libanius himſelf in different parts of his works, Fabricius recapitulates the titles, beſides various Counſels (συμβυλαι ‡) to the Emperor Theodoſius, mentioned in the beginning of his oration for the temples of the Heathens. And many more, which Fabricius has omitted, might be ſpecified from ſeveral of his epiſtles.

‡ Tranſlated by Dr. Lardner, " Orations, and the counſel delivered in them."

A MONODY

# A MONODY * by LIBANIUS,

## On NICOMEDIA,

## Deftroyed by an Earthquake †.

A. D.
358.

**H**OMER never fuffers even a tree to perifh
without commiferation ; but, as if he himfelf
had been the planter or gardener, when he fees it
ftretched on the ground, he fings a lamentation

---

\* A mournful fong, recited by one only on the ftage,
without a chorus, was called Mονωδια. And mention is
made of a *Monodiaria*, or of a woman who fung a monody.
WOLFIUS.

Libanius, in his XXXIft Epiftle, mentions two Monodies
which he compofed on this occafion ; one (which is now
before us) relating to the city, the other, no doubt, to
Ariftænetus, Præfect of Bithynia, who perifhed in it (fee
the next note) ; but the latter is loft. " I alfo," fays he,
(Ep. xxv.) " am one of thofe who are overwhelmed by
" that great calamity. For Ariftænetus, O Jupiter, has
" perifhed ; and, befides this, we have fuffered another
" ftroke, as fate has not fpared the head of Hierocles."
All the ancients fpeak of Nicomedia as a place of great
note : Pliny calls it " a famous and beautiful city :"
Ammianus, " the mother of all the cities of Bithynia."
In this city the Roman emperors refided, when the affairs
of the empire called them into the eaft. Conftantine the
Great chofe Nicomedia for the place of his abode after he
retired from Rome, and there remained till the buildings
that he had begun at Byzantium were finifhed. This city,
once fo famous, is now but a fmall village, known to the
Turks by the name of Schemith ‡. UNIVERSAL HISTORY,

‡ According to Pococke, Ifmir.

At

† At break of day, on the 9th of the calends of September, the sky, which before was clear, was obscured by thick
dark clouds; and the light of the sun being veiled, neither
near nor contiguous objects were discernible. Then the Supreme Deity throwing, as it were, fatal thunder-bolts, and
removing the winds from their very hinges ‡, the fury of
the storm abated; and to these hurricanes and whirlwinds
succeeded an horrible earthquake, which totally overthrew
the city and suburbs. And on account of the declivity of
the hills, some houses fell upon others, all resounding with
the dreadful crash of the ruins. Mean time the lofty roofs
re-echoed with various cries of those who were seeking their
wives and children, or dearest friends. After the second
hour, but long before the third, the sky, now fair and clear,
discovered the funereal carnage. For some, crushed by the
overwhelming force of falling rafters, perished under the
weight of them: some, buried up to the neck, though they
might have survived if they had had timely assistance, died
for want of help; others hung fixed to the tops of standing
beams; many men were killed a little before by one blow;
then were seen promiscuous slaughtered bodies; some, the
roofs of their houses falling in, were confined unhurt, victims
to anguish and famine. Among whom Aristænetus, who
governed the diocese lately desired with vicarial power, to
which Constantius, in honour of his wife, had given the
name of the Eusebian Piety ||, by this calamity, long tor-
tured, expired. Others, crushed by sudden bulky ruins,
are still covered by the same heaps. Some, who had their
sculls fractured, or had lost their arms or legs, between
life and death, imploring with earnest intreaties those who
were assisting others, were deserted. And the greater part
of the inhabitants might have survived the sacred and private buildings, had not flames, widely dispersed, for fifty
days and nights, consumed whatever was combustible.

AMMIANUS.

See also an Epistle on this subject from Libanius to Julian,
Vol. I. p. 303.

‡ *Ventosque ab ipsis excitante cardinibus.*
Not unlike to this are Milton's " winds," that
———— rush'd abroad
From the four hinges of the world.        *Par. Reg.* IV. 409.
|| After the example of the Julian Piety, a name given to Po'a in
Istria (of which see Plin. l. III. c. 19.)        LINDENBROG.

3                                     over

over it *. And can I permit Nicomedia, where I
increaſed my knowledge of the liberal arts, eſpecially eloquence, and acquired, beſides, a degree
of reputation which I had not before, to be deſtroyed, can I ſee ſuch a city, a city no longer, reduced to aſhes, unmourned, unwept? This concern I ſhare in common with the vulgar; let
her alſo participate of the oratory which ſhe
cheriſhed. As, if I had been a muſician, and had
gained many victories there in muſical conteſts,
ſhould I have ſuffered others to lament without
joining in the lamentation?

Let me now addreſs the Gods, ſuppoſing them
preſent, and thus endeavour to eſtimate our calamity.

When, ſitting in the palace of Jupiter, with the
other Gods, you, O Neptune, were enraged on
account of the wall which the Grecians had built

---

* Homer deplores the deſtruction of plants in Iliad ıx
and xvııı.                                    MORELL.
——————— a monſtrous boar,
That levell'd harveſts, and whole foreſts tore.
                                         POPE, ıx. 659.
Much more expreſſive in the originıl.
In the xvıııth I find a plant, or a tree, mentioned only
thus,
Like ſome fair olive, by my careful hand
He grew, he flouriſh'd, and adorn d the land.
                                    POPE, 175 and 512.
If Libanius had been acquainted with the Pſalmiſt, and
unprejudiced by Paganiſm, he could not have overlooked
that beautiful alluſion of the " vine brought out of
" Ægypt," and the complaint of its being " rooted up,
" burnt, and cut down." Pſ. LXXX. 8—16.

Q 3                                            at

at Troy to cover their ſhips, was not their negleĉt
of the Gods, when they laid the foundation, the
principal ſubjeĉt of your complaint * ? And therefore, when Troy was taken, you judged right in
thinking it neceſſary to deſtroy that wall; which
you eaſily accompliſhed by turning againſt it the
rivers that ruſhed from Ida †. But in the foundation of this city what was the offence that induced you to treat it in the ſame manner ? Did not
its firſt founder ‡, deſigning to build a city on the
ſhore

* Hom. Il. VII. 450.
See the long walls extending to the main,
No God conſulted, and no viĉtim ſlain, &c. POPE, 535.
† Ibid. XII. 17.
Then Neptune and Apollo ſhook the ſhore,
Then Ida's ſummits pour'd their watery ſtore ;
Rheſus and Rhodius then unite their rills, &c.
.   .   .   .   .   .   .
Theſe, turn'd by Phœbus from their wonted ways,
Delug'd the rampire nine continual days ;
The weight of waters ſaps the yielding wall,
And to the ſea the floating bulwarks fall.
Inceſſant cataraĉts the Thunderer pours,
And half the ſkies deſcend in ſluicy ſhowers, &c.
POPE, 15.
This is a noble paſſage in the old bard; ſtorm, inunda-
tion, and earthquake magnificently combined.      B.
Milton alludes to it in his viſion of the Deluge, b. XI.
————— ————— Then ſhall this mount
Of Paradiſe, by might of waves, be mov'd
Out of his place, puſh'd by the horned flood,
With all his verdure ſpoil'd, and trees adrift,
Down the great river to the opening gulf,
And there take root, an iſland ſalt and bare,
The haunt of ſeals, and orcs, and ſea-mews' clang. 829.
‡ Nicomedia is ſaid to have been firſt built by Olbia,
and had its firſt name from him. It was afterwards re-built

ſhore oppoſite to that where it now ſtands, or rather
where it once ſtood, begin his work from you?
Were not the altars covered with victims, and ſurrounded by a crowd of worſhippers? But by an
eagle and a prodigious ſnake you diverted their attention to the hill; of theſe, the former with her
talons ſnatched the head of the victim from the fire;
and the latter, large and reſembling thoſe which
are bred in India, iſſued from the earth. The one
cleaving the ſea, and the other the air, repaired to
the brow of the hill. The people followed, led,
as they thought, by the guidance of the Gods.
Theſe omens were all deceitful. The city was at
firſt overwhelmed by the torrent of war *. Be it
ſo. Your own Corinth † alſo, and the land of

by Nicomedes I. king of Bithynia, though Olbia ſeems
rather to have been near it, and that the inhabitants of it
were tranſplanted to this place. POCOCKE.

Nicomedia, Aſtacus, and Olbia are ſpoken of by
Ptolemy as three neighbouring but diſtinct cities. Strabo
writes that Nicomedes, the ſon and ſucceſſor of Zipœtes, deſtroyed Aſtacus, and transferred its inhabitants to Nicomedia.
UNIVERSAL HISTORY.

* This muſt probably have been in the reign of Nicomedes III. who was twice driven from his throne by Mithridates the Great, king of Pontus.

† Among other names which Corinth anciently had we
find that of Heliopolis, or city of the ſun, for which this
reaſon is commonly given; that the poets feign Apollo and
Neptune to have contended for it, and that Jupiter having
appointed Briareus, the Cyclop, their umpire, he adjudged
the Iſthmus to the latter, and the Promontory, which commands the city, to the former. UNIVERSAL HISTORY.

Q 4 Cecrops,

Cecrops *, your beſt beloved, have experienced
the ſame fate †. Another founder came, who,
making the Gods his principal leaders, and, by the
ſuperior magnitude of his offering, rendering your
minds more propitious, reſtored the city. How
then, like the land of Ætolia, for the offence of
Œneus ‡, did ſhe deſerve to be puniſhed with contempt? Is it right, has it been uſual, for the Gods
to deſtroy with their own hands works like theſe,
in which they have co-operated with mortals, and
to imitate the paſtime of children, who are accuſtomed to pull down what they have erected § ?
Or did it become you, O Neptune, to enter into a
conteſt with your niece for an Attic city not then
in being, and to overflow a citadel ſo diſtant from

* An Ægyptian fugitive, who introduced religion into
Greece, and founded the Athenian monarchy. See note *
p 233.

† Corinth was ſurpriſed by Antigonus and Aratus, taken
and burnt by the Romans, &c. Athens was deſtroyed by
Mardonius, taken by the Lacedæmonians and Sylla, &c.

‡ Oeneus, king of Ætolia, or Calydon (its chief city)
ſacrificing to the reſt of the deities, neglected his duty to
Diana, who in conſequence ſent a wild boar to ravage and
deſtroy the country, which was killed by his ſon Meleager,
and his company. See Hom. Il. IX. 530.

§ Thus Tibullus, ——— _puer è virgis extruet arte caſas._
                            l. II. el. I.
And Horace of a boy, ——— _amata relinquere pernix._
                                 MORELL.
Libanius had here, no doubt, in his view that paſſage in
the Iliad to which Julian alſo refers in his XLth Epiſtle.
See p. 166.

the fea \*, yet to difplay no regard for fuch a great
and important city as this, but even to fubvert it
from the foundations? What city was more beautiful? I will not fay larger, for in fize it was exceeded by four †, but contemned all that increafe
of extent, which would have wearied the feet of
its citizens ‡. In beauty alfo it yielded to thefe,
and was equalled, not excelled, by fome others :
for, ftretching forth its promontories, with its arms

\* Cecrops not knowing what name to give to his new-
built city, an olive-tree, and a fountain of water (or, as
others fay, a horfe) appeared. The oracle, being confulted,
anfwered, that " Neptune and Minerva were contending
" for the honour of naming it, that the olive was the gift
" of Minerva, and the fountain (or horfe) that of Nep-
" tune ; and that that which they efteemed moft benefi-
" cial to mankind fhould adjudge the prize to the giver."
The men and women being affembled to give their judgement, the former gave it for the God ; but the women,
who were more numerous, gave it for the Goddefs ; and
the city was named from her *Athena*. Neptune, in revenge
of the affront, overflowed their territories. APOLLODORUS.

Here we have an account of the Poθιος mentioned by Libanius, which Morell has rendered *Procella*, though it
fignifies properly " the violence and force of water, a billow
" of the fea :" as, in the poem on Hero and Leander, the
poet fays, he ftood on the fhore,

Μαινομενων ροθιων πολυηχια βομβον ακωω·

where βομβος excellently expreffes the heavy found occafioned
by the fall of the waves.                                                   B.

† Rome, Byzantium, Antioch, and Alexandria.

‡ Τοσυτον αλιμασασε τε μιγιθυς, οσον εμιλλι λυπεσιν των οικη-
λορων τες ποδας. This is an odd paffage, and feems to me a
puerile conceit, Morell's marginal reading, ισ. παιδας (for
ποδας) is pleafant enough. I wonder he fhould think any
alteration neceffary, as he underftood the true fenfe of the
place ; for men may be fatigued as well as children. I have
no doubt that he was a great walker.                          B.

it

it embraced the fea. It then afcended the hill
by four colonnades extending the whole length.
Its public buildings were fplendid, its private
contiguous, rifing from the loweft parts to the
citadel, like the branches of a cyprefs, one houfe
above another, watered by rivulets, and furrounded
with gardens *. Its council-chambers, its fchools
of oratory, the multitude of its temples, the
magnificence of its baths, and the commodi-
oufnefs of its harbour I have feen, but cannot
defcribe. This only I can fay, that, frequently
travelling thither from Nice †, we ufed on the
road to difcourfe on the trees, and the foil, abundant in all productions, and alfo of our families,
our friends, and ancient wifdom. But after we had
paffed through the intricate windings of the hills,
when the city appeared, at the diftance of a hundred and fifty ftadia ‡, on all other fubjects a profound filence inftantly enfued, and, no longer engaged either by the towering branches of the
gardens, or by the fruitfulnefs of the foil, or by

---

* In like manner, Dr. Pococke defcribes the prefent town
as " fituated at the foot of two hills, and all up the fouth
" fide of the weftern one, which is very high, and on part
" of the other : it is near the N. E. corner of the bay. All
" the houfes have fmall gardens, or courts, to them, efpe-
" cially thofe on the hills. The gardens are planted with
" trees §, and the vines, being carried along on frames built
" like roofs, make the city appear exceedingly beautiful.
" There are very few remains of the ancient Nicomedia."
    † Thirty-two miles.                                        Pococke.
    ‡ About nineteen miles.

    § Κητοι αιωρυμινοι τοις κλαδοις are the words of Libanius.

the

the traffic of the fea, our whole converfation turned on Nicomedia. And yet mariners, or thofe who labour at the oar, and enfnare the fifh with nets, or hooks, naturally attract the obfervation of travellers. But the form of the city, much more fafcinating, by its beauty tyrannifed over our eyes, and fixed their whole attention on-itfelf. Similar were the fenfations of him who had never feen it before, and of him who had grown old within its walls. One fhewed to his companion the palace, glittering over the bay ; another the theatre embellifhing the whole city ; others various other rays darted from various objects: which furpaffed it was difficult to determine. Revering it as a facred image, we proceeded ; in our way to Chalcedon, it was neceffary to turn, till the nature of the road deprived us of the fight *. This feemed like the ceffation of a feaft.

A city fo great, fo renowned, ought not the whole choir of the Gods to have furrounded and protected, exhorting each other to decree that it fhould never be fubjected to any calamity ? But now fome of you have deceived, others have deferted, and none affifted her. And all thefe particulars, which I have mentioned, once were, but remain no longer. What a beautiful lock has For-

* He firft mentions the pleafure arifing from the profpect of the city, as they approached ; and then their concern at lofing fight of it, as they proceeded from it to Chalcedon. B.

tune

tune now fevered from the world *! How has fhe
blinded the other continent by thus bereaving it of
its illuftrious eye! What a deplorable deformity
has fhe diffufed over Afia ; as if her moft fpacious
grove had been felled, as if her moft confpicuous
feature + had been lopped off! O moft injurious
earthquake, why didft thou perpetrate this? O departed city! O name of it in vain remaining! O
grief difperfed over land and fea! O dire intelligence, diftrefsful to the hearts of all ranks, of all
ages! for what heart is fo ftony, what heart is fo
adamantine, as not to be wounded by this relation?
who is fo deftitute of tears as now to with-hold
them? O dreadful misfortune, which has reduced
the innumerable ornaments of the city to one
ruinous heap! O unpropitious ray ‡, what a city
didft

* Thus Pindar ftyles Ætna " the front," or forehead,
" of the fruitful earth," ευκαρποιο γαιας μιλωπον, Pyth. I.
and Nicomedia was a beautiful city " high-mounted on a
" hill," as Sandys fays of fome other. I am afraid the hill
of Nicomedia hardly deferved the name μιλωπον γαιας; but
a panegyrift may make mountains of molehills.         B.

† Βορρυχος, οφθαλμος, what next? αλσος, ριν (" The lock,
" the eye, the grove, the nofe.") In the name of propriety, what has αλσος to do here? Are we to underftand it
of the hair of the head?          B.

  This idea feems anticipated by βορρυχος. The metaphor
indeed feems here loft, " a grove," or " wood," being no
feature, like the others. Pw. feemed in Englifh to require a circumlocution.

‡ Ω δυςυχης ακλινος, οιαν μεν προσιβαλλι την πολιν ανασχυσα·
οιαν δι αφηισα καλιδυ. Morell tranflates ακλινος tridentis radius.
But why fhould it not mean (as ufual) the " fun's ray?"
Ανιχω and κατακδυνω are ufed for the " rifing and fetting of the
fun."

didſt thou ſmite at thy riſing, what a city ſunk with
thee! The day had almoſt advanced to noon *;
the tutelar deities of the city abandoned the
temples, and ſhe was left like a ſhip deſerted by
its crew. The lord of the trident ſhook the earth,
and convulſed the ocean; the foundations of the
city were diſunited; walls were thrown on walls,
pillars on pillars, and roofs fell headlong. What
was hidden was revealed, and what had appeared
was hidden. Statues, perfeƈt in beauty, and complete
in every part, were blended by the concuſſion in one
confuſed maſs. Artificers, working at their trades,
were daſhed out of their ſhops and houſes. In
the harbour was much deſtruƈtion, and alſo of
many worthy choſen men colleƈted about the Præ-
feƈt †. The theatre involved in its ruins all who

fun." I do not recolleƈt that αϰῖιν is uſed abſolutely, as
here, for the " prong of the trident." The trident too
is thruſt under the foundation. See the beginning of the
Phœniſſæ of Euripides, where Jocaſta, addreſſing the Sun,
complains of his darting an " unpropitious ray" on Thebes.
Ἥλιε, θοαῖς ἱπποισιν, ϰ. τ. λ.
  O thou, that glorying in thy fiery ſteeds,
  Rolleſt the orient light, reſplendent Sun,
  How inauſpicious didſt thou dart thy beams
  That day on Thebes, &c. POTTER. Poſſibly Libanius may allude to it.    B.
 * Μικρον μιν απιιχιν ημερα πιρι πληθεσαι αγοραχ ωχι.
Literally, " it was near high market." But Ammianus
ſays, that it happened at break of day; and George Ce-
drenus, in the night.
 † Ariſtænetus, the great friend and patron of Libanius,
who, in ſeveral of his epiſtles to him, celebrates his eloquence and ſweetneſs of manners. See p. 227. note *. He
was afterwards buried at Nice, of which he was a native.

were

were in it. Some buildings, which had long ftood
tottering, and others which had yet efcaped, with
all who were in them, fhared at laft the general
fate. The fea, violently agitated, deluged the
land. Fire, which abounded every where, feizing
the rafters, added to the concuffion a confla-
gration * ; and fome wind, it is faid, fanned the
flames. Much of the city, much of the ramparts,
ftill remains. Of thofe who have efcaped, a few
ftill wander about wounded.

O all-feeing Sun, what were thy fenfations on
feeing this? Why didft not thou prevent fuch a
city from leaving the earth? For the oxen pro-
faned by the famifhed mariners † fuch was thy
refentment as to threaten the celeftial powers that
thou wouldft give thyfelf up to Pluto ‡ ; but for
the glory of the earth, for the labour of many
kings, for the fruit of prodigious coft, deftroyed
in the day-time, thou haft no compaffion.

O faireft of cities, on what a faithlefs and fro-
ward hill didft thou fix thy feat ; which, like a
vicious horfe, has difmounted its excellent rider?
Where are now thy winding walks? where are thy

---

* Thus at Lifbon, Meffina, and in all great earthquakes,
fire has been their conftant attendant.

† Hom. Odyff. xii. Libanius has before taken Neptune to tafk ; he here reprimands Apollo.

‡ Alluding to what Apollo fays on that occafion in the
fame book of the Odyffey.
  " Vengeance, ye Gods, or I the fkies forego,
  " And bear the lamp of heaven to fhades below."
                                        POPE, 450.

porticoes? where are thy courfes, thy fountains, thy courts of judicature, thy libraries, thy temples? Where is all that profufion of wealth? Where are the young, the old? Where are the baths of the Graces and of the Nymphs? of which the largeft, named after the prince, at whofe expence it was built, was equal in value to the whole city *. Where is now the fenate? Where are the people? where the women? the children? where is the palace? where is the circus †, ftronger than the walls of Babylon ‡? Nothing is left ftanding; nothing has efcaped; all are involved in one common ruin.

O numerous ftreams, where now do you flow? what manfions do you lave? from what fprings do you iffue? The various aqueducts and refervoirs are broken. The plentiful fupply of the fountains runs to wafte, either forming whirlpools, or ftagnating in moraffes; but drawn or quaffed by no one, neither by men nor birds. Thefe are terrified

---

* As Diocletian, according to Lactantius, embellifhed Nicomedia with a great number of ftately buildings, with a defign of equalling it to Rome, poffibly thefe baths might be part of them, and named after him, as we know his baths, now magnificent in ruins, were at Rome; which, fays Ammianus, with no fmall exaggeration, " feemed rather a " province than a building."

† He [Diocletian] built there feveral bafilics, a circus, a mint, an arfenal, a palace for his wife, and another for his fon.      Lactantius.

‡ The walls of Babylon were fo celebrated among the ancients as to grow proverbial. Libanius mentions them in like manner in his cxcvith Epiftle.

by

by the fire which rages every where below, and, where it has a vent, flames into the air. This city, once so populous, now in the day time is deserted and desolate, but at night is possessed by such a multitude of spectres, as I think must crowd the inhabitants of the infernal regions after they have passed Acheron.

Celebrated of old were the disasters of Lemnos [*], and the Iliad sings the woes of Troy. Their remembrance will be slighted, but the excess of our calamities any one may hence determine. Former earthquakes, though they destroyed some parts of the city, spared others; but this has overwhelmed the whole. Other cities have also perished, but never one of such a magnitude. If it had been deprived only of bodies infected with the plague, or of those persons who, contrary to the laws [†], were celebrating

brating

---

[*] Great misfortunes were proverbially styled " Lemnian ;" some say, from the slaughter of the Attic women, and the children which they had by them, by the Pelagians, who inhabited Lemnos ; others, from the murder of their husbands, on account of their offensive breath, by the Lemnian women. See Ludolph Kuster on Suidas, tom. II. p. 441. Bayle's Dictionary, vol. II. p. 1780. and Erasmus, in his Chileades. WOLFIUS.

Libanius, in his xxivth Epistle, thus alludes to this passage; " I said little when I expressed the ruin of Nicomedia by the misfortunes of Lemnos."

[†] Κατα νομον. It seems a little hard that people should be destroyed for sacrificing " according to law ;" yet κατα νομον is certainly " according to law." Let us suppose an error of the press, and make it νομω. He alludes to some event, which I do not recollect. I suspect that he has taken a line from some Greek poet, and accommodated it to his purpose. B.

Though

brating a general facrifice without the city, and had not itfelf fallen, the ftroke might have been fupportable. The whole would not have been defolated; now both lie proftrate, and the form of the city is confufed with the flaughter of the citizens.

Lament therefore, every ifland and every continent, peafants and mariners, cities, villages, cottages, every thing that is connected with human nature; and let tears prevail over all the world, as in Ægypt whenever Apis dies *. Even rocks fhould now be indulged with tears, and birds with reafon, to join in an elegiac fong. O harbour, which fhips now carefully avoiding, rather fteer into the ocean, their cables flipped, which formerly wert filled with loaded veffels, but now cannot boaft even a pleafure-boat, and art more dreaded by mariners than even the manfion of Scylla! O difappointment to travellers, who no longer frequent the road, which, gloomy and in the form of a crefcent, beautifully winded round the dykes f the haven, but embarking fail to-

---

Though Libanius, like Julian, was probably acquainted with the Mofaic hiftory, I will not affirm that he here alludes to it; but certain it is, that this paffage has no diftant affinity to the earthquake that fwallowed up Korah and his company, for offering unhallowed incenfe, and to the plague that deftroyed their abettors. *Numbers* xvi.

* When Apis dies, they behave as if they had loft their deareft children, and bury him in the moft fumptuous manner. Nor do the people ceafe from lamenting till the priefts have found a calf with the fame marks.

DIODORUS SICULUS.

wards the hill, to which they formerly haftened [by land], trembling as at Charybdis, and unable to conjecture in what part of the sea they used to stand on the shore! O deareft of cities! in your ruin you have involved your inhabitants; you have deftroyed them by your fall; fo that all mankind apply themfelves to fupplications, thinking the extinction of their whole race determined. After the lofs of this moft valuable poffeffion, nothing hereafter, they apprehend, will be fpared. Who will fupply me with wings to waft me thither? Who will place me on an eminence to view the diftrefsful fight? For a lover has fome confolation in being furrounded by the objects of his affection, though in ruins *.

* For the notes on this and the following Monody, marked B, I am obliged to a learned and amiable friend.

# A MONODY by LIBANIUS,

ON THE

Daphnæan Temple of Apollo, deftroyed by
Fire, or, as it is faid, by Lightning *.

FELLOW-citizens, whofe eyes, like mine, are
now involved in darknefs †, this city we fhall
no longer ftyle beautiful or great ‡.

A. D.
362.

---

\* The Greek title of this Monody is more perfect in the
Royal MS. which I have followed, than in the Bavarian;
in which it is only ftyled, " A Monody on the Daphnæan
" Temple of Apollo." But the corollary, which is added
to the infcription here adopted, does not give the fentiments of Libanius, who had conceived an idea, that fome
incendiary by a fmall fpark had kindled this great confla-
gration, as he fays, in the beginning; and foon after, that
he may obviate the opinion of thunder from heaven, he
adds, that " it happened in a clear and cloudlefs fky;"
which to the orthodox increafes the miracle, of which St.
John Chryfoftom, the contemporary of our Libanius, in his
1ft Difcourfe on the Martyr St. Babylas, p. 725. " As
" foon as the bier was brought to the city, lightning
" fell from heaven on the head of the image, and con-
" fumed every thing." And the Emperor Julian too was
well aware of this; " he knew that the blow came from
" heaven;" though he afferts, in the Mifopogon, that " the
" temple was deftroyed by the negligence of the keepers,
" and the prefumption of the impious." MORELL.
After the interment of St. Babylas, Apollo gave oracles
as before; and Julian caufed a fuperb colonnade to be built
round his temple. But in the night of the 22d of October,
362, a fire confumed the wood work of that ancient edi-
fice, and the ftatue itfelf; nor could Julian, who haftened

to the place, fupply any remedy. That fire was afcribed
by the Chriftians to the divine vengeance, and by Julian to
the refentment and jealoufy of the Chriftians. He fufpected
the facrift, and the minifters who kept the temple, of being
in a confederacy with them. But thofe idolaters, being put
to the torture, accufed no one. On the contrary, they
conftantly affirmed, that the fire began from above; and
fome peafants, who were that night on the road in their
way to the city, faid, they faw fire from heaven fall on the
temple, though the weather was very calm, and there was
no appearance of a ftorm. Julian, however, either by way
of reprifal, or to prevent the Chriftians from triumphing,
ordered the great church of Antioch to be fhut, and its
riches to be carried to the imperial treafury.

LA BLETERIE.

See alfo Vol. I. p. 247, 248.

† What darknefs hangs over the eyes of the Antiochians ?
Is it the darknefs of a cloud, which
   With mifts and films involves their mortal fight ?
Such as the Pallas of Homer boafts to have removed from
Diomed, and the Venus of Virgil from Æneas ? Or is it the
gloom of forrow, which, hanging over the eyes of the
mind, obfcures the ufe of reafon and thought ?  MORELL.

‡ On the beauty and extent of Antioch, fee Philoftratus
on the Life of Apollonius, l. I. c. xii. p. 21.  " Apollonius
" came to Antioch the Great," &c. and our Libanius, in
his oration to Theodofius the Great, on the fedition, in behalf of the Antiochians, where, in the conclufion on the mif-
fortunes of that city, he adds, as here, " our city is be-
" come different, or, to fpeak more truly, it is no longer
" a city." Aufonius celebrates it among the famous cities,
   *Tertia Phœbeæ lauri domus Antiochia.*
   With the Phœbëan laurel grac'd, the third
   Is Antioch.
After the firft fentence, Chryfoftom in the fame place
declares, that Libanius added fomething of the fable of
Daphne, and perhaps it was the fable which Philoftratus,
in the above mentioned paffage, calls " Arcadian," and
explains as follows : " He entered the fane of Daph-
" nœan Apollo, to which the Affyrians afcribe the Ar-
" cadian fable. For they fay, that Daphne, the daugh-
" ter of Ladon, was there transformed; and the river
" Ladon flows among them, and the laurel-tree is ho-
" noured by them, on account of that virgin."  *Ibid.*

. . . [A king

··· [A king of Perſia, one of the anceſtors of him who is now at war with us, having by treachery taken and burnt the city, as he was preparing the ſame fate for Daphne, was ſo thoroughly diverted from his purpoſe by the Deity, that, throwing away the torch which he brandiſhed, he proſtrated himſelf, and adored Apollo : ſo appeaſed was his reſentment, ſo checked was his fury \*.] He, though he led an army againſt us, thought proper to preſerve this temple, and the beauty of the image reſtrained his barbaric fury, But now, O heaven and earth, who and whence is that traitor, who wanting neither light † nor heavy-armed foot ‡, nor

---

\* This I have not publiſhed in the Greek, becauſe it was not in our Royal and Bavarian MS. And John Chryſoſtom himſelf, though he did not inſert it in its proper place, hurried away by the eddy of his diſcourſe, yet afterwards pays it as a debt, or brings it back as a fugitive, with this introduction, " You read this in the beginning of the " Monody, " A king of Perſia," &c. [as above]. But who was this king of Perſia, unleſs it were Sapor, the ſecond king, who, according to Zoſimus, ſucceeded Artaxerxes the firſt king ? The ſame took Antioch, and held it till the Emperor Gordian, having defeated the Perſians in ſeveral battles, diſpoſſeſſed king Sapor, and recovered Antioch, with Carrhæ and Niſibis, all which were under the Perſian dominion, as Julius Capitolinus relates in his Gordian.

MORELL.

† The light-armed foot of the Greeks fought with arrows, darts, and ſlings ; and were placed either in the van to begin an engagement, or on the flank of the wings to gall the enemies cavalry, and prevent their breaking in.

‡ The heavy-armed ſoldiers engaged with long ſpears, broad ſhields, and cutting ſwords. The Grecian cavalry was not very numerous.

R 3                                        horſe,

horfe, has confumed the whole with a fmall fpark ? Nor was our temple deftroyed by a violent ftorm, but in a ferene and cloudlefs fky. Hitherto, Apollo, your altars thirfting for blood, you have remained the conftant and careful guardian of Daphne; and though neglected, and fo far contemned as to be ftripped of your outward ornaments, you acquiefced. But now, when many fheep, many oxen, have been offered to you; when the facred lips of an Emperor * have impreffed your feet; feen by him whom you have exalted, feeing him whom you have proclaimed, and delivered from the hateful neighbourhood of a certain dead body †, which difturbed you, you have withdrawn from the midft of your worfhip.

How can we now expect to be honoured, in future, by thofe who have a veneration for temples and images ! When fatigued in our minds, of what a relief, O Jupiter, are we deprived ! How pure, how free from all tumults, was the region of Daphne ! how much ftill purer was the fhrine ! like a haven formed by nature within a haven; both being tranquil, but the inner affording the moft tranquillity. Who did not there lofe his difeafes, his fears, his forrows ? Who there wifhed

* Julian. The Pagans ufed religioufly to kifs the images of their Gods, if they could, and putting their hands to their mouths, they wafted kiffes to them at a diftance. From this cuftom fome derive the word *adoro*. Thus Job, XXXI. 27. *If my mouth hath kiffed my hand*, &c. WOLFIUS.

† The remains of Babylas. See the Mifopogon, Vol. I. P. 247.

for

for the ifland of the blefled? Ere long will be the
Olympic games *; that annual feftival will convene
the cities; thefe cities too will come, bringing oxen
as victims to Apollo. What then fhall we do?
Where fhall we fecrete ourfelves? Which of the
Gods will open the earth for us? What herald,
what trumpet, but will excite tears? Who now will
ftyle the Olympic games a feftival, as this late mif-
fortune fuggefts fo dire a lamentation?

Bring me my bow of horn †,

fays the tragedy. I add, a little in the fpirit of
prophecy,

That thus I may attack, and thus deftroy,

The vile incendiary.

O impious deed! O facrilegious foul! O daring
hand! Surely this was another Tityus ‡, or Idas §,

* Of Antioch. In the adjacent fields a ftadium was
built by a fpecial privilege, which had been purchafed from
Elis; the Olympic games were regularly celebrated at the
expence of the city; and a revenue of thirty thoufand
pounds fterling was annually applied to the public pleafures.
                                                      GIBBON.

In three of his Epiftles Libanius urges three of his
friends to fupply thefe games with wreftlers; and in his
Life, pp. 59 and 68, he mentions two orations which he
compofed on that folemnity, which are not now extant.
A third is in his works, Vol. II. p. 538.

† Δος τοξα μοι κερουλκα. Euripides in Orefte, 268.

‡ Struck by Jupiter with a thunderbolt, for attempting
to ravifh Latona. See Odyff. XI. 575. and Æn. VI. 595.

§ — matchlefs Idas, more than man in war.
   The God of day ador'd the mother's charms,
   Againft the God the father bent his arms.
                                   POPE, Il. IX. 672.

Let us not imitate that daring Idas, who bent his bow,
it is faid, againft the God; for this is waging war with
Apollo.                                        LIBANIUS.

R 4                                              the

# A MONODY BY LIBANIUS,

the brother of Lynceus, not an archer, indeed, like
the one, or a giant, like the other, but a proficient in
nothing fave frenzy towards the Gods. The fons of
Aloëus *, while they meditated mifchief againft the
Gods, you, Apollo, quieted by death; but him, bringing fire from afar, your arrow did not arreft, tranf-
fixing his heart. O wicked hand of Telchin † !
O injurious fire ! What did it firft catch ? Where
did the evil begin ? Seizing the roof, did it defcend
to the inferior parts, to the head, the face, the cup ‡,
the tiara, or the flowing robe ? Vulcan, the dif-

* Othus and Ephialtes, who being of a gigantic ftature,
and threatening to make war againft the Gods, were tranf-
fixed and flain by the darts of Apollo and Diana. See
Æn. vi. 582.

† The Telchines, who inhabited Rhodes, were the inven-
tors of feveral arts and other things beneficial to mankind.
They are alfo faid firft to have made images of the Gods,
and fome of the ancient ftatues were furnamed from them.
Thus among the Lindians Apollo was called Telchinius.
Juno was alfo ftyled Telchinia. . . They were called en-
chanters; and were faid to produce, when they pleafed,
clouds and rain, and to generate hail, and to be invidious
in teaching their arts.           DIODORUS SICULUS.
Thus it appears that the Telchinians were a people of
great ingenuity, by which they got a bad name, like our
Roger Bacon, and the German Fauftus, who is fuppofed at
this very day to have dealt with the Devil; fo that this
exclamation, Ω δεξιας Τελχινος, ftanding in immediate con-
nection with the preceding fentence, Telchin here muft be
Apollo. And perhaps he means to give Apollo a rap here,
as he did Neptune [and Apollo too] in the other Monody. B.
    ‡ The coloffal figure of the deity almoft filled the ca-
pacious fanctuary. He was reprefented in a bending atti-
tude, with a golden cup in his hand, pouring out a libation
on the earth; as if he fupplicated the venerable mother to
give to his arms the cold and beauteous Daphne. GIBBON.

penfer of fire, though indebted to the God for his
former obliging difcovery *, did not rebuke this
wafting flame.   Nor did Jupiter, who has the
command of rain, pour water on it, though for the
unfortunate king of Lydia he extinguifhed the funeral pile †.

What was the firft fuggeftion of him who
undertook this enterprife? whence this rafhnefs?
how could he retain his fury? how could he avoid
abandoning his purpofe through reverence for his
beauty of the God? My fancy, O my countrymen,
prefents me with the form of the God, and fets
before my eyes his image, the complacency of the
afpeft, the tendernefs of the fkin expreffed in the
marble, the fafh over his breaft confining the golden
robe, fo that fome parts of it fubfided, and others
rofe.  What mind had fuch fervour that the whole
appearance of the ftatue could not calm? For the
God feemed in the aft of finging; or as when he
was once heard playing on his harp at noon.   The
fong was in praife of the Earth, on whom, gaping
to receive the virgin, and then contracting to con-

* Alluding to that paffage of Homer, Odyffey VIII,
where, in the loves of Mars and Venus, fung by Demodocus,
　　Warn'd by the God who fhed the golden day,
　　Stern Vulcan homeward treads the ftarry way,
　　　　　　　　　　　　　　　BROOME.

† Crœfus, being placed by Cyrus on a funeral pile,
praying to Apollo was faved by a fhower of rain, which
extinguifhed the flames,  See Herodotus, I. 87.  Julian
afcribes this miracle to Jupiter.

ceal

ceal her, he feemed to pour a libation from the golden cup.

At the eruption of flames the traveller exclaimed; the guardian of Daphne, the domeftic prieftefs of the God, was alarmed; the beating of bofoms, and fhrill fhrieks, echoing through the fpacious groves, foon reached the city, diffufing univerfal grief and horror. The prince *, whofe eye had fcarce yet yielded to fleep, at the dreadful intelligence fprung from his bed. Tranfported with fury, and wifhing for the wings of Mercury, he rufhed forth to inveftigate the caufe. Inwardly he burnt no lefs than the temple. The rafters now fell, fcattering the fire below, which deftroyed all that was within its reach; [the ftatue of] Apollo immediately, being near to the roof; then other ornaments of the temple, the Mufes, the ftatues of the founders, the fplendid marbles, the beautiful pillars. Crowds of fpectators ftood by lamenting, but unable to affift, like thofe, who from land beholding a fhipwreck, can afford no relief but their tears. The Nymphs, leaving their fountains, loudly exclaimed; fo did Jupiter, who fat not far diftant, lamenting, as became him, the tarnifhed honours of his fon; fo did alfo an innumerable throng of Dæmons who inhabit the foreft. Nor lefs was the lamentation of Calliope, in the middle of the

* Julian.

city,

city *, when the high-prieft of the Mufes was injured by the flames * * * * †.

As propitious may'ft thou now be to me, Apollo, as Chryfes rendered thee, when he imprecated vengeance on the Greeks, full of indignation, and " dark as night ‡." Since while we were offering facrifices to thee, and were reftoring whatever had been purloined from thy temple, the object of our worfhip has been fnatched away from us; like a bridegroom, who, while the garlands are weaving for his nuptials, dies.

* I have an idea that there was a ftatue of Calliope in the middle of Antioch, to which Libanius here alludes; and alfo in one of his Epiftles. See Vol. I. p. 324. And from a paffage in his DCCXXXVIIth Epiftle, to Rufinus, it feems to have been erected to that chief of the Mufes by the great-great-grandfather of that friend.

† Something here is wanting.

‡ Νυκτὶ ἐοικώα. Hom. Il. I. 47.
Breathing revenge, a fudden night he fpread.    POPE 65.

THE

# H I S T O R Y

OF THE

# EMPEROR JOVIAN.

From the French

Of the Abbé de la BLETERIE.

————— *Infelix brevitate regendi.*

THE

# AUTHOR's PREFACE.

AS the empire and religion are at the death of
Julian in a kind of crifis which interefts the
curiofity of the reader, the Life of that prince
would remain in fome degree imperfect, if the
Hiftory of Jovian were not annexed to it. Though
he reigned only a few months, and though, in our
age, when fingularity alone may fupply the place
of merit, his character may be lefs interefting than
that of his predeceffor, I may venture to fay, that
his hiftory prefents fome memorable facts, and
fuggefts more reflections than the long reigns of
many other fovereigns.

It is characterifed by two remarkable events,
one good, the other bad : I mean the re-eftablifhment of Chriftianity, which is feen to re-afcend
the throne of the Cæfars never again to leave it;
and that fatal treaty of peace, which announces
and begins the fall of the Roman greatnefs. It is
thus that *he who dwelleth in the heavens laughs* at
the defigns of his enemies. Julian flattered himfelf with reftoring his empire to its ancient fplendor.

6 He

He had, or feemed to have, moft of the talents neceffary for the execution of this plan ; yet the imprudence of Julian muft have been the caufe, or, at leaft, the occafion, of the ruin of the empire. Julian made no doubt of fuppreffing the Chriftian religion : but Providence had decreed that he fhould be the laft Pagan Emperor. The war which he waged with Sapor was preparatory to that which he meditated againft us [the Gauls]. He thought that the conqueft of Perfia would give him fufficient leifure and authority to complete by force of arms the work which his cunning and his artifices had only fketched ; yet it was really that war which preferved the Chriftians from the other which he was preparing againft them ; it was that war which took him out of the world; and gave the Romans an Emperor who was zealous enough to make Chriftianity triumph by means worthy, of the true religion.

Hitherto the reign of Jovian has remained loft; as it were, in general hiftory. I fhall be thanked, perhaps; for fnatching it from oblivion. I have treated it with all the care of which I am capable, and I dare not fay how much it has coft me. Hiftory is not a compilation of facts collected at random, a brilliant collection of pretty thoughts, a tiffue of learned differtations. It is neither a pa- negyric, nor a fatire; it ought to be an impartial and difinterefted narration, fimple and natural, though fentimental, always eafy in its ftyle, even

2                                                       when

when it offers the refult of many refearches and
difcuffions. It ought, if I may fo fay, to render
the reader contemporary with the events, to inftruct without fatiguing him, to enlighten without
dazzling him, to make him think, and to give him
the pleafure of believing that he thinks for himfelf,
not faying every thing, and leaving nothing to be
wifhed, allowing neither too much nor too little to
conjecture, and removing apparent contradictions
by lucky difcoveries; in a word, it fhould fupply
the place of original authors to thofe who have it
not in their power to read them, and enable thofe,
who can confult them, to read them with more
pleafure and emolument. I have endeavoured to
write in this manner the Hiftory of Jovian. I do
not flatter myfelf with having fucceeded; happy
if connoiffeurs find fome marks of refemblance
between the execution and the idea.

# HISTORY

## OF THE

## EMPEROR JOVIAN.

IT may be feen, in the Life of Julian, that that
prince, after paffing the Tigris above Ctefiphon,
by an extravagance which even fuccefs could not
excufe, burned his fleet and provifions *. He was
defirous

*. He deftroyed, in a fingle hour, the whole navy, which
had been tranfported above five hundred miles, at fo great
an expence of toil, of treafure, and of blood. Twelve, or,
at the moft, twenty-two fmall veffels were faved, to accompany on carriages the march of the army, and to form oc-
cafional bridges for the paffage of the rivers. A fupply of
twenty days provifions was referved for the ufe of the foldiers; and the reft of the magazines, with a fleet of eleven
hundred veffels, which rode at anchor in the Tigris, were
abandoned to the flames, by the abfolute command of the
Emperor. The Chriftian bifhops, Gregory and Auguftin,
infult the madnefs of the apoftate, who executed, with
his own hands, the fentence of divine juftice. Their authority, of lefs weight perhaps in a military queftion, is
confirmed by the cool judgement of an experienced foldier
[Ammianus], who was himfelf fpectator of the confla-
gration, and who could not difapprove the reluctant mur-
murs of the troops. Yet there are not wanting fome fpecious, and perhaps folid, reafons, which might juftify the
refolution of Julian. The navigation of the Euphrates
never afcended above Babylon, nor that of the Tigris above
Opis. The diftance of the laft-mentioned city from the
Roman camp was not very confiderable; and Julian muft
foon have renounced the vain and impracticable attempt of
forcing

firous of penetrating into the heart of Affyria; but at the end of fome days march, finding neither corn nor forage, becaufe the Perfians had laid all the country wafte, he was obliged to approach the Tigris. Being unable to pafs it for want of boats, he took for the model of his retreat that of the ten thoufand *, and refolved to gain, like them, the country of the Carduci, called in his time

---

forcing upwards a great fleet againft the ftream of a rapid river, which in feveral places was embarraffed by natural or artificial catarafts. The power of fails and oars was in-fufficient; it became neceffary to tow the fhips againft the current of the river; the ftrength of 20,000 foldiers was exhaufted in this tedious and fervile labour; and if the Romans continued to march along the banks of the Tigris, they could only expeft to return home without atchieving any enterprife worthy of the genius or fortune of their leader. If, on the contrary, it was advifeable to advance into the inland country, the deftruftion of the fleet and magazines was the only meafure which could fave that valuable prize from the hands of the numerous and aftive troops which might fuddenly be poured from the gates of Ctefiphon. Had the arms of Julian been victorious, we fhould now admire the conduft, as well as the courage, of a hero, who, by depriving his foldiers of the hopes of a retreat, left them only the alternative of death or con⁴ queft. Recolleft the fuccefsful and applauded rafhnefs of Agathocles and Cortez, who burnt their fhips on the coafts of Africa and Mexico.                                  GIBBON.

*  ———————————— the martial throng,
  Up Tigris' banks who wound their march along;
  O'er wilds and mountains held their toilfome way,
  By hofts affaulted, and the folar ray;
  By thirft, by famine, by eternal fnows —
  Whom heaven and earth united to oppofe.
  Unconquer'd ftill the Greeks each peril meet,
  Regain their fhores, and dignify retreat.      IRWIN.

Corduenne, a name which is ftill found in that of Curdes and Curdiftan. Corduenne, then fubjeft to the Romans, is fituated on the north of Affyria. Thus marching on that fide, Julian had the. Tigris on his left, and went up towards the fource of that river.

Superior in every attack to the lieutenants of Sapor, whether they waited for him in line of battle, or contented themfelves with infulting him on his march, he was ftill advancing, when on the 26th of June, 363, repulfing the enemy with too much ardour, he received a wound, of which he died the night following *.

At the death of Julian the Roman army was in a ftrange fituation; victorious, but in want of every thing. Corduenne, its only refource, was ftill far diftant. To reach this province it muft traverfe without provifions, beneath a burning fky, a ruined country, fuftain in this march the continual at-

---

* The defection of this great man from the pureft of all religions cannot be defended, though it may be accounted for; and his averfion and difcountenance to Chriftians fuit not the informed and liberal mind of Julian in other points. It will fuffice to fay, that his life feems to have belied the name of Apoftate, which he brought upon himfelf by his deviation from the faith in which he was educated. If the paths of Virtue lead to the temple of Truth, he invariably trod them; and may charitably be fuppofed to have arrived, by an indirect courfe, at the divine goal. The circumftances of his death are fo fimilar to thofe of Epaminondas, that we muft be rejoiced to find their lives were equally dignified by purfuits that rendered their end immortal.            IRWIN.

tacks

tacks of the Perfians, always formidable though
vanquifhed, becaufe they were as ready to rally
as to fly, and, befides, as the death of Julian had
raifed the hopes of king Sapor.

It feemed difficult to remain without a chief; the
moments were precious. On the 27th of June,
therefore, at break of day, the officers met to
choofe a fucceffor to Julian, who had juft expired.
The creatures of that prince *, and thofe who
ftill remained of the old court †, having neither
the fame interefts, nor the fame views, all earneftly
defired an Emperor of their own faction; but as
neither of the two factions had had time to concert among themfelves, all their fuffrages, not one
excepted, were united in favour of Salluft the
fecond, Præfect of the Prætorium of the Eaft. This
illuftrious Pagan, whofe virtue cannot be fufficiently admired and lamented, completed the jufti-
fication of that choice by the firmnefs with which
he refufed to load himfelf with a burthen too op-
preffive, he faid, both for his age and infirmities.
A fubaltern officer ‡, then feeing the embarraffment
into which the perfevering refufal of Salluft had
thrown the affembly, faid to the generals, " What

* Nevitta, Dagalaiphus, and the Gallic officers.    B.
† Arintheus, Victor, &c.              B.
‡ Thus I tranflate that expreffion, *honoratior aliquis miles.*
I fufpect that Ammianus thus defcribes himfelf.        B.
   The modeft and judicious hiftorian defcribes the fcene of
the election, at which he was undoubtedly prefent (xxv. 5.)
                                        GIBBON.

S 3                          " would

" would you do, if the prince, inftead of march-
" ing in perfon, had given you the command of
" the army? You would only think of extricating
" yourfelves from this dilemma. Act, as if he
" were ftill living; and when we have once reached
" Mefopotamia, in concert with the army of ob-
" fervation we will choofe an Emperor, whofe
" election cannot be contefted." This perhaps
would have been the beft advice; but fome on a
fudden exalted their voices in favour of Jovian, and
by their tumultuous clamours drew away all the
reft, without giving them time to confider.

FLAVIUS CLAUDIUS JOVIANUS, aged about 33
years, was the firft of the Emperor's guards *. He
had conducted the corpfe of Conftantius to the im
perial city; and as, according to cuftom, fitting in
the funereal car, he received in fome fort the
honours which were paid to that prince, it was
imagined, after the event, that this honourable, but
tranfient and mournful, employment had been the
prognoftic and image of his future grandeur †.

The

---

* Jovian was not captain of the guards, as fome have
thought; but only what was called *domefticorum ordinis primus*. What rank this was we know not. *Domeftici*, or *pro-
tectores domeftici*, are certainly the body-guards,        B,
    The *primus*, or *primicerius*, enjoyed the dignity of a fe-
nator, and though only a tribune, he ranked with the military dukes. *Cod. Theodofian. l.* vi. *tit.* xxiv. Thefe privileges
are perhaps more recent than the time of Jovian. GIBBON.

    † Wherever the Emperors paffed, deputies were fent
to them: they were harangued, famples of the provifions
intended for the troops were prefented to them, the horfes
were

The nobility of his family afcended no higher than count Varronian, his father, born in the territory of the city of Singidon in Myfia, and probably a foldier of fortune, who, for his merit, had been appointed to the command of the Jovians: Such was the appellation of a body of troops formed by Diocletian, who, it is known, had taken the fur-name of Jovius. It was owing perhaps to his regard for the troop of which he was chief, that Varronian made one of his children bear the name of Jovian. This officer, full of years and glory, ftill enjoyed his high reputation in retirement. Some even pretend that it conftituted the prin-cipal merit of his fon. But to refute them it is fufficient to fay, that though Jovian had declared that he would rather quit the fervice than renounce the Chriftian religion, Julian did not ceafe to keep him near his perfon, and to take him with him, when he fet out on his fatal expedition. Julian was well acquainted with his talents. A confeffor of the faith, whom an apoftate and intolerant monarch thought worthy to retain a place of con-fidence, was certainly no ordinary fubject. The Pagans themfelves do juftice to his valour, and if

were fhewn to them, &c. which the public maintained for the ufe of thofe who travelled by order of the court. The fame ceremonial was obferved with regard to the Emperors after their deaths. On that occafion he who attended the corpfe acted and fpoke, without doubt, in the name of the late Emperor. It was a kind of fovereignty which expired on the tomb of the prince. See Amm. *l,* xxi. *c. ult,*    B.

they

they fometimes fpeak of him as a timid prince, this reproach falls rather on the politician than the warrior.

To finifh his portrait, without copying the Chriftian authors, who might here perhaps feem lefs credible, I will chiefly confine myfelf to the teftimony of Ammianus and Eutropius, both Pagans, who were in the Perfian war, and of whom the former ferved in the guards with Jovian. With the fentiments of a generous and beneficent foul this prince united affable manners, a fund of gaiety which induced him to joke with thofe who approached him, fufficient application and activity, but too little experience. He had fuch a knowledge of mankind as promifed difcernment in the diftribution of employments; fome literature *, and great regard for men of learning; an extreme attachment to his religion, but a great refpect to confcience, which he thought accountable only to God. Zealous without bitternefs, and moderate without indifference, he profeffed orthodoxy; but he perfecuted neither heretics, nor even Pagans. It is faid, that thefe excellent qualities were accompanied with fome faults. Ammianus accufes him of loving wine and the table, and fome other pleafures ftill more unbecoming a Chriftian. Men are apt to be inconfiftent, and their belief has not always a fufficient influence on their morals.

---

* This feems to me the fenfe of thofe words of Ammianus, *Mediocriter eruditus, magifque benevolus.*     B.

" But,"

" But," fays the fame author, " the refpeƈt which
" he owed to his purple would have correƈted
" them *." Jovian was in ftature much above the
common ftandard, and large in proportion, fo that
it was difficult to find an imperial habit that would
fit him. He was round-fhouldered, as he appears
alfo on his medals, and had a majeftic air, but a
heavy walk. The gaiety of his mind fparkled on
his face and in his eyes. He is ranked among the
good princes. Perhaps he would have been placed
among the greateft, if he had afcended the throne
at a junƈture lefs fatal, and if he had reigned
longer.

The army was ftill ignorant, it feems, of the
death of Julian. It was beginning to leave the
camp, in order to march, when the new Emperor
appeared, and, invefted with the marks of his
dignity, repaired to the different quarters to fhew
himfelf to the foldiers. The name of *Jovian* refounded on all fides; but the refemblance of this
name to that of *Julian* caufing a miftake, fome
cried, JULIAN AUGUSTUS. Their cries, foon approaching by degrees to the vanguard already at a
diftançe from the camp, were repeated with the
moft lively tranfports. It was imagined that the
wound of Julian was not dangerous, and that he
was leaving his tent, according to cuftom, in the

---

* Thefe are the hiftorian's own words, *Edax tamen et
vino venerique indulgens ; quæ vitia imperiali verecundiâ forfitan
correxiffet.* B.

midft

midft of acclamations. But this tranfient joy was immediately fucceeded by affliction and tears, as foon as the prefence of Jovian announced what had juft happened.           /

Such is the recital of an eye-witnefs, a Pagan indeed, but an impartial writer; I mean Ammianus Marcellinus. His teftimony does not allow us to underftand literally what Theodoret wrote about half a century after him, of the perfect unani- mity with which all the army demanded Jovian for Emperor, while the officers were affembled for the election. Nothing, however, obliges us to re- ject what the fame father adds : " Jovian," he fays, " was placed on a tribunal prepared in hafte ; the " names of Auguftus and Emperor were given " him. The prince then faid to the foldiers, with " his ufual franknefs, that, being a Chriftian, he " could not command Pagans, and that he faw the " wrath of the living God ready to fall on an army of " idolaters." " You command Chriftians," exclaimed with one voice thofe who heard him. " The reign " of fuperftition has been too fhort to efface from " our minds and our hearts the inftructions of the " great Conftantine and his fon Conftantius. Im- " piety has not had time to take root in the fouls " of thofe who have embraced it *."

While Jovian received the homage of the army,

<hr/>

* Ammianus, calmly purfuing his narrative, overthrows this legend by a fingle fentence : *Hoftiis pro Joviano extifque infpectis, pronuntiatum eft,* &c. xxv. 6.       GIBBON.

an enſign of whom he had reaſon to complain *, fearing his reſentment, deſerted to the enemy. He found Sapor, who had juſt joined his troops, at the head of a conſiderable reinforcement. This fugitive, admitted to an audience of the great king, told him, that " Julian was no more; and that the ſervants " of the army had tumultuouſly ſupplied his place " with the phantom of an Emperor, one only of " the body-guard, a man without vigour, without " courage, without capacity." At this unexpected news the monarch ſtarted with joy. The valour of Julian, and the rapidity of his conqueſts, had ſo alarmed him, that he paid no attention to his hair, and ate on the ground as in the greateſt ca- lamities. The Perſians, even after the death of that formidable enemy, repreſented him, in their hiero- glyphical paintings, under the emblem of thunder, or of a lion vomiting flames ; ſuch was the terror with which he had impreſſed them. Sapor, who ſaw himſelf at the ſummit of his wiſhes at the very time when he thought himſelf on the brink of de- ſtruction, flattered himſelf that the Romans would no longer ſtand before him, and detached a body of cavalry ✝ full ſpeed to fall on their rear-guard, with the troops that had fought the preceding day.

Sapor had no doubt that the Romans were on their march; but the election of Jovian had ſuſ-

---

* He was an enemy of Varronian. By mangling the re- putation of the father, he deſerved the hatred of the ſon. B.
✝ Perhaps the ten thouſand *Immortals,*         GIBBON.

pended

pended their departure; and this prince thought of deferring it till the next day. The Pagans, for all were not converted, having offered some sacrifices of thankfgiving for his election to the empire, the augurs found in the entrails of the victims that all would be loft, if they remaiued in the camp, but that they fhould gain fome advantage, if they began their march. As the Emperor knew how much fuperftition can affect courage, he did not hefitate to purfue the latter. The Romans had fcarce left their entrenchments when they faw themfelves attacked. Their cavalry was at firft put into diforder by the elephants which preceded that of the Perfians; but the legionaries fo vigoroufly fuftained the fhock of the hoftile fquadrons, that they forced them to retire. On the fide of the Barbarians, befides fome elephants, a great number of foldiers were left on the field. The Romans, however, paid too dearly for that advantage, as it coft them three of their braveft officers *.

After having paid them the laft duties, as well as the time and place would permit, they encamped near a caftle named Sumera † ; and on the next day, for want of a better defence, they entrenched

---

* Tribunes.

† On the banks of the Tigris, about one hundred miles above Ctefiphon. In the ninth century, Sumere, or Samara, became, with a flight change of name, the royal refidence of the Khalifs of the houfe of Abbas. The obfcure villages of the inland country are irrecoverably loft; nor can we name the field of battle where Julian fell.

GIBBON.

them-

themfelves in a valley furrounded by eminences which left only one outlet. From the top of thofe hills, covered with trees, the Perfians rained on the camp a fhower of arrows, which they accompanied with the bittereft taunts, calling the Romans " traitors, and the murderers of their " Emperor." Thofe reproaches originated from the frivolous difcourfe of fome deferters, and the endeavours which the great king ineffectually employed to difcover who had delivered him from Julian. Sapor having offered a reward proportioned to the importance of the fervice without any one appearing to claim it, he concluded that Julian had been killed by one of his own fubjects ; as if it were impoffible for that rafh prince to have been ftruck either by a dart thrown at random *, or that the horfeman, who wounded him, might himfelf have loft his life.

Libanius indeed has difplayed all his rhetoric to give fome colour to this accufation. This fophift abfolutely infifts that the fatal blow, which fhortened the days of Julian, came from a Chriftian hand directed and employed by the chief of the Chriftians †. By this Libanius probably means fome

---

* Thus Ahab was killed by *a certain man* who *drew a bow at a venture.* 1 Kings xxii. 34.

† Ειδολης πληρων τω σφων αυλων αρχονλι. *Implens acceptum ab eo qui præeft illis mandatum.* Perhaps it fhould be tranflated *præerat* ; as the oration of Libanius was not compofed till the reign of Theodofius. I have retained in the French

some diftinguifhed bifhop, whom he makes the
author of a confpiracy, formed againft the life of
Julian. He pretends that he was privately acquainted with all the particulars of that dreadful
tragedy, and that there needed only public authority to unravel and afcertain its horrors. Libanius, however, utters only conjectures that are
eafily confuted by other conjectures as probable as
his ; and as to the pretended confpiracy, the profound filence of all writers of the fame religion is
a proof either that they had not heard it mentioned, or at leaft that they confidered it as a fable *.
Thofe authors, and Zofimus himfelf, fay exprefsly,
or plainly fuppofe, that Julian was wounded by
a foldier of Sapor. The malignity of Zofimus is
well known : all the evil which he has not faid of
the Chriftians, and which others have faid of them,
has much the air of a calumny.

French the equivocal expreffion of the Greek. It is impoffible to know what bifhop Libanius had in view. It is
furmifed that it might have been either St. Bafil or St.
Gregory of Nazianzus. For my part, I think that in the
time of Julian there was no bifhop in the Eaft who deferved
the name of " chief of the Chriftians" better than St.
Athanafius.        B.

   * Above fixteen years after the death of Julian, the
charge was folemnly and vehemently urged in a public
oration, addreffed by Libanius to the Emperor Theodofius.
The fufpicions are unfupported by fact or argument, and
we can only efteem the generous zeal of the fophift of
Antioch for the cold and neglected afhes of his friend.
                                        GIBBON.

After

After all, that a rhetorician, like Libanius, a
Pagan even to madnefs, fhould think the Chriftians
capable of attempting the life of Julian, is not
furprifing. That it is poffible for an ignorant and
fanatical Chriftian to think that he fhall immor-
talife himfelf both in this world and the next, by
delivering the church from an implacable perfecutor, hiftory unhappily affords too many examples.
But that an ecclefiaftical hiftorian, like Sozomen,
fhould be tempted to canonife fo deteftable an
action, might perhaps not be credited on my af-
fertion. Let him fpeak for himfelf: " It is not
" improbable," fays that writer, " that one of
" thofe who then ferved in the army might have
" reflected, that the deftroyers of tyrants were
" highly extolled, not only by the ancient Greeks,
" but by others even to our times, as men who for
" the common liberty of all did not hefitate to die,
" having chearfully affifted their countrymen,
" friends, and relations. No one certainly," continues Sozomen, " can eafily blame him, who, for
" the fake of God and his religion, has acted fuch
" a manly part *." Sozomen, it feems, had ftudied
profane antiquity more than the morality of the
gofpel and the fpirit of true Chriftianity. Let it
be obferved, that this hiftorian was not a father

---

* *Sozom. Hift. Ecclef. l. vi. c. 2.*
Sozomen applauds the Greek doctrine of *tyrannicide*;
but the whole paffage, which a Jefuit might have tranflated, is prudently fuppreffed by the prefident Coufin.

GIBBON.

of

of the church, that he has no authority in matters
of doctrine, that his language is here contrary to
all tradition, that he wrote towards the middle of
the fifth century; and that he is the firſt in whom
we perceive ſome marks of that anti-chriſtian fanaticiſm. But it is time to reſume the thread of
the hiſtory.

While their enemies, poſted on the heights, were
inſulting the army, a detachment of cavalry forced
the gate of the camp, called the Prætorian gate;
and were very near penetrating even to the imperial
tent: but they were repulſed with loſs. The
Romans afterwards encamped at Carche; from
whence on the ſucceeding day, July 1, they arrived near the city of Dura *, which muſt not be
confounded with another of the ſame name, ſitu-
ated in Meſopotamia. Four days were there loſt
by the obſtinacy of the Barbarians. As ſoon as
the army was on the march, they harraſſed it by
continual ſkirmiſhes, ſometimes in rear, ſometimes
in flank. If it faced about to receive them, by
degrees they gave ground, being only deſirous of
retarding its march, and leaving to famine the
care of fighting for them.

The fear of the worſt miſfortunes makes men
credulous and ready to adopt the moſt hazardous expedients. On a ſudden a report being ſpread that the

* Dura was a fortified place in the wars of Antiochus,
againſt the rebels of Media and Perſia. (Polybius, l. v.
c. 48. 52.)    GIBBON.

frontiers

frontiers of the empire are not far diftant; on this falfe fuppofition the foldier will no longer coaft the Tigris, but clamoroufly infifts on being allowed to pafs it. The Emperor, with the principal officers, oppofes this rafh projeƈt in vain. In vain, fhewing this river always fo rapid, and then fwelled by the melting of the fnows of Armenia, he reprefents that moft of them cannot fwim, that the enemy is mafter of the two banks, and that, if they gain the other fide, it will only be to fall into his hands. Thefe fage remonftrances are difregarded. The clamours increafe, threats are added; every thing breathes fedition. It was necef- fary to allow a number of Gauls and Germans * to attempt the paffage. Jovian flattered himfelf that if they perifhed, the reft would become more traƈtable, or, if they were fo lucky as to fucceed, he might reafonably make an attempt to tranfport the army.

By favour of the night, five hundred able fwim- mers crofs the Tigris with more eafe than could have been expeƈted, and find the Perfians, who guarded the oppofite bank, buried in a profound fleep. They make a great flaughter, and as foon as the day begins to break, they raife their hands, and throw their cloaths into the air, to announce their fuccefs. The army, anxious to follow them, urges the engineers to ƈonftruƈt a kind of [floating]

* The text of Ammianus gives *Sarmatis*; but it is pro- bably faulty. Soon after, the fame author calls them Ger- mans.                                                                 B.

Vol. II.                    T                    bridge,

bridge, which they propofed to make of fheep
fkins faftened together *. They laboured on it
two days; but it was impoffible to fix it on
account of the violence and rapidity of the ftream.
The foldiers, having confumed the provifions that
they had left, became defperate, and rather chofe
to perifh fword in hand than languifh under the
horrors of a flow and cruel death.

Ths Perfians, on their fide, had alfo much to
lament. The intoxication of Sapor was already
difpelled; from the moft prefumptuous confidence,
he relapfed into an extreme perplexity; he faw his
country laid wafte, his towns taken by affault, his
troops, always defeated when they dared to wait
for the enemy, having no refource but in flight,
and confiderably diminifhed by the lofs of an innumerable multitude of men, and almoft all the
elephants. Every day fome new check made him
perceive that the valour of the Romans was not
buried + with Julian. Animated with the genius
of that conqueror, they feemed to think as much,
and perhaps more, of revenging him than of fur-
viving him. Famine itfelf could not force from
them the leaft propofal of peace. Was Sapor
certain of avoiding a battle? And if he muft fight,

---

* Covered with a floor of earth and fafcines. A fimilar
expedient was propofed to the leaders of the ten thoufand,
and wifely rejected. It appears, from our modern travellers, that rafts floating on bladders perform the trade
and navigation of the Tigris.                    GIBBON.

+ *Enfevelie.* A flight inaccuracy. Julian was not then
" buried."

                                                    what

what had he not to fear from men refolved to determine their fate, either by gaining a complete
victory, or at leaft by rendering their defeat fatal
even to the conquerors? Could he flatter himfelf
with annihilating the Roman army, he was not
ignorant that Julian had left in Mefopotamia 40,000
men, under the command of his relation Procopius:
at length the vaft provinces of the empire might
eafily furnifh other legions, who, by attacking
Perfia when exhaufted and terrified, might over-
throw the throne of the Artaxerxides already tottering.

Amidft thefe melancholy reflections, he was informed of the fuccefsful temerity of the Gauls and
Germans. This exploit of a handful of determined men alarms him, and makes him fenfible of
what a whole army of defperadoes will be capable.
Immediately he turns all his thoughts towards an
accommodation with the Romans; he does not
hefitate to make the firft advances, proceeding to
effentials, and defiring, at any rate, to commence
a negociation, which, in the prefent circumftances,
muft infallibly terminate to his advantage. Thus,
contrary to their expectations, the Romans faw the
Surena (he was the general of the Perfian cavalry),
arrive in their camp, with another lord *. " The
" Great King our mafter," faid the deputies to

---

* Sextus Rufus (de Provinciis, c. 29.) embraces a poor
fubterfuge of national vanity. *Tanta reverentia nominis*
*Romani fuit, ut à Perfis primus de pace fermo haberetur.*
GIBBON.

Jovian and the principal officers, " is not dazzled " by prosperity ; he knows the situation to which " fortune has reduced you; but he knows still " better the uncertainty of human affairs. Sapor " respects unsuccefsful virtue, even in his enemies. " He esteems you enough to seek your alliance, " and to offer you peace on equitable terms."

As the Romans were supported only by despair, the hope of peace weakened them at once, and made, it may be said, their arms fall from their hands. Jovian, in particular, was eager to enjoy the empire, and to insure to himself its poffeffion by repairing speedily to the capital. How did he know, but that, in his absence, some ambitious leader, Procopius for instance, then at the head of an army, might feize the diadem ? At that time, those who affumed the purple did not even deign to feek pretexts to colour their enterprife ; and Procopius, as he was related to Julian, might allege the rights of confanguinity. The propofals therefore of Sapor were embraced with eagernefs. They were vague, embarraffed, equivocal, and liable to great difcuffions. At all events, this able poli- tician defigned to protract the negociation, in order to famifh the Romans more and more.

The Emperor, on the contrary, impatient to con- clude it, difpatched, without lofing a moment, Salluft, with Arintheus *, to draw from Sapor himself

* Libanius puts the general Victor in the room of Arintheus. The latter was reckoned one of the greateft captains

himſelf ſomething determinate. They had many
conferences equally long and intricate by the
management of the old monarch, who negociated
peace as he waged war. The more the Romans
advanced, the more he retreated. He formed ſuppoſitions upon ſuppoſitions, and raiſed difficulties
upon difficulties. Now he required time, then he
would no longer grant what he had promiſed, and
promiſed what he had refuſed. Beſides, he ſeemed
to think it ſtrange that the death of Julian was
not revenged; for he ſtill thought that that prince
had been killed by a Roman *; and as the deputies probably did not allow the fact, " if one
" of my generals †," added he, " had loſt his

captains of his age. Prodigies are related of his valour.
He was of an extraordinary ſtature, yet ſo well made,
that, St. Baſil ſays, he was conſidered as the model of a
man. His ſtrength was equal to his courage. His looks
alone had made him gain ſome battles. He received
baptiſm before his death. We have a conſolatory letter
written by St. Baſil to the widow of Arintheus, who had
been the protector of the churches, and the friend of St.
Baſil. We have alſo a letter from the ſame ſaint to this
general, in which he praiſes him for his generoſity and
liberality, of which every one perceived the effects. See
M. de Tillemont on the Emperor Valens, _Hiſtoire des
Empereurs_, tom. V. p. 100. B:
    * For the Perſians alſo had heard this report, and, in
conſequence, before Jovian made peace with them, the
common ſoldiers reviled the Romans as traitors and murderers of the greateſt of princes, as we learn from Ammianus, xxv. 6. OLEARIUS.
    † Libanius heard theſe words of Sapor to the Roman
ambaſſadors, no doubt, from Salluſt himſelf, with whom
he was extremely intimate, as four of his epiſtles to Salluſt
ſufficiently atteſt. _Ibid._

T 3                          " life

" life in a battle, thofe, who, being near his
" perfon, had the cowardice not to die with him,
" fhould not efcape my juft refentment. I would
"; inftantly fend their heads to the family of that
" officer." We here difcern the ideas and language of an Eaftern monarch. Sapor, by affecting
to intereft himfelf in revenging Julian, was alfo
defirous perhaps of teftifying his efteem for that
prince, with a view to infinuate, that he had little
regard for his fucceffor, and that he no longer
feared the Romans.

They became lefs formidable every moment. A
devouring famine confumed them, while by chi-
canery and affected delays he trifled with their
deputies. " We paffed four days," fays Ammianus, " in a ftate more cruel than the fevereft
" punifhments. During that time, if the Emperor,
" difcovering the artifices of Sapor, before he
" fent deputies to that prince, had continually
" gained ground, he would certainly have arrived
" at the ftrong places of Corduenne, which then
" belonged to us; and which would have fupplied
" us with provifions in abundance. We were but
" a hundred miles diftant *."

---

* About thirty leagues.                              B.
It is prefumptuous to controvert the opinion of Ammianus, a foldier and a fpectator.  Yet it is difficult to underftand, how the mountains of Corduenne could extend over
the plain of Affyria, as low as the conflux of the Tigris
and the great Zab: or *how* an army of fixty thoufand
men could march one hundred miles in four days.

GIBBON.

I wifh

I wifh Ammianus had clearly explained the poffi-
bility of this march. If I am not miftaken, this
is his idea. Sapor himfelf had occafion for a peace,
and only offered it to his enemies becaufe he feared
to encounter them. Jovian therefore fhould have
oppofed craft to craft, fhould have expreffed lefs
eagernefs for peace, fhould, however, have given
good words to the envoys of Sapor, fhould have
purfued his route, fhould have fent deputies to
that prince, and have treated on his march. Sapor,
from the fear of being forced to a battle, or of
thwarting the accommodation, would not have attacked the Romans, and would have been taken
in his own fnare. Ammianus was a foldier: he
underftood his profeffion, and knew the country.
He faw things near, and he faw them with reflection; to be convinced of this we need only read
him. The judgement of an hiftorian like him muft
embarrafs the defenders of Jovian.

When Sapor thought he had fubdued the Romans by famine, he threw off the mafk, and,
fpeaking with authority, he declared, firft, that
he infifted on their reftoring to him, for fo he expreffed himfelf, the five provinces beyond the
Tigris *, formerly conquered by the Emperor

---

* Moft of thefe provinces were on this fide the Tigris
with regard to the Romans. In calling them " beyond the
" Tigris" they conformed to the language of the Perfians,
whom they were on the other fide of that river. As to the
particular names of the provinces, they are not the fame
in all authors. B.

Maximian-

Maximian-Galerius from King Narseus, his grand-father; viz. Arzanenia, Moxoënia, Zabdicenia, Rehimenia, and Corduenne. Secondly, that besides these, there should be ceded to him fifteen castles, the city of Nisibis, that of Singara in Mesopotamia, and another important place called the Castle of the Moors (*Castra Maurorum*). Thirdly, that they would engage to interfere no more in the affairs of Armenia, and even refuse king Arsaces the assistance which he might demand against the Persians.

" It would have been a thousand times better," says Ammianus, " to have tried the chance of " arms than to have accepted any one of these " conditions." In fact, under pretence of a restitution, which is not honourable but when it is voluntary, to cede five provinces, annexed to the empire for about seventy years, was to pay a ransom the more humiliating as there were added to it almost all Mesopotamia, and even Nisibis, which had been possessed by the Romans ever since the wars of Mithridates; Nisibis, the bulwark of the East, and the rock which wrecked the pride of Sapor *.

By

---

* He acquired, by a single article, the impregnable city of Nisibis, which had sustained, in three successive sieges, the effort of his arms.    GIBBON.

The treaty of Dura is recorded with grief, or indignation, by Ammianus (xxv. 7.) ; Libanius (*Orat. Parent.* c 142. p. 364.) ; Zosimus (l. III. p. 190, 191.) ; Gregory Nazianzen (*Orat.* IV. p. 117, 118. who imputes the distress

to

. By binding his hands with regard to Armenia,
Jovian furrendered at difcretion, to a revengeful,
perfidious, and cruel prince, Arfaces *, the faithful ally of the Romans, to whom he was connected
by the neareft and moft honourable ties, as Conftantius had made him efpoufe Olympias, daughter
of the Præfect Ablavius, who had been contracted
to his brother the Emperor Couftans. Sapor was the
declared enemy of the Chriftians; and, what muft
perfonally affect Jovian, Arfaces, by his attachment
to Chriftianity, had merited, like Jovian himfelf, difgrace from Julian. King Arfaces had been effentially
ferviceable to the empire. He had juft ravaged
the provinces of Perfia bordering on Armenia.
That was his crime in the fight of Sapor, and the
fecret reafon, but eafy to be gueffed, for which
he required them to refufe him affiftance.

    Thefe confiderations could not efcape Jovian;
but he was befieged by a crowd of flatterers, who

to Julian, the deliverance to Jovian); and Eutropius (x.
17.) The laft-mentioned writer, who was prefent in a military ftation, ftyles this peace *neceffariam quidem, fed ignobilem.*
                                                        *Ibid.*
    * See p. 186. The unfufpicious Tiranus was per-
fuaded by the repeated affurances of infidious friendfhip
to deliver his perfon into the hands of a faithlefs and
cruel enemy. In the midft of a fplendid entertainment, he
was bound in chains of filver, as an honour due to the
blood of the Arfacides; and, after a fhort confinement in
the Tower of oblivion at Ecbatana, he was releafed from
the miferies of life, either by his own .dagger, or by that
of an affaffin. The kingdom of Armenia was reduced to
the ftate of a Perfian province.  '            *Ibid.*

                                    inceffantly

inceffantly reprefented to him Procopius as an
enemy more dangerous than Sapor *. . . His fear
of Procopius was well grounded; and it may be
faid that his revolt † juftified it two years after, if,
neverthelefs, this fear itfelf did not occafion his
revolt.  Befides, there is the greateft probability,
that the irreparable lofs of four days, imprudently
confumed in inactivity, had rendered the army
utterly incapable of fighting, and reduced Jovian
to the indifpenfible neceffity of accepting the peace.
Thus the treaty was perhaps lefs the work of his
timid policy than of his inability.

Be that as it may, to the difgrace of the Roman
name, this prince received the law from Sapor, and
agreed to all the articles propofed.  All that he
obtained, and that with difficulty, was, that the
garrifons of the places ceded as well as the
inhabitants of Nifibis and Singara, fhould retire
into the territories of the Romans.  Arfaces was
included in the treaty, of which he did not fail
to be foon after made the victim.  On both fides a
peace, or rather a truce, of thirty years was fworn,
and in the mean time hoftages ‡ were given for the
performance of the treaty.

* La Bleterie has expreffed, in a long direct oration,
thefe fpecious confiderations of public and private intereft.
                                        GIBBON.
This harangue being imaginary, I have omitted it.

† For an account of his revolt and death, fee p. 221.
note

‡ Remora, Victor, and Bellovædius, tribunes, on the
part of the Romans; and Binefes, with three other Satraps,
on that of the Perfians.                AMMIANUS.
                                        Rufinus

Rufinus and Theodoret, deceived by probability, pretend that Sapor furnished the Romans with provisions *. Nothing was more natural; but without doubt, the Persians had no magazines, and subsisted themselves with difficulty in an exhausted country. At least, it is certain that the Romans gained by that disgraceful peace not even the permission to deviate from the banks of the Tigris †, where the roads were rough and craggy, in order to cross the country to the place where they intended to pass that river. Thither they proceeded by long marches, continually tormented by famine, to which was also added want of water. Many, collecting their expiring strength, withdrew from

* Such a fact is probable, but undoubtedly false. See Tillemont, *Hist. des Empereurs*, tom. IV. p. 702. GIBBON.

† In the neighbourhood of the same river, at no very considerable distance from the fatal station of Dura, the ten thousand Greeks, without generals, or guides, or provisions, were abandoned, above 1200 miles from their native country, to the resentment of a victorious monarch. The difference of their conduct and success depended much more on their character than on their situation. Instead of tamely resigning themselves to the secret deliberations and private views of a single person, the united councils of the Greeks were inspired by the generous enthusiasm of a popular assembly; where the mind of each citizen is filled with the love of glory, the pride of freedom, and the contempt of death. Conscious of their superiority over the Barbarians in arms and discipline, they disdained to yield, they refused to capitulate; every obstacle was surmounted by their patience, courage, and military skill; and the memorable retreat of the ten thousand exposed and insulted the weakness of the Persian monarchy. GIBBON. See p. 256. note *.

the

the body of the army, and endeavoured to fwim
crofs the Tigris.   Moft of them perifhed; the reft
fell into the hands of the Perfians and Saracens
pofted on the other fhore.   Thefe Barbarians, incenfed by the maffacre of their companions whom
the Gauls and Germans had flaughtered, put to
death all who efcaped the waters, or if they fpared
fome of them, it was only to fell them, and fend
them to fuch a diftance that the Romans could
never reclaim them.

When the Emperor and the army were arrived
at the place of paffage, which no author, not even
Ammianus, has taken care to point out to us, after
fome flight preparations, the trumpet gave the
fignal.   It is impoffible to exprefs with what pre-
cipitation every one, caring only for himfelf,
haftened to outrun his companions, and braved
danger, to efcape, as foon as poffible, from that
fatal country.   Some on bad hurdles, by way of
rafts, drew after them their horfes fwimming;
others were carried on bladders; all availed themfelves of what was offered them by chance, or of
what neceffity, ever fruitful in expedients, made
them contrive.   Twelve fmall flat boats, the remains of the fleet of Julian, ferved to tranfport
the Emperor, with the principal officers, and made,
by his order, as many voyages were neceffary to
complete the tranfportation.   " Thus," fays Ammianus, " by the divine goodnefs, we all paffed
                                                " fafely,

" fafely, excepting fome who had the misfortune
" to be drowned."

Immediately after, advice was received that the
Perfians, out of the fight of the Romans, were
conftructing a bridge, no doubt that they might
intercept the ftragglers and the baggage ; but feeing themfelves difcovered, they did not dare to
execute their perfidious defign. Thus the Perfians, it appears, had materials for a bridge. Why
then did not Jovian infift, as a preliminary, that
they fhould facilitate his paffage? Sapor was too
great a gainer by the treaty to have made a difficulty
of a condition which he could with eafe perform.
This feems worth remarking, as another proof of
the inability of Jovian.

The Roman army, continuing its march with
extreme diligence, encamped fome leagues from
the Tigris, near the town of Hatra *, fituated on
a hill in the midft of a vaft defert, formerly inhabited by the Scenites Arabians : it had been
reckoned impregnable, but had now been long
abandoned. Perhaps the Romans, when they faw
Hatra, confoled themfelves a little on their difgrace, by recollecting that which had befallen,
under the ramparts of that place, the two greateft

* So called by Ammianus, by Dio, (*lib. ult.*) Τα Αγρα,
and by M. de la Bleterie, *Atra.*.

M. d'Anville (fee his maps, and *l'Euphrate et le Tigre*,
pp. 92, 93.) traces their march, and affigns the true pd-
fition of Hatra, Ur, and Thilfaphata, which Ammianus
has mentioned.　　　　　　　　　　　　GIBBON.

3　　　　　　　　　　　　　　　generals

generals that had filled the throne of the Cæfars. Trajan had made the taking it a point of honour, but nature abfolutely armed againft him, in defence of the befieged; and what may be confidered as a prodigy of another kind, Severus, who, after having raifed the fiege, attacked it a fecond time, called back his foldiers very unadvifedly, when they were juft ready to ftorm the place, and when he ordered them to return to the affault, he could never make himfelf obeyed. This prince, as well as Trajan, thought he fhould have perifhed before that town with all his army. Artaxerxes, the founder of the fecond monarchy of the Perfians, was not more fuccefsful, and Providence * feemed conftantly to declare in favour of Hatra. However, the frequent attacks of the Romans, and the danger to which the town was expofed, efpecially in the laft fiege, might make the Scenites Arabians think, that the liberty, of which they were always fo jealous, and which they ftill preferve, was lefs endangered in their tents than under the fhelter of the ftrongeft walls. They abandoned Hatra We no where read that it was taken, and yet it had been long deferted when Jovian arrived there. The Romans were now informed, that they had a plain

* In this Dr. Delany, a learned Englifh divine, thinks he difcovers the marks of the vifible protection of God to the defcendants of Ifhmael, agreeably to the promifes made to Hagar and Abraham, Gen. xvi. and xvii. See the work, entitled, *Revelation examined with Candour*, vol. II. differt. IV.                                                        B.

of thirty leagues to traverfe, where nothing was
to be found but wormwood and fuch kind of herbs,
with a little putrid and brackifh water. They provided therefore fome frefh water, and killed fome
of the camels and other beafts of burden, whofe
unwholefome flefh prolonged their lives at the expence of health.

In about fix days march they met, near the caftle
of Ur, a place dependent on the Perfians, a con-
voy of fome provifions, which Jovian, immediately
after his election, had fent the tribune Mauricius
to feek in Mefopotamia. This weak fupply, the
fruit of the oeconomy of the two generals Procopius and Sebaftian, enabled the Emperor to recover
breath, and to take meafures to make himfelf
acknowledged through the whole empire. He
might even confider this affiftance as an act of obedience on the part of Procopius and his collegue,
whofe fubmiffion neceffarily drew after it that of
the Eaftern provinces. But who could infure to
him the Weft, till Illyricum and Gaul had acknowledged him? The troops of Illyricum and Gaul
had often difpofed of the purple, and occafioned
great revolutions. They were indeed lefs formidable fince the time of Conftantine. That prince,
more on his guard againft civil wars than againft
the invafions of the Barbarians, had, by good or
bad policy, weakened the authority of the generals
by dividing it. He had alfo difperfed in the inner
.part of the provinces the legions long ftationed on
the

the frontiers, where the proximity of their quarters placed them within the reach of keeping up
correfpondences, of fecretly forming and fuddenly
executing confpiracics. Neverthelefs, in fpite of
thefe precautions, the recent examples of Vetranio *
in Illyricum, and of Magnentius † and Julian in
Gaul, did not allow a doubt that the legions might
again make Emperors there; and the diftance muft
increafe the uneafinefs of Jovian.

He difpatched therefore, with the neceffary
orders to fecure to him thofe important provinces,
two confidential men, Procopius, fecretary of ftate,
who muft be diftinguifhed from the relation of
Julian, and Memoridus, a tribune. The whole
family of Jovian was in Illyricum; his wife, his
fon yet in the cradle, Count Varronian his father,
and his father-in-law Count Lucillian. Both, after
having quitted the fervice, enjoyed the repofe of a
quiet life. But the infirmities of age without doubt
rendered Varronian incapable of acting, as the
orders of the Emperor were addreffed to Count
Lucillian. The meffengers carried him the com-

* Vetranio, an aged general, beloved for the fimplicity
of his manners, who had long governed the martial countries of Illyricum, affumed the purple in 350. But Conftantius, having feduced his troops, and undermined his
throne, at an interview with the ufurper, appointed at Sar-
dica, by the defection of his followers, Vetranio was de-
pofed and banifhed to Prufa, where he lived fix years in the
enjoyment of eafe and affluence. *Abridged from* GIBBON.

† For an account of the ufurpation of Magnentius, fee
Vol. I. p. 175. note *.

miffion

miffion of mafter-general of the horfe and foot.*.
Thus invefted with two employments which were
ufually feparated, he was to take with him fome
officers of merit and known fidelity, whofe names
were mentioned in a private difpatch, and to repair
immediately to Milan, from thence to watch over
the remainder of the Weft, and to refort, in cafe
of commotions, where-ever the exigence of affairs
might require his prefençe. The Emperor took
from Jovinus the command of the troops in Gaul,
and conferred it on Malarich, by nation a Frank,
long attached to the fervice of the Romans. Thus
he freed himfelf of a man whofe fuperior talents
rendered his fidelity fufpeted, and put in his place
a foreigner, who, not being able to have any pretenfions to the empire, would always confider the
good fortune of his benefactor as the foundation of
his own, and would confine his ambition to ferving
him well. The meffengers had alfo orders to
announce on their journey the death of Julian and
the election of his fucceffor, to convey to the go-
vernors of the provinces the letters of Jovian, and
to publifh every where that he had terminated the
war by an advantageous peace. They travelled
night and day, without ftopping ; but, more expe-
ditious and more fincere than they, Fame out-
ftripped them, and declared the truth.

---

* In M. de la Bleterie, *le brevet de généraliffime de l'infan-
terie et de la cavalerie:* in the original of Ammianus, *ma-
giflerii equitum et peditum codicillis.* For obvious reafons I
prefer the latter.

Jovian wrote, without doubt, at the fame time to the fenate of New Rome, and efpecially to that of the Old, which ftill retained fome kind of pre-eminence, praying them, at leaft for form-fake, to confirm what the army had done in his favour. It was at that time probably, that he nominated himfelf conful for the enfuing year, with his father Count Varronian, who had learned, in a dream, if we credit Ammianus, that he fhould be ap-pointed to the confulfhip, but who certainly knew not that death would prevent his taking poffeffion of that high dignity *.

If the Pagans of the army had been fenfibly affected by the lofs of Julian, it was no lefs dif-treffing to the others, of whom there were fuch num-bers throughout the empire ; and, without doubt, the latter, not being conftrained by the prefence of their new prince, abandoned themfelves to their grief with more freedom. " This intelligence," fays Libanius, " was a ftroke that pierced me to " the heart. I caft my eyes on a fword, and wifhed " to rid myfelf of a life that would henceforth be " more cruel to me than death. But I recollected " the prohibition of Plato, and the punifhments re- " ferved in hell for thofe who difpofe of themfelves

---

* Count Varronian thus dying foon after he had heard of his fon's good fortune, and before he had feen him, Jovian declared his infant-fon Varronian conful with him-felf, in the room of his grandfather ; " becaufe," adds Ammianus, " the old man was foretold in his fleep that " the higheft magiftracy fhould be borne by that name."

" without

" without waiting for the command of God. Be-
" fides, I réflected that I owed that hero a funeral
" oration *."

Libanius acquitted himfelf of that duty by con-
fecrating to the memory of Julian two difcourfes,
which have been tranfmitted to us. The firft †,
which feems to have been compofed immediately,
is only a very fhort and yet fufficiently tedious lamentation, with more wit than fentiment, and more
pedantry than wit. The fecond ‡ is an hiftorical
elogium, laboured at leifure, in which the orator
follows Julian ftep by ftep, and always fhews the
bright fide of him. This piece, perhaps the beft
of his works, and worthy, almoft in every refpect,
of the pureft antiquity, makes, on the whole, a remarkable contraft to the eloquent difcourfe of St.
Gregory of Nazianzus §.

At Carrhæ in Mefopotamia, a city entirely devoted to Paganifm, the meffenger who brought
the firft account of the death of Julian, was near

---

\* *De vitâ fuâ.*

† Ιυλιαιος, η Επιταφιος ιπι τω Ιυλιαιω. (" A funeral ora-
" tion on Julian.") This difcourfe was publifhed imperi-
fectly by Morell; but more correctly, with Latin tranflation
of Olearius, by Fabricius, Bibl. Græc. Vol. VII. p. 223.

‡ Υπιρ τω Ιυλιαιω τιμωριας. (" On revenging Julian.")
Spoken before the Emperor Theodofius, 379, firft publifhed
by Olearius, 1701, and afterwards, with his tranflation and
notes, by Fabricius. See p. 224. note ‡.

§ Though in the editions of this Father the work is divided into two, it is, however, only one and the fame
difcourfe, as is proved by the judicious writer who has
given a French tranflation of it; printed at Lyons, in 1735,
a tranflation much lefs known than it deferves to be. B.

being

being ftoned to death, and really was fo, according to Zofimus. Such was the defpair of the Pagans. They faw their reign vanifh like a dream, the flattering hopes which they had conceived from the youth and zeal of Julian pafs away in fmoke, Hellenifm ready to be buried in the tomb of its reftorer, and the Chriftian religion again invefted with the purple, and more ftrengthened than ever, at the very time when, thinking it arrived at its fatal period, they only waited the return of Julian to give the laft blow. Many had perfecuted it without difcretion, and had been betrayed into the greateft exceffes. What probability that the moft moderate Chriftian prince would let crimes, at which Julian himfelf had been forced to blufh, pafs with impunity !

On the other fide, the Church, in the tranfports of a fudden deliverance, bleffed by its canticles the God ever faithful to his promifes, whofe arm had exterminated the new Sennacherib. But the Chriftians, it muft be owned, did not all confine themfelves to the legitimate fentiments which this kind of refurrection planted in their hearts. Inftead of a Chriftian joy, pure in its motives, humble and modeft in its effects, mixed with compaffion for a perifhing enemy, and with fear at the profpect of profperity; many gave themfelves up to the merely human emotions of a proud and outrageous joy, and feemed already to threaten the vengeance of a religion which teaches only patience and forgivenefs.

givenefs. Thofe of Antioch, perfonal enemies to Julian on fo many accounts, infulted at once the memory of the Pagan, the philofopher, and the author. In this great city, fo voluptuous, and which thought itfelf fo Chriftian, there was nothing but public entertainments, nothing but facred and profane feftivals. In the churches and oratories of the martyrs were feen dances, and the tumult of public fhews; and the theatres refounded with religious exclamations. There was publifhed the victory of the crofs; there was apoftrophifed, though abfent, the philofopher Maximus, the oracle and the perverter of Julian. " Foolifh " Maximus," they exclaimed, " what is become of " thy predictions? God and his Chrift have con- " quered."

But if the Church triumphed, the empire was covered with difgrace, and had received a deep wound, of which it never recovered. Thus the tranfports with which the intereft of religion, efpecially when joined with animofity, at firft infpired the people, were no fooner abated, than the public rejoicings gave place to uneafinefs and alarms. To inveigh againft Julian, to impute the calamities of the ftate to his apoftacy and fenfelefs conduct, publickly to expofe the fhocking remains of the human victims which he was accufed of having facrificed in his abominable myfteries, this might be a kind of confolation, but it was not a refource. Jovian alone gained by it, becaufe he

U 3                                        had

had the advantage of fucceeding a prince that was hated, and confequently refponfible, in the opinion of the multitude at leaft, for the firft faults of his fucceffor.

By the ceffion of the provinces beyond the Tigris, and of Nifibis, Syria was going to become almoft a frontier, and the city of Antioch remained expofed, with the reft of the Eaft, to the incurfions of the Barbarians. Whoever had ftill a Roman heart muft confider, that for the fpace of about eleven centuries, neither the annals of the republic, nor thofe of the monarchy, furnifhed an example of an event fo grievous, fo ignominious, all things confidered, as the treaty of Jovian; that if, in former times, fome generals had fubfcribed to difhonourable conditions, the fupreme authority, which then refided in the people, by declaring thofe treaties null, had made all their infamy fall on their authors; that the majefty of the empire, after it was concentered in a monarch, had been no doubt deeply humiliated by the captivity of Valerian, who had grown old in the chains of another Sapor; but that this majefty had degraded and annihilated itfelf in the perfon of Jovian, who had forfaken the fundamental principle of the policy of the Romans, who yielded nothing by force, nor were ever more haughty, or more intractable, than when they feemed crufhed; that this precious maxim, efcaped from the wreck of the republic and of ancient manners, had fupported

to

to the prefent day the empire which it had formed; but when that was once abandoned, the Emperors would in future be feen fucceffively to cede the provinces, to difmember the ftate, under a pretence of faving it; in fhort, that it was eafy to forefee the fall and total ruin of that vaft body.

Without extending their views fo far, the inhabitants of Nifibis, fufficiently occupied with their own calamity, trembled to fee themfelves at the mercy of Sapor, and of Sapor provoked. They retained, neverthelefs, fome hopes founded on the importance of their fortrefs, their paft fidelity, and their recent fervices. They could not believe that Jovian would deliver them to Barbarians; and they flattered themfelves, that if, from a regard to his oaths, he did not dare directly to infringe the treaty, fenfible at leaft of the juftice of their remonftrances, he would not deprive them of the liberty of defending themfelves againft an enemy, whom they had already fo often repulfed.

The army, however, after having confumed the little provifions that it had received, again endured fo ftrange a famine, that they were on the eve of eating human flefh. If a bufhel of corn was found by chance, " which happened," Ammianus fays, " but feldom," it was fold for at leaft thirteen pieces of gold. By degrees, as the horfes were killed, the arms and baggage were abandoned; fo that there is perhaps lefs exaggeration than malignity in the picture which Libanius draws of the

ftate

ftate of the troops at their return: " Our foldiers,"
fays he, " returned without arms, without cloaths.
" They afked alms, being as naked, for the moft
" part, as people who efcape from fhipwreck.
" If any one retained half his buckler, a third
" part of his fpear, or even one of his boots, which
" he carried on his fhoulder, he confidered himfelf
" as a hero. All thought themfelves fufficiently
" juftified, by faying, that Julian was dead, and
" that it was not furprifing that the Romans fhould
" appear in the deplorable ftate in which the Per-
" fians would have been, if that conqueror had
" lived."

It is fuppofed, that the army re-entered the territories of the empire at a place named Thifal-
phata. It was there, at leaft, that Procopius and
Sebaftian, with the officers of the troops of Mefopotamia, came to pay their duty to the Emperor,
who received them gracioufly. Jovian foon repaired to the gates of Nifibis, and encamped under
the walls, without liftening to the prayers of the
inhabitants, who conjured him, with reiterated intreaties, to lodge in the palace, like his prede-
ceffors. He was afraid to fhew himfelf, and was
ftill more afraid, no doubt, to confine himfelf in a
Roman colony, of which he had put the Barbarians
in poffeffion.

That very evening he committed an act of de-
fpotifm more fuitable to the fufpicious character
with which he is reproached, than to the delicacy

of

of confcience on which he piqued himfelf. At the beginning of the night, on his rifing from table, an officer, who had diftinguifhed himfelf in the laft war at the taking of Maogamalcha *, was put to death. He was dragged out, and thrown into a dry well, where ftones were heaped over him. He was named *Jovianus*, like the Emperor, and had had fome votes to fucceed Julian. To remain a fubject, after having appeared worthy to reign, is a fituation fo delicate, that the greateft circumfpection is fcarce fufficient to ward its dangers. Of this Jovianus was not aware. Ambition or vanity made him utter fome expreffions the more fufpicious as he occafionally invited fome officers to his table; and " to this," fays Ammianus, " his deftruction " was certainly owing." The tragical end of this unfortunate man, who feems to have been more imprudent than culpable, is related by none of the modern writers who mention Jovian †. I queftion whether they would have omitted a fimilar paffage in the hiftory of his predeceffor.

On the next day Binefes, a lord of the Perfian court, who attended Jovian, to ferve as an hoftage, and at the fame time to urge the execution of the

---

* Whilft the Barbarians defended themfelves, finging, according to their cuftom, the praifes of their king, and braving the Emperor, faying, he might fooner fcale the walls of heaven than take Maogamalcha, the legions entering by the mouth of the mine, furprifed them, maffacred them, and threw down the ramparts. B.

† A fubfequent hiftorian, Mr. Gibbon, ironically ftyles it " a *royal* act."

treaty

treaty of peace, efcorted, no doubt, by a guard which the Emperor gave him, entered Nifibis, and difplayed on the citadel the ftandard of the Great King. The fight of this fatal flag, and the order which the inhabitants received to retire fomewhere elfe, threw them into the utmoft confternation. At firft they had imagined, that Jovian had engaged to deliver up the city with all its inhabitants. One would think therefore that it muft have been fome abatement of their grief to learn that their perfons would not fall into the hands of Sapor. But befides their not being able, as I have faid, to perfuade themfelves entirely that this engagement would take place, the banifhment, to which they faw themfelves condemned, appeared to them as terrible as flavery. Several perhaps would even rather have chofen to live flaves in the bofom of their country, that is, fubje&ts of the kings of Perfia, than to preferve in exile, in poverty, in the miferies of a new eftablifhment, a chimerical liberty under the Roman Emperors, princes as abfolute in fact * as thofe who bore the fceptre of Arfaces and Artaxerxes pretended to be by right.

It is very ufual with hiftorians, when they relate the ruin of illuftrious cities, to recount in few words their origin and the principal events which rendered them diftinguifhed. May I therefore be allowed to fay fomething here of the famous Nifibis,

---

* Witnefs the inftance juft related.

as

as the Romans then loft it for ever, and as it in a
a manner even perifhed itfelf by the total tranfmi-
gration of its citizens ? Nifibis, if we may credit
the oriental hiftorians, is the fifter and contemporary of Babylon, Nimrod alfo being its founder.
According to fome, he gave it the name of *Chalya*;
according to others, that of *Achad*; and it is, fay
thefe, the fame city of Accad which is mentioned
in Genefis, among thofe of which the fon of Cufh
laid the firft foundations in the land of Shinar.
It took afterwards the name of Nifibis ; and if we
had a right to infift on an uncertain etymology *,
we might conjecture that it was already, or then
became, a place of ftrength. One of the kings of
Syria who fucceeded Alexander, gave it the name
of Antioch of Mygdonia, and certainly it was fo
called, as may be feen in Polybius, (*l.* v.) in the
reign of Antiochus, furnamed the Great. It was
fituated in the north part of Mefopotamia, two
days journey from the Tigris, near mount Mafius,
in a pleafant and fruitful plain, watered by the
river Mygdonius,.which interfected the city. Notwithftanding its antiquity, Nifibis does not begin
to figure in hiftory till towards the latter time of
the Roman republic.

    Tigranes, king of Armenia, having taken it
from the Parthians, being himfelf attacked by

---

* נצב fignifies, it is faid, in Phœnician, " columns,
" heaps of ftones." It means in Hebrew, " a monument,
" a ftatue," &c. but it alfo fignifies in the Bible " a gar-
" rifon, ftatiouary foldiers." 1 Sam. xiii. 12.    B.

Lucullus,

Lucullus, there lodged his treafures. He thought them fafe in a city furrounded by two walls all of brick *, of a prodigious thicknefs, which a broad and deep ditch fecured from being undermined, and alfo put out of the reach of machines. Thus it defpifed Lucullus, when he ventured to appear before Nifibis in the depth of winter. But by the favour of this contempt, and of a tempeftuous night, he carried the place by fcaling, fixty-eight years before the Chriftian æra. After the defeat of Craffus, it again became fubject to the kings of Armenia. Occupied by their civil wars, the Romans did not think of retaking it; and the policy of Auguftus, who fixed the limits of the empire to the banks of the Euphrates, was a law to his fucceffors till Trajan. Thus for more than a hundred and fifty years the Romans faw without jealoufy Nifibis and its territory in the hands of the kings of Armenia, their vaffals, or of the kings of Adiabena, vaffals of the Parthians. Trajan, the moft warlike of the Emperors after Julius Cæfar, exploded the ftatemaxim introduced by Auguftus, and carried his victorious arms far beyond the Euphrates. The taking of Nifibis was one of the firft exploits on that fide; but Hadrian foon abandoned it, with the

* Nifibis is now reduced to one hundred and fifty houfes; the marfhy lands produce rice, and the fertile meadows, as far as Moful and the Tigris, are covered with the ruins of towns and villages. See Niebuhr, Voyages, tom. ii. p. 300—309.　GIBBON.

new

new provinces which Trajan had conquered in the East.

Lucius Verus, the brother and collegue of Marcus Aurelius, retook it; and in the time of Severus befieged twice, once by the people of Mesopotamia revolting againft the Romans, and the other time by Volagefus king of Parthia, it defended itfelf with fuch vigour and fuccefs, that Severus, who firft firmly eftablifhed the Romans in Mefopotamia, not contented with fortifying Nifibis, and making it the capital of a particular province, raifed it even to the dignity of a colony, and made it take the name of *Septimia*. In the time of Alexander the fon of Mammea, Artaxerxes, who had juft dethroned Artabanes, the laft king of Parthia, and reftored to the Perfian nation the fceptre which fhe had loft for about 555 years, endeavoured, but ineffectually, to make himfelf mafter of Nifibis.

Under one of the fucceeding Emperors it was taken either by the fame Artaxerxes, or his fon Sapor I.; but by taking it he only procured the younger Gordian the honour of re-conquering it. Julius-Philip, the murderer and fucceffor of Gordian, deferved by fome benefactions to be confidered as a new founder of the colony, as on a medal which fhe caufed to be ftruck in honour of Philip, fhe took the name of *Julia* with that of *Septimia*. The captivity of Valerian, and the effeminacy of Gallienus his unworthy fon, ceded to Sapor I. moft of the Afiatic provinces. It

I                                                           was

was neceſſary for another Barbarian, named Odenathus, the chief of ſome Saracens, more Roman
than the Emperor himſelf, to take care of the intereſts of the empire ; and he ſaved it in the Eaſt.
Niſibis firſt ſubmitted to that prince, whoſe ſervices Gallienus rewarded with the title of Auguſtus.
It ſeemed again ſeparated from the empire in the
reign of Zenobia, the widow of Odenathus ; but
it was re-united by Aurelian. The Perſians having
made themſelves maſters of it after the death of
Carus, the terror of the arms of Diocletian forced
them to abandon it.

In ſhort, the æra of the glory of Niſibis, and
the moſt brilliant parts of its hiſtory, muſt be
ſought in the IVth century after Jeſus Chriſt. In
the reign of Conſtantius, Sapor II. as has been
ſaid, was thrice foiled before its ramparts. Of
thoſe three ſieges, the moſt memorable is that of
the year 350 *, deſcribed by Julian with no leſs
elegance than energy, in his two firſt orations,
which the orator has found the ſecret to render
intereſting in a certain degree, though they are
panegyrics, and the panygyrics of Conſtantius. To
give an idea of that ſiege, I will add, that Sapor
having learned that the revolt of Magnentius, and
the progreſs of that uſurper, called Conſtantius into
the Weſt, deſirous of availing himſelf of that
juncture, invaded Meſopotamia at the head of an

---

* The other two ſieges were in 337, and 359, according to Spanheim. Mr. Gibbon, though he refers to this
author, has (in his margin) by ſome miſtake, placed the
three ſieges in 338, 346, and 350.

innumerable

innumerable army, and that, after having taken
fome caftles, he on a fudden invefted Nifibis. At
firft he befieged it in form; but neither the ram,
nor the mine, nor the tortoife, having any effed, he
turned the courfe of the river Mydonius, hoping to
reduce the inhabitants by drought. From this, happily, the fprings and the wells preferved them. The
Great King then conceived a defign worthy of Darius and Xerxes. He furrounded the place with a
high and ftrong mound, and ftopped the river below
it. The waters ebbing filled a bafon that was prepared for them, and rofe almoft as high as the
rampart, which was not more above their level than
was neceffary to prevent the city from being
overflowed. Sapor then equipped on this lake a
fleet of barks filled with machines to batter and
fcour the walls, and with foldiers to affault them.
This new mode of attack continued feveral days
with an amazing lofs on the fide of the Barbarians,
and with prodigies of intrepidity on the fide of the
Romans, till a weak part of the bank breaking,
buried in the waters great numbers of the befiegers.

Sapor, feeing his reputation endangered, ftopped
the Mygdonius above the city, and difcharged the
river againft the walls, of which it threw down a
hundred cubits, 152 feet. Though he played inceffantly on the breach, the inhabitants raifed a new
wall fome paces from the old one, with fuch expedition, and defended it with fuch vigour, that they
repulfed all the affaults. The king, in the violence
of

of his paſſion, ſhot an arrow into the ſky to revenge
himſelf, as far he could, of the deity himſelf. But
he made that impious prince ſtill more ſenſible of
his power by an army of gnats, whoſe ſtings ſo
enraged the horſes and elephants, that they cruſhed
in pieces ſeveral thouſand ſoldiers. At length,
after loſing 20,000 men, he burnt his machines,
and raiſed the ſiege, which had laſted more than
four months. Count Lucillian, who commanded in
the city, and St. James, its biſhop *, divided the honour of having ſaved it; the former by his courage
and military talents, the latter by his fervent
prayers, which he interrupted only to animate his
people to fight for their liberty and religion; for
they all profeſſed Chriſtianity, of which Sapor was
the perſecutor.

Such was the city of Niſibis, which the ſon-in-
law of Lucillian ceded to the ſame Sapor. Thoſe,
whom he ordered to leave it and give place to Barbarians, were in general the ſame, who, thirteen
years before, had ſo well defended it. The ſenate,
in a mournful ſilence, and the people uttering lamentable cries, repaired to the camp of the Emperor, and, proſtrate at his feet, ſaid to him every
thing that grief and the love of their country ſug-

* The miracles which Theodoret (*l.* 11. *c.* 30.) aſcribes
to St. James, biſhop of Edeſſa, were at leaſt performed in
a worthy cauſe, the defence of his country. He appeared
on the walls under the figure of the Roman Emperor, and
ſent an army of gnats to ſting the trunks of the elephants,
and to diſcomfit the hoſt of this new Sennacherib. GIBBON.

geſted

gefted to them moft affecting. As the whole anfwer that he oppofed to their fupplications, to their
arguments, to their fighs, was the fanctity of an
oath ; " Sire," faid they, " if neceffity conftrains
" you to cede your rights to Nifibis, do not forbid
" us, at leaft, to fupport ours, fword in hand.
" We afk of you neither ftores, nor troops, nor
" money. By conquering Sapor we are all be-
" come foldiers. Confider us as foreigners. Aban-
" don us to ourfelves, or rather to Heaven, the
" protector of juftice and innocence. That will
" continue to render invincible fuch Romans as
" fhall fight for their altars, for their hearths, for
" thofe walls which they have cemented with their
" own blood. After we have repulfed Sapor, the
" only ufe that we wifh to make of our liberty is
" to give ourfelves back to you."

Jovian anfwered, that he had exprefsly fworn
to deliver up the city, and that he was incapable
of eluding an oath by vain fubtleties. Then
Sabinus, to whom his birth and riches gave a diftinguifhed rank among his fellow-citizens, faid to
him with equal fpirit and boldnefs : " Conftantius,
" always at war with the Perfians, was almoft al-
" ways unfortunate ; he fhivered at the name of
" Sapor, and this terror embittered all the mo-
" ments of his life. Conftantius, however, over-
" whelmed with misfortunes, Conftantius, reduced
" to the neceffity of efcaping almoft alone, and of
" eating a morfel of bread in the cottage of a

" poor woman, ſtill preſerved Niſibis. What do
" I ſay? He never ceded to the enemy an inch
" of ground; but Jovian no ſooner comes to the
" empire than he ſurrenders the bulwark of the
" Eaſt." Jovian heard theſe reproaches unmoved,
ſtill intrenching himſelf in arguments drawn from
a point of honour and conſcience.

It was cuſtomary for every city to offer new
princes a crown of gold. In the critical ſituation
to which the inhabitants of Niſibis were reduced,
they were particularly careful to perform that duty.
The Emperor, who did himſelf juſtice, being very
ſenſible that he did not deſerve the crown, eſpecially
from them, refuſed that which they preſented to
him. But the inhabitants, with a perſeverance proof
againſt all refuſals, conjured him to receive it,
thinking, without doubt, that he would allow himſelf to be affected by that mark of attachment and
reſpect, and that, if he accepted their homage, he
would contract a kind of engagement with them.
Jovian, in order to extricate himſelf from their im-
portunity, ſeemed at length to accept it; and inſtantly a lawyer, named Silvanus, exclaimed, with
a loud voice, " In like manner, great Emperor,
" may you be crowned by the other cities!" At
this ſpeech he was ſo exaſperated, that he immediately ordered the inhabitants to evacuate the city
in three days, and ſent ſome troops to haſten them,
with orders to put any to death who ſhould remain
there after the time preſcribed.

3                                           This

This terrible decree filled Nifibis with confternation. Inftantly nothing was heard but groans,
cries, imprecations againft the government, and
frightful howlings. To fee fome women of rank
forced by their fovereign to banifh themfelves from
the fcenes of their birth, from the places where
they had happily paffed their days in the bofom of
opulence, forced, I fay, to abandon all their pof-
feflions, and, what was more diftrefsful, to remove
for ever from the tombs of their hufbands, their
parents, their children, whofe afhes remained at the
difcretion of the Barbarians, was a fight capable
of moving Sapor, if he had been prefent. Sometimes they tore their hair and their faces, fometimes
they clafped in their arms the doors of their houfes,
bathing them with tears, and bidding them a laft
farewell. In a word, there was feen the image of
a city taken by affault, and all the fymptoms of
grief and defpair which great calamities produce
among the orientals, whofe paffions were always
more expreffive than ours. But who could defcribe
the anguifh of heart which muft be felt by thofe
brave men who had fuftained three fieges, and
who would have thought themfelves happy to
fhed the remainder of their blood for a country,
which they confidered not only as the place of
their birth, but alfo as the theatre of their glory,
and the monument of their valour! Every one
feized in his hafte, and as if he had ftolen it, any
thing, that he could carry away, of his own effects;

for,

for, to complete their misfortunes, beafts of burden were wanting, fo that a large quantity of valuable furniture was obliged to be left.

The roads were foon covered with thefe poor fugitives, who, groaning under their burdens, and ftill more oppreffed by the weight of their affliction, were going to feek the firft afylum that providence fhould be pleafed to offer them. Moft of them retired under the walls of Amida, where Jovian ordered a walled fuburb to be built for them, which was called the town of Nifibis. Amida, founded by Conftantius, and almoft ruined by Sapor, thus increafed by the ruins of this ancient city, and repaired its loffes with fo much advantage, that it became the capital of what the Romans retained in Mefopotamia. As foon as the inhabitants of Nifibis were departed, Jovian difpatched the tribune Conftantius to expell thofe of Singara, another Roman colony, and to deliver the five provinces to the officers of Sapor. Thus this famous treaty was literally executed, a treaty, which may be regarded as the epocha of the fall of the empire, and whofe execution expofed Jovian, more than the treaty itfelf, to the reproaches not only of Pagan, but of fome Chriftian authors. Are their reproaches well founded? This is a problem, whofe difcuffion will be more properly placed at the end of this hiftory *.

After

---

* The Abbè de la Bleterie, though a fevere cafuift, has pronounced, that Jovian was not bound to execute his promife;

After having fulfilled his engagements with the
Perfians, the Emperor ordered Procopius to convey to Tarfus in Cilicia the corpfe of Julian, agreeably to the laft will of that prince. In the funeral proceffion, which muft have been a fortnight
at leaft on the road, the cuftoms of the Pagans
were obferved, of which the moft fantaftic was, to
enliven the funeral pomp of the great, and even
of the Emperors, at the expence of thofe whom
they pretended to honour. They added humour
and fatire to the demonftrations of grief. Ilere
were heard mournful fongs and lamentations, and
tears were feen to flow : there drolls and buffoons
danced and acted fome jocofe fcenes, or one of
the troop, in a mafk which reprefented to the
life him whofe obfequies were celebrated, imitated
his gefture and his voice *, and made him utter,
in a ludicrous ftrain, the language moft proper to
characterife him. The inferior perfonages loaded

promife ; fince he *could not* difmember the empire, nor
alienate, without their confent, the allegiance of his people.
I have never found much delight or inftruction in fuch political metaphyfics.                                  GIBBON.
   Not being convinced or edified by the Abbè's reafoning, I have not tranflated his differtation.
   * Of this we are informed by Suetonius in the following
remarkable paffage : " At the funeral of Vefpafian, Favo,
" the chief of the comedians, who played his part, and imi-
" tated, as is cuftomary, his words and actions while alive,
" afked the managers of the folemnity aloud, " What
" would be the expence of the funeral pomp ?" and they
" anfwering, ' a hundred millions of fefterces,' the pretended
" Vefpafian exclaimed, " if they would give him but a
" hundred fefterces, they might throw him into the river." B.

this

this principal performer with railleries and affronts. The pretended Julian muſt have been highly ridiculous, as the copy was always more extravagant than the original. Neither the faults of that unfortunate prince, nor perhaps his good qualities, were ſpared. He was reproached in the bittereſt terms for his apoſtacy, his temerity, his defeat, his death. To conceive how far the licentiouſneſs was carried, it muſt be remembered that the actors revenged themſelves on the enemy of the ſtage, and that they were ſure of the applauſe of the Chriſtians.

As ſoon as Procopius had acquitted himſelf of this commiſſion, alarmed at the fate of Jovianus, and at the falſe report that was ſpread, that Julian, his relation, had wiſhed, at the point of death, to have him for his ſucceſſor, he thought that his life was in danger. He therefore ſecreted himſelf, and had the art to elude the ſearches of Jovian, and afterwards thoſe of Valens. About two years after the death of Julian, he appeared again in order to aſcend the throne, from which he fell almoſt the ſame inſtant *.

From Niſibis Jovian took the road to Antioch, and came to Edeſſa, which ſhould have been dear to him for the ſame reaſon † that had made it odious to his predeceſſor. He was in that city on the 27th of September, according to the date of a

---

* See p. 221. note †.

† Julian would not paſs through Edeſſa, becauſe that city was ſtrongly attached to Chriſtianity.　　　B.

law,

law *, which excufes the foldiers from going to
forage more than twenty miles, or one day's journey,
from the camp. Julian, the reftorer of military
difcipline, had obliged them to go in fearch of it
to that diftance; but perhaps fome officers fent
them ftill farther. Jovian, interefted in conciliating
the affection of the troops, delivered or preferved
them from that fatigue, to which there was no
right to oblige them; and the fpirit of his law
agrees exactly with that of Julian.

The Emperor continuing his march by long
ftages, and received very forrowfully on his route,
entered Antioch in the month of October, and
could not difpenfe with making fome ftay there,
notwithftanding his impatience to go and fhew himfelf at Conftantinople, and afterwards, no doubt,
in the provinces of the Weft. His troops were in
extreme want of repofe. Antioch, the abode of
plenty, and the centre of all the conveniences of
life, was the propereft place in the world to recover them; and prudence did not yet allow Jovian
to feparate himfelf from an army, whofe fuffrages
were the only right that he had to the empire.

During fix weeks, more or lefs, that he paffed
in the capital of the Eaft, he applied himfelf
chiefly to regulate what concerned religion. That

---

* This law is dated in the confulfhip of Jovian and Varronian, and confequently the date is falfe, at leaft in that
refpect. It is well known, that the dates marked in the
Theodofian code are fo faulty, that fcarce any ftrefs can be
laid on them.                B.

portion of public affairs, fo effential and always
fo delicate, then required extreme difcretion.
Julian, with his pretended toleration, which had
been no more in fact than a perfecution aukwardly
difguifed, in which the injuftice of oppreffion was
aggravated by the infolence of-difhonefty, had in
a manner fet all the fubjects of the empire at variance. The people were incenfed againft the
people ; cities were divided ; families were dif-
united; the ferment of minds was fo violent, that
it feemed as if it could not be calmed but by the
extinction of one of the parties. The unexpected
revolution, which again gave the Chriftians a
prince of their religion, was not fufficient to reftore tranquillity. There was room to fear, that,
under the appearance of zeal, the animofity of
fome ill-informed Chriftians, indulging itfelf in
fome unworthy reprifals, might drive the Pagans,
with whom patience was founded on no religious
principle, to extremities. Already the temples were
every where * fhut; the blood of victims flowed
no longer ; the priefts of the idols abfconded ; the
philofophers trimmed their beards, and quitted the
cloak, to refume the common drefs. This was not
a panic fear : they had unworthily abufed their
credit. St. Gregory of Nazianzus, at the conclufion
of his difcourfe againft Julian, exhorts to the for-

---

* Τα ιιρα των Ελληνων παντα απικλιιθη. Suppofing that Socrates is not miftaken in faying that the temples were
every where fhut, this could not have happened before the
law which we fhall prefently mention.                    B.

givenefs

givenefs of injuries in a manner that would induce a belief, that, on that occafion, he confidered obedience to the precept as a great effort of virtue. One would be apt to think, that, though he inveighs with fuch warmth againft the Pagans, and againft the memory of Julian, it is a ftroke of Chriftian policy; and that by taking, as it were, in the name of the church, and by public authority, a lawful vengeance, he means to prevent and difarm that of individuals.

The war kindled between the Chriftians and Pagans was not the only one of which religion was either the pretext or the caufe. Not to mention fome fects that were obfcure or of little account *, every thing that bore the Chriftian name was divided between the faith of Nice and the herefy of Arius. The moft vehement controverfies are often no more than difputes on words. Here, under the appearance of difputes on words †, and even on letters, there were real divifions as to fundamental tenets; and the difputes were managed with as much animofity, as if incomprehenfible truths had been in queftion. The Arians, whom the favour of Conftantius had put in poffeffion of the churches of Conftantinople, and of the principal

---

* Such as the Valentinians, the Marcionites, the Montanifts, the Manicheans.                            B.

† The terms ομοουσιος, " confubftantial," " of the fame fubftance," confecrated by the council of Nice, and ομοιουσιος, " like in fubftancc," which moft of the Arians admitted, only differ an iota more or lefs.        B,

fees

fees of the Eaſt, ſubdivided into pure Arians and
demi-Arians, agreed only againſt the Catholics.
In leſs than fifty years they had made ſixteen formularies of faith *, and it was doubted whether they
had made the laſt. Arianiſm was a cruel ſect, and
even by that, according to St. Athanaſius †, bore
on its front a mark of reprobation. To cruelty
it knew how to add cunning and artifice. Deceived by its equivocal forms ‡, under Conſtantius
the whole world was ſurpriſed to find itſelf Arian
without thinking of it; but error did not long enjoy this imaginary triumph. A reunion founded
on duplicity had only produced a more cruel
diviſion.

On the other ſide, thoſe who acknowledged the
divinity of the Word, did not all agree as to the
reſt. Some, by an exceſs of delicacy, rejected the
term " conſubſtantial," as not being in ſcripture;
and though they admitted the tenet meant by that
word, all had not, like Athanaſius §, equity enough
to compaſſionate their weakneſs, and to reckon them
among the orthodox.

An obſtinate ſchiſm, formed by miſtake, and
perpetuated by imprudence, rent the city of

---

* The enumeration of them may be ſeen in the Eccleſiaſtical Hiſtory of M. Fleury, l. xiv. 23.     B.

† Ath. Hiſt. Arian. ad Monachos, t. 1. p. 382. Edit.
Bened.                                  B.

‡ At the Council of Rimini.     B.

§ Athan. de Synodis, l. 11. p. 755.     B.

Antioch.

Antioch *. There were feen two Catholic bifhops, befides one Arian. At Conftantinople, and elfe-where,

* In the year 330, under the reign of Conftantine, having fucceeded in depofing and banifhing St. Euftathius, bifhop of Antioch, the moft zealous of the Catholics began to hold their feparate affemblies. As they ftill acknowledged Euftathius, the name of Euftathians was given them. The fee was fucceffively filled by feveral bifhops, more or lefs attached to the Arian cabal, with whom the great number of Catholics of Antioch, either through love of peace, or from weaknefs, did not fail to communicate. Things remained in this ftate during the reign of Conftantius. But in 361 (the laft year of that prince) Anianus, the Arian bifhop, having been banifhed, and, befides, Euftathius having died in his exile, they were defirous to elect a bifhop who might re-unite the church of Antioch. The Arians and the moderate Catholics caft their eyes on Meletius, the moft amiable and moft peaceable of men. Every one thought him of his own party. But in that the Arians were miftaken. Meletius was no fooner elected than he declared for the Catholic faith. The Euftathians, however, obftinately refolved not to acknowledge him, becaufe the Arians had had great fhare in his election. On the other fide, the Arians, enraged at being deceived in him, caufed him to be banifhed a month after, to the great regret of the moderate Catholics, who, retaining an inviolable attachment to the holy bifhop, would no more affemble, as they had hitherto done in the churches of the Arians, and offered to unite themfelves with the Euftathians, or zealous Catholics. But thefe refufed to admit them to their communion. There were then at Antioch therefore three parties; the Arians, the Euftathians, and the Meletians. After the death of Conftantius, in 362, Lucifer, of Cagliari in Sardinia, whom that prince had banifhed into Syria, a man celebrated for his courage, and his fufferings in the good caufe, but whofe views were too confined, ordained as bifhop the prieft Paulinus, whom the Euftathians already confidered as their head. Lucifer thought that the Meletians, more pacific than the others, would accept Paulinus, who, befides, was very worthy of the prelacy; but

where, the Macedonians *, orthodox, at leaſt in appearance, as to the conſubſtantiality of the Son, denied that of the Holy Ghoſt. The Donatiſts, thinking that there was no church, or even ſacraments, out of their ſociety, carried fanaticiſm in Africa to a decree of madneſs. The Novatians †, whoſe hereſy was to erect a deſperate rigour into an article of faith, kept up ſome good underſtanding with the Catholics, who diſtinguiſhed them extremely from the other ſectaries; and it may be ſaid, that they merited that diſtinction by the purity of their manners, and by their attachment to the ancient doctrine as to the divinity of Jeſus Chriſt. They had ſupported with heroic courage the Arian perſecutions: but ſome had ſhewn ‡, that for the defence of their faith they knew how to employ other arms than thoſe of true Chriſtians.

As the moſt natural effect of a foreign war is to ſuſpend civil diſſentions; in ſpite of the artifices of

out this imprudent ſtep only ſerved to put an end to the ſchiſm. Thus there were ſeen in the ſame city three biſhops, Euzoius the Arian, Meletius, returned from his exile, and Paulinus, both Catholics. This diviſion did not terminate till long after, under biſhop Alexander, to whom the Euſtathians re-united themſelves in 415.                B.

* So named from Macedonius, archbiſhop of Conſtantinople.        B.

† The Novatians did not admit to penitence thoſe who had fallen after baptiſm.        B.

‡ Under Conſtantius the Novatian peaſants of Mantinium in Paphlagonia, armed with ſcythes and axes, cut in pieces four companies of ſoldiers, who had been ſent to oblige them to embrace Arianiſm.        B.

Julian

Julian to foment the flame of difcord, there ap-. peared in his reign between the moft oppofite communions a kind of truce refembling peace. Excepting only the Donatifts, who committed exceffes againft the Catholics, for which the magiftrates thought it their duty to acccunt to the Emperor; excepting, I fay, thofe madmen, the Chriftians had feemed to forget their domeftic divifions, and to employ themfelves in concert in offering up prayers for their common deliverance. But as foon as the election of a Chriftian prince was known, the flumbering difputes began to awaken, and the chiefs of the different communions were eagerly defirous of going to meet the Emperor as foon as he was in the Roman territories; either to engage him, or at leaft to render him favourable to their party.

Amidft fuch a diverfity of opinions, Jovian, as I have already faid, had the happinefs to know the truth. He had preferred Chriftianity to his fortune, and openly profeffed the Catholic doctrine. If the purity of his manners did not perhaps anfwer to that of his faith, at leaft he ardently wifhed, it cannot be doubted, to fee all his fubjects re-united in the bofom of the true religion. But Jovian was too well inftructed in the nature of religion itfelf to offer violence to any one. A confeffor of the faith become a perfecutor would have been a kind of prodigy. Who fhould be better acquainted with the rights of confcience than he

.6                                                           who

who himfelf had been obliged to claim them? He
was convinced that faith perfuades, but does not
command; that to employ fire and fword, in the
progrefs of the gofpel, is to combat at once the
fpirit of the gofpel, and the principles of reafon;
that fear only makes hypocrites; that God rejects forced homage, and that if he difapproves
error, he detefts perjury; that the excellence of
the end propofed cannot fanctify unlawful means;
that, befides, in order to fucceed, the means muft
be fuited to the end, and thus that confciences can
no more be carried by force of arms than ramparts
by arguments *.

But, befides, if Jovian had thought it lawful and poffible to convert men by the dread of
punifhments and death, it would have been rifking
too much at the beginning of a new reign to irritate
the Arians, who ftill retained, among the Chriftian
communions, that air of fuperiority which had
been given them by the protection and favour of
Conftantius. It would have been ftill more dangerous to attack Paganifm in front, which, under
Julian, had recovered ftrength, and had even become again the religion of the ftate. It muft be
fuppofed, that the Pagans, feeing themfelves at the

---

* Thefe truly Proteftant doctrines flow from the pen of
a nominal Papift, but are as different from thofe of the
murderers of Cranmer in former times, and of thofe of
Calas in the prefent, as light from darknefs. Such liberal
fentiments in fome ages and countries would have configned
the author to the Inquifition.

difcretion

difcretion of a prince who was a zealous enemy to idolatry, were extremely alarmed, and that many expreffed fo much uneafinefs as to occafion fome to that weakly eftablifhed prince. With a view therefore to confirm them, and alfo to confirm himfelf, he haftened to make a law, by which he maintained them in the free exercife of their religion, and permitted them to re-open the temples, where, by forcible means, and without the authority of the prince, they had been fhut fince the death of Julian.

" You underftand," fays Themiftius, a Pagan philofopher and fenator of Conftantinople *, in a panegyric on Jovian, which he pronounced before him, " that there are fome things which a fo-
" vereign cannot reftrain. Among thefe are the
" virtues, and efpecially religion. A prince,
" who fhould make an edict to enjoin his fubjects
" to love him, would not be obeyed. Could he
" flatter himfelf with being fo for commanding
" them to have fuch or fuch a religious perfuafion?
" Fear, without doubt, will effect tranfient meta-
" morphofes, But fhall we confider as men con-
" vinced, thofe men more changeable than Eu-
" ripus †, perfuaded by their variations to be the
" adorers of the purple, and not of the divinity;
" thofe ridiculous Proteufes who difhonour human
" kind, and who are fometimes feen in the temples

* See the Epiftle to him, Vol. I. p. 4.
† This narrow fea, between Bœotia and Eubœa, ebbed and flowed feven times in 24 hours, or oftener, or feldomer, as the wind fat.

" at

" at the feet of the ftatues and altars, and fome-
" times at the holy table in the churches of the
" Chriftians? Thus, inftead of ufing violence, you
" have made a law which allows every one to pay
" to the Deity the worfhip which he fhall think
" the beft.   As the image of the Supreme Being,
" you imitate his conduct.   He has placed in the
" heart of man a natural inclination which leads
" him to religion ; but he does not force him in
" the choice.   Thus the coërcive laws, which
" tended to deprive man of a liberty which God
" leaves him, have lafted at moft during the lives
" of their authors ; inftead of which, your law,
" or rather that of God himfelf, fubfifts in all
" ages.   Neither confifcations, nor exiles, nor
" punifhments can annull it.   The body may be
" imprifoned, tormented, deftroyed ; but the foul
" takes her flight : fhe efcapes from violence, bear-
" ing in herfelf this indelible law, this liberty of
" thinking, of which it is impoffible to deprive
" her, though the  tongue  fhould be  forced
" to articulate fome words. . . . . . The wifdom
" of your edict allays our cruel divifions.   This,
" Emperor, beloved by God, you know better
" than any one : The Perfians were lefs formidable
" to the Romans than the Romans themfelves ; the
" incurfions of thofe Barbarians lefs dangerous than
" the accufations fuggefted by the fpirit of party
" to deftroy citizens.   Continue to hold the ba-
" lance even.  Allow all mouths to addrefs prayers
" to heaven for the profperity of your empire. . .

" A law

" A law fo juft muft penetrate all the fubjects of
" our divine monarch with refpect and love, thofe,
" among others, to whom not contented to reftore
" liberty, he explains the tenets of their religion
" as well as the ableft of their teachers."

Thus, in the prefence of Jovian himfelf, fpoke
Themiftius, one of the moft illuftrious magiftrates
of his age, and deputed by the body to harangue
the Emperor. His authority fufficiently authen-
ticates the law of Jovian, though it no longer exifts,
and though other writers feem to have been ignorant of it. The panegyrics of princes fometimes
praife them for virtues which they do not poffefs,
but never for laws which they have not made. It
cannot be denied that Themiftius, in the difcourfe,
part of which I have juft quoted, lays down, on
occafion of that law, fome very philofophical and
even very Chriftian maxims. But as truth is very
feldom found in the mouths of Pagans without any
mixture of error, to the folid arguments which
condemn cruelty and violence he adds the pretended impoffibility of knowing how the Deity
would be adored, and the imaginary honour which
redounds to the Supreme Being from the variety
of worfhips which divide the world. This philofopher confounds political toleration with indifference, while Jovian, by the light of the gofpel,
perfectly diftinguifhes them.

The fame edict, which permitted the temples to
be re-opened, ordered the abominable fanctuaries

of impoſtures and witchcraft to be ſhut. It ſuffered
the public ſacrifices, and the worſhip formerly au-
thoriſed, to remain ; but it forbade enchantments,
magic, and all worſhip viſibly founded on im-
poſture. Though the Roman laws had always condemned theſe practices, the fooliſh ſuperſtition and
credulity of Julian had brought them extremely
into faſhion. The wiſeſt among the Pagans muſt
greatly praiſe his ſucceſſor for the care which he
took to proſcribe what they deemed foreign to their
religion, and likely to do it diſcredit. It ſeemed
to them, no doubt, performing a legitimate act of
the pontifical power, which they ſtill aſcribed to
the Chriſtian Emperors, and of which Conſtantine
had uſefully availed himſelf, to effect the deſtruction
of idolatry.

Properly ſpeaking, the Pagan religion had no
dogmas ; it conſiſted of a heap of practics, and
the Sovereign Pontiff had a right to ſuppreſs ſuch
as he thought abuſive *. Conſtantine, therefore
having formed the plan of diſſolving it by little
and little, and of deſtroying it by degrees, without ſhocking the Pagans, had confined it within
very narrow bounds, by retrenching ſometimes a
worſhip contrary to good manners, ſometimes a ſuſpicious practice; here ſubverting a temple that
was become the ſchool of libertiniſm, there inter-

---

* See the Diſſertation of the Baron de la Baſtie, on the
Sovereign Pontificate of the Roman Emperors (Part III.)
in the *Memoirs of the Academy of Inſcriptions and Belles
Lettres*, t. XV.                          B.

dicting an oracle whofe priefts manifeftly abufed the public credulity. It appears that Jovian did not pretend to tolerate Paganifm but in the ftate to which Conftantine had reduced it. On that footing only it could in fact be fuffered, and the moderate Pagans required nothing more.

The political toleration of Jovian was effective and fincere. Inftead of feeking pretences to difturb the Pagans, he did not avail himfelf of the moft natural occafions. He might, without injuftice, have abandoned to the feverity of the laws feveral priefts of the idols, and the philofophers who had abufed the confidence of Julian. Neverthelefs, it is not to his reign that the rigours which, Li- banius fays *, were exercifed againft them, muft be

---

* As Libanius did not pronounce his fecond funeral oration on Julian till eighteen months after the death of that prince, and confequently more than ten months after the death of Jovian, I know not why M. de Tillemont ap- plies to the reign of the latter the bitter complaints of that orator. " At prefent," fays that orator, (*Orat. Parent.* 148, *et feq.*) " thofe who declaim againft the Gods are treated " with refpect, while the priefts, thofe who are only guilty " of ferving the Gods, undergo unjuft trials. That which " they have employed in divine worfhip, that which the " flame has confumed on the altars, they are forced to " furrender. Are they unable to pay? They languifh in " fetters. The temples have been deftroyed, or remain " half-built, to ferve as a ridicule for Chriftians. The " philofophers are put to the torture. To have received " fomething from the Emperor is to have contracted a " debt. What do I fay? It is to have committed a theft. " In the midft of fummer, at noon-day, a man is expofed " quite naked to the heat of the fun. Befides what he

.Y 2 " has

" has received, he is afked what every one fees he has not
" received. It is well known that this is to require an
" impoffibility; but it is a pleafure to burn him; he muft
" expire in this horrible torture. The profeffors of elo-
" quence, accuftomed to live with the great, are driven
" from their doors, like infamous murderers. That nu-
" merous fwarm of young difciples who always accom-
" pany them, feeing their mafters thus treated, conceive
" that knowledge is good for nothing, and feek a better
" protection. In every city the members of the public
" council unjuftly difpenfe with the fervice, which their
" country has a right to expect from them; and no one
" checks fo outrageous a diforder. Nothing is every where
" feen but exactions, forced fales, confifcations, indigence,
" poverty, tears. The labourer choofes rather to beg than
" to cultivate the earth. He who to-day gives alms, to-
" morrow will be obliged to afk them. The Scythians, the
" Sarmatians, the Celts, in a word, all the Barbarians be-
" gin again to infult us on all fides," &c.

The odious ftrokes of this picture do not relate to Jovian.
Indeed, during his reign, the bifhops, and other Chriftian
preachers, were in great efteem, and fpoke againft Paganifm with full liberty. It is alfo very poffible, that at
the news of his election, in places where the Chriftians
were the ftrongeft, the populace might deftroy fome temples.
Thofe which Julian was building remained unfinifhed, becaufe Jovian would not furnifh the expence, and the zeal
of idolaters cooled. I alfo fuppofe that Libanius, and his
fellows, did not find the fame accefs to the great: fome magiftrate might have refufed him admittance; a very fenfible
affront to that fophift, who treated Julian as an equal. But
this is all that can reafonably be afcribed to the reign of
Jovian. According to Libanius, it was " the height of
" fummer," (μεσυ θερυς) when the philofophers were perfecuted. Now Jovian did not enter on the territories of the
empire till towards the beginning of autumn, and died before the end of winter. Befides, the philofopher tormented fo cruelly is plainly the famous Maximus. But
Prifcus and he were brought to trial at the beginning of the
reign of Valentinian and Valens.

As to what Libanius fays of the venality of exemptions,
and of the oppreffion of the people, no author reproaches
Jovian with any thing like it; on the contrary, the patrician
Petronius,

be aſcribed. It is true, that, after the death of
Julian, their protector and their dupe, ſome philoſophers were called to a ſevere account for the
immenſe ſums, which, it was ſaid, they had drawn
from him; and this perhaps is the only time that
the royal treaſure has purſued men of letters. But
thoſe enquiries were not made till the reign of Valens. Eunapius, alſo a Pagan, and as plaintive
as Libanius, affirms that Jovian continued to honour the philoſophers * who were in the train of
his predeceſſor. We may at leaſt conclude, from
that expreſſion, that he had ſome regard for them.
Themiſtius reckons as a merit in him his protecting
philoſophy at a time when almoſt every one elſe
declared againſt it, and recalling it to court in a
leſs diſgraceful habit. Fear had at firſt driven the
philoſophers from it; but they ſoon recovered
their courage; and Jovian allowed them to appear
there again, but in the common dreſs. It may,
however, be preſumed, that they were not ſeen
there with a very gracious eye, and that they muſt

Petronius, the father-in-law of Valens, a monſter of avarice and cruelty, rendered immediately the government of
his ſon-in-law highly odious, and ruined a multitude of
families, by enquiring what was due to the treaſury for
near a century paſt. See Amm. xxvi. 6. In ſhort, the
two brothers reigned when the Barbarians, being no longer
reſtrained by the fear of Julian, again took up arms. Thoſe
people had ſcarce had time to hear of his death, and to
make ſome preparations, during the reign of Jovian.  B.

* Τιμᾶν τους ανδρας διιλιλισιν. Illos viro honore proſequi non
deſtitit.

Y 3                                                ſuſter

suffer some mortifications, and perhaps infults,
from the courtiers, which the Emperor did not
take the trouble to avenge; and that, if I miftake
not, is the meaning of what Themiftius fays, in a
difcourfe addreffed to Valens; that " it is a ftain to
" the glory of Jovian to have fuffered infults to
" be offered them, though, as to himfelf, he offered
" them none."

Libanius continued inceffantly to bewail Julian,
and to praife him in his writings. Some would
have made it a ftate crime, and Jovian was advifed
to fend him to confole himfelf with his hero. But
he thought it beneath an Emperor to trouble himfelf with what a fophift might write. He was
fenfible alfo that by putting an author to death, his
works, inftead of being fuppreffed, are affured of
immortality. As Jovian fpared a Maximus and
a Libanius, we may judge what tranquillity was
enjoyed by fuch Pagans as could be reproached
with nothing but their religion. It is certain,
that at Conftantinople facrifices were publickly
offered for the folemnity of the confulfhip of
Jovian.

If this prince, in quality of common father and
chief of the body politic, thought himfelf obliged
not to reftrain the confciences of his fubjects, he
did not forget that he owed a ftriking protection
to the religious fociety of which he was a member.
It appears by his medals that he replaced in the

I                                           *Labarum*

*Labarum* \* the monogram of Jefus Chrift. Not
content with having thus declared that Chriftianity
was the religion of the empire, he formally declared by a letter †, which he wrote to the gover-
nors

\* The principal ftandard which difplayed the triumph
of the crofs was ftyled the *Labarum*, or *Laborum*, an obfcure though celebrated name, which has been vainly derived from almoft all the languages of the world. It is defcribed as a long pike interfected by a tranfverfal beam.
The filken veil, which hung down from the beam, was cu-
rioufly enwrought with the images of the reigning monarch and his children. The fummit of the pike fupported
a crown of gold, which inclofed the myfterious monogram, at once expreffive of the figure of the crofs,
and the initial letters of the name of Chrift. The fafety
of the Laborum was entrufted to fifty guards of approved
valour and fidelity.                                    GIBBON.
Julian had replaced in the ftandards the antient Latin
letters, S. P. Q. R.
† This letter, mentioned by Sozomen, is, I fancy, the
very law of which Themiftius gives the elogium. He fays,
plainly enough, that this law was the firft of thofe of
Jovian; and Sozomen afferts, that Jovian did not defer a
moment (ωδεν μιλλησας) to write to the generals of the provinces. It is probable, that the law contained two heads.
The Emperor there declared, firft, that the Chriftian religion was that of the ftate, &c. Secondly, that he did
not pretend to deprive any one of the liberty of following
and exercifing any other, &c. The Pagan philofopher
dwells only on the fecond head, which was advantageous
to the Pagans: the ecclefiaftical hiftorian mentions only the
firft, which favoured the Chriftians. Each of them com-
ments in his own way on the article which interefts him,
and gives it too much latitude. In reading Themiftius,
one would think that Jovian had put all religions on the
fame level; but Sozomen, whofe text I am far from underftanding rigoroufly, fays, that this prince declared Chriftianity the only religion of his fubjects. M. de Tillemont did
not know how to reconcile the law that Themiftius mentions

nors of the provinces, all Pagans no doubt, as
they had been put or left in place by Julian; en-
joining them to act so that the Christians might
assemble in the churches : for in several places they
had either been destroyed or converted to profane
uses. He recalled all who had been banished on
account of religion, restored to the clergy, to
virgins, and to widows the privileges granted by
the Christian Emperors, and re-established the diftribution of corn which the demesne allowed to
every church for the subsistence of widows and
orphans. The famine which then afflicted the
empire obliged him to reduce to one-third that
pious donation of Conftantine; but he promised to
give the remainder at the first return of plenty.

He made also a law, which we still have; addressed to Sallust the Second, Præfect of the prætorium of the East, denouncing capital punishment
to those who should dare to steal away, or even
solicit in marriage, the virgins consecrated to God *.

Thefe

with that referred to by Sozomen. I flatter myself that
this learned writer would have approved the method of
agreement here proposed.                                B.

The Abbé de la Bleterie judiciously remarks, that Sozomen has forgot the general toleration, and Themistius the
establishment of the Catholic religion. Each of them
turned away from the object which he disliked, and wished
to suppress the part of the edict the least honourable, in his
opinion, to the Emperor Jovian.              GIBBON.

* The following are the very terms of the law. *Imp.
Jovianus A. ad secundum P. P. Si quis, non dicam rapere, sed vel
attent-*

These scandalous marriages had grown common under Julian. To accomplish them, some had employed violence, and others seduction. An officer, named Magnus, the same who was, under Valens, and perhaps from the time of Julian, treasurer of the Emperor's houshold *, had burned, by his private authority, the church of Beryta in Phœnicia. Ecclesiastical history represents Count Magnus † as

unprin-

*attentare, matrimonii jungendi causa, sacratas virgines vel invitas ausus fuerit, capitali sententiâ feriatur. Dat. XI. Kal. Mar. Antiochiæ, Joviano A. et Varroniano Coss.* Instead of *invitas,* we should perhaps read *invitare.* Sozomen seems to have read *intueri,* as he translates the Latin word by these; ακολαϲως προϲαλεποϲα, *impudicè aspicientem.* There is no probability that this was the sense. The date of this law is also false, like a number of others. Jovian did not take the consulship till a month at soonest after his leaving Antioch; and, besides, he was no longer in this world on the 19th of February, 364, as he died between the 16th and 17th of that month. **B.**

The new law which condemned the rape or marriage of nuns, is exaggerated by Sozomen; who supposes that an amorous glance, the adultery of the heart, was punished with death by the evangelic legislator. **GIBBON.**

\* Thus, I think, *Comes largitionum comitatensium* should be translated. · **B.**

† It was he who, in the time of Valens and of the governor Palladius, persecuted by an inferior order the Catholics of Alexandria, to oblige them to receive the bishop Lucius. Having caused nineteen, as well priests as deacons, to be apprehended and brought before his tribunal, some of whom were more than fourscore years of age, he said to them, "Embrace, wretches, embrace the opinion of " the Arians. If your religion be true, God will pardon " you for having yielded to necessity. You will please the " most clement, august Valens." After having put them

in

unprincipled, a flave to the court, ardent to diftin-
guifh himfelf in all perfecutions, and committing
with the bafenefs of a fubaltern fome crimes of
fupererogation.   He was very near being beheaded
by Jovian.   Powerful interceffions obtained his
pardon ; but he was condemned to re-build the
church of Beryta at his own expence.

   ·   Athanafius, the perfonal object of the hatred
and perfecution of Julian, hearing of the death of
that prince, had on a fudden re-appeared in the
midft of his people, who were agreeably furprifed.
As the orders of Julian had not then been revoked, a Pagan or an Arian might have made an
attempt on the perfon of the holy prelate.   How
was it known whether the new Emperor would not
be difpleafed that Athanafius fhould fhew himfelf
publickly in Alexandria, without the leave of the
fame authority which had banifhed him from all
Ægypt ? But his fears were immediately difpelled
by a letter from Jovian, conceived in thefe terms :
" To the moft religious friend of God, Athanafius,
" Jovian.   As we admire beyond all expreffion the
" fanctity of your life, in which fhine forth the

---

in prifon, and caufed them to be fcourged and tormented,
he banifhed them into an idolatrous country, made them
fet out immediately, urging them himfelf, fword in hand,
without giving them time to take neceffaries, without waiting till the fea became calm, without being moved by the
cries and tears of the whole Catholic people.   *Epiftola Petri
Alexandrini apud Theodoret.* l. IV. 22.        B.

                                              " marks

" marks of refemblance to the God of the uni-
" verfe *, and your zeal for Jefus Chrift our Sa-
" viour, we take you now under our protection,
" moft refpectable bifhop. You deferve it by that
" courage which has made you reckon as nothing
" the moft painful labours, and regard as an ob-
" ject of contempt the rage of perfecutors and
" menacing fwords. Holding in your hand the
" helm of faith, which is fo dear to you, you ceafe
" not to combat for the truth, nor to edify the
" Chriftian people who find in you the perfect
" model of all virtues. For thefe caufes, we re-
" call you immediately, and we order you to return,
" to teach the doctrine of falvation. Return there-
" fore to the holy churches ; feed the people of his
" God. Let the paftor, at the head of the flock,
" offer up prayers for our perfon : for we are per-
" fuaded that God will diffufe on us, and on thofe
" who are Chriftians like us, his moft fignal favours,
" if you grant us the affiftance of your prayers."

It appears by the order contained in this letter,
that the Emperor was ignorant, or chofe to be
ignorant, that Athanafius had refumed the public
exercife of his functions †. Be that as it may,

---

* The word " celeftial" faintly expreffes the impious
and extravagant flattery of the Emperor to the archbifhop,
τας προς τον Θιον των ελων ομοιωσιως. GIBBON.

† He might be ignorant of it ; for St. Gregory of Na-
zianus fays, that the order for the recall of Athanafius was
difpatched the firft of all. *Greg. Naz. or.* XXI. B.

Jovian

Jovian wrote to him again, to afk inftruction of him
as to the tenets which were then the fubject of
difputes. Not that he was not a confirmed catholic.
The letter juft quoted would alone prove it *;
and, befides, thus to confult the great Athanafius,
the man of the church and the bulwark of the
faith, was loudly to declare himfelf for the doctrine
of Nice. But not to mention the difpute which
had been raifed concerning the divinity of the Holy
Ghoft, the Arians, by their fophifms and captious
formularies, fome of which were rather infuffi-
cient than erroneous, had introduced into a con-
troverfy, fimple in itfelf, more difficulties than
were neceffary to embarrafs a foldier like Jovian.
Thinking himfelf then obliged by the ftate to
labour on the great work of the re-union of Chriftians, and refolved to employ only perfuafion, he
had need of fome palpable but decifive and keen
arguments to convince the fectaries, without entering into thorny difcuffions, which would have
been above his reach, and in one fenfe beneath his
dignity.

Athanafius entered fully into his views; convened fome intelligent bifhops, and anfwered him

---

* Theodoret (l. ıv, c. 2,) fays, that he ordered thofe,
who had adhered to the faith of Nice in its purity, to be
put in poffeffion of the churches. If that be true, the
order was not rigoroufly executed. It appears, however,
that Jovian gave a church new-built to the Catholics of
Antioch (of the communion of St. Meletius) ; which feems
to prove that under Julian the Chriftians might build
churches. B.

in

In the name of the whole patriarchate of Alexandria. After congratulating the Emperor on the care which he took to inform himself of the truth *, the holy teacher proves that he muſt attach himſelf to the faith of Nice. It is the faith of the Apoſtles and martyrs. They were in poſſeſſion of that doctrine when Arius came to ſow his errors. All the churches have received, and ſtill receive, the deciſion of Nice; the ſmall number of Arians that oppoſe it cannot form a prejudice againſt the reſt †

of

* We have this letter in the Hiſtory of Theodoret, and among the works of Athanaſius. In the letter, as it is quoted by Theodoret, is a half phraſe in which Athanaſius ſeems to promiſe Jovian a long and tranquil reign, as the reward of his deſire to be inſtructed in heavenly truths: Και την βασιλειαν μετ᾽ ειρηνης πολλαις ἱων περιοδοις επιλελησιις " and " you will govern the empire many years in peace." As Jovian reigned a very ſhort time, Baronius imagines, that theſe words are an addition of ſome Arian, who was willing to make Athanaſius paſs for a falſe prophet; but in authors who are not inſpired ſuch ſort of expreſſions ought to be regarded as wiſhes, and not as promiſes, much leſs as propheſies. B.

Before his departure from Antioch ‡, he aſſured Jovian that his orthodox devotion would be rewarded with a long and peaceful reign. Athanaſius had reaſon to hope, that he ſhould be allowed either the merit of a ſuccesful prediction, or the excuſe of a grateful, though ineffectual, prayer. In ſome MSS. this indiſcreet promiſe is omitted; perhaps by the Catholics, jealous of the prophetic fame of their leader. GIBBON.

† Συμψηφοι τυγχανωσιν αἱ κατα τοπον εκκλησιαι . . . παρεξ ολιγων των τα Αρειου φρονωων . . . και τινες αλλιγωσι ταυτη τη πιστει η δυναιλαι προκριμα ποιην πασσι τη οικουμενη. " All the churches " every where agree . . . a few excepted, who embrace

‡ This letter was rather previous to his coming to Antioch, and indeed occaſioned it. See p. 334.

" the

of the world. At length Athanafius, willing to
guard Jovian againſt the hereſy of Macedonius,
obſerves, that the ſame council of Nice has ſufficiently eſtabliſhed the conſubſtantiality of the Holy
Ghoſt, by ſaying, that it is " glorified with the Fa-
" ther and the Son." Thus this able divine adapts
himſelf to the neceſſity and capacity of the prince,
and does not omit to ſupply him with peremptory
arguments, drawn from preſcription, and the conſent
of the churches as to a formal and determined tenet.

The Emperor was ſo well ſatisfied with the letter
of Athanaſius, that he wiſhed to converſe with him,
and ordered him to repair to Antioch. The holy
biſhop obeyed the more willingly, as he had already
reſolved to go to court; not from taſte (for no
biſhop was ever leſs a courtier), but for the intereſts

" the opinion of Arius *, and though ſome contradict this
" faith, we know that they cannot prejudice the whole
" world." Athanaſius, by reducing the Arians to ſo ſmall
a number, ſeems to differ from the common opinion; but
it muſt be obſerved, 1. That the biſhops who had ſub-
ſcribed to the council of Rimini, had recovered their fall
after the death of Conſtantius. 2. At the very time when
hereſy ſeemed to prevail, many of thoſe who received the
forms propoſed by the Arians, received them in a Catholic
ſenſe. 3. As the moſt determined of the Arians did not
ſcruple to ſay, that Jeſus Chriſt is God, the Chriſtian
people, who knew only the Supreme God, underſtood that
Jeſus Chriſt was the only and ſame God with his Father,
and underſtood in a good ſenſe the ambiguous expreſſions
with which the error was envelopped. This occaſioned the
ſaying of a father of that time: " The ears of the people
" are more holy than the hearts of the prieſts." B.

* This aſſertion was verified in the ſpace of thirty or forty years.
GIBBON.

of the church, and from deference to the advice of
his intimate friends. However advantageous his
reputation was, he always gained by a perfonal
acquaintance. Jovian liked him extremely, and
gave him his confidence. It is, honourable for
that prince to have placed it fo well. Athanafius
was the greateft man of his age; and perhaps,
taken all together, the church has never had a
greater. God, who deftined him to combat the moft
dreadful of herefies, armed at once with the
fubtleties of logic and the power of the Emperors,
had endued him with all the gifts of nature and of
grace, which could render him proper to fill that
high deftination.

He had a juft, quick, and penetrating mind; a
generous and difinterefted heart; cool courage, and,
it may be faid, uniform heroifm, always the fame,
without impetuofity or extravagance; lively faith;
unbounded charity; profound humility; a chriftianity, ftrong, fimple, and noble, like the gofpel;
a natural eloquence, abounding with penetrating
ftrokes, ftrong in fubftance, going directly to the
point, and of rare precifion in the Greek writers
of that time. The aufterity of his life rendered
his virtue refpectable; the gentlenefs of his manners
made him beloved. The calmnefs and ferenity of
his foul were painted on his face. Though he
had not an advantageous perfon *, his external appearance had fomewhat majeftic and ftriking. He

* See note *. p. 141.

was

was not ignorant of the profane fciences, but he avoided making a parade of them. Skilled in tho letter of the fcriptures, he alfo poffeffed their fpirit. Neither Greeks, nor Romans, ever loved their country fo much as Athanafius loved the church, whofe interefts were always infeparable from his. Long experience had inured him to ecclefiaftical affairs. Adverfity, which enlarges and refines when it does not crufh the genius, had given him admirable penetration to difcover refources, even human, when every thing feemed defperate. Threatened with exile when he was in his fee, and with death when he was exiled, he ftruggled for near fifty years againft a league of men fubtle in arguments, profound in intrigues, acute courtiers, mafters of the prince, arbiters of favour and difgrace, indefatigable calumniators, barbarous perfecutors. He difconcerted, confounded, and always efcaped them, without giving them the confolation of feeing him make one falfe ftep; he made them tremble even when he was flying before them, and when he was buried alive in the tomb of his father *. He read hearts and futurity. Some Catholics were perfuaded that God revealed to him the defigns of his enemies; the Arians accufed him of magic; and the Pagans pretended that he was

* Under Valens he concealed himfelf in the fepulchre of his father, and remained there four months. Among the ancients, particularly in Ægypt, fepulchres were buildings in the open country, fo confiderable that there were apartments in them. *M. Fleury*, l. XVI. 10. B.

verfed

verfed in the fcience of auguries, and that he uⁿderftood the language of the birds *; fo true it is that his prudence was a kind of divination. No one difcerned better than he the feafons to difclofe or to conceal himfelf; thofe of fpeech or filence; of aftion or repofe. He knew how to 'fix the inconftancy of the people (the Alexandrians, which is faying all), to find a new country in the places of his exile, and the fame credit at the extremity of Gaul, in the city of Treves, as in Ægypt; and the very bofom of Alexandria; to keep up correfpondences; to procure protections; to unite the orthodox; to encourage the moft timid; of a weak friend never to make an enemy; to excufe weakneffes with a charity and goodnefs 'of' heart, which fhewed, that, if he condemned rigorous methods in matters of religion, it was lefs from intereft than principle and character.

* This we learn from Ammianus: " It was faid, that " being thoroughly fkilled in foothfaying, and in what " was portended by augural birds, he fometimes foretold " future events." It is related on this fubject, that as Athanafius was paffing through the ftreets of Alexandria on the eve of a feftival which the Pagans were to celebrate with great feftivity, a raven was heard to croak. " What " fays that bird ?" exclaimed the Pagan populace. Athanafius anfwered fmiling, " He fays, cras" (which fignifies in the Roman language, " to-morrow)," " and declares to " you that the Emperor of the Romans forbids you to cele" brate your feftival." On the morning after, the prohibition of the Emperor did not fail to arrive. SOZOMEN. B.
A prophecy, or rather a joke, is related by Sozomen, (l. IV. c. 10.) which evidently proves, if the crows fpeak Latin, that Athanafius underftood their language. GIBBON.

Julian, who did not, persecute the other bishops, at least openly, considered the taking away his life as a piece of great policy, thinking that the fate of Christianity was attached to that of Athanasius. This honourable distinction seemed to have completed the glory of the holy bishop, when he repaired to Jovian. He was then about seventy years old; but his career was not ready to close. After having made him triumph over three former Emperors *, God destined him to gain other victories over Valens †.

We are ignorant of the particulars of the advice which Athanasius gave to Jovian; but we may be certain, that he confirmed him in the design of labouring only in a Christian manner to re-unite Christians; and that he made him understand that it was previously necessary to inspire all parties with principles of kindness; to teach them to bear with one another; to desire and to seek peace, till it should please God to accomplish it. At the same time he disclosed to him the snares of the sectaries, some of whom at least had formed projects of conquest on a prince who was not sufficiently instructed in theological matters to distin-

* That is, of Constantine (in the latter years of his reign deceived by the Arians), Constantius, and Julian. B.

† The Jansenists have often compared Athanasius and Arnauld, and have expatiated with pleasure on the faith and zeal, the merit and exile, of those celebrated doctors. This concealed parallel is very dexterously managed by the Abbé de la Bleterie. GIBBON.

guish

guifh by himfelf what characterifes error, when it borrows the features of truth.

Arrian and Candidus, pure Arians, ordained bifhops by the famous Ætius *, both relations of the Emperor, were gone to meet him at Edeffa ; and Jovian, if we may believe Philoftorgius, had, in fpeaking to them, expreffed a kind of neutrality which might give them fome hope, though his anfwer might be only the effect of his moderation. They had followed him, without doubt, to Antioch ; and it is alfo known that Euzoïus, bifhop of that great city, and fome other Arians, already practifed upon the eunuchs of the palace, having not forgotten that, by that method, they had gained the favour of Conftantius, and reigned in his name. All the leaders of parties befieged Jovian to obtain his permiffion to perfecute their enemies. We may judge of their refpective pretenfions by the petition of the Macedonians, who demanded to be put into poffeffion of the churches which were occupied by the pure Arians. The Emperor contented himfelf with replying, " I hate difputes : I love and ho- " nour thofe who have peaceable views, and who " concur in union." Thefe words, proceeding from the mouth of the fovereign, and coming from the bottom of his heart, were an effectual ftroke, and immediately chilled the warmeft difputants. They held a council in Antioch, where the Arians of the party of Acacius of Cæfarea in Paleftine

* See Vol. I. p. 2. note *.

com-

communicated with Meletius, one of the two Catholic bishops of that city, and subscribed to the form of Nice. The sincerity of their signature is questioned ; but if they betrayed their conscience, it was not the fault of Jovian, who declared plainly that he would not constrain any one, and who said it sincerely. He was not so successful in terminating the schism of the Catholics of Antioch, divided between Meletius and Paulinus. Fraternal dissensions are always the most obstinate.

Though Jovian shewed very great regard for Athanasius, the Arians of Alexandria, supported clandestinely by Euzoïus, made some attempts to prevent his returning to his church. After the tragical death of their bishop, George of Cappadocia, which happened in the time of Julian *, they had cast their eyes on a priest named Lucius, a man of very bad looks, and of a still worse character, who did not fail to justify their choice by the cruelties which he committed in the persecution of Valens. The Arians of Alexandria, for some reason that is not known, had not yet caused him to be ordained. They sent deputies to Jovian, and Lucius at their head; wishing to have him for their bishop, or, at least, any other that the Emperor would give them to the exclusion of Athanasius. The Catholics of Alexandria sent deputies also, on their part, to oppose the efforts of the Arians; the latter addressed the Emperor several

---

* See the IXth and Xth Epistles of Julian, p. 17—23.

times.

times. We have the original relation of the different audiences which he gave them *. It is a curious remain in many refpects. Above all, Jovian is there feen drawn to the life: he there fhews firmnefs, fenfe, judgement, and equity, fomething blunt and military, a lively difpofition, and, if I miftake not, a tafte rather than a talent for raillery. But I am wrong to foreftall the reader; let him judge for himfelf †.

[The Emperors, who originally were only generals of the army, were accuftomed to exercife with their foldiers. There was near every city a place for exercife, called, " The field of Mars," or, " The field.]" One day, when Jovian [attended by his guard] was going on horfeback through the Roman gate to the field of Mars, Lucius, Berniccus, and the other [deputies of the] Arians, approached him, faying, " We beg " your power, your majefty, your piety, to give " us audience." ' Who, and whence are you?' faid Jovian. They anfwered, " Sir, we are Chrif-" tians," ' Whence, and of what city ?' added the Emperor: "Of Alexandria," replied the Arians. ' What do you defire of me ?' faid the Emperor. " We befeech your majefty," faid they, " to give " us a bifhop." ' I have ordered Athanafius,' re-

* *Petitio Arianorum ad Jovian. inter opera Athan. t. I. p. 782.* B.

† I give this account entire, having taken care to inclofe within crotches all that is not in the acts themfelves, and yet was nycceffary to facilitate the underftanding them.

Z 3

plied

plied Jovian, ' to return to his fee.'   " Sir," said
the Arians, " Athanafius has been banifhed many
" years for crimes of which he is not cleared."
Then a foldier [a Catholic, of the Emperor's
guard], in the tranfport of his zeal, took the
liberty to fay, ' Sir, give yourfelf the trouble
' to examine, who are thefe people, and whence
' they come.   They are the miferable remains
' of the faction of Cappadocia, the agents of
' George, of that villain, who defolated the city
' of Alexandria, and the whole world.'   At thefe
words, the Emperor fpurred his horfe, and went
to the field.

They prefented themfelves a fecond time, and
faid, ' We have feveral heads of accufation againft
' Athanafius, which we are able to prove.   It is
' thirty years fince he was banifhed by Conftan-
' tine and Conftantius, of immortal memory.   He
' has been banifhed lately by the beloved of God,
' the moft philofophical * and moft happy Julian.'
" The accufations of ten, twenty, thirty years,"
faid the Emperor, " are obfolete.   Speak no more
" to me of Athanafius.   I know why he was ac-
" cufed, and how he was banifhed."

[So firm an anfwer did not repulfe the Arians.
They returned to the charge a third time.] " We

---

* It is difficult to conceive that perfons who profeffed
Chriftianity, and, befides, were fpeaking to a Chriftian
Emperor, fhould have been fo irreligious, fo abfurd, as to
give Julian thefe epithets.

Muft there not have been fome interpolation here ?   B.

" have,"

" have," faid they," " new complaints againft Atha-
" nafius." [The deputies of the Catholics of Alexandria beginning, as it feems, to fpeak at the fame
time], " Jovian faid, '·When all fpeak together, it
' is impoffible to underftand who is in the right.
' Choofe two perfons on each fide ; for I cannot
' anfwer both of you.' The Catholics began. " Sir,"
faid they, " thefe men, whom you fee, are the re-
" mains of the deteftable George, the fcourge of
" our province. They do not fuffer in the cities any
" fenator". . . . The Arians [wifhing to cut fhort an
account which would have covered them with confufion, and perceiving, befides, that Lucius, a crea-
ture of George, would never be approved by the Emperor, interrupted the Catholics by faying], ' Be fo
' kind, Sir, as to fet over us whomever you pleafe,
' except Athanafius.' " I have already told you," replied the Emperor, " what concerns Athanafius is
" fettled ;"—and in an angry tone, he faid to his
guard in Latin, " Feri, feri," that is to fay, " Strike,
" ftrike *." [The order, without doubt, was not
executed, as the Arians perfifted.] ' Sir,' faid
they, ' if you fend back Athanafius, our city is
' ruined ; and, befides, no one affociates with him.'
" I have, however,' faid Jovian, " made en-
" quiries ; and I am affured, that he thinks well,
" that he is orthodox, and that he teaches found

* Jovian fpoke Greek to the Alexandrians. It is probable that the Emperors always fpoke Latin to their
guard. B.

" doctrine."

" doctrine." ' It is true,' replied the Arians, ' that
' he speaks well ; but he thinks ill.' The Emperor said, " I require no other testimony than that
" which you have given him. If he thinks ill, he
" must give an account of it to God. We men
" hear words ; God alone knows the bottom of the
" heart." ' Sir,' said the Arians, ' allow us to
' hold our affemblies *.' " Ah !" replied Jovian,
" what hinders you?" ' But, Sir,' added they,
' Athanasius declares us heretics and dogmatists.
" His place obliges him," said Jovian. " It is the
" duty of those who teach the truth." ' Sir,'
proceeded the Arians, ' he has taken away the lands
' of the churches †.' " You would make me be-
" lieve," said Jovian, " that you are brought
" hither by other views than those of the faith.
" Retire, and live in peace. Go to church ; you
" have an assembly to-morrow." [This was on
a Saturday, or the eve of some festival.] " After
" the assembly, every one shall subscribe his pro-
" fession of faith. You have here some bishops
" and Nemesinus ‡. Athanasius also is here. Those
" who are not instructed in the faith have only to
" apply themselves to him. I give you to-morrow,
" and the day after. I am now going to the field

---

* Συναγισθαι.

† This perhaps is the meaning here of the word τα
τιμωνη.　　　B.

‡ This Nemesinus is not known ; he might be an officer
employed by the Emperor to effectuate the re-union. Under
Constantius we find *Nemesianus,* intendant of the finances,
*somes largitionum.*　　　B.

" of

" of Mars." A lawyer, a Cynic philofopher, then
faid to Jovian, ' Sir, on account of the bifhop
' Athanafius the treafurer-general has taken fome
' houfes from me.' Jovian anfwered him, " If the
" treafurer-general has taken fome houfes, is Atha-
" nafius refponfible for it ?" Another lawyer,
named Patalas, then faid to him, ' I have a charge
' againft Athanafius.' " What bufinefs," faid the
Emperor, " has a Pagan like thee to trouble him-
" felf with Chriftians?"

[During this time Lucius kept behind the other
deputies. The bad fituation in which he faw his
affairs was likely to increafe the confufion which
his difadvantageous perfon might already have occafioned in him. He would have mingled in] the
crowd of the people of Antioch, who were collected round the Emperor. But fome feized him,
and having made him advance, againft his will,
' See, Sir,' faid they, ' what a fubject they wifh to
' make a bifhop !' [It muft be remembered that
Athanafius had a countenance full of noblenefs
and dignity *.]

Neverthelefs the fame Lucius [depending perhaps on fome private recommendation] ventured
to appear again before the Emperor at the
gate of the palace, and begged an audience.
Jovian ftopped, and faid to him, ' Lucius, is it
' thou to whom I am fpeaking ? How cameft thou
' hither? By fea or by land ?' " By fea, Sir," replied Lucius. ' May the God of the univerfe, may

* See p. 141, note.

' the

'the fun * and the moon,' faid the Emperor,
'punifh the companions of thy voyage, for not
'having thrown thee into the fea! May the fhip
'be eternally the fport of outrageous waves, and
'never arrive in port!' [Thus he delivered himfelf from that odious man by an ironical impre-
cation, in which the learned editors of Athanafius
difcover much wit †. I queftion whether every one
difcovers as much; nor do I know whether they will
not be furprifed at this fantaftic affemblage of the
fun and moon with the God of the univerfe in the
mouth of a prince in other refpects fo religious.]

The Emperor, having learned that the Arian
cabal were ufing indirect meafures at court, and
that Euzoïus had engaged Probàtius, the great
chamberlain, and the other eunuchs of the palace, to fpeak to him in favour of the Arians
of Alexandria, was enraged to fee that the fucceffors of Eufebius and Bardion ‡, who had made
a traffic of the favours of Conftantius, fhould pretend to fucceed to their credit. He made his
eunuchs undergo the torture to difcover the
bottom of the intrigue; and faid, " that he would
" treat in the fame manner the firft [of his do-
" mefticks] who fhould dare to folicit him againft
" the Chriftians." After having begun the work

---

* It is in the Greek Κομήτης ηλιος, " the blazing fun." B.
† See the Latin Life of Athanafius, which is prefixed to
the new edition; *et facetè quidem*. B.
‡ Braudion in the French; but in the Greek, Βαρδιων.

of

of re-union, as far as time would permit, under the eyes and direction of Athanasius, he allowed him to return into Ægypt, and remained impressed with esteem for his virtues and talents *.

With such zeal for the Christian religion, Jovian, one would think, must have succeeded at An-tioch better than his predecessor. But the city was filled with Arians, or with persons who thought themselves such; and the Arian sects deemed themselves persecuted when they could not persecute. Besides, the inhabitants of Antioch re-mained in possession of the faculty of despising all their sovereigns, or at least of turning them into ridicule. What prince could have found favour in their sight? They did not spare Marcus Au-relius. Some Emperors had punished those info-lent people. Most had connived at their insults.

* Athanasius at the court of Antioch is agreeably re-presented by La Bleterie. He translates the singular and original conferences of the Emperor, the primate of Ægypt, and the Arian deputies. The Abbé is not satisfied with the coarse pleasantry of Jovian; but his partiality for Atha-nasius assumes, in his eyes, the character of justice.
GIBBON.
As soon as Athanasius had gained the confidence, and secured the faith, of the Christian Emperor, he returned in triumph to his diocese, and continued, with mature counsels and undiminished vigour, to direct, ten years longer, the ecclesiastical government of Alexandria, Ægypt, and the Catholic church. The true æra of his death is perplexed with some difficulties. But the date (A. D. 373, May 2.) which seems the most consistent with history and reason, is ratified by his authentic life (*Maffei Offervazioni Letterarie*, tom. III. p. 81.) Ibid.

Julian

Julian had lately revenged himfelf with his pen. But Antioch was a city that was incorrigible, was reckoned fuch, and abufed its reputation. Jovian was not well received. The treaty of peace, and the ceffion of Nifibis, furnifhed the jokers with a thoufand farcaftic ftrokes. They had ridiculed Julian for his beard, his diminutive ftature, his temerity. As for Jovian, he was treated as a fecond Paris: " he has," it was faid, " the good looks and per- " fon of the Trojan prince. He has, like him, " ruined his nation. O that he had perifhed in " the war! He fhould be fent back into Perfia " to commence another treaty. His perfon was " formed at the expence of his mind. The meafure " of his ftature is that of his folly." The walls were covered with abufive bills, the ftreets and fquares were ftrewed with verfes of Homer, applied, or parodied, in the moft infulting manner *. In the Hippodrome a man of the dregs of the people made the fpeҁators laugh by repeating, with a loud voice, fome low jefts on the ftature of the Emperor; and at the idea of this wretch being ap- prehended, the people revolted. This fedition might have had dreadful confequences, if the præfeҁt Salluft the fecond had not quelled it; and that required all his authority.

* The libels of Antioch may be admitted on very flight evidence.                                         GIBBON.

Thefe

# HISTORY OF JOVIAN.

Thefe facts, though taken from the fragments·
of a Greek monk *, an hiftorian little known, are
no more than probable and fuitable to the character
of the inhabitants of Antioch. But what the
fame writer adds merits no belief. " There was,"
fays he, " in Antioch, a fmall temple, of very
" elegant architecture, built by Hadrian, in ho-
" nour of his adoptive father, Trajan. Julian had
" converted it to a library, and entrufted the care
" of it to the eunuch Theophilus. Jovian, at the
" inftigation of his wife, reduced it to afhes, with
" all the books that it contained." But, what is
more furprifing, the author makes Jovian march to
this expedition at the head of his feraglio, with a
torch in his hand †, juft as Alexander formerly,
with the courtefans of Greece, burned the palace
of Perfepolis.

I am far from fufpecting the Greek monk of in-
venting fo ridiculous a ftory, and of intentionally
blackening Jovian. He copied, without difcernment, fome enemy of that prince, Eunapius perhaps, an hiftorian very envenomed againft the
Chriftian Emperors. That the morals of Jovian

* John of Antioch, whofe hiftory began with the cre- ·
ation of the world, and clofed with the reign of Phocas. B.

† Αὐἰων των παλλακιδων υφαπίωσων μἱλα γιλωἶος την πυραν.
" The harlots themfelves with laughter lighting the pile."
SUIDAS.

He might be *edax, et vino Venerique indulgens.* But I agree
with La Bleterie in rejecting the foolifh report of a Bac-
chanalian riot (*ap. Suidam*) celebrated at Antioch, by the
Emperor, his *wife*, and a troop of concubines.    GIBBON.

were

were not very regular we may believe, if we pleafe, on the word of Ammianus Marcellinus, though according to the judicious reflection of Ammianus himfelf, on the fubject of another Emperor, the malignity, or corruption, of mankind, is accuftomed to lend frailties to princes who have them not *. However, if Jovian had lived in a public and fcandalous irregularity, the Chriftians would not have loaded him with praifes at a time when no one had any thing more to hope or fear from him. The concurrence of the Emprefs with the miftreffes of the Emperor is alfo fomething very fingular. But by what caprice could the wife of Jovian, Cariton, to whom her father, Lucillian, had, without doubt, given a Roman education, fuitable to the rank which he himfelf held in the ftate, have wifhed to burn a temple, which was no longer a temple, but a library? To annihilate the remains of profane literature is a Muffulman tafte, which never prevailed among Chriftians, efpecially in the fourth century, when the moft celebrated men in the church were at the fame time the moft converfant with the fciences of the Greeks. Befides, we fhall prefently fee that the wife of Jovian was not then with him. In fhort, the filence of Ammianus and Zofimus completes the deftruction of this calumny, and even renders what I have juft

---

* It is fuppofed that they would do all that they can with impunity. *Quod crimen etiamfi non invenit malignitas, fingit in fummarum licentiá poteftatum.* B.

mentioned,

mentioned, of the ribaldry of Antioch againſt Jovian, in ſome degree ſuſpicious.

Neither of them ſay a word of what happened
during his reſidence in that city. Ammianus contents himſelf with relating ſeveral natural events
which the Pagan ſuperſtition conſidered as fatal
preſages. The ſtatue of Maximian, placed in the
veſtibule of the palace, loſt on a ſudden the
[brazen] globe (a ſymbol of the empire) which
it held in its hand. A dreadful noiſe was heard
in the council-room. Comets were ſeen in the
day-time \*. The Emperor, too intelligent to be
alarmed by theſe pretended ſigns of the wrath of
heaven, but filled with a thouſand anxieties on account of the provinces of the Weſt, of which he
had received no intelligence, ſet out with his army
in the month of December. Forced marches, and
the rigour of the ſeaſon, deſtroyed a great number
of men and horſes.

At Tarſus he paid the laſt duties to Julian, according to Socrates, and gave him a ſolemn funeral. Ammianus only ſays, that he ordered his

---

· \* Ammianus, who is very ready to diſplay his erudition,
here relates the various ſentiments of the ancient philoſophers on comets, and concludes with the opinion of
Pythagoras, which ſeems then to have had the preference :
" that they are ſtars, like the reſt, but that we are igno-
" rant of their revolutions." *Stellas eſſe quaſdam cæteris
ſimiles, quarum ortus obituſque, quibus ſint temporibus præſtituti,
humanis mentibus ignorari.* B.

tomb

tomb to be decorated *. This order was executed
under Valentinian and Valens, with much attention, on their part, and even with sufficient magnificence. To give some idea of it, it is enough
to say, that Libanius was satisfied. Thus three
Christian Emperors, whom Julian had molested on
account of their religion, concurred in granting
him that frivolous reward of his frivolous virtues,
or rather that prerogative annexed to the rank in
which God had placed him in the world. Humanity, decorum, policy, and even religion autho-
rised their conduct; and Jovian did not foresee,
that, at the end of twelve centuries, his having buried the dead, and expressed some regard for the
talents of the man, the Emperor, and the nephew
of the great Constantine, would be imputed to him
as a crime †.

Though we have no incontestible proofs of the
apotheosis of Julian, there is no doubt that the

* Zonaras says the same in these words; *ξ Αντιοχιας δε
εις Ταρσον γεγονως, και το μνημα κοσμησας τυ Ιυλιανυ σταντος.*
" Going from Antioch to Tarsus, he honoured Julian by
" adorning his tomb." He also relates that the corpse of
Julian was afterwards removed from Tarsus to Constantinople; which is confirmed by Cedrenus.　　VALOIS.

† Baronius, in his Annals, considers the premature death
of Jovian as the punishment of his having commanded the
adorning the tomb of a wretch who deserved to be thrown
into the highway, *hominis alioqui ne cæspititiâ quidem sepulturâ
digni.*　　B.
　　The Abbé de la Bleterie handsomely exposes the brutal
bigotry of Baronius, who would have thrown Julian to the
dogs.　　GIBBON.

senate

fenate of Rome, whofe members were ftill almoft
all idolaters, paid him an honour due by right to
the Emperors, unlefs a procefs was inftituted againft
their memory. Even the Chriftian princes were
deified. - There was no medium : they muft be
ranked among the Gods, or numbered among the
tyrants. Many cities, in which Paganifm prevailed,
affociated Julian with their tutelar deities. Some
of his credulous adorers thought that they perceived fome effects of his power ; while it was faid
by the Chriftians, that the afhes of that apoftate
ftirred in the tomb. A report was even fpread
that the earth, by a violent fhock, had difcharged
them from her bofom. There, however, they remained, when, writing in the reign of Theodofius,
Ammianus judged the city of Tarfus little worthy
of fuch a treafure. This hiftorian, a foldier, wifhed
to have feen Julian on the banks of the Tiber
among the firft Cæfars * ; and Libanius, entirely
a man of letters, would have been better pleafed
with him in the Academy by the fide of the divine

* xv. 10. The paffage deferves to be tranfcribed :
*Cujus fuprema et cineres . . . non Cydnus videre debuit, quam-
vis gratiffimus amnis et liquidus; fed ad perpetuandam gloriam
recte factorum præterlambere Tiberis, interfecans urbem æternam,
divortiumque veterum monumenta præftringens.* B.

" Whofe obfequies and afhes fhould not have been feen
" by the Cydnus, though a moft pure and limpid ftream,
" but, to perpetuate the glory of his good deeds, fhould
" have been laved by the Tiber; which interfects the
" eternal city, and chills the monuments of the ancient
" Gods."

Plato *. Either in the field of Mars, or in the Lyceum, Julian would have been placed with propriety. On the contrary, he would have been remarkably mifplaced, if, as the modern Greeks pretend, he had been afterwards removed from Tarfus to Conftantinople, and interred among the Chriftian princes in the church of the Holy Apoftles. Who could have made that auguft temple fo ftrange a prefent? This kind of digreffion will, I hope, be excufed. To the hiftory, that I am writing, nothing that relates to Julian is foreign.

Jovian, continuing to make long marches, paffed through Tyana in Cappadocia, where Procopius, the fecretary of ftate, and the tribune Memoridus, who had been difpatched into the Weft, brought him the following intelligence. Lucillian, his father-in-law, on arriving at Milan, had learned that Malarich, that confidential Frank appointed by the new Emperor to command the troops in Gaul, in the room of Jovinus, refufed to accept that employment. Upon that, the Count had fpeedily paffed the Alps, and repaired to Rheims, with Valentinian and the tribune Seniauchus. He

---

* Orat. Parent. c. 156. p. 377. Τυλον εδεξαλο μεν το προ Ταρσων της Κιλικιας χωριον, ουχι δ'αν δικαιολερον το της Ακαδημιας πλησιον Πλαλωνος.　　B.

"The fuburb of Tarfus in Cilicia received him; but "he had a greater right to be buried in the Academy near "the tomb of Plato."

The hiftory of princes does not very frequently renew the example of a fimilar competition.　　GIBBON.

had

had found Gaul tranquil and fubmiffive to Jovian.
But without confidering that the authority of his
fon-in-law was not fufficiently eftablifhed, he undertook to proceed againft fome officers with a
premature feverity. A criminal, apprehenfive of
being punifhed for his mifdemeanours, fought an
afylum among fome troops of Batavians *, who
were probably quartered in the neighbourhood of
Rheims. To induce them to take him under their
protection, he affured them that Jovian was only
an ufurper who had revolted againft Julian ; but
that Julian was living, and would foon make that
rebel fenfible of it, if he had not already ; and that
the moft effential fervice which fubjects could render to their lawful fovereign was to exterminate the
emiffaries of a tyrant, who came to furprife the
fidelity of the people, and to engage them in their
revolt. This Roman, indifcreet as he was, found
credit among people that were fimple, and befides
affectionate to Julian. They took arms, and maffacred Lucillian and the tribune Seniauchus. Valentinian (who in a few months was to reign) owed
his life to the care which his hoft took to fecrete
him. The Batavians, having foon difcovered the

---

* Ammianus only fays, *ad militaria figna confugit*, without mentioning the Batavians. Zofimus names them,
but extremely mutilates all this hiftory, and places the
fcene at Sirmium. It appears, however, by the *Notitia* of
the empire, that there were Batavians at Condren, in
the fecond Belgic, of which Rheims was the capital. *Præ-
fectus Lætorum Batavorum Contraginenfium, Noviomago Belgicæ
fecunda.*    B.

impofition,

impofition, returned to their duty. As, on the refufal of Malarich, Jovinus had retained the command of. the. troops, he difpatched the principal
officers to Jovian, to affure him of the fubmiffion of
the army and himfelf *. Procopius and Memoridus, accompanied by Valentinian, proclaimed the
approaching arrival of his deputies.

The Emperor, to reward the zeal of Valentinian, gave him the fecond [fchool, or] company
of targetteers, of his domeftic guards, and fent
Arinthæus immediately with a letter to Jovinus,
by which he confirmed that general in his poft,
and enjoined him to punifh the author of the impofition, and to fend the principal leaders of the
fedition.to court, loaded with irons.

At the little town of Afpuna †, in Galatia, the
deputies from the army of Gaul met Jovian, who
having given them a public audience with extreme
fatisfaction, made them prefents, and ordered them
to return immediately to their refpective employments.

He entered Ancyra ‡ at the end of the month
of December; and on the firft day of January,
364, he there celebrated the folemnity of his
confulfhip. In the room of Varronian, his father,

* The moderation of Jovinus, mafter-general of the
cavalry, who forgave the intention of his difgrace, foon
appeafed the tumult, and confirmed the uncertain minds
of the foldiers. .GIBBON.

† As he defcended from mount Taurus. Ibid.

‡ The capital of Galatia.

who

who died conful elect, he had chofen for his collegue young Varronian, his fon. He had been
brought from Illyricum to Ancyra, where the Emperor immediately conferred upon him the title of
*Nobiliffimus*; a title invented for the brothers of
Conftantine, and afterwards given to the fons of
the Emperors *. They quitted it only to affume
that of Cæfar. Other princes had often raifed
their fons to the confulfhip before the time fixed
by the laws; but a conful in the cradle had never
yet been feen. Jovian thought it a debt to the
memory of his father to fubftitute to that illuftrious
veteran an infant who bore his name. After
all, this dignity, which was ftill called the fummit
of human grandeur, had no longer any functions.
It ferved merely to denominate the years, and to
perpetuate the form of the ancient government.
On the day of the ceremony, when the young
prince was to be placed, according to cuftom, in
the curule chair, he expreffed by obftinate cries a
reluctance, which feemed a bad omen, and which
was foon after confidered as a kind of forefight †.

---

* The fame is now the title of our dukes.

† *Cujus vagitus, pertinaciter reluctantis, ne in curuli fellâ
veheretur ex more, id quod mox accidit portendebat.* Amtnian.
xxv. 10. Auguftus, and his fucceffors, refpectfully folicited
a difpenfation of age for the fons or nephews, whom they
raifed to the confulfhip. But the curule chair of the firft
Brutus had never been difhonoured by an infant. GIBBON.
See p. 290.

From Ancyra Jovian repaired to Dadaſtana, a
ſmall city, or town, on the frontiers of Galatia and
Bithynia, but which belonged to the firſt of theſe
provinces *. There, if we credit Socrates, he received the deputies from the ſenate of Conſtantinople, who came to compliment him on his con-
ſulſhip. Themiſtius, the chief of the deputation,
there pronounced, according to the ſame hiſtorian,
the panegyric of the Emperor, in which nevertheleſs are obſerved all the marks of a diſcourſe
pronounced the very day that Jovian took poſſeſſion
of the conſular dignity. The piece, however, is
written with great elegance and dignity ; but, like
all that comes from the pen of Themiſtius, is rather
too much loaded with learned alluſions. Some
ſtrokes of flattery appear in it concerning the
election of Jovian, and on the peace made with
Sapor. The author extolls, with much more juſtice, the patronage with which the prince honours
men of learning. The elogium principally turns
on his mildneſs and equity with regard to matters
of religion. The ſame orator gives him a commendation which is alone worth a panegyric; namely,
that his elevation had made no change in his manner of treating mankind. He neither forgot nor
ſlighted thoſe who had been his equals. He did not
affect to make his ſuperiority perceived by thoſe who

---

* The Itinerary of Antoninus fixes Dadaſtana 125 Roman miles from Nice, 117 from Ancyra. Weſſeling, Itinerar.
p. 142.    GIBBON.

might

might have made him fenfible of theirs. His friends, his benefactors, did not difcern the change of his fituation, but by the effects of his gratitude and liberality. He collected at his court the moft virtuous men in the empire : he invited thither, he attached to his perfon, thofe whom difgrace, or exile, had eftranged. " There were feen," according to the expreffion of Themiftius, " watching " over the fafety of his reign, the wife Neftor, the " free and generous Diomed, the Chryfantus of Cy- " rus, and the Artabazus of Xerxes." I fufpect that Salluft the fecond is the Neftor; Valentinian might be the Diomed. I am not fufficiently acquainted with the court of Jovian to guefs the two others. It is not only in modern times that orators, by way of being eloquent and figurative, exprefs themfelves in a manner fometimes ænigmatical to their contemporaries, and almoft always unintelligible to pofterity,

The endowments of Jovian, acknowledged by the Pagans themfelves, his attention to find out perfons of merit, and that talent, which in a prince may fupply the place of all others, of knowing mankind, of eftimating their worth, and properly employing them, announced to the Romans a wife government. Some faults, which I have not difguifed, he committed. Raifed on a fudden from a ftation of little eminence to the fupreme power, to which he had never afpired even in a dream, in a manner dazzled and feduced by the fatality of cir-

cumftances,

cumſtances, he made ſome ſlips on the moſt rugged
and ſlippery ground in the world.   But the faults
of inexperience and ſurpriſe often turn to the advantage of thoſe who commit them, when they
have good ſenſe and juſt intentions.   Jovian was
young : he might have acquired what he wanted.
Ammianus could not have had a mean opinion of
him, as, when he reproaches him with ſome vices,
that author preſumes that he might have corrected
them through reſpect to his diadem.   Every thing
may be hoped from a monarch who reſpects himſelf
ſo far as to find motives to become virtuous even in
independence, the uſual ſtumbling-block of virtue.
The choice, which Jovian made, of his confidents
and miniſters, gives room to believe, that he was
capable of receiving advice ; and, as it is obſerved
by one of the greateſt men of the laſt age, " ſtates
" are generally better governed under a prince of
" moderate abilities, who knows how to hear and
" follow good advice, than by a ſovereign of a
" ſuperior genius, who is attached to his under-
" ſtanding, and thinks himſelf infallible *."

The two capitals, the provinces, the armies, had
acknowledged Jovian.   The church was about to
enjoy a profound peace : the ſtate, united within
itſelf, hoped to repair its loſſes : Jovian ſeemed

---

* Grotius, in his hiſtory of the war of the Netherlands,
l. vii. under the year 1598. *Uſu compertum . . . multa
ſæpe ſalubrius geſta ſub principe qui aliorum bene repertis aures
et juſſa commodaret, quàm ſi cui ſapienti fiducia contumaciam
addidiſſet.*        B.

able

able to promise himself a long and glorious reign. Conſtantinople was preparing to receive him magnificently, and, impatient to poſſeſs him herſelf; conjured him to get the ſtart of the prince his ſon. Rome; who alſo flattered herſelf with ſoon ſeeing the Emperor, was already ſtriking medals to celebrate his arrival; his wife was coming to meet him with the pomp of an empreſs; when, in the night between the 16th and 17th of February [364], he was found dead in his bed, after having reigned only ſeven months and twenty days. This was the third Emperor who diſappeared in leſs than three years and a half.

It is pretended that he was ſuffocated by the fumes of charcoal that was lighted in his chamber, to warm it, and to dry the walls which had been newly plaiſtered *. The danger to which Julian had been expoſed at Paris †, might have put him on his guard againſt a like accident. Others aſcribe his death to indigeſtion ‡, or to the attack of an apoplexy. The cauſe was neglected to be aſcertained; without doubt, becauſe it was thought natural: but this very negligence made many imagine it to be the effect of the wickedneſs of men. Am-

---

* See Ammianus Eutropius, who might likewiſe be preſent, Jerom, Oroſius, Sozomen, Zoſimus, and Zonaras. We cannot expect a perfect agreement, and we ſhall not diſcuſs minute differences. GIBBON.

† See the Miſopogon, Vol. I. p. 236.

‡ Occaſioned either by the quantity of the wine, or the quality of the muſhrooms, which he had ſwallowed in the evening. GIBBON.

mianus,

mianus, by faying, that " his death, like that of
" Scipio Æmilianus, was followed by no enqui-
" ries," infinuates, that he loft his life by fome
fecret attack *. St. Chryfoftom fays exprefsly,
that " Jovian was poifoned by his domeftics."
Would the eunuchs of the palace have formed a confpiracy to deprive themfelves of a mafter who feemed
not to be of a temper to fuffer himfelf to be governed, or were they fet at work by fome ambitious man, fuch as Procopius, who, neverthelefs,
did not avail himfelf of that crime? Still it is certain, that the fufpicion could not fall on the fucceffor of Jovian. It was not till after having offered the empire to Salluft, born to deferve it, and
conftantly to refufe it †; it was not till after having caft their eyes on various fubjects, among others
on Januarius, a relation of Jovian, that the army
fuddenly determined [Feb. 26], in favour of Valentinian ‡, who was then abfent §. The Chriftians

* Ammianus, unmindful of his ufual candour and good
fenfe, compares the death of the harmlefs Jovian to that
of the fecond Africanus, who had excited the fears and
refentment of the popular faction.          GIBBON.
† He enjoyed the glory of a fecond refufal; and when
the virtues of the father were alleged in favour of his fon,
the præfect, with the firmnefs of a difinterefted patriot,
declared to the electors, that the feeble age of the one, and
the unexperienced youth of the other, were equally incapable of the laborious duties of government.      Ibid.
‡ Valentinian was the fon of Count Gratian, a native
of Cibalis, in Pannonia, who, from an obfcure condition,
had raifed himfelf, by matchlefs ftrength and dexterity, to
the military commands of Africa and Britain; from which
he

tians bitterly lamented Jovian, and thought that
God had only fhewn him to the world, becaufe the
world was not worthy of him *. A proof that it
was not the fpirit of party that caufed their tears
to flow, is the good that is faid of him by the Pagans. Valentinian and Valens did not prevent the
fenate of Rome-from placing him among the Gods †.
His corpfe was carried to Conftantinople into the
church of the Holy Apoftles ‡, where, long after,
his tomb was feen among thofe of the other Au-
gufti.

His wife furvived him feveral years; an inftance
as memorable, but ftill more ftriking, of the in-
fignificance of what is ftyled grandeur. She had
loft in a few months a father-in law, a father, a
hufband, of whofe elevation fhe only heard to feel
more poignantly his lofs. That which is the refource of all other mothers, completed her unhap-
pinefs. She had a fon; but a fon deprived of the
higheft hopes, and fufpicious to the government.

he retired with an ample fortune and fufpicious integrity.
The city of Nice in Bithynia was chofen for the place of
election. Valentinian affociated his brother Valens in the
empire, in one of the fuburbs of Conftantinople, thirty days
after his own elevation. GIBBON.

§ In his quarters at Ancyra.
* *Oftendunt terris hunc tantum fata, neque ultra
Effe finunt.* VIRG.
† This feems to me the meaning of thefe words of Eu-
tropius: *benignitate principum qui ei fuccefferunt inter Divos
relatus eft.* B.
‡ The fad proceffion was met on the road by his wife
Charito. GIBBON.

The

The empire was elective, and young Varronian
not having been chosen Cæsar, had no right to
pretend to it. Besides, Jovian had not had time to
ingratiate many dependents. It was feared, however, that Varronian would sooner or later aspire
to the place which his father had filled. He was
still living in the year 380. A barbarous policy
had already deprived him of an eye; and his
mother constantly trembled for the life of that
unfortunate child, who had no crime but that of
being the son of an Emperor *. She was, without
doubt, a Christian, and no one had ever more need
of the solid consolations which Christianity alone can
give. It is not certain that Jovian had conferred
on her the title of *Augusta*. No medal of this
princess now exists, though those of Jovian are not
scarce. She was placed, after her death, in the
tomb of her husband.

* Chrysostom, *tom. I. p.* 336. 344. *edit. Montfaucon.* The
Christian orator attempts to comfort the widow by the examples of illustrious misfortunes ; and observes, that " of
" nine Emperors (including the Cæsar Gallus) who had
" reigned in his time, only two (Constantine and Con-
" stantius) died a natural death." Such vague consolations
have never wiped away a single tear. GIBBON.

An

# An ABSTRACT of an ESSAY,

### By the Abbé de la BLETERIE,

## On the Rank and Power of the ROMAN EMPERORS, in the Senate *.

*From Les Memoires de l' Academie des Sciences et Belles Lettres, at Paris, tom. XXIV.*

THE object of this Memoir is to shew the error of thofe who confider the imperial go-vernment as a monarchy, and to prove that it was in fact an ariftocracy, the head of which, invefted with the power of the civil and military magiftrates, the confuls, tribunes, and generals of the ancient republic, was, after all, only the firft magiftrate; powerful enough indeed to opprefs his country, when willing to expofe himfelf to the rifk of act-ing the tyrant, but alfo liable to be punifhed as fuch whenever fhe could affert her rights. With-out admitting this point, the hiftory of the Em-perors muft appear a heap of the groffeft contra-dictions, a confufed chaos of unaccountable facts and events, a downright fchool of fanaticifm and rebellion; whereas, by adopting it, every obfcu-rity vanifhes, every difficulty is removed; and we

---

* The Abbé de la Bleterie delights to purfue the vefliges of the old conftitution, and fometimes finds them in his copious fancy.   GIBBON.

are

are no longer furprifed at feeing the fenate proceed judicially againft a Nero, and other fuch
monfters, both before and after their deaths.

In the fenate the Emperor fat between the two
Confuls. His curule chair did not, by any thing
that appears, differ in any refpect from theirs.
The privilege, granted to Caius *, of fitting on a
tribunal fo high that it was impoffible to reach
him, did not defcend to his fucceffors. Neither
Tiberius nor Auguftus had ever any guards in the
fenate. Tiberius, indeed, in the twentieth year of
his reign, afked leave to introduce with him Macro,
Præfect of the Prætorium, accompanied by a fmall
number of other officers; and the fenate permitted
him to bring in as many military men as he thought
proper; but this conceffion, of which that prince,
as he never returned to Rome, never had occafion
to avail himfelf, became fo precarious, as to be renewed for Caius, and then for Claudius, after
whom the Emperors generally appeared in the
fenate with one or two Præfects of the Prætorium.

The meetings of the fenate were either ordinary,
the number of which was fixed to two for every
month, or extraordinary, being called, as the exigence of affairs feemed to require, by the Conful
in poffeffion of the *fafces*, the Prætor, in the abfence of the Confuls, or the Tribune, in certain

* Caligula.

cafes,

cafes, which it is not eafy to determine. The Emperors, without being Confuls for the year, had the privilege of calling extraordinary meetings of the fenate; firft, as invefted with the tribunitian power; fecondly, by virtue of the conceffion made to Auguftus, A. U. C. 732; thirdly, as perpetual Confuls. Moft of the Emperors, when at Rome, were prefent in the fenate; and all, or almoft all of them, acknowledged themfelves inferior to it, at leaft in fome refpects. They addreffed it as fuppliants or petitioners. " I pray you, I conjure " you, I befeech you, confcript Fathers," are their common expreffions. Some of them ftyle the fenators their lords and their patrons; others call them the princes of the world, and give them the title of " Your clemency, your majefty," &c. The Emperors chofen by the army always applied to the fenate to confirm their election. But what were the prerogatives of the Emperor in this auguft affembly?

Either the Emperor was Conful for the time being, or Conful elect, or neither the one nor the other. In quality of Conful for the time being, he convened the fenate, prefided in it, propofed the affairs upon which it was to deliberate, collected the fuffrages, and finally difmiffed it; all functions attached to the confular dignity; but it was only alternately with the other Conful, his collegue, that he performed them. For a long time, the Prince, when in the exercife of the con-

fular

fular power, wore the fame kind of robes as the
other Confuls * ; which robes were kept in the
capitol, to fhew that both one and the other held
from Heaven, and their fellow-citizens, the powers
of which thofe robes were the enfigns †. .

As Conful-elect, the Prince performed the functions attached to that dignity. The Confuls elect
gave their votes firft, and it appears that the Emperor fubmitted to this cuftom. In the early days
of Rome, the Confuls for the time being never
gave their votes in affairs of their own propofing ;
and if they fometimes voted during the Imperial
goverment, it was never but in matters which the
Emperor himfelf had laid before the fenate.

The Emperor feldom profided in the fenate,
though actually prefent, unlefs invefted with the
ordinary confular dignity. This the Abbé de la
Bleterie proves by a paffage in Pliny the younger,
who, fpeaking of Marcus Prifcus, fays, that Trajan then prefided in the fenate, " for he was
" Conful." The Prince was often prefent only in
quality of fenator. We read that feveral Emperors
reckoned it an honour to be members of the Senate,
and to pay the tax called *glebæ fenatoriæ præftatio*.

---

* That drefs was a robe of purple, embroidered with
filk and gold, and fometimes ornamented with coftly gems.
                                                    GIBBON.

† The Emperors themfelves, who difdained the faint
fhadow of the republic, were confcious that they acquired
an additional fplendor and majefty as often as they affumed
the annual honours of the confular dignity. *Ibid.*

They

They never left the houfe till the Conful had difmiffed the fenators in the ufual form, by the words
" *Nihil vos moramur, Patres confcripti.*" There
are many inftances to prove, that the Emperor
ufed to give his opinion in the fenate; and that
the Conful called upon him for it. This is fufficient to fhew the error of Salmafius and Muret,
who, from the Emperor's collecting the votes, concluded, that he never gave any himfelf; it being
an eftablifhed cuftom, that whatever member collected the votes never gave any himfelf, and the
prince was, befides, fuperior to all the other magiftrates. But, as the prince did not always prefide, neither did he always collect the votes, nor
was he fuperior to the ftate, of which the Conful
was both the organ and the reprefentative, when,
as prefident of the affembly, he called upon the
members for their votes. Accordingly, the fenate
often decided againft the opinion of the Emperor,
and its decrees were always confidered as the voice
of the ftate. Sometimes, it is true, the will of
defpotic princes was blindly followed by the fenators; but even then the fenate deliberated and
decided fovereignly. On this occafion M. de la
Bleterie obferves, that authors, in general, are too
apt to exaggerate the abufe which the Roman Emperors made of their authority. From the year of
Rome 727, the epocha of the lawful authority
of Auguftus, to the firft year of Diocletian, and
U. C. 1037, there elapfed 310 years. Now let

us, on the one hand, add together the reigns of
all the bad Emperors, and, on the other hand, the
reigns of thofe who were fometimes good and
fometimes bad, and we fhall not be able to make
out above 120 years of oppreffion for the Romans;
and even in this interval we fhall find proofs of the
Roman liberty fubfifting, at leaft *de jure*, though
oppreffed *de facto*; fo that there remain 190 years,
during which the government was conformable to
law, and favourable to liberty.    This learned
Academician has, befides, obferved, in order to
invalidate a fact related by Tertullian, that authors
are apt to infift too much on the flavifh fubjection
of the fenate to the will of Tiberius.    That Emperor, having received from Paleftine an account
of the miracles performed by Jefus Chrift, wrote
to the fenate to propofe placing him among the
Gods ; which propofal was rejected.    It is true,
indeed, that the fenate was, at that time, both the
inftrument and the victim of that Emperor's cruelty,
and that, therefore, it would not have refufed to
comply with his defire, had he difcovered fuch
earneftnefs to have it granted as might have been
deemed an order.    But the fenate, no doubt, was
aware, that, in order to amufe the people with a
fhadow of liberty, he afked, with little earneftnefs,
what he was not folicitous to have granted.    Nor
was much refolution requifite to humour this gri-
mace.

But

But if, on the one hand, the fenate had a right to decide againft the opinion of the Emperor, the Emperor, on the other, by virtue of his tribunitian power, had a right, by his *veto*, to hinder the decifions of the fenate from being carried into execution. Befides, he prefided " extraordinarily," without being Conful, by virtue of a fpecial conceffion, which conftituted cne of the moft confiderable branches of the Imperial power. This prerogative is known by the name of *jus relationis,* or " right of propofing matters in the fenate." This was primitively the ordinary funftion of the Confuls, in the abfence of the Prætors, and, in certain cafes, of the Tribunes. When, in the year of Rome 731, Auguftus divefted himfelf of the Confulfhip, which he then exercifed for the eleventh time, he likewife refigned that confular prerogative. Upon which, the fenate confirmed to him, in perpetuity, the tribunitian power, with the privilege of propofing, at every fitting, any one fubjeft that he thought proper ; whereas the Conful had an unlimited authority of propofing as many as he pleafed. Soon after, the fenate conferred upon him the right of convening it as often as he thought proper. In 735, the fenate offered him, for life, the ordinary and extraordinary powers of the confulfhip, and he accepted them, but without affuming any title that indicated fuch perpetual confulfhip; without depriving the annual Conful of the right of performing the

public

public ceremonies, and propoſing affairs to the deliberation of the ſenate, and perhaps too, without
accepting the lictors and faſces, that were likewiſe
offered to him. He accepted, however, firſt, the
precedence in the ſenate; ſecondly, a tribunal,
with a right of trying cauſes, and, probably, the
general inſpection of the finances; and, thirdly, the
prerogative of acting as he thought proper in the
preſſing exigencies of the ſtate, without waiting
for the orders of the ſenate.

Auguſtus confined himſelf to the prerogative,
that had been granted him, of propoſing any one
ſubject he thought proper, at every meeting, ſo that
neither he, nor his ſucceſſors, unleſs they happened
to be annual Conſuls, ever enjoyed an unlimited
right of propoſing matters to the deliberation of
the ſenate. Accordingly we find this right conferred at every change, with fixed bounds, *jus ter-
tiæ, quartæ, quintæ relationis.* As often as the
Emperor propoſed any affair to the deliberation of
the ſenate, he became Preſident of it, if he was
not ſo already in quality of annual Conſul, and
uſed to aſk the votes as a mere Conſul might have
done, but with one remarkable difference. Originally, and even under the Emperors, the magiſtrates in office never gave their opinion in affairs
of their own propoſing. The Conſul who pre-
ſided, and propoſed the buſineſs on which the
ſenate was to deliberate, did not call upon his
collegue, nor the Prætors, nor any of the Curule
magiſtrates,

magiſtrates, for their opinion. He firſt addreſſed himſelf to the Conſuls elect, to the Prince of the ſenate, or firſt ſenator, to the Prætors, and other magiſtrates, elect, in ſhort, to all the members of the ſenate not actually in office. He might indeed re-capitulate the arguments on both ſides, and weigh them one againſt another, but without pretending to conclude upon them; which precautions were, no doubt, employed to ſecure to all the members a proper liberty of ſpeech. But when the Emperor propoſed any affair, the Conſul and other magiſtrates were allowed to give their opinion. This is expreſsly obſerved by Tacitus, (*Ann.* III. 17.) in ſpeaking of the charge brought againſt Piſo, and his wife Placina, for the murder of Germanicus. The Abbé de la Bleterie is of opinion, that this conceſſion, to the Conſuls, of voting, was by way of compenſation for the two ſpecial privileges they had before, one, of propoſing any affair they thought proper, the other, of hindering the ſenate from deliberating upon it; and that this conceſſion extended by degrees to the other magiſtrates.

This entertaining and inſtructive Memoir is followed by another, containing " an anſwer to ſome " objections." The firſt objection is, that the deciſions of the Roman ſenate might be, and were ſometimes, actually amended, and even reſcinded, by the judgements of the Emperor; and that the Emperor continued in the poſſeſſion of this pre-

rogative

rogative till the reign of Hadrian, which began 140 years after that of Auguſtus. This we find in the Digeſt, *ſciendum eſt appellari à ſenatu non peſſe principem*; *idque oratione Divi. Hadriani effectum* *.
Till then, therefore, the decrees of the ſenate were ſubject to the reviſion of the prince, whoſe authority, of courſe, muſt have been ſuperior to that of the ſenate, and the whole nation.

This prohibition of Hadrian, ſays the Abbé de la Bleterie, proves indeed that appeals uſed ſometimes to be made from the ſenate to the Emperor, and that the Emperor finally decided upon theſe appeals ; but it does not prove, that theſe appeals, or the deciſions given upon them, were according to law. The legal authority of the Emperor reſulted entirely from his power as both Conſul and Tribune. Now, neither the ordinary power of the Conſul, nor even the extraordinary power, by virtue of which the Conſuls might act, in preſſing emergencies, without conſulting the ſenate, gave him any right to alter the decrees of the ſenate, not even while the republic ſubſiſted in its primitive form, when the ſenate was only the national council, and ſtill leſs under its new form, when the ſenate repreſented the whole nation. As Tribune, the Emperor had a right firſt, to interpoſe both judicially and by force in favour of the oppreſſed, and obſtruct the execution of all ſentences, even thoſe that were national : ſecondly, a

---

* *Lib.* xlix. *Tit.* 2. *a quibus appellare.*

new

new right of trying all caufes brought into his
court, either in the firft inftance, or by appeal,
and of pardoning thofe who had been condemned
at any other tribunal whatever. But the author
has elfewhere proved, that the only appeals that
could be made from the fenate to the Emperor,
were thofe which preceded a final fentence. Befides,
to pardon and to abfolve are different things, and,
in general, inftead of giving it himfelf, he ufed to
afk the fenate for the pardon of criminals.

Suetonius, it is true, feems to fay, that Tiberius cancelled fome decrees of the fenate, *confti-
tutiones quafdam fenatûs refcidit*; but, perhaps, thefe
decrees had not as yet gone through the ufual
forms. For example, a *fenatûs confultum* was confidered as little better than the projeft of a law,
till it had been depofited in the *Ærarium*. In fuch
cafes, therefore, the oppofition of the Emperor
did not exceed the bounds of his authority as Tribune. Perhaps too the hiftorian means no more
than that Tiberius engaged the fenators to alter
fome of its decrees; an interpretation which no way
clafhes either with the text or the ftyle of Suetonius.
For example, he tells us, in another place *, that
Vitellius, uncle to the Emperor of the fame name,
" accufed Pifo of the murder of Germanicus, and
" condemned him," *accufavit, condemnavitque*. Now,
the fame perfon could not be both judge and ac-
cufer; and it is, befides, well known that Pifo was

* *In Vitell. c. 11. 2.*

B b 4 con-

condemned by the fenate on the accufation of Vitellius. This therefore muft have been the meaning of Suetonius; and the word *refcidit* will admit
of the fame latitude. Befides, the paffage of Suetonius can only be underftood of the beginning of
the reign of Tiberius, who not being as yet firmly
feated on the throne, and being, befides, under ap-
prehenfions from Germanicus, would hardly have
ventured to give any umbrage to the fenate by annulling its decrees.

Suetonius, likewife tells us, that Vefpafian cancelled the decree *, by which the fenate had voted,
divine honours to Galba † : *decretum Vefpafianus
abolevit.* The Abbé de la Bleterie, by combining
what Tacitus and Suetonius have faid on this fubject, proves, that, at the requeft of the younger
Domitian, the fenate by way of reparation for the

* Here we may obferve that the fuperiority of the fenate
over the Emperor, if we may truft to Father Hardouin,
is proved by the decrees of that body granting divine honours to thefe princes. *Neque enim confecrat,* fays he, *aut
in Divos reponit, nifi poteftas fuperior eo qui confecratur ;* a
principle, from which he has drawn the following conclufion, which M. de la Bléterie has corroborated by fo many
other proofs : *Atque hinc intelligis id, quod multis aliunde con-
ftat argumentis, Imperatores Romanos fenatui fuiffe fubjectos, à
quo utique confecrabantur ii, qui hunc fibi poft obitum deferri ho-
norem in vitâ meruiffent.* Note 18. on the xxxvith book of
Pliny, Sect. 14.

This argument fcarce proves the fuperiority of the fenate
to the living reigning prince. All that can well be deduced
from it is, that the fenate was fuperior to the Emperors
when they were dead, according to the old adage, *A
living dog,* &c.

† Galba, c. XXIII.

insults offered to Galba, ordered, first, that his statues should be erected again; and, secondly, that a column and a new statue should be erected to him in the forum: that Tacitus mentions only the first of these orders, and Suetonius only the second. The first was executed; the second required time; and Vespasian, who suspected Galba of having formed a design upon his life, gave himself no trouble to hasten the execution of it; and the senate, being informed of the Emperor's suspicions, suffered the project of the statue and the column to drop; so that this part of its decree was abolished by the mere non-execution of it; and the term employed by Suetonius may signify no more, and not a formal abrogation.

By a short view, which our learned author takes, of all the Emperors before Hadrian, it appears that Caligula was the only one among them who can be proved to have made any encroachment on the jurisdiction of the senate; and it was, no doubt, in order to prevent such encroachments for the future, that Hadrian, who was perfectly well acquainted with the rights of the Roman people, and never decided any important question without the advice of the senate, whose interest he had very much at heart, brought in the law mentioned in the Digest. After all, this law only forbade appeals, after judgement had been formally given by the senate; till then, the parties might appeal from the senate to the Emperor, who, in quality

of

of Tribune, might interpofe, of himfelf, *ex officio*, fo as to hinder the fenate from ever proceeding to judgement, though he had no right to judge him-felf, or call the affair to his own tribunal.

The fecond objection to this doctrine of the Abbé de la Bleterie is drawn from an epiftle quoted by Julius Capitolinus. Macrinus, Præfect of the Prætorium, having caufed Antoninus Cara-calla to be affaffinated, was chofen Emperor by the army *, who did not believe him acceffary to that murder. This election required confirmation by a national act. The decree of the fenate, as re-prefenting the nation, that conferred on the new prince all the prerogatives of which the Imperial authority was the refult, was ftyled, firft, *lex im-perii*, and afterwards, under Juftinian, *lex regia*. Macrinus, therefore, wrote to the fenate, requeft-ing them to ratify what had been done by the army. He fays, in his epiftle, that in conjunction with the troops, he had decreed divine honours to Caracalla, adding, " You will likewife decree them " to him, confcript Fathers : we have a right, as " Emperor, to command you to do it ; neverthe-" lefs, we only requeft it of you." *Et vos, Patres confcripti, ut decernatis, cum poffimus imperatorio jure præcipere, tamen rogamus.*

But this epiftle bears fo many marks of forgery, that it is furprifing M. de Tillemont fhould have been the only one who has difcovered the impofture;

* See the Cæfars, Vol. I. p. 163.

though

though Tillemont, neverthelefs, for want of having narrowly examined the nature of the Imperial government, confidered the Emperors as real monarchs.

Our learned Academician fhews, that this pretended epiftle is full of contradictions, and of expreffions, which not only clafh with probability, but cuftom, and even truth. He alfo proves, that it muft have been forged by fome friend of Elagabalus, an implacable enemy of Macrinus and his fon Diadumenus. We likewife find, in the hiftory of Auguftus, two epiftles afcribed to the laft, though it is evident that they were forged with a defign to blacken Diadumenus, and to make him pafs for a monfter, of which Elagabalus did well to rid the world.

For farther particulars the reader muft be referred to the Memoir itfelf, in which he will meet with deep refearches, folid reflections, and great purity of ftyle.

ADDI-

# ADDITIONAL NOTES.

## VOLUME I.

P. 14, l. 18. Carterius. *

* Libanius, in his Life, p. 59, mentions a Carterius, who was in many refpects notorious for his folly, particularly in daring to offend the auguft Emperors. The perfon above-named muft probably have offended Conftantius, or he would not have wanted the intereft of Julian, and the affif-tance of Araxius. Libanius alfo mentions another Carte-rius, in his ccxlviiith Epiftle (probably the fon of the former) as an orator whom the fenators of Arce in Phœ-nicia had enrolled among them. And in his dlxxth he apologifes to Maximus for his deferting the Mufes, and following Mars. Araxius was præfect of Paleftine. Li-banius has fix Epiftles to him.

P. 121. note †.

To the "Rhodian fhower of gold" Libanius alfo alludes in his dccclxxiiid Epiftle; and Ammianus, xvii. 7.

P. 149. To note * may be fubftituted this.

* Julian has here in view that paffage of Homer, in the firft book of the Iliad, [ver. 607.] where he fays, that "every God has his manfion and throne † fabricated by "Vulcan with his own hands;" and which he repeats in another place.                    SPANHEIM.

Ib. l. 18. When therefore they rife at the entrance of their Father † &c.

†. This is alfo taken from a paffage of Homer, in the fame book [ver. 533.] to this effect; that "at the approach "of their Father Jupiter all the Gods rife from their "feats, and go to meet him, and that no one waits for "him." I find, however, that the poet fays the fame thing of Apollo, in the Hymn which is afcribed to him, in praife of that God.                    Ibid.

† In this paffage Homer mentions only their manfion, or houfe, δωμα.
—— their ftarry domes ——
The fhining monuments of Vulcan's art.                    Pors, 778.
The

The ſhining ſynod of th' immortals wait
The coming God, and from their thrones of ſtate
Ariſing ſilent, wrapt in holy fear,
Before ʒhe majeſty of heaven appear, &c.    POPE, 690.
P. 151. To note † add.

† The authority of Julian, no douht, is highly reſpeɛtable;
but if a perſon in youth carry the marks of a bad diſpoſition, and deliberately commit atrocious aɛtions, when his
intereſt required them, we are ſtill warranted to queſtion
the ſincerity of his converſion, though, in a different ſtate
of his intereſt, even the whole tenor of his life ſhould
change.                                        FERGUSON.

P. 290. To note † add.
Theſe Abantes are alſo mentioned by Libanius in his
Orat. XIX.

P. 305. To note † add.
The Jupiter, who laments with tears of blood the death
of Sarpedon, his ſon, had a very imperfeɛt notion of happineſs, or glory, beyond the grave.            GIBBON.
Libanius, " on hearing of the death of Julian," repeats
this alluſion, by ſaying, " I looked up to heaven, expeɛting
" tears mixed with blood, ſuch as Jupiter ſhed upon Sar-
" pedon; but I did not ſee them; though perhaps he
" poured them on the corpſe, and, like the duſt and blood
" attendant on a battle, they were ſeen by few."   In Jul.
Imp. Necem.

P. 312. note ‡.  Ουτ' ιν λογω ʉτ' ιν αριθμων.  Subſtitute this.
Libanius quotes this oracle again in his MCXVIth Epiſtle:
" But now he who is ignorant of the laws is truly an
" Ægian *, of no name or rank." On which the tranſ-
lator has the following note:
    * Αιγιυς.] In the MS incorreɛtly Αιγιυς, called Αιγιυς, from
Αιγιοι. a city of Achaia, as we learn from Stephens de
Urbibus, p. 36, who quotes this oracle given to them,
    Υμεις δ'Αιγιεις ʉϊε τριλοι, ʉϊε τιλαςλοι,
to which others add the following,
    Οʉϊε δυωδικαλοι, ʉτ' ιν λογω, ʉτ' ιν αριθμω.
Compare Th. de Pinedo on this paſſage, p. 36. To this
our author refers. Eraſmus, in his Adages, p. 393, applies this to the Æginenſians, deceived by the ſimilitude of
the name.                                      WOLFIUS.
The ſcholiaſt on Theocritus applies it to the inhabitants
of Megara.
    Υμεις δ'ω Μεγαριις, κ. τ. λ.

                                               P. 316.

P. 316. note *.

Calliopius, it appears from feveral other Epiftles, was alfo an affiftant to Libanius in his inftruction of youth, one of his ufhers.

P. 324. l. 8. Calliope is alfo honoured, &c.

† See Vol. II. p. 251. note *.


## V O L U M E   II.


P. 14. Epiftle VIII. " You are come, Telemachus.'

Libanius begins his Legation to Julian (πρισβιιλιος προς Ἰυλιανον) with the fame quotation.

P. 45. Epiftle XXII. To LEONTIUS *.

* Confular of Paleftine in 363, as appears by the title of a law, XII Cod. Theod. tit. 55. De Decurionibus.

This Leontius feems to be that governor of Paleftine whom at that time, together with Alypius, Julian is faid by Ammianus to have given a fruitlefs commiffion to re-build the temple of Jerufalem. [See p. 74. note.] To the fame there are feveral Epiftles of Libanius. He afterwards governed Paleftine as Pro-conful under Theodofius the Great.

GODEFROI.

P. 46. Epiftle XXIII. To HERMOGENES †.

† Libanius often mentions an Hermogenes, as Prætor of Syria, and ftyles him in his Life, p. 39, " the beft of " magiftrates." He has alfo two Epiftles to him, viz. the MDXLIxth of Wolfius, and the XIIth of Zambicari, l. III. By the latter he appears to have had a houfe at Corinth. Ammianus too mentions him, XIX. 12. See Valois on the paffage, and Godefroi in the profopographia of his Theodofian Code, p. 365.

P. 69. l. 16. The garden *.

* The fhort defcription, which Julian here gives, of this Syrian garden, may be added to the few particulars of ancient gardens which Mr. Burgh has collected in a note on Mr. Mafon's Englifh Garden, p. 130. The extent is not mentioned, but by its comparifon to that of Laërtes it muft have been fmall. Of its difpofition, however, we are informed, which was far from happy. The pot-herbs and fruit-trees were planted in the middle, the latter, in that hot

hot climate, not requiring walls to force them, and there was not only a grove of cypresses, but a row of those trees was also ranged along the walls, it being, like the Italian gardens described by Bishop Burnet, walled round, and by this double fortification, as it were, completely excluded from a view of the country.

P. 90. l. 1.

" Diogenes," says Libanius, " was a native of Synope, " and the uncle of Aristophanes." See Vol. I. p. 317.

P. 148. l. 7. swallows †.

† In like manner his master Libanius (Ep. XLIV.) compares chattering and long letters to swallows, birds that are noisy in the summer, and fly to and fro. WOLFIUS.

P. 199. Add to note *.

By the Epistles above-mentioned of Libanius, Eutherius appears to have been præfect of Armenia, and to have had a son under his tuition.

P. 227. Add to the second paragraph of the note:

In a subsequent work Libanius deems both these events presages of the death of Julian. " This," says he, " was " predicted by the temple of Apollo destroyed by fire. " The God forsook the earth, as it was soon to be pol- " luted. This was also foretold by the earthquakes con- " vulsing all the ground as harbingers of approaching " disturbance and confusion." In Jul. Imp. Necem, p. 258.

P. 246. Among the gardens of antiquity to which Milton, b. iv. compares and prefers his " Paradise of " Eden," is

" That sweet grove
" Of Daphne by Orontes."

P. 247. Add to note *.

Libanius in his Life, p. 47, 8. mentions the Olympics which were celebrated on his 50th birth-day, which must have been in the year 364, the year after the death of Julian. " At these," says he, " I had an ardent desire to " be present ; but on the first day was imprisoned, not by " the Prætor, but by a severe attack of the gout."

INDEX.

# INDEX

## TO

## VOLUME II.

*Boftre-*

C c 3 *Homer*,

# I N D E X.

Labarum,

## L.

                                                     *Momus,*

# I N D E X:

# INDEX.

Since

\*\*\* Since this work has been printed off, I am enabled, by the *Nouveau Dictionnaire Historique* \*, (*4me edition*, 6 *tomes*, 8*vo*, à *Caen*, 1779), to add the following account of a writer to whom I am much obliged.

BLETERIE (JOHN PHILIP RENE de la), born at Rennes, died in an advanced age; in 1772. He was a man of learning, was much attached to religion, and his morals did not belie his principles. His knowledge, being folid and diverfified, rendered his converfation interefting and improving. He publifhed feveral works, which have been well received by the public. 1. *The Hiftory of Julian the Apoftate* †, Paris, 1735. 1746. 12mo. a curious performance, well written, and diftinguifhed at once by its impartiality, precifion, elegance, and judgement. 2. *The Hiftory of the Emperor Jovian*, with tranflations of fome works of the Emperor Julian; Paris, 1748, 2 vols. 12mo. &c. &c.

---

\* The work fo ftyled, *ou Hiftoire abregée de tous les hommes qui fe font fait un nomme par le Genie, les Talens, les Vertus, les Erreurs, &c. depuis le commencement du monde jufqu'à nos jours, par une Societé de Gens de lettres,* is of itfelf a library.

† This work, it is obfervable, is not fo entitled by the author, but folely *Vie de l'Empereur Julien.*

| Page | Page |
|---|---|
| 17. note † l. 1. r. "Julian | 145. r. 'Conftans' |
| "was truly." | 165. note * l. 3. r. 'Phædon' |
| 26. note † l. 6. r. 'χρυσων' | 169. note * l. 1. r. 'φευδη,' |
| 31. note * l. * r. "common | 206. l. the laft, r. 'confectam' |
| "reading" | 214. l. 4. r. (1L) |
| 65. l. 13. r. 'Chalcis' | 240. note * l. the laft, r. |
| 66. is mifpaged | 'Chiliades' |
| 82. note l. 3. r. 'υρσι τοιλω' | 259. is mifpaged |
| 95. note * l. 7. r. 'λωστιτω' | 279. note l. 3. r. "to whom" |
| this this | 284. l. 3. r. the bottom, r. |
| 97. note ‡ l. 7. 'F. Mar- | 'as were' |
| tinius,' &c. belongs to the | 291. note † l. 3. r. 'a Latin' |
| next note | 333. note † l. 3. r. 'πασι' |
| 102. note † l. 1. r. 'ταιδιαν,' | 341. l. 17. r. 'Bernicius' |
| 173. l. 13. After 'friends add | to note † add B. |
| ‡ and prefix the fame re- | 361. note * l. 1. after 'Am- |
| ference to the note be- | "mianus', add a comma |
| ginning "Julian, it ap- | |
| pears," &c. | |

F I N I S.